SAN DIEGO PUBLIC LIBRARY

S0-BKF-117

8919

FIC   Brackenbury,
        Rosalind.

        Sense and
          sensuality

JUL 1 0 1987

$14.95

DATE			

STORAGE

San Diego Public Library

© THE BAKER & TAYLOR CO.

SENSE AND SENSUALITY

A NOVEL

ROSALIND BRACKENBURY

8919

Taplinger Publishing Company
New York

First American Edition

First published in the United States in 1987 by
TAPLINGER PUBLISHING CO., INC.
New York, New York

© Rosalind Brackenbury, 1985
All rights reserved
Printed in the United States of America

No part of this book may be reproduced or transmitted in any form or by any
means, electronic or mechanical, including photocopying, recording, or any information storage and retrieval system now known or to be invented, without
permission in writing from the publisher, except by a reviewer who wishes to
quote brief passages in connection with a review written for inclusion in a
magazine, newspaper, or broadcast.

Library of Congress Cataloging-in-Publication Data

Brackenbury, Rosalind.
    Sense and sensuality.

    Originally published: Brighton, Sussex:
Harvester Press, 1984.
    I. Title.
PR 6052.R24S4   1987   823'.914   86-14576
ISBN 0-8008-7062-X

SENSE AND SENSUALITY

The school play, that year, is *The Walrus and the Carpenter*. A group of the younger children are to perform as oysters. She is one of them. She is nine. The play will be performed at the end of the summer term for the parents, directed and produced by the two women who keep the school, the two teachers; out upon the parched lawn, there, on a blazing July day, once the tables have been cleared away, once the seniors have been round handing out lemonade. The Walrus, the Carpenter, the ranks of little oysters sweat on the bank, await their turn. There is a gramophone, to play an overture, and a child ready to wind it up, to set the needle in the groove. The parents sit and wait, sweat runs down the backs of their necks, stains the silk print dresses, the best shirts; it is the hottest day of a hot summer. The grass is more brown than green, marked and dented where cricket matches have been played, holed for rounders. Yet in some places there are still daisies. An aeroplane seems always to be there, droning in the distance; a summer sound, remote as bees.

And it is time for the performance, already; it is the moment; it is the last time that they will be there, he and she in their oyster suits, crouched beneath the curved pink cardboard shells cut out and painted in the art lesson, the last time, this afternoon, sweating, close.

She glances sideways without turning her head, to admire again the black down that grows already on his forearms, browned by the sun. His knees, up beneath his chin, clasped by his hands, fascinate by their squareness, their bony strength. His black head turns slightly upon his neck, so that he can squint into the sun and watch what is happening, there, on the lawn, where the teachers in their best flowered dresses run heavily about, putting finishing touches, and beyond, there on what they call 'the loggia', where the parents sit,

5

hands folded, programmes folded and handkerchiefs cornered to keep off the sun, peering to sight their children. She does not know which are his parents; if he has any. He has this way of squinting into the light, as if it baffles him. She thinks he might have been born this way, complete. His brown eyes screw up slightly at the corners beneath thick black eyebrows and his look is belligerent, enquiring. She copies his look, without realising it, until her face, her own face, might be his. Her own parents wave to her, and she does not respond.

They have all of them changed into their costumes in one of the classrooms, at the dress rehearsal, yesterday, and now, today, for the performance. She has a blue-checked summer dress with puffed sleeves and a sash that ties behind, and she has a vest, knickers, sandals. Her legs, brown as his and scarred with constant falls, are bare. It takes her only a minute to take off everything but the knickers and slip on the fine muslin top and pants that her mother has made. Her blue dress lies upon the top of a chair. He is slower, struggling with buttons. Off come his blue aertex shirt, the snake belt, the grey shorts that hang unevenly to his knees. Underneath, he has on a white cotton vest and pants. She can see the brown smoothness of his back, the slight down of black hair, the muscles of his shoulders as he bends away from her to take off his socks. Stripped to his underpants, barefoot, he turns suddenly to stare at her; his belligerence, his enquiry, a mask. Who is he? His brown, furred flesh so close, so available, it could be her own. Not herself, no, and not a brother; but something like. She wants to reach and stroke him as if he were a cat; no, more as if he were simply herself, her extension. But the teacher calls curtly to him – Michael, what are you doing, haven't you got your costume on yet, come on, we're starting in five minutes. Alice, get out of his way. Come on, boy, can't you even do your own tapes up yet? Get a move on!

The oyster costumes, flimsy, transparent, are fastened with tapes on the shoulders, making the sewing of them easy, using as little material as possible. They are very thin, but then, these are the younger children, the oldest only eight and nine and they do keep their pants on underneath. Some of the littler ones look really sweet in them, chubby, holding hands, chanting beneath their shells. If you

6

are ready, oysters dear, we will begin to feed . . . And it will soon be over now, the costumes and the shells packed away, not to be worn by them again, and it will finish, this heat, this brilliant summer day, and the strain of it all, end of term for teachers, time spared for parents from business, from life; and for her, this strangeness, with her parents clapping over there and her grandmother waving, holding her parasol, will be over; and she will never be an oyster with him again. He will be sent away, encased in a stiff uniform, sent away to another school. He will be in training to be a man.

After the play, they go to sit on the bank again, in the blazing sun, so that the heat strikes at the backs of their necks, from which the hair is evenly cut away. There are two silver birch trees at one end, shading part of the bank, and beneath them some of the children huddle to be out of the sun, the fat pale ones, the fair ones, the pink and freckled ones; while he and she sit out there in the sun's full glare, their twin black heads tipped forward upon their arms. In the distance, she sees her mother wave a pale arm, signalling to her to put on a sun hat, but she takes no notice. With him she will sit out in the full sun, darkening her skin so that it matches his, so that their two sets of arms, clasped again around their knees, will be identical, matching. She wants to be so like him that she is him, indistinguishable: so as to know what it is like to sit there, so complete, silent, full mouth unsmiling, eyes fixed on a far point, to be lightly furred all over, to have broad brown hands with elastoplast on one finger, to be male. The two of them wear their shirts and shorts now, for the gym display. In it, she will shine by doing a rapid series of cartwheels all round the lawn. He will be the one to balance perfectly at the very top of a pyramid of people. Each of them has to offer his, her practised excellence. They will be the best, they will be twinned in perfection. The applause that will ring out for her, for him, will be shared, will be eternal. And for this afternoon, she basks in it, as in his proximity.

Michael Foley. He it was then, the first in a long line, yes, as if this prototype, once created, has to be struck to life again and again, in all the corners of the world. The man with his back turned in the cinema queue, his hair growing in just such a way; the man glimpsed in a

7

crowd, in a photograph, on a beach, poised in just that way to dive and swim away; the stranger opposite in the train, staring out for just a minute from behind his newspaper; the friend's husband, introduced for a blinding moment in a dark hallway, but not quite, not quite, for otherwise the dinner party will explode and the glasses crash from the table, otherwise the friend will turn foe and come rushing with a poison bottle, with a knife— The man in dreams, half-remembered at waking; the man in reality whose glance, innocent and unknowing, recalled that half-aggressive, half questioning squinting up into the sun, which in itself, that summer day, nineteen-fifty-one, end of the summer term, parents' day in the afternoon, yet echoes something else, something as yet inaccessible, freak of genetic inheritance, perhaps, quirk of joining cells, whatever it is that makes us fly together, fish, fowls, animals, humans; together, rather than apart.

The day ends. Children go home, some of them holding silver cups, prizes for effort and for French. Marks have been read out, honours distributed. Ninety out of a hundred has the same exaggerated triumph as ninety degrees in the shade. It is a summer for extremes, for exuberance. And yet she and he have no cup, no honour but the startling evanescence of their fame, there for an afternoon and then perhaps forgotten, their gymnastic elegance, and the sudden private flowering of their love. For is that not what we call it, the overwhelming longing to discover everything about another person? She looks at him and knows the precise direction of her feelings, and only after a moment looks away. He is puzzled; he pushes with his blunt head forward, against veils, against uncertainties. She looks at him, this girl, and then springs away, into a dizzying series of cartwheels that turn the green lawn, the birch trees, blue sky, moon faces, all, for her into kaleidoscope; it spins around her, the speed of her movement turning the whole wheel of the world, she at the hub, the pivot; become the force that makes everything else turn about her whirl. For a moment, then, the world and she are concentric, unified. He watches, not understanding. That if she goes fast enough, fast enough, she will remain at the centre of her world. When she has finished, having circled the lawn twice – spring from hand to hand to

8

foot to foot to hand, and her wrists jarred each time – she collapses on to her bottom, legs splayed out, and there is a hard spatter of applause. It is hard to recognise for a moment as the claps of hands, for her; but then she relaxes into it, sprawled there, far from the proper gymnast's pose that should have been legs together, hands at sides, demure; she knows it for what it is. But should have sprung up again, sooner, remembered her training, eyes down, figure erect, should have taken it with proper deference, not stayed there sprawling, grinning for minutes too long, as if she could not be bothered to get up, panting the while and feeling the world still whirl around her, still hers. The clapping, hesitates, dies away; was too spontaneous, is quickly hushed. Hands return to laps; the child is a show-off, not to be encouraged; somebody should tell her not to sprawl there, showing her knickers, in that shameless way, looking so pleased with herself, it is not proper. One of the teachers makes a mental note, to tick Alice Linnell off later; but forgets. So she gets up slowly and walks back across the mown and trodden expanse, her gleaming gym shoes streaked with green, a smear of brown across her bottom where she has sat too long having skidded to the ground; and takes her place again beside him, sitting there impassive, hands linked across the knobs of his brown knees, acknowledging her return with a ghost of a sideways smile.

After a minute he mutters – you'll get told off for just sitting there like that. But you were jolly good.

It is the crown of the afternoon; and she does not need it, has not even awaited it, his praise. She knows she is good; feels it in each spring and turn of her body, in the firm contact of palms with earth and grass, in the controlled spring of each leg, in the movement, the whirling, and the way she experiences herself, whole, at the hub of it all. But now he says it, she is dizzy still, and it crowns her achievement.

She says – Don't care, anyway. Even if they do.

They lay their arms close together, comparing tans; how the little hairs rise on each arm, they note; and, almost touching, feel the warmth of each other already, flesh feeling the anticipation of flesh, so that there is no need to touch, just look, just be there. He shows her a

9

scar on his wrist where a dog has bitten him; she shows him the twin scars on her bony knees where she fell in the drive. He mutters to her the date of his birthday, a month earlier than hers, and tells the names of cars and racing drivers. His hand scores a fast passage between long grasses, a low zoom-zoooom comes from his throat. Over there, they are still making announcements, handing out prizes. The tall shiny figure of the headmistress, her bosom spilling over in tight blue, and the flash of a silver cup changing hands, and again the spatter of applause, distant as at a cricket match, momentarily changes the air. It is all very far away. They have done it, their performance, the play and the gymnastics. 'Some of us are out of breath and all of us are fat,' he murmurs to her, signalling towards the teachers, and their mutual prolongued and stifled giggles are gratifying as shared sweets. She stretches her legs out in front of her on the bank, on the tickling grass, on the hard earth, and shifts her bottom into a new position. He stretches his out too, in defiance of the teachers' edict that the watching children should sit tidily cross-legged all afternoon. Both of them have white creases behind their knees and pins and needles in their toes. In smudged gym shoes, whitened this morning with wet gleaming stuff from a pot, their feet touch, as they compare leg lengths. She admires her new white socks that fit so neatly just above the ankle bone. She loves her legs, the smooth brown length of them these days. Some people have loose socks that drag down at the heel, displaying a raw redness. But his socks, like hers, are white and neatly turned over. His shins are lean, his knees turn in slightly, she finds him completely admirable in every detail, as admirable as herself. For an hour, for an hour and a half, they indulge it, then, this complete unstinting mutual admiration, with only a few words muttered, a few glances exchanged straight from eye to eye, and the proximity – an inch, no less, between – of their two hands bent back in the grass where they lean, bracing their elbows, upon their wrists. Not long, before the afternoon, the day, ends. It is the last part of the last day of the last term of this school year; she never sees him again. Not as a nine-year-old schoolboy, that is, and not beside her in perfect relaxation of friendship on a grassy bank throughout a long hot summer afternoon.

PART I

1

She was born towards the end of a great war, which for so long afterwards was known as 'The War' that it seemed possible to forget that there had been any other, or might be more to come. Throughout her early childhood, the phrase which she seemed to hear more often than any other was 'before the war'. Before the war, things had been different; but the great change, the watershed, had happened irrevocably before her time, so that she would never know. Pre-war, she learned, meant good quality, longlasting, reliable, elegant, moral, safe. But she herself was a war baby. Conceived, as her parents told her several times, at a point in history at which to conceive babies was madness; conceived as the world seemed to explode and then begin its long burning, as the last, the worst stages of the insane happenings took place. Was it then for hope against hope, for faith in the future, for a stake in a new world born from ashes? Or simply from a blind burrowing into the oldest form of reassurance? She would never know. But was conceived, carried, born, and survived; in spite of war and rationing and poor food, not enough milk and vitamins and a mother who might have been shocked daily into miscarriage through fear, anxiety, and a rushed, mismanaged birth in an understaffed hospital in wartime, in the capital city upon which bombs dropped, nightly. Survived.

Into a world that was not as it had been, pre-war, but was lastingly changed. Seen from a distance, with hindsight, through history, it was to be known for its austerity. Not for many decades was the country to submit again to such cold, such discomfort, such hunger. The images of this time, seen from the standpoint of history, were of queues, of ration books, of badly dressed, ill-nourished people, the women strangely masked with make-up as if to hide a bitter truth. They were in black and white, on old film. It was easy to feel nostalgia for them, later, when prosperity was real again, if only for a while; to think, ah, there was the chance, there was the moment, to rebuild the world, to start it all anew. But what she remembered was different. With a child's perception, she could see only the world as it was to her, as it had always been. And it was in two colours, always, not black and white. The colours might vary, but there they were, always in subtle opposition to each other, always contrasting: the richness of reds and golds and yellowy greens set against the harshness of pale, light colours, blueish colours, cold colours, the colours of pale eyes. For a long time, she did not see them consciously, let alone analyse them, but moved easily, with hardly a jolt, from the aura of one colour to that of another, absorbing their influences, allowing them to mould her. With each came an intensity of feeling, a strong current, a tug at the direction of her whole being. That was why, later, the black and white of film, of newsreel, seemed inaccurate, never did justice to the truth about that time; whereas the gaudy colours of the Cinemascope films she went to see distorted in the other direction, were too garish, unsubtle, missed the point. The swarthy, sweating flesh of the heroes of the Cinemascope vision caused her, for some reason, intense anxiety: it was too much, as were the crimson lips and the jutting white breasts of the heroines. But this is to go too far ahead already . . . .

She survived, and was for two years alone her parents' child, and they were twin trees, bending over her, one of them in khaki that was untouchable, the other in the softest of wool, perhaps angora, and a necklace of pearls. That is, at least, how they appear in the photographs of that time; again, the lasting image, the permanent one, outlives the varied subtler ones of memory. There they are, on a piano somewhere, on some polished piece of furniture, he with his rakish army cap and a mouth set firm against something that he sees approach, she gracious, leaning, in the position the photographer chose. Studio portraits. Against a time, a future time, in which the reality, the flesh, may have ceased to exist. They were, to her, reality.

14

But the details, it seems are easy to forget; there are themes, there are songs, there are smells, there are the coat-tails of memory; there are the colours still. She remembered the feel of the softness, of angora wool. In the darkness, the apple-firmness of a smiling cheek. And for many years, the large male hand that came from somewhere above her, that grasped hers uncritically, that swung her along.

There was softness and hardness, and in between, herself, Alice: made up of both, partaking of both, yet vulnerable still, because of having no boundaries.

When her brothers were born, one after the other, with the predictable time gaps in between, when she was no longer the only child, small between the two tall trees, she went out into the woods with somebody, a nursemaid, a girl hired to take her for walks, and found two tall leaning pine trees that stood one on each side of a little stump, and invested them with the power, the safety. The little stump, she named. And each afternoon took presents, offerings. Nearly always when she returned – the girl reluctant, not understanding, or sometimes with an older woman, more tolerant of fantasy – the presents would still be there, leaves of bracken a little shrivelled, sweets grown sticky, a pine cone or a smooth stone rolled to one side. Whatever might have fallen apart, there were still the marks of her magic, remaining. Nothing would be random any more. The leaf wrapped around a cone was a parcel, even when the leaf dried and fell away to show its skeleton, even months hence, even years.

She conducted a marriage service between the two trees. Next, there was a christening for the little stump, and a birthday, and a birthday, and a Christmas party. The stump and the two trees never moved, never changed; and yet each time there was a slight anxiety of finding them, of taking a particular path through the pine woods, getting to the right place, the right conjunction of trees, bushes, paths, sky. Recognising the place. And each time, the relief of recognition: they were there, nothing had changed. In her dreams there were woods, paths, trees undifferentiated from each other, unrecognisable, unnamed, and there was the search, for the right conjunction. Somewhere, only just out of reach, there was recognition. The essential thing, the relationship between the three objects, those particular

15

ones, in that particular sequence, to be hunted for, again and again. Later on, she returned to look for those trees again, out of curiosity to find that little stump upon which she had poured out such devotion, and could not find them, or be sure. Of course, undergrowth grew up even in pine woods, memory tricked one, the path across the pine needles, lightly trodden, could easily have changed course. Trees were cut down and new ones grew up. Woods were not static, but were growing, living things. The small stump, moss-covered, worn with caresses, could simply have rotted away.

She grew: and I tell her story now, not to seek out the symbolic meanings in past actions, not to go along with that facility of thought that makes the past responsible entirely for the present, but to discover anew the rich seams of life, the flowing underground rivers, to ask – how is it that we come to interpret the world around us? To make patterns of experience, to make them explicit. This is how it was . . . .

Brothers, then, siblings, but male, all male; and that perfection of male beauty that was finished off with the fat little bunch of grapes between the legs, that dangled or was squashed tight when the ankles were held together neatly in the air, pink feet bunched, for the towelling nappy and then the fine muslin one to be laid beneath the pink, globed bottom; that would rise and squirt even as the legs were pinioned, spread, and the nappy about to cover it all, so that the woman who held the legs, giant safety-pin between her lips contorting her true expression, would grunt or laugh and have to hunt for another square of white, clean, cleaner, nothing but the cleanest for this baby – all this. Look at him, isn't he beautiful? Come and look at your little brother. No, not too close, don't touch him there. Just look. Aren't you a lucky girl?

Her first brother, she heard, was like Winston Churchill, the second like Gandhi, the third like Aneurin Bevan. Thus, each had his public persona; all he had to do was grow into it. The first was pink, the second yellow, the third black. This was how she saw them, although of course there were the gaps in between. Each time, she stood at the side of the decorated cot and stared in. There was the meaninglessness, the puzzle of babies, of their flesh. Why? What did it mean? What was the point? She did not ask these questions, but there was the blankness of feeling, of no-feeling. What am I supposed to feel, to say? By the time the third one was born, there was the consciousness that this creature, this blob, would grow up to be another boy. Your little brother. Another little brother. Why? Why?

Her mother, feeding babies. A dark, greedy head at her breast. The warm room, the putter-putter of the gas fire, the tight drawn curtains, the special low nursing chair, the withdrawal from the cold and clatter of the rest of the house. The quiet, the refuge. Her mother, shut away with this infant. She came in, stood, stared, at the exposed breast, so white and so strangely coming out from all those clothes, at the baby, at his grasping and uncurling fist. With the last one, she was allowed, even encouraged, to hold him on her knee. People joked with her, assuming that she liked babies, there had been so many of them. This one, her grandmother said, would be a schoolboy, looking up to her, admiring her as she made her way, grown-up, into the world. She would give him half-a-crown, to spend on tuck. She tried to believe it, to see it this way; but felt, inwardly, dismay.

And all the time, there were the colours, the contrasts. The nursery was cream, with the angry red of the gas fire at its centre. Her mother's flesh, white, and the new baby a dusky flushed red with the blackest of hair. And she, Alice, dizzy, spun between two extremes, would be ill with it unless she penetrated the secret, unless she understood why. A thin, bony girl, burning with energy, she ran the length of the house, skidded on polished floors, galloped shouting along corridors where nobody heard her, found chill empty rooms, the larder, the dining room, the downstairs lavatory, in which her breath made patterns in the air, and secret, hot rooms, the boiler room, the airing cupboard, the place between the fire and the rack where the nappies dried. From one to the other, searching, sniffing; from the furniture polish, cold-book smell of the drawing room, the velvet-curtain smell of the dining room, the cold-fat smell of the larder where the killed pigs hung; from there into the pungent coke-smelling boiler house where the cats hid and the brushes were kept for blacking shoes, or the burnt-linen smells of the airing cupboard, the nappies

17

that smelled of boiled pee. Her domain, this. In which to search and find the clues, that would make sense, that would make coherence. It was snowing, outside. The world outside was all white, and had been white it seemed forever. It was the worst winter of the century. And in the house was such cold that she woke in the morning and did not dare to put her hands out of the bed. It was an austere time. It was all she had ever known. People spoke of it later naming it, describing it. The war had left its marks – tiredness, a lethargy born of malnutrition and long effort, an inability to rise above the demands of everyday. There was not enough to go round – of food, of energy, of heat, of time to spend with children when new babies were born. Everything was in short supply; this she learned early. All there was plenty of, was space. Aimless in the freezing corridors, she explored the ambiguous messages of freedom.

Yet there was the other side, too, there was the contrasting colour, the rich red-gold against the pale mean blue; there was the other world, her grandmother's house. Not that it was warmer, for money did not necessarily buy heat, and the heating system was as antiquated and inefficient as any other. There were still the big high-ceilinged rooms with only a log or coal fire giving heat, so that the only way was to crouch on the hearth rug and turn oneself as if on a spit. But there was the colour, the smell, the warmth, the touch of luxury. Instantly recognisable, for ever after: in the feeling of material, in a word, a name, in the taste of wine, the cold touch of fur, in colour, in sensation, in all falling away into physical ecstasy, in all joyful surrender. The red and the gold of life.

Alice decided to become a magician, so that throughout her lifetime one could be transformed into another, so that substances would never limit her, so that the colours could meet and flow. She practised, in secret, her art. Alchemy was not a word she had heard, yet from this time onward all her concentration would go towards this, the transformation of matter: until the base metal should become indistinguishable from gold.

In her grandmother's house, the vivid taste of life existed particularly in small cream-filled chocolate biscuits, shell-shaped, that had been sent in a square tin from friends in South Africa, to relieve the English at war, Apfeldorn wafers. The pure sensation, and then the after-ripple, the sense of what had passed, and afterwards (when the tin was closed) the torment. Addiction: to the moment, when the teeth broke through the thin crust of wafer to find the firm sweet cream beneath. The sensation just behind the front teeth, against the palate, that could neither be prolongued nor repeated. The second bite less than the first, the third less than the second; that first incision and discovery of the cream within, the essence of sensual experience, to be sought again and again. In war-time, ration-book-time, when hundreds of people, thousands of people, lived close to starvation, Apfeldorn wafers, sent from South Africa, in a tin. There was also, in her grandmother's house, chilled Coca-Cola, the first ever tasted in the neighbourhood, and there were individual bottles of peppery tomato juice, poured and shaken with Worcester sauce. There was a round tin with a worn pattern of flowers on the lid that stood by the bedside full of digestive biscuits in case of night starvation. In her grandmother's bedroom, smelling of lotions and powder, a breakfast tray was brought up each morning and her grandmother lay elegant in a crêpe de chine nightdress, smiling, awaiting her after-breakfast visit. In the morning room, where the portraits were and the folded newspapers and the drinks trolley with the cut-glass decanter and the sober whisky glasses, there was the quiet morning flicker of the fire beside which *he* sat. There were his clean hands with the well-cut nails, his barbered beard, his gold watch too. And it was everywhere here, heady, pervasive, in this house; narcotic, addictive; thoroughly pre-war. The red and the gold. The contrasting colours of life.

When her grandmother died, and she was seventeen, she went with her mother into that bedroom, which smelled still of the perfumed lotions, which housed still the cupboardfuls of clothes, in which the aura of breakfast in bed and Balkan Sobranie still lingered powerfully; and together they opened the cupboards and drawers, laid bare the magic, examined the stuff of which the dream was made. Her mother, distressed, was simply angry at there being so many objects to dispose of. Each one, perhaps, reminded her of her loss; each one gave her a new obligation. But Alice stood before the rows of shoes, shoe-treed, polished, made of suede or fine leather, gazed at the drawers full of shawls, silk scarves, fine underwear, fingered the pots and bottles, the lotions for eyes and body, against wrinkles, against marks of all sorts, against wear and tear, laughter and sorrow, sorted the nail polishes, the soaps, the creams and cream removers, in a daze. There were the gloves, like thin hands folded in their narrow drawer compartments, wrapped in tissue paper, white gloves, kid gloves, leather gloves, silk gloves; next to them, the scarves, head-squares and cravats, silky, sinuous, and cashmere, and knobbly wool; then the handkerchiefs, some with the slightest pink stain upon them, where somebody had pressed them to her lips. There were the blouses and cashmere cardigans, the smocks her grandmother had liked to wear, for they concealed the cruel high corset she had to put on as soon as she got out of bed; then there were the wardrobes full of dresses, coats, jackets, furs hidden in plastic shrouds, hats in hat boxes, berets, turbans; and, finally, the collection of shoes. In her mind, that image, of at least thirty pairs of well-kept shoes, remained the most powerful. Even their tongues polished, even their soles cared for; like well-stabled, well-groomed horses, they waited in their rows to go out. Her mother's feet were too big for them, her own too small. She hardly wanted them used, only cherished, only admired. She guessed, accurately, that never again in her life would she come across anybody who owned at least thirty pairs of shoes.

And so the picture, the pattern, begins to emerge. Austerity on the one hand, luxury on the other. Throughout her life, the two poles upon which experience was to be hung. The sensible and the sensual. Sense, you could say, and sensuality. These were what she was given, the colours on the palette, the two extremes between which all others, more muted, less clear, more subtle, less obvious, must play and adjust and readjust themselves. On one hand, a freezing house with too many children in it, in which a man, her father, reads the *New Statesman* and reckons up his bills for the month, frowning, and a woman, her mother, scrubs nappies and muddy clothes in a sink with no detergent until her knuckles bleed. On the other, a room in which a

woman lies in bed reading the newspaper after breakfast and gets up
into silk underwear, in time to come down for a glass of sherry before
lunch; in which there are thirty pairs of shoes; in a house where
Apfeldorn wafers may be had. The post-war and the pre-war. The
new world, perhaps, and the old. And she, Alice, whoever she is,
finding her way between them, all the while.

2

She lay in bed in the chill bedroom and watched the flicker of light
that came from between heavy curtains, the cold light of winter, weak
light of winter sun. It must be nearly time to get up, dress, go down for
breakfast. The bedclothes were heavy, pinning her in place: cold stiff
linen, blankets tightly tucked, puffy slippery eiderdown anchored by
one more blanket to stop it slithering off her in the night. There were
patterns of frost upon the window. When the taps in the basin were
turned on, they would cough and spit water. Everything in the room
was heavy, silky, brocade; surfaces intricate to the fingers, untouched,
like a museum. She was alone here, alone and free. She thought of the
noises of home, the rush and hurry of early mornings, her mother up
in the cold dawn already, making porridge, feeding babies and cats,
and the storming and stamping of her brother as he was forced into his
school clothes, and strapping of satchels, thrusting on of balaclava
helmets, fastening of gloves that had elastic running eerily through
coat sleeves and across the back of the neck; the cold, always the
intense cold, and the sudden small square of heat that was the gas fire,
and the smell of singed underclothes, of scorching hair. Rush, noise,
voices shouting, and her self somehow lost, somehow left behind, a
small vital part of herself still curled up tight in bed. Now, here, she
was all here and herself, in this bed. Distinct from all the others, from
the formless mass of them. Her feet reached to the still cold extremities, her legs slid across the smooth delicious plains of linen, at the
centre was her complete self, warm, reliable. Her hand slid down to
find the comforting certainty of it again.

And today was New Year's Day. The old year, the old decade, had died in the night. At some point, when she had been asleep, the old year had twisted shrivelled, blackened, died, and the new one had sprung to life. She had wanted to watch for that moment, to spy on it: catch that momentous passing. But had slept instead, her head upon this pillow like a meringue, legs curled high as a foetus', hands folded between her thighs. Thus she slept every night; and time moved on, midnight passed, not to be examined.

A new year, a new decade, and her ninth birthday. Upon Christmas Day, in church, her mother, vast in a brown coat, had whispered to her, had pulled her out from the pew, pushed her across the aisle, whispered to Mrs Davies who sat staring, fur hat, eyes round with what was confided to her; all around in a blast of sound they sang 'O Come All Ye Faithful' and she stood beside Mrs Davies, her heart thudding, and mouthed the words like a goldfish, and dared not turn, dared not follow her mother with her eyes to see where she was gone. There was the smell of fur and the dust of hassocks and the church floor. A boy stared at her, Andrew Davies, and the familiar sensation of sickness stirred in her stomach. Her mother had gone out in the middle of church, but she could not move; only fight down the sickness, think of something else, quick, the book thrust into her hand, the page, the known tune, Christmas dinner, no, that would not do, the great brass eagle with its taunting beak, the stained-glass window, miles away, there, in the colours of blood and the sky. The hymn ended. Let us pray. And the darkness behind her gloved hands hid her, the smell of fur beside her intensified as Mrs Davies knelt to pray, the voice of the vicar murmured over her and she willed his words to work, magic. At the end of the service (the peace of God which passeth all understanding) there was everybody's confusion, what to tell the child, and who to take her home. Why had she been there with her mother in the first place? Did only women go to church on Christmas Day? Her father was at home in his study, drawing plans as if it were any weekday, wearing the same old jersey. Her brothers could perhaps not be trusted to behave. So, she had been there, and her mother, seized with the first cramping pains of labour, in the second verse of that long Christmas hymn, had left her, handed her over, cast her afloat, into that sea of people.

All night, there had been noises in the house, comings and goings, creaks, lights on, doors opening. Between tea and supper, she had passed her father on the landing and his glance had been wild. She had hurried past him, to her room. Don't look at me, his glance had said, and don't ask. It was as if she had surprised him naked coming out of the bathroom. And there had been Christmas dinner, too much to eat, the overladen platefuls, the taste of burnt raisins charring the mouth afterwards. It had been like a plug to block off the sickness, mouthful after mouthful. Eat, everybody said, you must eat. Her grandmother presided; said, 'I'll take one of the chicks home with me – Alice perhaps. Alice can come and stay with me tomorrow.

Alice had known it would be she; chosen quickly by her grandmother like that. Let the boys and the man live hugger-mugger, get by. The grandmother and Alice would retire to the world of Apfeldorn wafers, white linen. She breathed out, pushed the rest of the Christmas pudding to the side of her plate, now that there was a choice. Her grandmother smiled at her, a little painfully. Alice knew how it was for her grandmother to be here, in this house, at this table, and for her own daughter to be up there producing a baby, locked up there in some secret world of pain. She smiled back, a social smile, a smile for between women.

In the morning, somebody had come into her room – who had that been? A messenger, from what had been going on out there. The room was creamy yellow and a knot in the light cord made spooky shadows on the ceiling. She had shared it with her brother William when they both had chicken pox, because it was easier; but lately, she had been in it on her own. The messenger said – 'You've got another little brother' and she knew what had been happening all along, there was no need to explain. She thought – they must be mad. Another? Were there not too many already? What did they think she wanted with all these brothers? What were they trying to do?

In her grandmother's house, away from it all, she awoke to the silence of the morning; and solitary, female, free, but a little too scared to move out of the confines yet of the huge bed, welcomed the new year.

Brothers, boys, men: everywhere the insistent beauty of the male form, the lithe thinness of them, the way they moved, knees bony, elbows angled, buttocks small and fine napes bared by scissors. In the house in which the rooms were large and spare, the corridors long, so that one person crying could be isolated, not heard; where the air in winter was so intensely cold. In the shared playroom and in the bedrooms with the high swinging lamps, in the hall, behind the long curtains, in the back corridors where the green linoleum was scuffed and torn, on the slippery back stairs where the paint went only to eye level; in the bathroom where scalding water jetted suddenly into the scarred bath and then went cold, where there was steam in the air, or breath. All around her, forever, the imprint of masculinity, sign of the norm. Naked boys in the bath, pink in the passageways and half-pyjamaed, taunting her so that she ran and slapped and then was slapped in turn – it was his fault, he started it – but you are the eldest and a girl. And waking early in the cold was hard, dressing in scratchy grey school socks, gartered at the knee, putting on wool vests and stiff aertex shirts, coming down to the warm island of the kitchen to eat porridge and bicker while the cats at the window pressed moon faces to the frozen glass. Hard. And they eyed each other, watched, waited; taunted, flared to anger. There were rules, traditions. All this was imposed, it seemed from within. You could not drink from a cup that another had touched with his lips, nor eat a cake that another had fingered. Limits, boundaries, fears. He's touched it, I can't eat it now. It's his, I won't use it. The touch of the other, forever taboo. Islanded, they moved yet close within each other's orbit. She saw one in tears, punished for something that he had not done, and the pain went through her, was hers, intimate. Another, goaded beyond endurance, hurled his plate of cold cabbage to the floor. Tears, slaps, recriminations. The cold food set back before him, to be picked at through a whole long afternoon; for her, the discomfort, all that time, of knowing he was in there with his plate of cabbage, a prisoner. Yet after all, he was the other: he, not I, not she. She learned to avert her eyes, to say that it was not happening, finding the pain of another's hurt impossible to bear.

Yet in the other house, she awoke and the day was free, empty.

There was no blood here, and no cries. There would be breakfast laid downstairs for her alone, for her grandparents breakfasted in their rooms. There would be the sunlight coming in and the softly polished silver, the butter dish, the little triangles of toast. Cereal in a bowl, a milk jug, individual salt and pepper pots and the big handful of a sugar shaker, all for her. There might be scrambled eggs, or bacon, a choice. In the room there would be silence, so that she could hear the birds outside and the slow thaw-drip into the water butt. Glassy light; a fine fragility of early winter day. And afterwards, when she had wiped her mouth upon the stiff smooth folded napkin that had lain bridging her knees, she would go upstairs, through the rays of dusty light, through the blinding dancing sparks, blinking as she went, her hand on the banister, feeling her way. She would shut her eyes for a moment in the passageway at the top, to see what it felt like to be Blind Pew, and tap-tap her way along, feeling the doors, scaring herself, till she came to the certainty of the third one along. Always the knock, then, and the high-pitched call 'Coo-ee' – and the door pushed open upon thick carpet, the muted pinkish light within, the face in the pile of hair upon the pillow, the tray pushed to one side, the beautiful ringed polished hands idle upon the sheet: the welcome, the acceptance of herself. Sometimes, there was also something that was a little too stuffy, a little too airless, too perfumed, perhaps, that made her hold back for a minute, reluctant to be kissed. To kiss her grandmother was to bend over the vertiginous low neck of her nightdress, to guess at heavy, ageing breasts, to be enveloped for just too long a time in too sweet an odour; it was at once alarming and fascinating, because in some way not quite real. Enchanting, stifling, the odour of the boudoir, centuries old; of indoor women. And the fear, never quite explained, of what might show, what might be glimpsed below the surface. Silk, powder, perfume and beneath, what, the wolf's pelt, the snapping shining teeth? What lay beneath the skin of a grandmother?

She came close, kissed, withdrew. There were crumbs of toast left upon the plate, lip-marks upon the cup, the fine sheet was crumpled slightly, the soft grey-blonde hair fell back upon a pillow on which there was the slightest pink mark, lipstick or rouge. And in the dim light, suddenly, she wanted something clean, cold, airy: the stark winter outside, an unfurnished room.

– Hallo, chick, and what about you this morning? Did you have a nice breakfast? Draw back the curtains, will you, darling, and let in the day.

As if she knew, as if she guessed: just as, years later, she would fix her clear green-brown eye upon her granddaughter, close to, and ask her quite sternly – Well? Are you heart-free? And Alice would have to blush and look away, for fear of disappointing her: fearing that love must always give its self away in the eyes. Heart-free? Never, or rarely. And her grandmother, pleased at her embarrassment, would go on to tell her of the successes of her youth. Did I tell you about my young middy, the one I met at my very first dance? I quite fell in love with his shiny buttons. Oh, and do you know, he even asked for a lock of my hair—

The difference, Alice could not help noticing, was that whereas all the boys in her grandmother's stories were captivated by her, asked for locks of her hair, made an adoring endless chain through history, the ones she dreamed of were ignorant of her very existence. But then, her grandmother was beautiful. She incarnated the very word 'beauty' for ever after. In the portraits of her youth, auburn-haired, white-skinned, wide-mouthed, smiling, she had been very beautiful indeed. To keep the disappointment of a plain unloved grand-daughter from her, Alice invented dances at which boys looked longingly at her, queued to dance with her, longed to hold her in their arms. They were curly-headed, pink-complexioned, well-behaved boys, like the one in midshipman's uniform who had survived for sixty years in her grandmother's dream, he of the shiny buttons. They were not what she wanted, not really. But for the fantasy, for her grand-mother's favourite game, they would do. And they were safe, too. Dinner-jacketed to the chin, shiny-black-shod to the toes, stiffly positioned for foxtrots and waltzes, they were dolls, they were puppets; they never undressed or went to the lavatory or were sick or screamed abuse or broke her things; they were inhuman, like little gods. All her friends, at one point in her life, had them. They called in cars, escorted them to dances, sent Valentine cards, played tennis, asked for the Last Waltz. They belonged to the Young Conservatives and went to the Golf Club. (Young Conservatives? Her father snorted disdain. No such thing. Contradiction in terms.) But they were what was required, what was supposed to be desirable; and so she turned her back upon earlier, darker passions and did her best, and told her grandmother that no, she was not heart-free.

In the boudoir, then, in the bedroom, in the rose-tinted silken glow of luxury, what else was hinted at, never revealed? The trembling of a petal about to fall; and, falling, the bared dead head, its baldness. Tear down the brocade curtains, pull in the alien light, and what is seen? What, beneath the layers, the gentle surfaces? Beneath the charming midshipman's uniform, behind the blue blank eye of the doll, what remains, unyielding to potions, unassuaged by creams, remorseless as the passing time? She did not know, but felt it sometimes, and trembled.

– Happy New Year, darling.
– Happy New Year.

And the year was a gulf, empty, glittering clean, that had to be filled with something. A new brother born. Her ninth birthday. Treasure Island, Blind Pew, the tapping of twigs upon a window pane at night. An illness, perhaps, measles this time, or mumps. School, and a new desk, not marked yet with her initials. Empty white books, new paper, pencils, the smell of the stationery cupboard, the promise locked in there, of the blank sheets. But, what? What else? There was again this sense of the gap, the stretching emptiness, like skin. And of something in her that was scarcely anchored, scarcely controllable, that tugged, tugged to be away.

3

And to whom was it then that she spoke, as she crouched on the high flat branch of the sycamore tree that stretched above the peat stack, as, notebook and pencil in hand, she mouthed the words, trying them like bubbles in the air, searching for the spell that would come right,

27

would effect the transformations, would present, exactly, the world as she found it, but linked, connected, a fluid living thing? Her mouth spoke the words in silence, and there was nobody listening; they hunted for her, perhaps, elsewhere in the garden, they were out there calling her name. Alice? Alice! She was not answering. She was elsewhere, up among the green branches, hidden, in a place only she and the cats knew; she was compact up here, her knees beneath her chin, she chewed her pencil and the words raced through her, all that she had ever heard, since the moment she was born. It had to be today. It had to be now, this minute, this afternoon, this early summer time, this hour among the green leaves. Now, at last. There had to be a time when you began, when you seized it, this flying essence that was life; when you said – flinging out a hand, grabbing at what passed – Mine. Mine, she said; and hugged her knees, and felt the power run through her, push at her fingertips, her toes, her sex, spring tears into her eyes. Mine. Now. And the green world that enclosed her said nothing, but waited, and in the far garden among the rose trees, among the cabbages, they hunted for her and called her name. Enough, of feeling, of being caught up, this way and that, she said; enough of waiting, while somebody calls my name. Where are you? We were looking for you all afternoon. In the house, the chaos of people living, argument and embraces, the day-to-day, on-and-on, repeated chain. Her mother, standing at sinks; her father, coming in from trains; her brothers, separate from her, for whom she was not responsible. In the house, you could wait for ever, and the intense beauty of the world, of everything, could run through you and use you up and never be caught, be said. She did not know what she wanted: but to do something with it, this green afternoon, this time, her childhood. Mine. My life. My world. Mine, because I choose to make it so; because the feelings that riot through me will not be dammed. Mine, because I tell you of it, you, the other, whoever you are who sit here quietly beside me in my leafy perch, who want my version of it all, who want to know. She chewed her pencil and made holes with it in the soft places on her knees, and looked at the sky between the broad green leaves, and when something had settled at last inside her, when the person whom she did not know came close enough, so close that the silent words her lips practised could be heard and held, she began to write them down. The joy of it was so enormous that it pressed against her skin from the inside and she felt herself stretch and grow light, like a balloon. All afternoon and evening it was there, and she walked about lightly, quietly, holding it; knowing it was hers, now.

To be a poet. It was not what she said, it was hardly articulate even inside herself, for the word was to do with men, with adults. Yet she knew what she meant, as she crouched there in the tree with the notebook, writing her own name over and over again. It was a way of handling all this: the randomness, the overflowing of life, the contrasts, the red and the gold. It was a way past the sickening sensation that came with the too-beautiful colours of the sky at evening, a way through the impossible. For otherwise the world was too full, too rich: could never be lived in. Once, so recently, she had whirled at its centre, cartwheeling free and vivid at the hub of the universe. Now, quite suddenly, the same movements made her sick. She was sick of cartwheeling, of being admired. She had tried it, and it had not worked; had only made her dizzy, not powerful, not central. The magic was elsewhere.

She took a small leather-bound book from her parents' shelves, leaving a gap among the collected works of Kipling, and climbed back up into the tree with it, and let the words run through her until they became senseless, an incantation as rhythmic as her own body's pulse, absorbed into herself. There was no way that she could be a man or an adult; no way, then, to be what this was, to wield the magic, to be in charge of it and therefore of the world. But she sat among the green branches and every now and then, as she read, as she rocked beneath the leaves, there came a glimpse, blue between green, sun dazzling, of what might just be possible.

There were, of course, other people; and attempts, impassioned attempts, to make the two worlds meet.

The abduction of Colin – a failure, but nevertheless an attempt to bridge gaps, to show the ordinary boy from next-door the red-gold of

29

the extraordinary. He let her down. Became the prototype of men who lost their nerve at the last minute, thought of their wives, their jobs, their families, ran for cover. In whom the flame went out. Colin was thin, fair-haired, with knobby fists and knees and big feet and a scowl for most of the world; lived in the world of the pub, where late hours were kept, meals forgotten, where cars screeched their brakes late at night in the driveway, skidded on gravel. A road-house, people said of Colin's father's pub. A den of thieves, said Alice's father, scathing. Colin's father was rich, paid others to look after his son, ignored him. Alice's mother said Colin was neglected. Colin came through the fence at the top of the garden through a burrowed hole he had made himself, like a visiting fox to the farmyard. Stayed to play, hoped to be asked to tea, charmed nobody with his sullen manners; gave way to bursts of violence and was given for Christmas guns, bows and arrows, exploding caps. People said of him that it was a pity; and Alice and her brothers carried him into their house like a prize, like a hostage, and stuffed him with cake. When he and Alice quarrelled, he threw half a brick at her accurately enough and stood panicking over her as she groaned and clasped her bleeding head, his first thoughts of the police. But she did not tell; not until, years later, airily – the time the boy next door threw a brick at me – for she knew that his banning would curtail her own freedom, cut short the valuable stream of information that came from him, about pubs, cars, criminals, suspicious events, and divide her off from what was necessary, vital, the curious half-hating half-needing relationship she had with Colin now. He was slightly younger than she, and so she led. And yet, his knowledge, his weapons, his language, the freedom and secrecy of his way of life also compelled her to listen, to follow. She hated his hardness, his lack of imagination, the way he bored her with boasting stories; yet loved the mere fact of associating with him, the outcast.

Colin said that he hated girls. He said it regularly, making of her an exception, an accomplice in something she feared. When he tied Joanna from up the street to the sycamore tree in Alice's garden, capered around her, his conquest, showered her with sticks and pebbles, threatened her with a tin bucket over her head if she did not surrender – and what surrender more was possible? – Alice stood

30

apart, watching, divided. She was Colin's friend and associate. Joanna was nothing, a stupid girl, who deserved perhaps to be tied to a tree. And yet, the scene stirred deep fear in her, and antipathy. When he had tired of tormenting Joanna, she said to him as scornfully as possible – I don't know why you bother. And walked away, leaving him his pointless scene of triumph, his ridiculous victim, his unimpressive self.

Colin. She wanted him, wanted him with her. The plot was hatched between them during the twilight evenings, in the thick jungle of vegetation at the top of the garden, where he came in through the hedge. On the other side of the hedge, quite close, there was the weary, angry tone of the woman who was supposed to look after Colin when his parents were busy, who simply stood at the back door and shouted, in the sharpness of her tone – Colin' – all the irritation at her task. At the other end of their territory, at the back door of Alice's house, a light glowed, and Alice's mother called for her, too; and neither of them stirred. Alice was thrilled by what she had so easily brought into being, by his subservience, all at once, his subdued excitement, his dependence.

– Now, don't forget. Tomorrow, when you're supposed to go home for lunch. I'll bring you some food. Then you can get to the car while they're still eating, it'll be a cinch.

She did not imagine, then, the boy standing bawling in the cupboard in the darkness, howling to be let out; nor the angry searchers ransacking the house, turning upon her, blaming her; nor his look of accusation when he came out, the prisoner, and told them it was all her fault. But rather, thought of the thrill of their secret communication, the success of their plan; the smooth getaway and the time – hazily imagined, this – that they would spend together when they got there.

As it was, when she went down to the kitchen to eat her dinner, the next day, and Colin stayed willingly locked in the cupboard on the landing, silenced by her promise that she would bring him food directly, the woman who was supposed to look after Colin came from the pub, knocking.

– No, I haven't seen him, not since about twelve o'clock. She lied,

31

and they all watched her.

– Are you sure, dear?

The 'dear' was barbed, an accusation.

– He said he was going home. Honestly. I suppose he might – might have gone round by the heath. You might have only just missed him. That's it, you probably did, if he went the other way.

Alarm shook her, but she chose the lie, elaborated on it, felt then a little safer. The search party – Mrs Bolter, with her thin trap mouth, accusing and on her dignity, her parents, at once defensive and critical of her, her grandmother, disbelieving – all went out into the garden, calling, their voices spreading as they fanned out. Co – lin, Co – lin. Alice stayed near to the house, uncertain. Later, she said to him – Well, how could I have brought you anything to eat just then, with all that going on, it would have given the game away at once, wouldn't it, couldn't you have waited a few minutes, couldn't you have—? Trusted me, was what she wanted to say. But, no. Of course not. Colin trusted nobody, had not for years, probably never would again. Locked in a cupboard at ten years old by a girl who wanted to kidnap him, and who simply turned the key, promising food, and then went away. In a panic, he had drummed his fists upon the inside of the locked door, and shouted, in this alien house in which he was not welcome, shouted and yelled, for the last time, for somebody to come and let him out. The punishments that would be waiting for him outside would be a relief after this darkness, this waiting. The hour in the cupboard stretched, expanded, darkness and waiting enough to fill the whole of his lifetime, till there was nothing else. He banged, shouted, rattled at the handle, and they came closer. It was life or death, it was the end of him, the end of his tether. And they came closer. He heard the footsteps. Up the stairs and across the landing. As footsteps had come, and passed him by, all his life, since he lay in that cot in the dark room, harnessed, and they did not come. But this time, yes. Across the landing towards him, towards the locked cupboard, the cupboard that had no key.

– Alice! Do you know the meaning of this?

She handed the key, on its string. It had hung around her neck, invisible. The meaning was that she had failed, that she had been let down. There would be no sleek getaway now for Colin in the back of her grandparents' car, covered with a fur rug as she had imagined until the moment when he could emerge, because they were there, because they had arrived. It was all bungled, ruined, her dream, whatever it had been. The key was snatched from her. Waiting for Colin to come out was like waiting for a jack-in-the-box; you know the moment will come when the thing will shoot from its confines, but you are scared, waiting. But Colin did not shoot, had no spring. When he came, it was grasped by the arm by Alice's mother, snivelling. No other word for it, thought Alice. His red and resentful eyes flickered for a moment towards her. Coward, collaborator. She stood there, her face averted, and knew him led away, comforted, consoled, threatened, taken home, like a baby. She heard – 'She put me in there' and 'It was her fault. I wanted to go home, and she shut me in'.

And since nobody ever asked her for her version or what she had intended, since from now on all was shouting and punishment, she never said, never even articulated to herself this time, what it was she had been trying to achieve. But when it was at last time for her to leave on holiday, when the scenes and the noise were over and her grandmother was peering at her tiny watch and saying, really, dear, in spite of everything, I think we should be on our way; when she sat, the fur rug over her own knees, all alone in the back of the car waiting for her grandmother to get in, she knew that she was glad he was not there. It would have been too much to handle. He would have been there, at mealtimes, at bedtime, in the morning, boring her, getting in her way. Rescuing him would have been one thing, but having him there all the time, quite another. She did not want him, had never wanted him, not really. It was curious now, looking back, to think that she had thought she did.

She sat beneath the fur rug; in the back of the Rolls. (Perhaps it was the car that Colin wanted, after all?) The movement of it, the persistent thirty miles an hour, the closed windows, the back of the head of the chauffeur in front, his red neck, cropped hair, rigid cap; and the smoke that wreathed her, Balkan Sobranie, the sickly, heavy smoke; here it seemed was the essence of it, the closed and heady world in which her grandmother lived, in which Colin and all the others would be strangers, in which, if she stayed, she would be irretrievably alone. She sat, and was carried onward. Towards a destination, towards a holiday with relations, somewhere else. And yet, the journey encased, enclosed her; surely it would never end. Her hand went out to touch surfaces for reassurance, for solidity, found leather, metal, fur, the coldness of rings on flesh. Her grandmother's hand, with firm fingers, polished nails, pushing at her own cuticles, pressing them back. And she, Alice, was to travel always with her hands above the rug, the heavy fur, grey like a wolf's pelt, that lay across her knees. She was in the middle, between them, now, the two old ladies, her grandmother and her great aunt. Tall on each side of her, they smoked and talked across her. The smoke and the talk – censored – '*pas devant*' her grandmother would say warningly, elegant French accent used as a screen – flowed in and out of her lungs and above her head. And her hands wanted to go under that rug, find the warm place between her thighs, console her with the brief spurt of pleasure she had learned to conceal from the world. It was a challenge, to reach that height of dizzy pleasure without a sign, without a flicker, without even a change of breath; so that they would go on talking, smoking, not noticing. But their eyes seemed to be upon her hands. Somebody had decreed that her hands should be above that rug. And the movement of the car, the slight rock, the softness of the seats, the pressure of her sweaty thighs together was not enough; it merely maddened, instead of releasing. She began to cough. A ringed hand reached to wind the window a fraction down. There was Evian water for the journey. Outside, inaccessible, the rich green beauty of Sussex – was it Sussex? – countryside. Soon, she would say that she wanted to go to the lavatory, and be freed; for that announcement always alarmed them into commanding an immediate stop.

Once, travelling with her grandmother, she had gone into a wood, pulled her knickers down and suddenly noticed, immediately in front of her, a man with his penis hanging whitely out of grey flannel trousers. Her own rush of long-held urine went on, so that she could not scrabble up and run away at once, but simply stare. He could have been doing what she was doing, of course, but there was something about the way he stood there, something about the expression on his face and the way his penis went on hanging out, looking so pale and somehow ill, that made her think he was not. She pulled up her knickers at last, and ran, scattering hot drops down her legs, followed by his limp stare. Out of the wood she ran, out of the shadow and back into the sunlight, where the big black car gleamed and the man in uniform strolled and the two old women scrabbled in their bags. The group, before her, formed an oasis of safety. The edge of the wood, and the pale light grass, and the hot tarmac of the empty road and them. She ran up panting like a dog and told them, muttering so the man in uniform might not hear. Her grandmother shot into scandalised French to her sister; this was certainly a case of *pas devant* and told Alice that, poor man, he could not help it, he was ill, and that she was to forget all about it. That lunchtime, as they munched delicately small sandwiches of scrambled egg at a further roadside halt, she told Alice, for some reason, the life-story of the French artist, Henri de Toulouse-Lautrec.

Now, there was the taste of bitter chocolate in the back of her throat, and the flatness of Evian water from the bottle, and the pressing need between her legs, unidentifiable in its urgency. There was the morning behind her, and the scene of Colin's release from captivity, and her own disgrace. There was endless time, endless space, before her, in which she must go on and on at thirty miles an hour for ever, flanked by two old ladies, in a closed car. She said – I think I want to go. And thought of Toulouse-Lautrec again, as she had to now at such moments, and the way that the girls kicked their stout stockinged legs high doing the can-can. But, since the man in the wood, woods and even clumps of trees and hedgerows were out, and she would have to wait until they stopped in a minute or two, at what her grandmother called an 'otel. And there was bitter chocolate and Balkan Sobranie and Toulouse Lautrec and Colin and the limpness of the man in the wood and the movement of the car and the taste of the flat stale water, and she knew that in a minute all control would go, her muscles would be able to hold out no longer and she would do it, flood the back of the Rolls and the fur rug and all with the scalding pleasure and shame, if not.

– Stop! she cried – to herself, to them. And the car stopped, Mr

Parkes having daughters of his own and acting out of impulse, and she was saved.

Her grandmother had married late in life the man her sisters called 'the little nugget'. But to Alice when young, there was nothing little about her step-grandfather. Immense, immovable, he presided wherever he was, before well-laid fires, beside drinks trolleys, at meal times behind silver and cut glass, in the backs, always the backs, of cars. When she met him, she would have to walk straight up to him to kiss him, as if encountering royalty, and submit to the fierce hard bristles of his beard. And then his clean fingers with their flat, manicured nails, would slide into one of the slit pockets in his waistcoat and bring out something to show her: his gold watch on its chain; a cigarette case; the actual nugget for which he was named. There, in the morning room, beside the flickering fire, beside the whisky in its decanter and the glass he had poured, paler with water, and the Bath Oliver biscuits in the tin, he waited. For what? She wondered what he did when other people were out of the room; was he equally regal, equally still when alone? Above and around him there were the portraits, of men equally still, equally bearded, that seemed to study her with their eyes. The room was full of men's eyes; and her grandfather's, blue, watery yet suddenly imperious when he waved his stick, rang his bell, exclaimed with irritation. Upstairs, there was his bedroom, at the far end of the corridor, into which she never went. He did not sleep anywhere near her grandmother, but at the other end of the house, so that it was hard to remember that they were married. Upstairs, perhaps, he would be an invalid, a tired old man, a querulous figure in pyjamas; but downstairs, he ruled and stared. Sometimes he talked to her – of the Jameson Raid and Cecil Rhodes and Smuts, of Cannes and the Côte d'Azur – but it was always the objects that held her attention, the smooth lobe of the watch, the hard corners of the little nugget, his wealth.

Later, she understood that it was he who had created it, this world, in which she came and went, a small girl in the back of a Rolls Royce: world of luxury and ease, world of the red-gold glow and the sudden suffocation, world of riches. She knew that it was wealth, money.

From the power of South African gold, from mines in which black men toiled endlessly. He had it, he was it: the little nugget, they called him. Was he gold through and through, was even his heart made of it, the hot and molten metal that hardened, cooled; was it what ran even through his arteries? When he died, what would happen? Would the gold run out of him, powdered gold like dust, like sawdust, out of a punctured doll? Or would it pour from him and into the rest of them, into her, firing her veins, pumping her life for her, cutting her off forever from the Colin Dawsons that she fleetingly desired, from the Michael Foleys who would have been her equal? She thought that it would not: that whatever she touched – leather, fur, metal, precious stones – would remain outside of her, a substance remote from her own flesh. For she was herself, Alice Linnell, human, fallible, flesh-and-blood. Only the flesh and blood of others and their warmth, their breath, Michael Foley's breath and the scar upon his knee, the way the downy hair grew upon the flat of his wrists and at his nape, only this could be real to her in the way that her own flesh was real. For the sense of her own reality was there, flesh, beneath the fur of the travelling rug, flesh and therefore fallible, human, therefore not gold, not metal. She carried it within her, this knowledge of herself, carried it tight between her thighs and in the deep recesses of her mind; knew that she would not always be swept on like this, imprisoned in luxury, closed off from the green and glowing countryside beyond, full of both fear and beauty.

4

Where, then, did the image of the two hotels, the image of that far-off seaside holiday, fit in? It was earlier, certainly, for the summer was that first summer after the war, when the beaches had been cleared at last of barbed wire and sharp spikes of metal and it was possible, for the first time for so long, to plan a seaside holiday. The concrete pillboxes on the coasts of both England and France looked still too new and too raw to be seen as ruins; there were landmines still, and notices warning of them, and instructions to pick nothing mysterious up from the beach; but people, ordinary people, could go to the beaches again, and sink their bare toes in sand that was no longer grey and trodden only by boots, and walk into the welcome sea until waves frilled at knee height, at rolled-trouser height, and even go right the way in, and swim. What it meant to her mother, Celia, Alice would never know, only guess, only imagine. If the whole of Edwardian childhood could have been captured, encapsulated, its essence presented, it would have been in seaside, in holiday, in long summer months of dry heat and whistling windy cold, both, during which Celia and her cousins had played, walked, sat, picnicked on the beach. To be cut off entirely from all seaside activities, to be refused the beach, the sea, must have been for all of them not only a depriva-tion of pleasure, but of memory. The beaches, fenced, wired, inacces-sible to the public, were a whole middle-class generation's childhood and youth and happiness, wired and mined, made inaccessible too. But now, at last, the interdiction was lifted, socks and shoes and clothes could come off, pale skins, tired bodies slack with malnutrition and fatigue could rush into the sea again, under the sun, and be held once more by that rich, salt, rocking wave from which they had once come. The sea. They told Alice what it was like, what joy it was.

– You'll see, darling, we can go to the beach, you'll be able to go in the sea!

You'll be able to have a childhood, to dream, to live; not to be ruptured in mid-life from the sources of energy and pleasure, not to be dried out, landed, left gasping in the dying cities for breath.

They bought her bucket and spade and sunsuit and hat, the trappings of childhood on the beach. Her brother, the next one born, had a smaller, identical version. Very small, she stood on the beach in the baking sun, sand stretching away from her on all sides, and looked back at the two hotels. Next to each other they stood, red and white, with a gap in between. In the red, brickish, meat-coloured one she belonged, with her mother and brother; and in the white, cool one with the flag flying outside on the dried strip of lawn and the red and blue flowers in window boxes, her grandparents. She had to re-member to go back into the right hotel, the one in which she belonged.

But yet knew the other, where the carpet offered deep soft pile to her feet, tired from the beach, and where water gushed strongly from wide-mouthed taps. Tired, lost in the corridors of the wrong hotel, she had searched one afternoon for her grandparents and had found only cool corridors, fans whirring, a tree in a pot, a man hurrying in black with a shiny white front and glassy hair, a bathroom in which taps suddenly sang and rushed water and were hard to turn off. There were rooms and corridors; as in her own, the red hotel, but smoothly white-painted here, more identical; no scratch marks or odd door handles to relieve the sameness. Even walking fast, her own footsteps made no sound here; she had the feeling that if she were to call out, her voice would be noiseless. She retraced her own steps, back past the open mouth of the lift with its criss-cross shining doors and laundry baskets, back past the tiled bathroom where the bath stood proud on lion feet, back down the wide, shallow stairs. Out again, then, into the hot pale whirring afternoon. They had been in there, somewhere, her grandparents, resting; in their separate bedrooms, the feet of their beds raised on bricks so that the blood would drain to their heads, the curtains barely drawn upon the heaviness of afternoon; two effigies, on their backs, hands folded, eyes open, for as she had never seen them with their eyes shut, it was impossible to imagine; alert, they were, and listening in vain for her step, her breath, her voice. But their hotel was padded and soaked up sound. Suddenly panicking, she ran across the hot tarmac, up the path, past the faded hydrangeas in tubs, in through the front door of the other hotel that smelt of gravy and the tarnished metal of the gong. The gong that she and her brother fought over, each claiming the right to stroke the worn leather knob against the worn, pitted metal – bonnnggg – and bring the other guests to dinner. The dining room, with its gravy stains, egg-stains, on the stiff hanging cloth. The emptiness of arranged chairs, laid tables. And up the stairs of her own, familiar hotel, where she knew to turn right, to go up three more little steps, turn left, go past the mirror and find the first door on the left, number fourteen, where her mother would be; the door with the paint (brown) slightly worn where a foot had gently pushed at it for summers and summers before the war, to open it with a tray laden with things for early morning tea. The room with the flowered curtains sucking against the pane in the slightest draught, the bed with the pink cover, the worn, multicoloured, used, touchable things; and in the next room, adjoining, the two beds, hers and her brother's, and the things they had brought that had an odd, transported look, away from the home. The airlessness in the corridor and the freshness in the rooms, where her family opened windows to the sea. At last.

Looking back at the two hotels from the beach, she saw that they looked equal; it looked like an equal choice. To go right and into the white one, or left and into the red one; facing them, that was, with one's back to the sea. If you were to be coming out of one of them, left and right would be the other way round. In the red one, there was an unknown man in a striped towelling dressing gown, gargling in the bathroom in the middle of the night, grey hairs sprouting. There were doors open in the mornings upon dishevelled scenes – bedclothes all flung about, breakfast trays with toast crusts soaking in brown liquids and cigarettes stubbed out with lipstick on them, and burnt matches. Muttering women on their knees blocked the corridors with grey metal buckets and bad-smelling mops. At lunch one day in her grandparents' hotel, the white one, she heard her grandmother say – But, darling, I'm sure we could make arrangements, surely Richard would not mind? When her father came, still wearing khaki trousers although the war had ended, he took a plate of fish from the table in the red hotel and marched with it into the kitchen, holding it far away from him, with his look of disgust. But the red hotel, it seemed, was already paid for, and there would be no refunds, for smelly fish or men gargling in the bathroom or the lumps that her mother said she could feel, like the princess and the pea, no matter how many blankets went between the mattress and her, on her bed. The red and the white, were a fact, and the alleyway dividing them, and the rival patches of grass outside them, one with the flag on a white flagstaff, furled sullen in the windlessness of today, the other with only a board on legs, advertising cut-price facilities for children. The white hotel, Alice thought, was definitely pre-war. The red, she supposed, was what came after. And there was no real choice: or only the choice between losing oneself and being found.

She was alone, alone on the beach. Quite suddenly, they were none of them to be seen, only the line of the front, and the blue sky, and the two hotels, looming. Behind her, the gentleness of the sea, its sounds, awoke memories. And that, and the suddenness of being alone, the vast sky above her purple at its apex and drowning her with heat, began the familiar ache of feeling inside, the drumming emptiness that clamoured to be filled. She put her hand between her legs, inside her damp and crusted bathing suit, and felt it there, the suck of the sea, the salt, the overwhelming heat, the aloneness; the world, and she herself, stranded, at its centre. Standing there, with the two hotels like cliffs before her, she nearly fell with the sharpness of the pleasure. And then it was into the red hotel that they dragged her, up the steep steps, hurting her feet – quick, quick, wherever were you, we were out of our minds with worry, anything could have happened to you, anything, what do you mean by – In through the sudden engulfing doors of the red hotel, into darkness in which rings of light still whirled, up the stairs, along the corridor, quick, past all the landmarks that she had known differently, in her own time; quick, into the bedroom that had been a haven; and, quick, her yellow bathing suit, stripped off, lay like a soiled skin on the floor, sand-ribbed. The dried sand fell like dust from her body where their hands grasped. And it was in the red hotel, on the bed with the lumps, that she was spread out like a fish, like seaweed, and the innocent pod of her private pleasure probed like a shell that would not give up its creature. Words like 'doctor' and 'ointment' and 'rash' flew to and fro above her, as the brown of her body fought to conceal the white, the tenderly pink. Their hands were stronger, though, strangely firm, and the voices punishing although the words were not. She heard 'something to prevent it' and 'disturbing time' and the voices taut with anxiety. And in her mind she struggled to imagine herself not here, but there; there, in the other hotel, her feet soft upon endless carpets in endless cool corridors where doors opened upon tiled bathrooms and silent men carried bouquets of flowers along, past the discreet closed doors. In the white, in the cream, in the spotlessness, sandlessness, guiltlessness, silence of the other hotel.

For the rest of the time she shunned the beach and its uncontrollable size. Here, in the municipal gardens, the sky was more neatly confined, by trees, roofs, a summer house, with its pointed gable; the blue and red flowers grew like paper ornaments in their squares of dried earth, the grass edges were trimmed short by a man with long shears who walked sideways like a crab to do it, and the whole was kept in place by a metal gate. There were gravel paths, and benches. Her mother and grandmother sat on the benches, knitting, talking, relieved to be out of the sand, out of the glare, and she and her brother William played trains. The stations were the benches and there was an exactly predictable space between each bench. Scuffing the gravel with their sandals, chuffing along, hands held up for buffers, they chugged and steamed and whistled hour after hour, day after day. The rest of the holiday was divided up into the gaps between stations, the time it took to get from one to the next. The bench upon which the adults sat was the terminus, where the trains stopped to refuel. And, chugging, chuffing, her eye on the fat legs of William, who chugged and chuffed a little breathlessly ahead, she made herself all machine, all metal; fuelled, set, programmed, controlled. It was a good game, the adults said, doing their bit as the trains came round, with lemonade and ginger biscuits. Funny, they don't seem to want to go on the beach any more. And if Alice wanted to scream, scream with the boredom of it, scream with the mechanical motion, the control, and did not, it was on account of the remorseless position of them, their proximity, their difference, those two hotels.

She eyed her brother William, and wondered. As he went round and round, puffing with heat because she had ordained it, playing trains until he dropped, shorter than she was, fatter, short haired, chubby cheeked, out of breath. Was there an inside to him, she wondered, that was at all similar to her own? Beneath that pink skin that flushed easily with the sun, beneath that silken fringe of brown hair, behind those blue eyes, between those fat spread fingers trying to be buffers, what was there? She wanted to trip him, pounce on him, shake him, make him spit it out. As her mother had done once when she had nearly swallowed a peach stone in her grandmother's greenhouse a year ago. Beat him and shake him and then hold out a hand for him to retch and spit. What would come out? A small stone, disappointing in its size, finite, easily disposed of? She wanted to puncture him, to discover whether any hot streaming silky shameful pleasure such as inhabited her, would come spurting out.

When, that evening, they discovered what she had done to her doll, its belly rent open with nail scissors, its smashed smiling face awry, she heard the anxious muttering tones begin again, that were like distant thunder, only with no true storm. She thought that she would never discover, now, what her brother was like inside. Closed off from him, from his appeal, from his noisy admiration for her, from his frustration, his anger, she would wind him up and set him on his way: so many times round the gardens for the rest of the holiday, stopping and starting, whistling and puffing; while the dangerous sea and its whispering, creeping tides, remained at bay.

Yet there they were, increasing in number, growing up around her, the boys in whose rush of movement and noise she might go unnoticed. There was the small matter of their sex, theirs and hers, hidden equally by grey corduroy shorts that fastened by snake belts, and in winter, jeans; but this hardly mattered, surely, at their age, would only make itself apparent later on, when all was opened out, simplified, at adolescence. Beneath the convenient disguise, she grew, different from them, disturbed and segregated by this difference, as if set apart by what was unmentionable, because unmentioned.

They ran naked in the garden in summer, when their father turned the hose on them; darted beneath the rainbow curve of water, and shrieked. She ran faster than the others, fled in order to be all movement, invisible. Mrs Thompson from next door telephoned Celia to say – Don't you think your daughter is a bit too old now to be running about like that? It was done; she was seen, caught, made visible. Would not now go out naked like that any more, naked in the stream of water on the sodden grass, trusting in speed not to be seen. Noticed, picked out like that, she was slowed in her flight; fell. On hot days, from now on, she watched, moody on the step, while her brothers still ran and shrieked, their little penises bobbing, their wet round heads like seals'. She would not put on a bathing suit and join them, would not give in. The pleasure was over now, it had been

43

removed from her, she would not give them the satisfaction of com-
promise, nor run in the delicious spray with wet clogged cloth
between her legs where had been air. The summer dried out around
her, removed its oases. She contracted measles and had to lie in a hot
closed room, the curtains drawn against dangerous light, the radio
playing 'Shoes to set your feet a-dancing, dancing, dancing all your
cares away . . . '. Her mother sat in the half light and read John
Buchan in a soft voice, straining her eyes. Out on the bleached hard
lawn, down there, the boys danced beneath the hose-spray, laughed
and screamed, and her father in old flannels turned the cold hard jet
upon their tenderest parts and watched them jump away. Their little,
private hose-pipes that arched hot urine into the bushes, that
dangled, that could stiffen at a touch. Some boys, she learned, were
'Roundheads' and others 'Cavaliers'; it was the news from William's
school. But there was no explanation of why some had that concealing
flap of flesh and others the round purplish stump her brothers showed
her. She looked, listened; experienced the information as curiously
remote from herself. They told her, they included her. The old
question – what are they like? what are they really like? – continued to
puzzle her. But, after the initiation of measles, during which no male
of the household had come near her to visit or inquire, on account of
the infection, she tended to climb to the tree-house in the sycamore
tree alone and pull the rope up after her, as if she no longer wanted to
know. Their smooth bodies, predictable and all on view, they taunted
her from the bottom of the tree with the ill-aimed insults of childhood,
while up aloft she brooded, read poetry, and awaited adolescence as a
grumbling storm, now close, not far away. The drops upon the leaves
spattered. There was a tingling heaviness in the air. And her body,
that had been all hers to command, ached and twinged and would not
be reassured.

And the twin, the perfect other, the male counterpart of dream and of
the times before sleep, mirror-image, guardian of her self; where was
he? Brother and yet not-brother, self and not-self, imagined playmate
and actual person, surely existing somewhere there in the world? She
heard his laughter behind clumps of leaves, spied him fleet sometimes

between the trunks of trees, woke suddenly to the burning accuracy of his glance. He who uniquely recognised, mirrored, her power, her pride, her selfhood. He whose panache could crown and echo her own; so that, together, they would shine before the admiration of millions, of the entire world. With whom she was perfect, balanced, her perfect self. Where was he, in the time before the thunderstorm, in the remembered aloneness before the too-big sea? She searched, in her conscious mind, in her memory; and in dream, knew him retreating, disappearing, abandoning her at last.

High between the branches of the sycamore tree, on that hot evening of late summer when the gnats hung in clouds and the thunder rolled, she knew him finally departed, finally gone. As the first drops of the storm splatted among the broad leaves, she wept for his departure.

5

The train drew out of Waterloo station, laden as a troop train, uniformed arms coming out to wave. And of the couples who stood on the platform, who waved back, some were women in tears. Only the train (which was to pull out, gather speed, carry her inevitably away, in dreams, throughout decades) was filled – apart from the guard, the engine-driver – entirely with females. Female children, being sent away. The people on the platform consoled each other already. It's a good school, she'll do well, now, where shall we go for tea? Some of them – mothers – dabbed a little with a hanky, wondered briefly if they had been right. Others – fathers – fought with a sense of distaste, told themselves that of course, they had. And the children, already strangers, already anonymous in their brown tweed, brown stockings, brown berets and gloves; what of them? Beneath the tweed and the blouses and the regulation underwear, the plain bras and suspender belts, the lisle stockings, their bodies were similar, their memories and aspirations surely not so remote from each other, not so strange? Yet nothing was revealed. Each of them, sealed in her isolation, carried

45

with her, inside her, a world of remembered freedom, of embraces, of family meals, of childhood, of babyhood; dreams and fears. Yet to each other, they were opaque. Each one carried her self like a locked box, inaccessible. And stared out at her companions, swallowed tears as the train gathered speed, or exchanged trivial news, knowing its triviality, or combined to tease a newcomer. They had the same destination, would suffer the same things; and yet, in the closed carriages, enmity sparked easily, they drew back from each other, wary as caged cats, skin shrinking from any contact, eyes warning.

It was hard, then and later, for Alice to experience any of the others as a child, like herself. They were outside herself; creatures, neither male nor female in any sense that mattered; girls, neither children nor young women; just as the seventeen-year-old prefects with their eyes like policemen were neither young nor adult in any recognisable way, but sexless, related to no being she had seen before or would ever see again. Perhaps only prison warders, concentration camp guards, have this kind of otherness. Who were they? What sort of people consented to do these things? In what way, essentially, did they differ from herself and all that she had known until now?

What had happened? The universe, her universe, had changed dramatically, would not look the same again. Everything in her immediate world had now the hard, pale colour of institutional life There were the clean, stiff blouses laid out on Monday mornings, back from the laundry; exercise books had stiff shiny covers and pages of white; the walls were hard, cream-coloured gloss-painted, the steps of stone. A bell rang, and cold corridors were filled up with jostling girls, yet no flesh touched flesh, only cotton, only drill. Out on the playing fields, hockey sticks clashed in mud; and the trees, miles away, lost their leaves in the scorring wind. There were cold white plates at meal times upon which pink slabs of cold spam flipped flat. The bathrooms were chill off-white in early mornings, where girls stood in rows, stripped to pyjama trousers, waiting to wash. Their flesh pimpled with cold, breasts unlikely, stance an apology, heads ducked in the queue. The red, the gold of life, where was it: that glow, that had lit experience from within, long ago? There were sunsets, autumn sunsets beyond the buildings, beyond the playing fields, in whose extravagance some promise seemed to exist of beauty that was outside, beyond the glass, and might be eternal. There was the music of hymns, the rich words of the Bible, the King James version, prayers in the morning and the possibility, some days, some mornings, of feeling that certainty again, tasting those words, singing till her throat ached. There was the occasional hot pudding that would do for her palate and stomach what the words of hymns did for other parts: rhubarb crumble and custard, hot and running with acid juices, pink, streaming with sugar. And there was, resurrected, the possibility of falling in love.

Jane Appleby was plump, brown-eyed, dark-haired, seventeen, and her name was the truth about her, she was apple-round, apple-sweet, no plain Jane but honest English, a farmer's daughter from the West country, non-academic they said, no prefect; reassuring in her creamy-freckled firmness, in her voice that resonated with a buzz that was not upper-class English but underlined with something warmer, slower, not yet educated out. She wore three-inch heels in the evenings and her dresses dipped fashionably at mid-calf. She had a trilling voice, as she sang in the cloakroom the hit songs of the day. Her bosom stuck out like a firm shelf, for heads to be laid upon. Some people said that she was stupid. She had only cookery and Scripture at 'O' level and wrote in a round childish hand. And Alice fell in love with her. She heard her sing, copying Alma Cogan – I can't tell a waltz from a tango, I don't know what my feet are gonna do, I can't tell a waltz from a tango, darling when I dance with you. Her rosy lips pursed and woman's hips swinging, undisguisable, and the chirrup of easy welcome in her voice. Alice, twelve years old and skinny in her too-big too-new clothes, brown still from the summer sun, raw with angry scratched eczema patches on her elbows and knees, hung about the cloakroom that smelt of lacrosse boots and burning coke, and fell in love again. Doing so, condemned herself to sleepless nights, burning moments in corridors, aching urgencies, the daily life of a fantasy of consummated love whose details she had difficulty in inventing. Others did it; it was all the rage; falling in love with an older girl was what took up their time and energy, charged their empty hours, gave these existences meaning; filled the emotional and physical void that might otherwise have drowned them. But to Alice, nobody loved as she did. Soon, every moment of the day was tense with the promise of seeing Jane, the fear of saying the wrong thing to her, the plans for saying the right one. She rehearsed her speeches in lonely corners and rarely spoke them: waited in corridors for Jane to pass. Nothing else mattered. The glance of the beloved alone could assuage. Lessons were a time of deprivation in which she was locked away from the chance of seeing her; times between lessons were a brief scurry from one room to another, the corridors echoing with the possibility, each moment electric with hope and disappointment. Mealtimes, she might find herself eating at the same table as Jane; and feel her food go down in lumps as her hands went clammy and heart seemed to fill her body. Games periods, she might encounter her beloved slightly knock-kneed in divided skirt and hockey pads, breasts jutting beneath Aertex, dribbling a ball down the pitch, waiting for the perfect pass. At night, when all the younger girls hovered tense on the stairs and in the passageways longing for a glimpse of their loves, plotting a goodnight stolen kiss or more, air seethed with frustration and desire, both something none of them could have identified, or named. And the seniors, the prefects, the lost mothers, the future virile lovers, captains of the unattainable dream, strode past, locked doors, or sometimes it was said actually crept back, relented, came through the darkness to the bedsides of their admirers, bent down, kissed, actually kissed, the fevered cheek. The little girls lay awake in the dark, longing as they had longed in babyhood for the touch of the soothing maternal hand. Dreaming of the smooth breast and the loving eye, willing the love object to come close. It did not matter that the images they held in their minds, film images, were all of hard masculine lips crushing in their embrace, of bodies – theirs? others? – passionate in their urgency; that the urge was somehow to penetrate, to get back into the soft warmth of the beloved body, to hide in her, to be safe at last; it did not matter that the roles invented were now this, now that, now ravisher, now willing victim; in their minds, all havoc played, the possibilities were infinite, it was enough that she should come, that she should come close, tonight. What then? The passionate fusion of joined lips, the merging

48

(somehow) of two into one, the grasping of breasts with one's own (suddenly virile) hands, the initiation by the other (turned suddenly hero) into an unknown world of undifferentiated delight. Jane at her bedside, Alice dreamed and willed into being, Jane with her sweet-smiling freckled flesh, cream of the milk, apple, rhubarb crumble sweetness; Jane's soft pink lips and upholstered bosom and little hands with their bitten nails, her soft black hair, the mole upon her cheek, her eyelashes, her airs and graces, her out-of tune singing, her stupidity. It was enough that she should be there; the rest, whatever it might be, would follow. And she pleaded with her, silently, come to me, come; in order that the next stage might be unfolded, perhaps, in order that she should know.

Meanwhile, where all others failed, Felicity Ryan succeeded: in luring Elizabeth Courtney, captain of cricket and leader of the school choir, into her bed. The story flamed about them, transforming every detail of everyday life; they were transfigured. Through the attics at dead of night had crept Elizabeth Courtney, from the next door house; through the fire doors, in darkness, creaking on floorboards, her fingers touching soft edges of curtains, hard iron edges of beds, until she came to Felicity Ryan's bed, narrow as all the others, humped in the middle with the form of a sleeping girl; there she paused, felt rumpled sheet, rough blanket, softness of hair, warmth of flesh; there she— The story spread, was whispered, amazed. For those few brief hours, between midnight and first light, had Elizabeth Courtney (Fizz to her friends) really lain in Felicity Ryan's (Flick's) bed; close, closer than could be imagined, locked with her in that narrow, narrow space? The little girls murmured to each other, their hands damp and hearts like doorknockers. It was possible, then; the dream had substance, could be known. In the straight line as they waited for house prayers, faces still damp from washing, the hair tucked back behind their ears, a frisson ran through them so that the line quivered slightly, a taut wire in wind. A bell clanged. The seniors marched through, one behind the other, swing of skirts, stamp of sensible shoes, the air behind them trembled from their passage. They paused, stood. A girl cleared her throat, opened the Bible, began to read. Thin pages fluttered in the breeze – from where? The room was still, but a flutter, a breeze, a frisson ran through. Licked her fingers and turned a page. Her voice choked from silence. Cleared, began again. My beloved is mine and I am – hers. The lion shall lie down with the lamb. Words like salves, like cool ointment. She shuffled her feet, looked across at Jane, her senior. Bosom soft and shelving as a pigeon's, skin like nectarines to the touch. Nec–ta–rine. Fruit and feathers, feathers and fruit; and the stirring, behind the holy, dropping words, of all that had ever been forbidden. She raised her eyes, kept them raised when all eyes should be lowered, as the words came out, the edicts, the Thou Shalt Not and the God Sees; gazed straight ahead when all must stare at the floor, the dust, the cracks; looked for an answering look, a glimpse of brown eyes, just a glance, a glimmer; but Jane's eyes were cast down, for ever, and the reading ended, and there was a scutter of shoes and a dragging of chairs, and the curtains softly lifted at the windows, admitting the wanton breeze, and Let Us Pray.

We have done those things which we ought not to have done, we have left undone those things which we ought to have done; and there is no health in us. Twice a day, the general confession: twice a day for barefoot creeping through attics and sheets twitched aside, and whisperings, gigglings, settlings down; twice a day, as if that would do any good, against burning on the stairs, in the corridors, against offering tea-buns, fervently, against plotted kisses, dreamed embraces, against knowing, being known. The words rumbled around the room, rumble, rumble, rumble and AMEN. A sigh, as if of relief, just audible, came after. Now there would be streaming and stamping out into the cloakrooms, greasing of hockey pads, hunting for lacrosse boots, wriggling into aertex shirts, and the cluster round the board to see who was playing where, not left half again, oh God, I can't keep up, who's— And the littlest girls nearly squashed and trampled underfoot, one wailing, I can't find my— And out there, mud, a rinsed spring sky, the battered pitches, green blades poking, and a breeze that roused and teased. Once round the fields for talking before prayers. Punishments and pleasures mixed, so that never again would one be free of the other; the relief of running, studs sticking in mud, the release of limbs from cramped desks and kneeling upon cold floors, the intoxication of air, filling lungs, the wide world, wild sky, spring afternoon. Wind upon her cheek at last, tears sprung suddenly and splashed sideways; the boredom of longing released, unchained; Jane nowhere now as the air and light took hold of her and sped her along. She ran, tripped on a toecap, slid, fell, spreadeagled in mud, mud in her mouth and her eye, and the world tipped, circling above her, soundly embraced her below. Mud and sky; and in between, the thud of a body falling; in between sickness, breath flown out. Alice, are you all right? Alice, get up, do. Longer than was necessary, she lay there, booted, padded, armoured; her stick in one thrown-out arm, like a weapon lost; face downwards still in the mud. Alice! Are you all right? Hands would reach, pluck, drag her from the earth's embrace, soon enough; winded, she lay and let them do it, for more was too much, effort impossible, her moment's rest there all she could want just now.

Three hundred girls: it was bound to occur, of course, bound to crop up from time to time, this sort of thing, one supposed; three hundred girls at adolescence, within these walls, within these hallowed – well, since the beginning of the century, anyway, these chaste and encircling, solid, walls. Yes, there was a risk, there was a distinct possibility. But, on the other hand. Strictly observed. Rules to be obeyed. Slackness and laisser-faire. An example to be set, to be made. Stamped out at source. Irresponsible elements. Impossible to be too careful. A wary eye.

Elizabeth Courtney, heroine, captain of cricket, was expelled. In prayers, in the school hall, they heard that she had left the school for the good of others and for her own good. This was in accordance with the school motto, which said in Greek that the good of others was always one's own. She left no gold letters on the great boards that hung there, the honours board, marked with the names of those who had won scholarships, gone to university. She had bowled a fast left-hander, true, was remembered, revered, for her midnight attic journey, her devotion to sensuality (or homesickness, or loneliness); but, left without a word. Felicity Ryan, tear-stained, humiliated, famous, did not watch her go; but munched sweets hungrily, her locker door open, her face hidden in it, uninterrupted because nobody dared go near. Felicity Ryan, cherubic and giggly, her red hair a riot breaking free from kirby grips and elastic bands; whom nobody could envisage as seducer, child that she was, innocent; yet who had done it; and to whom for the moment nobody dared speak.

Alice vomited and was sent for a week to the San. Some of her vomit, tomato and egg-coloured from breakfast, sprayed her house-mistress's polished brown shoes. Nobody knew if she were really ill, herself included, or in disgrace too; disgrace was suddenly so ubiquitous, so all-pervading; it could fall like a knife into a chopping block and quiver there, so that nobody dared ask. Alice lay with a stiff sheet drawn tight across her breasts, tucked in under the arms, and a thermometer under her tongue, her lips tight closed upon it. Her hair was damp and smelt still of vomit. The sheets were cold as if specially chilled, and her toes pointed downwards, pressed by the weight of blankets. The nurse stood over her, bending so that one hand rested upon her pulse, cold fingers feeling for the life-beat with disapproval. She bent, counted, glared. A round watch dangled from a pin on her breast. Her bosom was two crackling peaks. Her lips, a cracked wound, cheeks powder-flaked, crumbling. (I have done those things that I ought not to have done and left undone those things that I ought to have done, and there is no health in us—) Outside, time passed extremely slowly. The sky was black. There was no Sunday, with church bells and greasy sausage and a clean shirt like a paper bag; no Monday, with mathematics and gym and cold meat and rhubarb pudding; no Tuesday, no day at all. No people. No cuddly Jane nor tear-stained Felicity, no daring, excommunicable Fizz. No people anywhere. No males, no females. Beings only with crumbling flesh and tall unmarked bodies like candles, wax where flesh should be, smoothness where should be hollows, declivities. Girls. Three hundred girls, smoothed, neutralised, made uniform. Nothing that hands could touch nor dreams catch hold of; no warmth or roughness of hair or contrasting silky smoothness of skin. Nothing hidden, nothing left. Candle wax beneath the clothes, filling the holes, smoothing away the differences, covering, setting, hardening, glossing. Candle wax, at last.

The nurse took the thermometer, peered at it against the light. The child had a fever; should be denied food, then, food and visitors. The mercury, rising, stated that this was so. And Alice, pale against the pale sheet, in the pale room with the pale light squared in the window, slid a questioning hand towards her own chilled thighs and felt nothing, nothing at all.

6

Years later, she cycled through snow, early in the morning when the world was still dark, to tell a woman about all this. To tell her grandmothers and brothers and penises arching streams and girls weeping quietly beneath covers, girls sent away to a far-off place. To tell a world in which there was still margarine for breakfast after the butter had run out, in which sweets were no longer rationed and yet children stole food from the larder; to tell how, post-war, it was cold still, and clothes fresh from the laundry chafed, and there were days on the calendar to be marked off, crossed off, wished away, the present moment in thrall to some vision of the future in which life might suddenly flourish and pleasure once again abound.

There seemed to be so much of it all to tell, once one began. Where to begin? Chronicling the small events which led up, as if inevitably, to this present despair. What to include? And what to leave out? And why?

Steam trains; trains pulling out of stations, hands waving, trains accelerating; accelerations of longing, of loss.

Rhubarb pudding, trickling pale pink juice, acrid saliva in the mouth at the thought of that acidity, doused in sugar.

The shape of hands, remembered from so long ago that they had no forearms, no arms to connect to; no face.

I had, she began, a mother, father, grandmother, three brothers, several cats, a dog, many friends, several occupations, innumerable talents, love to spare, a desire for poetry, an ability to turn cartwheels, exercise books filled, a hunger always for something more.

Now, she said, I have a husband, a child, a house, a degree, a sheaf of white paper waiting to be written on, and the same hunger for something more.

She did not tell of the red and the gold, and of how it had faded from life, so that the days were identical, grey; in spite of the black of night and the white of snow, in spite of all appearances. It seemed that there was no way to say this and be understood; had never been.

She sat facing a wall. Quite a pleasant wall, textured, not blank, not too hard too white too shiny, not a cell wall. A wall at which many, many people must have looked. It was said, that whenever you came for treatment, to be heard, these days, you looked at a wall. There was a window, in the corner of her vision, the curtains drawn against the darkness the snow, pale oatmeal nondescript giving nothing away. Well, curtains were for not giving away. There were sounds, sometimes, signs from the rest of the house, from downstairs, furnishing small clues, a dog whine, the sound of central heating coming on, the bubble of a coffee percolator. There was a dog, then, a small dog waiting in the kitchen to be let out, to be freed perhaps as soon as the session was over, longing to gambol and snuff the snow and lift a leg against her parked bike to release a hot yellow jet; dog prints in snow, she had seen them. Anything to disturb the smooth whiteness, the early morning blankness too-silent unmarked streets. And the wall, unmarked (though textured); an analyst's wall. Perhaps there was another person there, waiting for the coffee percolator (for one did not leave coffee to make on its own?) A silent person, sworn to silence, not to give anything away. A Freudian analyst's person, collecting and filing dreams. Perhaps there was a cat on the stairs. But, why should one want to imagine a cat on the stairs? The house was not quite silent, not quite empty, cats gave this sense, of silent presence, of creeping, waiting. Each time, Alice came through the house, followed the woman up the stairs, searched for clues, signs, instances: like a person on her way to solitary confinement.

The woman led the way, and everything about her was hidden, except for what she wanted to show. There were no heaps of dirty washing to be glimpsed through a half-open bathroom door, no unmade beds, no books put down hastily on the landing table, no teacups waiting to be taken downstairs. There were the stairs, the landing, the room; a fleet look took in desk, papers, books, a picture, a pot plant, all that was to be hidden from her in a minute, because she was to face the wall. The activity, the fullness of the room were to take place behind her. And, facing the wall, she was to select, to present: those aspects of the past which might explain the present, its blankness. She sat in a black mock-leather chair and heard the woman's voice behind her. It seemed to float, now into one corner, now into another. It said, sometimes, the most surprising things. But she could not see the mouth it came from, nor glance into the eyes for support or information, nor ground it in any way at all.

Now this is very interesting.

I think here we come to the centre of your problem.

You try at once to be the man and the woman –

You cannot accept to be a woman –

Freud would say—

Alice moved impatiently in the chair, wanting to escape; the connections made ran into her like deep insult. Yet this was what she had come for. She grew still again; and the voice behind her, commenting on her anger, would explain it, reduce it to the smallness of a clenched fist, even a tight muscle in the cheek, a small caught spasm in the stomach, nothing at all.

She began to cry. Her mother stood in the doorway: you can come out when you can behave yourself. Her housemistress sat at a desk, tapping her pen, her nyloned legs pressed tight together, heeled shoes digging at the carpet. Behind her, behind windows, clouds sailed. What is the meaning of this? Baffled, she began to cry. The doctor too sat at a desk, pen poised, notes available (a whole file somewhere, out of sight). She cried. Perhaps you should see a psychotherapist, he said. A lot of people would simply have given you pills. And so, she got up early, left her sleeping husband, her sleeping baby, because there were so many people on the list, and threw on her warmest clothes, boots, scarves, gloves, an Afghan coat that smelt of animals, and wheeled out her bike, breaking the night's close fall of snow on the garden gate, and marked her way with a clear wheel-line out into the street, as if everything were straightforward, switched on the yellow beam to light the cold mauve morning, straddled the saddle as men rode horses, and was off. Off through the sleeping town, the just-waking town, along with milkmen and students coming home from parties and locked-out yowling cats. Came here. Leaned her bike and stamped and shook her Afghan and rang the door bell and puffed cold in the warm hall and followed up the stairs and sat in the black armchair and heard the voice and tried to speak to explain, and cried. The voice said. Freud would say, Freud tells us. This is how things are. This is this, and that is that, because I say so. (She thought of a party game, played last New Year: this is a this. A this? A this? A this. This is a that. A that. A that? A that? When to get it wrong was to fall out of the game.) This is a this. It is interesting that you should think otherwise, an interesting aspect of your neurosis. The circle came full: closed, locked. Something moved in her stomach, but could not be admitted. Gradually, her tears dried, she could not cry any more, except for the occasional quiet tear for the sadness of inevitability. Patient, she waited for it all to be explained.

Patient. She became helpful, even eager, told dreams, remembered occasions when (because the circle was locked, and there was no other way), picked over memory, selected, presented. Her dreams, growing clearer, more vivid, were presents for the woman, brought a trace of glee to her tone. Daily, she came and carried dreams here on her bicycle as a good dog retrieves game, longing to deliver and be delivered. Yes, would say the voice, yes, that is very interesting, a most interesting dream. Freud would say— And the dream fell open, so beautifully, like an easily filleted kipper, so that there was the rich meat within. And yet, when the dram was taken, examined, as it were paid for; there was the sense of loss. Afterwards, she would slip on to her bicycle seat in the cold and pedal quite slowly away, slowed and weighted by something that she must take home with her and tell nobody and never put down and have always with her until it was purged quite away. The woman called it, her neurosis. She said that everybody had one, that it would be cured, eventually, after a long time, that she was bound to feel much worse before she felt better, that this was what happened, that you had to go right down into the neurosis before you came up. Cycling, Alice ground laborious at the pedals. Snow and the neurosis slowed her, made her nearly fall. A sense of great fatigue made it hard to go through the rest of the day, made it long, heavy, like the clogged wheels, the choked roads, the blocked doorways, packed with snow. The woman said: tell nobody, do not talk this over with anybody, keep what happens here to yourself. So, at mealtimes there were strangers at her table, the neurosis between her and the others, silent, an obtrusive guest. When she looked at her baby, she felt the neurosis inside her, looking out of her eyes, distorting her smile, spoiling the contact. She put the baby down, nervous that she might harm her. A mother with a neurosis was worse than no mother at all. The baby slept in a cork-lined room, decorated specially, that would soak up cries. Her bottles, bibs, nappies, were all sterilised, so that there was always something floating in sterilising liquid, bobbing up and down, always something boiling, to destroy germs. As Alice felt that she herself should be boiled, purged, sterilised; in order not to infect others with this thing, this neurosis, that had come at her out of nowhere, out of her past, a dark cloud with no predecessor, staining the horizon, darkening her house. And she wanted clean surgery, a cauterisation. That this pain should become so intense that it would burn itself out completely and leave her bare, scoured pure. Herself, clean as a picked bone, all hard edges. And all that was hot, pulsating, liquid, menacing: boiled, quite simply boiled away. Her life would be obvious then, visible as a scoured kitchen table, four-square, admirable. Her child would flourish. Her husband would love her. Her friends would sit comfortably beside her again. Wild skies would no longer move her to that old intense discomfort; winds would not torment her; a touch would not scald nor a memory dissolve her; ecstasies, whether of orgasm or poetry, would be banished forever; and that, it, the red-and-gold, sinful, compulsive, the stuff-of-life erotic encounter, gone for good, eradicated; safe, now.

She chose the words she wanted, the images. Mother. Kitchen. Bread. Husband. Work. Good, honest, safe, used words, words for the light of day. And the others, the banished words? Talismans from a long-ago childhood, words that raged and flowered like sunsets, like

57

the weather at sea? She closed the books, put away all the white paper that would have tempted her to excesses. Mother. Kitchen. Bread. Husband. Work.

But beneath each one of these words, a dozen, a score of others, that lurked, proliferated. Pick up: mother. And you find, sleepless nights, blood flow, cry, flesh, touch, skin, baby, hands feet mouth life and on and on and on. Or: bread. And again, yeast, flour, water, dough, touch, knead, feel, rise, heat, smell, taste, tongue, crumb and on and on and on. Nothing is simple. Nowhere may be brought down cleanly and simply, the lid, shutting all else out. Husband. That strange word, that foreigner. Hus-band. Not you, or you, or you, but an abstraction. Beneath which, wife. Knife, life. Wife, the other half, permanently cut, sliced, wounded. Hus-band. Dig deep, and find a man somewhere there, eyes lips teeth tongue hair penis; off with the collar and tie and zipped up trousers and what do you find? Brother. Lover. Twin, familiar. Dressed as something else, disguised, uniformed. But there.

And, work, she thought (as she stood there aproned in her kitchen, young wife, young woman still, sterilising bottles, the morning still early.) Work. A door shutting, and somebody going out. A man. Her father, going for the early train. Hating it, his captivity; work in town, home in the suburbs; a captive man. Work. And he, the man in husband's uniform, the one she had, shutting the door, steps down the passageway, ring of the bike bell at the corner. Work: a going away, a shutting off, an absence. Also, a drudgery, a washing and drying, boiling and sterilising, cooking and simmering, wiping of surfaces, sweeping of floors. Work, to tidy up the world. Which left great gaps: a clean floor, a wiped table. Clear, for what? Curious, that morning, she brought out again her folder of white paper and laid it on the cleaned, the emptied table in the kitchen. It was there, out there, visible again. For a while, she strode around in the house and garden, clearing armfuls of clothes from one place, dumping them in another, pegging the white nappy squares that smelt of bleach upon the frozen line; pegs in her mouth and her breath in cloud clouds, ice particles cracking underfoot. The radio said there would be a thaw. It would, one day, be spring. Unknown to her, a crowd of American musicians were arriving in London, preparing to play wild music and send audiences into frenzies of determination to have what they had never had, or had lost. The year would be known to history for revolution and rock music. The streets of the capital were full of freak-haired extroverts in silks and satins. Soon they would come to her, as all did; as the revolution in France had waited in the hospital delivery room as she gave birth to her daughter, as the months since then had been all private hope and public disappointment; as the public and the private event flowered each beside the other, inextricably joined by the time, the day, the hour.

Alone in her kitchen in this year of change, while the baby slept, she sat down at the table. Work? No, this was not work. Work was stitching laboriously, pricking one's fingers, joining, soldering, welding, exerting; work was at once an absence from life and a grinding necessity, stained with sweat and possibly even blood. While, for an hour, then for an hour and a half, then for two hours (and miraculously the child slept still) there was this letting down of something into something: bucket into water, hand into depths, this vein-tapping, listening, this contact with a pulse that beat on and on, had always, beat, heart-beat, blood-beat, life-beat, beat. Original pulse of the world from turning, cartwheeling. First flicker from another human's eyes. Touch of skins and knowledge of the other. Floods and fire.

Or, on the other hand, neurosis. She wrote, and covered the white sheets with this uneven black scratch of poetry, planting her own footmarks in the whiteness at last.

And since poetry seemed to flourish only when the child slept, the child was the reverse side of poetry, just as she was the flip side of the revolution in France, born on that day. Her life, a fragile glass at present, transparent with events. Alice, crouched over her kitchen table in a world that had hardly changed, heard with dismay that first waking cry that told of the baby's need. Mid-word, mid-way, she was yet jolted back into the present with the urgency of that need. A cry, stronger than word or phrase, jerking at the entrails still. And yet, with the mound of paper growing on the table, with the spider's dance of poetry changing it forever, there was a harmony. The streets of Paris that summer, and the child waking to scream in the garden; barricades smashed down and a new being opening toothless wide to the sky. Musicians with hair like black chrysanthemums and the words that were on their way to her: life, love, power. Words, and all that lay beneath them, all the confusing contradictory exhilarating frightening power of them. Collar-and-tie words, and the nakedness beneath. Names, signs, portents only: for all the chaos of being.

Now, we are getting close to the centre of the problem . . . .

When she left the woman in the upstairs room, to whom she had cycled all autumn and winter and spring, through cold and snow, it was more like leaving a mother than leaving her own mother would ever be, who, after all, was human, had room for doubt. In her mind, she left her first; sat there, resisting Freud, arguing. Wrote her own protest, registering some annoyance at Freud's interpretation of her own dreams; struck with her small shoe at all the machinery. The letters she wrote were filed, not seen again, made into an interesting aspect of her case. She struck with her hands at closed doors, making no impact. You can only come out when you are good. You can only come out when you have accepted, become what you ought to be. Like this, arguing, you are not a woman. Freud tells us what it is to be a woman. You are not yet one, you have not yet given in. Go on writing, by all means. Writing is a useful sublimation of desire. Freud endorses your writing. Writing can not do any harm. I am glad to hear you are writing. But anything you say will be filed away, an interesting aspect of your case, and will never go any further . . . .

When the first real day of spring came, and the washing rocked on the line in the garden, and clouds seemed chased down the streets by the wind so that all was white and blue and white again, dazzling; she opened her window pushed up the sash and leaned out. There had been a knock on the door, and there, down there, now, were two faces upturned in the street. Brown faces amazed at her suddenly opening up, up there, when they had expected a door opening below. She leaned, her arms on the sill. The wind leapt down the street, skittering

60

milk bottles and paper. They, in all the universe, stood still.
– We're looking for somewhere to stay. D'you know a hotel?
Americans. From the first wide smiling vowel onward. The man with
the hand to his eyes to shield them from the sun, taller than the
woman, who stood with her hand at her hip like a pioneer. Both in
blue jeans and coloured shirts and jackets and both with upturned
faces, asking, wondering, not hurrying away.

She called down to them – wait, I'll open the door. Thudded in her
socks to open up for them and catch them, bring them in. Off the
suddenly wide street where dust might blow and cattle run and they
be whirled away, on horse-back, never to return. But no, they were
here, they were solid. How had they come to her house? They were,
they said, planning on staying in town for a few days, just to look
around, looking for somewhere to hole up, you know, cheap, nothing
fancy. The man had slow, dazed, searching eyes, blue, and a blue,
holed sweater over his cowboy shirt that made them bluer; the woman
was honey-coloured, eyes, skin, hair in different tones of the same
colour, pale, dark, thick, runny, all honey, as if she had sprung simply
to life from one single source, one pair of genes, nothing conflicting
anywhere. Her tan jacket matched her tan hands. Nobody in England
was that colour at this time of year. Alice wanted to touch her, to see if
she was as warm as she looked. They hitched their jackets upon chair
backs, accepted coffee, asked all the questions as if they had endless
energy, endless fascination, or as if she were the most interesting
person they had ever met.

She hesitated, selected again. What to tell? Husband, baby, cold
morning cycle rides, neurosis, solitary confinement, staircase, black
leather chair? Or, sky, wind, chimney pots, puddles, washing line? Or
hot liquid inside versus cold scoured outside? Or gold versus grey? Or
what?

You're married, well, you have a baby, that's fantastic, what's she
called, where is she, do you really put them outside all the time, what
was it like, giving birth to her, gee that's just amazing, I've often
wondered, the most fantastic thing, and how old is she, did it change
you totally, it must be, well, I guess you know, yes, well, we're just
travelling together, yeah it is, just great, but one day, well, I guess

61

having a baby, that must be just the most amazing thing.

Honeycoloured warm laughing face up close to the child's small closed cold sleeping one; then eyes laugh into eyes and the child's mouth opens in a yawn, and colour comes back, and life. My child, Alice thought, my child. And I have only just noticed.

But, what shall I say? she thought. Move in. Stay here forever. Sleep in my room. Save me. Love me. Laugh with me like that. Tell me again that it is the most amazing thing in the world. Stay, stay here forever.

– Well, are you sure we won't be putting you out any? I mean, if that's really okay. Hey, Lally, isn't that great?

– I'd love to stay with you. I really would.

It was a declaration of love. With a light heart and step now she was able to do what should be done in one's own house; find bedclothes, towels, hand food, show them the rooms. One look at them had been enough. One look, to know that if they were to hear the word 'neurosis' they would laugh – not bitterly, not with cynicism, but with that easy assumption of the goodness of the whole of life that was theirs. She clutched clean linen to hand to them. They swung small bags, light travelling bags, into the corners of the room. They sat on the floor, leaned on cushions, easily. In her mouth were the words with which she would introduce them to Finn, when he came in; the extravagance of her certainty tinged with a small apology, a doubt. Please like them. Please be as certain as I am. Please see that through them, somehow, we shall be made whole.

He came in, his face immediately shrinking with the surprise. From the wide-open easiness of swinging back into his own house, thinking of anything, careless and unselfconscious, the narrowing of his look to take them in. Alice knew it well: his consciousness of the invader. She knew that he was angry, but would say nothing, until later, when he was safe, alone with her. But then she saw that his anger, his tightness, defending his own home, was dissolving in the warmth of the two Americans, in their delight with him, their questions, their appreciation of who he was. Narrowed brows and shrunken pupils and all, they saw and welcomed him; welcomed as he had never been welcomed home, he thawed and expanded quickly, and sat back among them, amazed, as she was. He took off his jacket, loosened his tie. He had been to work, in the uniform of work. But beneath that he was young, a young man, vulnerable; he was like that, and she had barely noticed, barely taken him into account. Now, she remembered, she loved him. He was young, like her, vulnerable, like her; once, they had been such friends. All this; as the two Americans looked on, and the room seemed to settle and relax, as if everything were, after all, in its right place. She breathed out, then, as she had not for months. Or even years, perhaps.

Later, Finn said to her – They seem so – He stopped, could not find the exact word. His hands out in the air, trying for it. She knew what he meant. The distance between the two of them had shrunk, to let her know more easily now what he meant. So often, he searched for his words, careful with what he would say; and she, tempted to fill the gaps, would suggest things. Inarticulate yet exact, himself a stranger in his own life, his own house, he would face her, his hands moving through the air, shaping what he could not say.

– Peaceful? he said finally. She had not interrupted.

Alice nodded. The bedroom was wide and disordered between them, the expanse of the shared bed, as he moved on his side, putting things away and she sat on hers, taking off her shoes. Finn made little piles of objects on the bedside table. He longed for it, peace, order, his vision of how things were. He took his own shoes and laid them in a row; drew the curtains tight, stood to unbuckle his belt. In the room adjoining theirs, the one lined out with cork, the baby slept, their daughter, her arms flung out above her head and pursed face blotched with sleep, lips rosy. At last, she slept. At last, the day was at an end. Peace seemed to exist in the wide shared bed, in sleep, in their bodies meeting, entwining. He would fall into a deep sleep, Finn would, and leave her floundering, half-dreaming half-thinking, with everything that worried her, like flotsam on a beach, washed to the surface of her mind. She lay, her body still through willpower, her mind racing; usually, at nights, letting him sleep, giving him the benefit, providing with her smooth outer surface, her body, what her inner self could not give. Beached, groaning, Finn slept his nights away; and if he turned to her to make love, it would be quite sudden and out of the far depths of sleep, so that to her it was as if he were hardly there; a shipwrecked man, a survivor, clutched her as he swam up from the depths, clutched her as he might a raft, a broken spar. And she was there – like a raft, like a broken spar – forever bobbing among the waves.

– Peaceful? she said. Yes.

She was in love with them both, with the warm brown couple downstairs on the sitting room floor on their wide mattress with their clean sheets already rumpled. In love particularly with the young woman, Lally, because of what she was: light, unfurnished, travelling the world. Her clear greenish-brown eye inquiring equally into all the corners, fearing nothing, Alice thought. She wanted now to be tucked in between them, down there, sharing in whatever made life appear so easy.

She lay awake, on her side of the bed (for marriage had already decreed these habits) and listened to Finn breathing in a near-snore on his, and did not pretend sleep, this time, nor court it. The dreams and images raced still through her mind, yes, and Finn's hands came out to her, unconscious, seeking, pulling her down; but there was more, there was something else. Tonight, she was breathing out, with the knowledge of it, of the possibility of change. They would be here for days more, and nights, here, in her house; and she would discover, how it came about.

Lally sat in Alice's kitchen in the morning sunlight and warmed her hands at a coffee bowl, her light hair swinging against her cheeks. Ned stood at the stove, frying bacon. Kate in her plastic chair bounced on the table top, and her fists flew up and the sounds that came from her that morning were bird-like and mellow, a chirrup for the delight in talking. She clutched a spoon, and then it flew through the air. She laughed, and her head went from side to side, seeking. Finn came in with his narrow pale face pointed to find his way through the morning, looking for cereal, coffee, clean socks, letters; finding them. His mile stones, without which he would lose his way. Ned came towards him, apron over his jeans, greeted him with big hands on his shoulders, with his warmth of bacon and breath. Alice loved Ned. For warming, transforming: both Finn and the house. She loved Lally, for

64

the way she sat there and smiled at the baby and picked up her spoon for her, many, so many times, for the way she sipped her coffee and the way her hair swung against her face, and for the slim brown strength of her hands. The sun came in through the dirty windows and lit the pile of rinsed plates on the sink that Ned had washed, and played among the dust and toys upon the floor. It was a new day, this. She thought – this is how things should be. And throughout the days, the new days, left her pile of paper in a corner gathering dust, the black writing broken off mid-page, and her bicycle propped outside against the coal-hole, appointments with the doctor cancelled; everything cancelled, except this, this warmth of living. For how long? They would go, leave, perhaps never return. Would she run after them, as they danced away, piping, over the hills? Or be shut out, left to return, to carry on, to be, as if nothing had been? She and Finn, outcasts again. She did not know.

On the evening before they left, they sat over dinner, the four of them, and candles burned in saucers between them, there were brown earthenware pots that had held rich stew and vegetables, a bowl in which the few last drowned leaves of salad strayed, bread scattered across the table in crusts, a jug of wine down to its purple lees. The baby slept upstairs, and they had eaten, the four of them, in near-silence, and had mopped up the last of the juices with the last of the bread, and turned now to look at each other, to see what came next.

Alice said – There's some fruit. Or yoghourt. Her voice was strained in the silence, it was effortful to keep on thinking, offering, handing things round.

Ned said – sit down. We're fine. I'll get it if we want any more.

She thought – You are my father, my mother, my friend. Tears spouted and began to pour from her eyes. Long ago, long ago she had wanted to weep for this absence. She saw Finn glance at her, his alarm. She had no handkerchief and no apology. The tears dripped on to the cloth, marking it among the wine stains, she sniffed, laughed, but let the tears come. Lally came and put an arm around her, but not as if to make her stop. She was there, simply, her head close.

Alice said – You're going tomorrow, I don't want you to, I don't want you to go – Her voice came out in a wail. It's all right when you are here. When you are here, there are no gaps, no contradictions. Life is one, whole, seamless. There is nothing that I have to shut out. And now, everything might change, but you are going. What else can I do?

She imagined the doors closing again; the possibilities shut out.

Ned said gently – Anything we have, you have too.

He sat there, healthy, free, American. Suddenly there came into her mind what people had said about Americans during the war, what she had heard: over-paid, over-sexed and over here. It was ridiculous. She turned her head from side to side, as if it were too much for her. It was easy, easy for them. Of course she could not have what they had. Of course not. What she had, her inheritance, would have to do.

He said – You can have anything you want. Anything.

Husband, love, baby, house, sky, puddles, chimney pots, bike, life. But that thing, that other, that wandered about still outside her, in the darkness, giving only a hint of its existence, a word, a tremor, the faintest sign; what of that?

She could not name it. Only, that. It. What was at the centre.

Lally said – We'll be here, still, we'll be in touch, always.

She thought – They love me. Why is it not enough?

Finn was in love with her, tonight, for her tears, for having cried; because he wanted to, and could not. He looked across the table at her with his tenderness, his acclaim, he reached out to her with his eyes; said, I will be here, with you, I will be here too.

The dinner table, her creation, the cleared space that was now littered, cluttered, covered with cloth, bowls, plates, glasses, knives, forks, corks, crusts: that had been clean, empty. On it, she had spread her papers, once, and begun on a chart of something, a map towards something, that remained unfinished. Was it then either this, or that? This love, this fellowship, or that lone, clean, climbing task? She looked at them all, from one to the other, from the smiling warm faces of the Americans, Ned and Lally, to Finn, his narrow fox-mask, slit eyes, smile arching now towards her, his fine boned head that her hands knew; and hesitated. They would go, and she would be left with it, the pain of their going, the emptiness, the sun gone in, the spaces at her table; and she and Finn would look at each other and remember, and decide to begin again; and then he would go out, and the door would close behind him, and she would be left again with it – It – and it was what she wanted, how she wanted it, after all. She would not shut it out, now, excluding it from her bed, her life; nor park it out there in the darkness, and draw curtains close; nor sit in a mock-leather chair and have it named for her, 'neurosis', 'problem' and wish it purged away. It was hers. Her hands went out to rearrange things, now, to clear a space: knife, fork, plate, glass, all moved to one side, and crumbs dusted away and tearstains dried and gone. The place in front of her, where her hands moved about on the table, emptied again. And then, Lally's slim brown hand with the rings and the wristwatch came out quite suddenly and closed in warmth on hers.

7

There was, of course, then, the other, the one she waited for, expected without expecting, knew without knowing, dreamed of occasionally to wake puzzled, excluded from her waking life. Had it only been a matter of time, then, before he made his appearance, put his head round her door in the way that people did come and put their heads round her door, announced himself, let himself in? She had not known that she was expecting anyone, again. You did not expect, made no plans, could not envisage it: but there, one day, was the knock at the door, the tap at the window, and there was a face, half-recognised, and there was the easy welcome, door opening, and beginning again. She was alone, with her cleared table, with her paper, her writing. Now, that was real. Who else, then, could possibly be expected? Her life was full, filled, peopled. In between these people, she made her narrow way; taking, using, what fell into her path. Every little scrap, to be used, reused, recycled, made again. Nothing wasted; but picked over, selected, distinguished, fitted together anew. No, she was not awaiting him: any more than she had consciously awaited Finn, or her children, or the Americans; any more than she could have imagined, made up, the people who came to her door.

It was cold, mid-winter. He came to the door this time with a sleeping child in his arms, little boots dangling, and let himself in. She made way for him. In the warmed, lamplit room, her room, allowed him to sit down. At once, she recognised him: who, that is to say, but not how. He was from far back, from before anything; from before speech, even, before choice. But she said nothing, only made cups of hot soup, stoked fires, rearranged cushions, looked at the time. He had come from far away, with his wife, his child, his sleeping child at this late hour, in this darkness, and had arrived here, and she had simply opened the door and let him in. People knocked, and she opened. It was her house, hers and Finn's. Finn, for some reason, had not gone to open that door, but had come, later, exclaimed, later, welcomed when all the welcoming had begun. Already, he and she were sitting close to the fire, and he had his boots off, and the children were stacked on the sofa half-awake, eyeing each other, his child grizzling with the cold and waking to heat, to flames; already the fire was burning higher, stacked late at night with more wood and the cups of soup were burning fingers and the night was alive with sparks, with possibilities. He came in late to this, Finn did, and warmed himself at the fire that was already there, as the years began in which this would be what happened. It was Christmas, and there were Christmas presents, dozens of things to be wrapped and unwrapped, to change hands, and there was a dark cold fir tree to be lit and food to be brought from the chill pantry and cooked and eaten; it was a time for festivities. Already, he and she sat close in the hearth and there was no need for presents. He brought her, nonetheless, a small clay pot that he had made himself. It was clay, and yet wrapped as jewellery. Opening it, she was confused, as to what it might be. She stroked it with her fingers, astonished. In his eyes, she saw her own astonishment. At the same time as the pleasure, there was pain: she registered it, like a beat of warning, like the crack somewhere of a door opening that has long been closed. The creak and groan of what opened, what would not close again, in her body, her heart. She did not know about him: and then looked, and did know, was certain. He had been a long time coming, from a long way away, his look said, and

68

now he was here, carrying presents, carrying children, warming himself at her fireside, here to stay; his look said, I am here, at last. So. Through all the tunnels and along the tracks of her long life, of his, that was what had been happening. Tired, through travelling to meet each other, here they were; and their feet touched just once accidentally in thick socks in the space before the open fire, and then they smiled, cleared the cups away, and said goodnight.

It was a time of miracles. In which the dark deadness of midwinter came alive and there were fires, sparks, at its centre; in a household in which all was coming and going, exchanges, jokes, questions, touches in passing. Alice saw the household in which she lived come alive again; it was as if the house itself lived, as if everything, everything were animate, charged with this life. She saw herself carry great laden plates to table, feeding people, and heard the sigh of pleasure as they fell to. In the far attics of the house she sat on a cushion with her pencil, her paper, and the words jetted from untapped springs, raw, wet, shocking the paper, marking forever the blanks and silences. She woke early, at this time, in the dark dawn, Christmas dawn, and got up to walk about exploring the house and its far corners, the places she had never visited. She stood early, so early in her kitchen, warming her hands at a bowl of coffee while the skin grew quickly on its surface in the cold, and stared out of the window at the pinkish spreading light, the extraordinary newness of morning; the creak on the stair, stocking-footed, told her, that he too was awake and there, coming towards her, taking and using the extremities of life, the unused early mornings and late at night times; and would soon, in a minute, stand behind her, just so close and no closer, looking out. He would come in not speaking, just smiling, with the slowness of a man walking as quietly as possible; she loved the way he took care with what he did, when it mattered. In every movement she saw it, this excellence, this skill. They were like dancers, skaters, acrobats; finely attuned and moving through space taking care with it, and daring all the time. She said – There is coffee. At some point, it was necessary to break the silence, or it would engulf her. She thought – it is for us always to break the silences. Or, will I one day dare to let them continue? At once, the foreignness of language, which they did not need, he thought. And yet, she needed it, needed it for now, to try for explanations, to try for ordinariness. Too much that was extra-ordinary would be like a comet in the sky – destruction in its fiery wake. So, she checked him, offered him coffee, spoke to him hesitantly in the words of another language, saving herself a little, putting things off. Soon, it would be breakfast time, and they would be there, all of them, children and adults, emptying out cereal packets and grabbing the milk and burning the toast and pouring coffee, and ordinariness would prevail and reassure. Still, there they would be, the two of them, with their private strange early morning between them, now and forever.

She could not tell how it was for him, this man, this stranger: to walk into her house and be all at once at its centre, after his journey-ing. He came in like somebody who has a right, who recognises it. And was yet careful, cautious even, at times: she saw him take tea towels and dry things from the rack, carefully, and wipe the surfaces in her kitchen clean; saw him attentive with others, with children, giving them his time. She saw his glance at Finn, his invitation. And Finn, wary, pretending he did not see. Scenting again the invader in his own house, seeing the man at his sink, the man who listened to his children, was in some way too close, there, smiling at the centre, with his wife. Yet he liked the man; glimpsed in him perhaps some old possibility of brotherhood. His own stance these days said: beware. Lonelier than usual, yet oddly stirred, he suffered the rituals of Christmas at his own fireside. Across laden tables he looked at him, quickly, the foreigner. His quick look flickered dreaming of treachery. He did not know, but was disturbed. There was between the three of them, somthing uneasy, like love.

He said – When are you leaving? He had not meant to be so blunt. But suddenly wanted his house, his family, his life, to be his own. It was too much, this sense of drama every day, and of rapid relentless change. He was tired with it; wanted some surcease, his head upon Alice's breast and the house all quiet around them, all silent.
– January 4th.
That was the day on which the tickets were booked. So there was the

whole terror of the New Year to face, the momentous turning over of the world at midnight, the chaos that might ensue. Finn sighed. He was in love with this man, in some sense, he knew it: for having come into his house and taken his responsibilities, lightening his load; for being there. Yet he needed an ally in his loneliness. There was the other woman, who was dark to him, quite opaque still, as if she might not know what was going on. Perhaps, on that account, she would be safe for him. He did not know, he doubted. Nothing had ever felt so difficult. He felt Alice slip early from his bed out into the cold, after her minutes of restlessness beside him. He felt discarded, used. The bed was blank and empty beside him, and he wanted to draw her back and down and have her, to himself. He wanted comforting, warmth; and she was alert as a blade, quivering with some tension, might stab him to death. So he feigned sleep, let her go: and felt the whole house wake, charged all at once with this same tension, as if an earthquake were about to begin. There was the sound of a kettle boiling, in the kitchen below, and a quiet clink of cups. He imagined it. A creak upon the stairs. A man's feet in socks, as he crept, crept about the place like a tomcat, stealing. A woman standing still in the kitchen, waiting as the kettle boiled and steam billowed, abstracted, looking out of the window, letting it all go on. He turned, pounded the pillow, looking for comfort. Something in him was profoundly stirred, out of the past, out of another time; he was a small boy in a room alone, hearing the movements of adults downstairs, a chink of china, a mutter of voices, he was hearing what he did not want, what he feared, to hear; he was blamed, accused, found wanting. He listened. The silence taunted him. There was – yes – a cold clink of milk bottles put down upon the step, and the back door opening then (but she was only bringing in the milk) and surely a voice (but could be speaking to herself, or the cat) and a shuffle, a rustle, something so slight that it could be imagined, that could have been, yes, the sigh of two people moving together, wordless because no words were needed, sighing with the closure of the gap between them, breathing out on the peaceful filling of that need? He did not know. Would never know. Was excluded, isolated, outside it all. And there would still be the New Year, all that, to go.

At the New Year, as the year changed, there was wind. The days of intense still cold ended in this long evening of rising wind, as if, Alice said, private in her attic for a moment, as if everything would blow open. She heard the wind, and the tree branches rattle at the window, and the vast sighing in the near woods. Birds would be blown from the branches, branches would even crack and fall; there would be split, maimed boughs; in the morning, the storm debris, the pieces. She listened in her attic room, where she sat to write but had not yet marked the paper. Downstairs, food was roasting, the meats were browning and crisping and the juices ran; and she had come away, for the moment, from everybody; climbed the dark stair to where she was awaited, here.

He had always been there, close, his breath just audible, somewhere at her side or even within her, his invisible self beating against her heart, so that she was not one, but two, twinned, finished off that way. She had moved, always with the invisible strength of his presence. And now, he seemed to be outside her – separate yet moving closer, a part of her no longer, become himself. He knocked. She knew he would knock, knew how it would sound, quiet yet insistent, a double knock, letting her know. She had heard him ascend the stair, had felt him come to find her. He would open the door, but would wait first for her call. She called – come in. Her voice sounded unnecessary. It was New Year's Eve, and the dinner was cooking, it was all down there, she was awaited. She did not know what would happen; apparently, could not choose. She sat in her chair, then, her paper still white before her, and only the bare twigs busily inscribing the pane, and let him come in. Of course. Of course, you. As if the long game of hiding and seeking were over, she sat there, hidden and yet found.

He said – Are you coming?

He said – They are looking for you.

He said – I knew where you were.

He said – Come.

Would he then be the summons to her to join the peopled world from which she hid? Among leaves, among branches, she had crouched, waiting, and he in his invisibility had crouched with her, whispering. Now, he came and fetched her out. She gestured towards her white page. It told him nothing. And he was all eagerness, all movement; he drew her out, towards the exhaustion of the dance. Come! But for a moment, just a moment, was stayed, stilled in his flight; as they came close together, brushed wings, feather touched; and she saw his bright dark gleaming eye up close, and the curved beak of him, the strength that could tear as well as caress. Birds. Yes, that was how he swooped and settled, soared and yet rarely came to earth. Come! Fly, dance, be one with the flock be caught in the movement, carried in the winds and currents. Come!

He led the way then, and she followed, touching all the way down the familiar surfaces of her house, the walls, cloth, furniture, dust of it, as if in farewell. The paper, she had screwed up and thrown at the waste-paper basket before she came down; but she had missed, and it lay there, a crumpled ball, unused, but discarded just the same. Outside the house the wind rose, whirled all it could carry, charged with it down the street. It was the wildest night, like an equinox. The moon was out, but blotted every moment and cleared again by huge clouds, travelling fast. The trees groaned, would crack. Something would crack, it was not known what. But nothing, everybody said, would be the same again.

When he had gone, she came back to the upstairs room, where the crumpled ball lay, the paper she had thrown away. She picked it up, smoothed it out, looked at the few lines written there; took a fresh sheet, found a pen, sat there, sighed with a long sigh, and began again. The spidery black pattern that walked the page began to run, to dance. The rest of the house was locked out, left in disarray. The words were hard to find, but she began, searching, discarding, discovering. Some of them had been there since first she sat, notebook in hand, and began her recipes, her smudged lists, her first descriptions of the world, they had ballooned then in her brain and swelled her cheeks and then been lost upon the air, never recaptured. Others were new. Others were from a new language, recently drawn from a source that had never been tapped before. They came up with the iron-taste of far down water. They were sour, sharp, they nourished. With the bitterness of them in her mouth and cold from the chill room stiffening her limbs, she began: and the red-gold, the torrent of it, flowed at last from the grey, so that she knew that they were one.

PART II

1

He said – I've brought you some flowers.
And there was the long slim cone of them, wrapped and pinned, a bouquet. It was hard for him not to stand back smiling with self-approval as she unpinned, unwrapped, and hard for her not to glance up gratefully, to bury her face in their coldness, to give him that easy moment. For she loved to be given flowers, and he knew it; and there had been some reserve between them that perhaps the simplicity of a gift might move. Chrysanthemums, flowers for the cold season, November flowers. Flowers for all that could not easily be said, or shown. Say it with flowers, said the posters. And then, say it with words. Flowers were for weddings, funerals, first dates, misunderstandings, missed birthdays, apologies, the hostess with everything; they were to cover lapses, embarrassment, lust, and corpses. Yet in themselves— She touched the cold faces of yellow chrysanthemums and the smell of them, acrid, wintry, reached them both. In the warmth of their kitchen, the smell and the touch of the cold outside, the winter streets, where flowers were sold. In the cold of the winter streets, hothouse flowers, from elsewhere; in among the holly and the dried flowers tied already for Christmas. These paradoxes. And he, whose key she had heard in the lock, whose step on the stair, whose bag banged down in the hall, whose voice calling – Hello? – who for so many years had let himself in, just so, into the houses in which she was; he, out of all this past, all this habit, giving her flowers.
  – I know it's a cliché.
  – It doesn't matter. They're lovely. Thankyou.
For, devoid of the clichés, carefully cliché-less, how arid the days could be, each knew. She took the tawny blooms and bit off their stalks and placed them in a blue jug. Stood the jug in the middle of the

table so that the flowers flamed at the centre of the room, so that the mess and unwashed teacups and books and newspapers were transformed. You put something beautiful there, at the centre, and everything was changed, the periphery did not matter. But still, she kicked muddy shoes and a cat's bowl out of sight, and stacked tea things, in case. He sighed. He had given the flowers, delivered himself. Now, he looked around, hungry, wanting something. There was a buttered scone left upon a plate, and he ate it up in big bites, standing close to the table. He still had his coat on, so that to embrace him would have been like putting one's arms around a coat stand. He swallowed the scone, and took off his coat then, and smiled at her; and the coat, dropped on a chair, slid to the floor along with a copy of *The Scotsman*.

He said – Have you been working?

Wanting to be asked about his own day, his work. Wanting also perhaps an explanation, some clue to the disorder around him. Tall and breathing out the cold still and wrapping his arms around her for warmth, for solidity, for the indoors comforting factual object she was; leaning back after a minute and looking into her eyes for the person she also was; establishing himself, home. He told her. There was a little packet with the flowers, that had fallen to the floor; later, she picked it up and read that if one dropped this powder into the flowers' water they would go on blooming longer: a bonus, she thought, in these days. But that was when she had moved away from him, from his close silent hug and his inquiry, and had begun to move around the room again, picking things up, moving things from place to place. Cups into dishwasher, bread into bin, jam into cupboard, bottle from shelf to table, glasses, and liquid from bottle into glasses for them both to sip. While he roamed, picking up crumbs, leaning against walls, waiting for novelties. She screwed up the paper in which the flowers had been wrapped and threw it away, missing the note which he had written to her; and he, who regretted having written it, said nothing. The flowers, his communication to her, filled the space between them as they sat to raise glasses, to drink; eye to eye and nothing said, as if words occurred to each of them but nothing was quite appropriate, only the ritual gestures, the known things.

Alice had said to the students in her class that morning: the use of symbolism is rarely a conscious choice, but rather something that presents itself to us, that forces itself upon us, as if in a dream. They had sat, pens poised, waiting to be taught. Restless, she fidgeted before them, looked at the polite, the expectant faces. Poetry? How to tell it, how convey it, the knowledge of the wave that came and picked you up and deposited you somewhere else, that immense movement of all that made you; that, and then the exacting toil, the picking over, the trying and rejecting and fitting and piecing and rejecting again, the trying to remake the world in this new mould? The questions were on scansion, on rhyme. When should assonance be used? Should one begin with haiku? How long should a poem be? Exasperated and loving as a parent, she sat upright before them, and made shapes with her hands in the air, and tried to explain. It was like explaining how to breathe, how to exercise: how to make love, or swim under water. It was like, like—

– Symbols, she said, can exist at many levels. The richness of them goes far beyond, sometimes, what we have already understood. Some poems, you can read over and over and over again, for the whole of your life.

Take for example—

Hothouse chrysanthemums. Yes, and a man who loved you, a close-ness that could hardly be described or shared, and a house in which all this took place. And years in which everything had changed and nothing had changed, and children growing, suddenly becoming adult, and the world outside, beyond the windows, outside the doors, always the beautiful demanding world, into which she must travel forth.

She said to him – I shall be getting the night train.

– I see.

– Eleven-thirty, so we have plenty of time for dinner.

– Do you want me to cook? I'll cook, if you like. Where are the children?

– Alex is round at the theatre, and Kate's next door.

In an upper room, the lights had been on and the television flickering

79

where they had left it, and school books flung about on the floor. The house seemed full to him of the noise of them, of their obtrusive presence; even though absent, it had the sense of a place suddenly, arbitrarily vacated; of doors that banged ajar.

– I'll cook if you like, what is there?

Once, she had made home-made bread so that the kitchen, the whole house of which the kitchen was the heart had breathed out a yeasty warmth. It had reminded him of the smell of her body after sex; or had the smell been his own? There had been great pots brimming with ratatouille and with daube; thumbed brown recipe books lying about with wine stains and torn pages marking the things he liked best to eat; a whole poetry of sensual memory, taste and anticipation. Wine had flowed easily in their kitchen in those days, from a cardboard box with a tap kept within reach on the kitchen dresser, dripping, staining, but always with some left if you tipped it enough. There had been French cigarettes too, to which visitors helped themselves; and she, aproned in a Provençal print, pregnant perhaps (or was that his fantasy?), perched on a high stool, smoking a Gauloise with her hair coming down and something rich, brown, meaty bubbling on the stove. At the thought, he salivated; but went on searching in the fridge, past the hardened yolk of egg in its tiny pot (the white had been used for Kate's face mask last week), past the fomenting last week's yoghourt (eat by November 5th) in the hope of finding something else.

Alice said – There's some paté, I think. Or, we could go out.

Briefly, he longed for the old days, the daubes, the triumphs of her reign in the kitchen, when to be female had meant being a good cook, when Elizabeth David had ruled, and graduate wives competed to swop foreign recipes. Now, it seemed that to be male meant being a good cook; to be liberated, masculine, in charge of one's life; only, it was late, for him, and he had never had the time, and now he was hungry. Pâté. He searched, found, sniffed; still had the feeling that life had cheated him of something.

She said – Or, there's the carry-out.

– What are you going to read, tomorrow?

Determined, he was, not to let it show, his disappointment, his hunger, his longing for a delicious dinner at home; not to be a man guilty of the expectation, not to play that role again. He said – No, let's have this pâté, and there must be some pasta, isn't there, and I'll make a delicious sauce out of nothing at all, I'll whip up something in a minute. I just need some onions, garlic, a tin of tomatoes, some herbs. Some wine. Have we got any wine?

With wine, one could eat anything. A crust, a bowl of rice. Wine was for forgetting: that the fridge was empty, a sauce burnt, a daughter about to swing round the door and say angrily – not spaghetti *again*. For forgetting a cold bed, too, and waking alone in the morning, and Alice gone away. He wanted to say – I need your warmth, don't leave me. Not for one night, not for one hour, not now. But handed her packets of cold flowers, instead and opened wine, and asked politely about her reading, and what time was her train.

– I haven't quite decided. It's not till the evening. But I thought, if I get the night train I'll have time to see everybody, and think about it, and not rush too much. I like getting there early in the morning, it gives you so much more free time.

Free time. What she had campaigned for and won. All those years, he remembered, when her time had been not free, but bound, not hers, but his, the children's, somebody else's apparently, out of her control. When to try to help, try to sort out something, to try to change things, had been to heap more fuel on the fire of her desperation, to goad her to more bitterness. Still, it seemed, she had to guard it, plan for it, her free time: take night trains in order to arrive in places early. Scheme, plot, organise, to cheat it, arrest it, the passing of her time.

Peacefully, he said – Well, you enjoy the night train, don't you? And I guess you can afford it, now.

Three books published, readings of her own work all over the country, an invitation to the States this spring, and her work at the university: if only he could have gone to her, like a seer, like a witch, at that time (the time of the simmering pots of daube and her endless cigarettes and her dissatisfaction) and said, here you are, look, in the crystal ball, there it is, it is all yours, this is your future. If only he could have done that, instead of watch, agonised, guilty, finally angry, as she made her own difficult way, alone. Here, a present for you. Not flowers, this time, not wine, but your future: work published and appreciated, money, fame, free time; your children grown, out somewhere; the night train south; everything you ever wanted.

He chopped onions and his eyes smarted, he sliced garlic thin against his thumb. He had wanted to help, not to be a monster; had been told, no, you are no help, you are part of the problem, and had retreated, hurt and puzzled; angry, finally, hitting back. Get back into your kitchen, have another baby, see if I care. And now, after all this time, there was her freedom, her departure, leaving him in his turn, free. A guiltless man at last, slicing garlic while his wife planned her trips, her readings. Garlic, he thought, to keep everything at bay: good against colds and vampires and the evil eye and probably a lot besides. Alice it was who had introduced him to the liberal use of it, as to so much else; and now he cooked with it with a kind of fervour of belief, his daughter complained that she was teased at school for smelling of it, and the smell hung about the house as if it were really bunched from the rafters, Hammer-film-fashion, and the vampires at the door. Anyone kissed by any member of this household would have to notice the smell, and recoil. Smiling, he grated it into Alice's dinner with some of the pleased skill of the old-time necromancers, weaving spells.

Alice at the station loved the smoky darkness and the cold and the sense of trains leaving. Stations and airports affected her this way; the roll of the departures and arrivals board as name succeeded name – Casablanca or Aberdeen, it made little difference essentially – and the sonorousness of announcements, telling of platform numbers and departure times. There was something deeply emotional about places where people rushed through, said goodbye to each other, met strangers, bought tickets to ride, vanished into air or darkness. He knew that she would say something in a minute about *Brief Encounter*; it was the way she strode and looked about her and then glanced at him, her eyes full of love. There was something strange about knowing a person so well and seeing her go so easily; a wrench within him somewhere, that made him look away. He thought of steam trains and war-time departures, conjuring for himself something that would have felt worse; for she was only going to London, would be back in a few days. She set the emotional scene, though, Alice did; and left him upon it, a player with his soliloquy before what felt like an empty house. She tilted her face, scrutinised him. Her hat brim shaded her eyes but the rest of her face was yellow in the yellow light. The cold seemed to swirl around them, down here in the depths, the depths of the rock, hewn out, while above them the towers and pinnacles in mist, the lit crags, the moon riding above abysses, the city they inhabited that was like a stage set, always, lending to any human gesture something intense, dramatic. He kissed her above the cold collar of her overcoat, and their breath steamed. A chaste kiss, suitable for goodbyes. Neither would admonish, now, nor advise; their farewells were wrapped about with discretion. And, returning, neither would ask.

The train was in from the far north, the people tucked already into their narrow beds, the blinds drawn tight. The train had an air of blindness, of secrecy. She stepped up, tightly belted, collared, a woman voyaging alone. A small wave for him, a swift smile; and her face, its vividness, averted. A guard consulted her ticket, told her where, and he was left behind already. He turned away up the platform, suddenly cold, suddenly wanting to be home. His way home, through the silent city across splashed, cobbled streets, awaited him; and his life, on, away from that moment. He was again a small boy at a railway station, seeing off, being seen off, he could not be sure which. But a woman with a fur-collared coat bent over him, he was kissed, he was bidden to be good, and his stomach turned to ice and water; he was labelled, dispatched, he was left luggage, he was part only of the impedimenta of war. Nameless and unmothered, with the injunction to be good, wherever, whatever, and that his only lifeline. Like a dog, told to sit, until its owner comes back, and the owner liable to forget. Now, he shook himself awake, 11.33 and the train to King's Cross leaving, and his car keys in his hand, and the forty-five years of his life so far all coiled tight inside him, his own. The child vanished for the moment, waving, mouthing: into thin air, until recalled. He turned up the car radio loud, found a late-night station playing jazz, and let it crackle through him until he got home.

With her little bag, Alice went into her compartment, to inhabit it. The guard retreated, promising tea and biscuits in the morning; and would she like a nightcap now? She went to the toilet even though the train was standing in the station and her pee would trickle straight through into a place where people teemed, instead of being sprayed out harmlessly over yards of empty track. Coming out, she passed a man in the corridor, he too with his coat collar turned up about his ears, and rubbing his hands together even in the air-conditioned warmth, as if he had had a long wait. They squeezed past each other, as the train moved and began to sway out of the station.

There was always the strangeness of undressing in the little compartment, as a train gathered speed, and places passed outside, and strange men stood leaning in the corridor, and others slept stacked and silent, invisible, just through a thin partition. The blind down, the door locked; as in all other compartments the blinds were down (beige, tightfitting) and the doors locked (with a reminder, to keep it locked at night, not to leave valuables) and the water rocked in the bottle of mineral water strapped to the wall, and the coat hangers rattled at the wall. And a mirror; before which, no escape, one undressed, coat, sweater, skirt, shoes already kicked aside (not to be lost) watch and earrings already removed, placed in the soap dish, then, petticoat, tights (did one go further than this, take everything off?). She unpacked her nightdress, ironed fresh for London, and took off her bra and pants, saw herself naked for a moment in the mirror on the back of the door (yes, still all right) and pushed her way up through Laura Ashley folds. The train squeaked rather than rattled, a subdued plastic sound, luxury fitted to utility, a newness still as of new shoes. The 125, yellow space-age engine, gobbling up the miles till Scotland vanished, telescoped up against England, and northern England became just a brief space on its way to London. It was like flying, more like flying than the old train-travel had been, when your head lolled and teeth chattered at each rickety stride of the train, and empty bottles rolled up and down the chilly corridors and the loo was blocked with paper, and the journey south took forever, forever, in a chilly drawn-out dawn. Alice cleaned her teeth in the smooth wide basin, drank some of the mineral water because it was there, examined her teeth in the mirror, wondering if she should have been to the dentist, sat down on the narrow bed. The tight cool sheet tucked, the regulation blanket; like school, like hospital, a bed for virginal dreamless straight sleeping. She got in, pushed her feet down between resisting hard sheets. Damn, her book was in her bag. The floor cold again and gritty to her feet – had somebody spilt sugar? She would not read, could not be bothered. Morning, she would need her wits about her, eyes unbagged. She smoothed on face cream, more each night, erasing wrinkles, pushing back time. And yet, when young, had not been happy. Better it was perhaps to be wrinkled and free, a night-time traveller, in nobody else's bed. She stretched, put out the light. A glow still in between the four close walls, not yet utter darkness. Ah, it was the sidelight, the discreet gleam. Extinguished, it let in the darkness, the train movement, the rush on through the unknown. Of course, it was the Borders, Northumberland, would be Yorkshire; but the straight onward rush could bear no resemblance to ordinary travel, through places that had names. Once, she had woken suddenly, the blind shooting upward released from its restraint, and a place out there that glared in at her as she lay, a gaunt lit city, towering building after building, hollow black windows, roofless wrecked shells of buildings, on and on, until she sat, nearly screamed staring out – Where is it, what has happened? In her just-woken mind, it seemed that what she feared had already happened, the bomb had gone off, this was the ruined, threatened world that awaited her. Then, the train had drawn in to a station, slowly, platforms elongating, and there had been the sign in the light summer dark 'Newcastle'. She had stood, uncaring, in her thin nightdress, and stared out, begging for information, mute against the glass; and at last had noticed that there were people, men in railway uniforms, people getting on, getting off the train. Luggage and clothes and faces intact. She had got back then into her narrow temporary bed, the blind pulled shut again; but had lain awake, all the hours it seemed till London, rehearsing in her mind the extent of the damage, the way it must have been. In her dreams, still, the yellow-lit gaunt-faced emptied city, like a premonition, only too readily conjured to reality.

Now, she lay flat beneath the sheet and blanket, her hip bones making promontories, breasts flattened against her chest, head tipped back upon the pillows, legs a little apart beneath the sheet, eyes open still in the darkness. Sleep would come. London and morning would be there, and people still, whole, and buildings, occupied. Behind her, there were Finn and Alex and Kate, in the house with the tall rooms, lying each of them in a separate room, snug beneath duvets, close to the floor, while the ceilings, the spaces, the darkness towered over them, piled them with sleep. And she, rocked like a baby by the moving train, carried on, as she wanted to be, on through life, into the future, further down the track.

The movement of the train; and another movement that echoed it, its familiar rhythm crowding the other out, rocking, rocking, yet faster, more urgent, a train that must hurtle on, faster, harder; and yet, no, slower again, gentle on smooth tracks, hardly rocking, hardly moving at all . . . She opened her eyes and saw the gleam of eyes in darkness above her, close, and felt the brush of a weight suspended above her, and from the touch of air knew her nightdress open all the way down the front, her breasts lying exposed, her belly too; while between her legs the rocking rhythm went on. She was being fucked, slowly, methodically, so that she had been almost asleep with it, almost lulled into unconsciousness again; and the train rolled her gently, as a pebble on the sea-shore, to and fro, to and fro. A mouth, whiskered, grazed her right breast, a tongue traced a saliva path cold from breast to belly, she was being touched as grass is touched by the delicate nostrils of grazing animals that search, that sniff out delicacies, in among the grasses, the summer plants. In a moment, she would come; it would be impossible not to, with the somnolent train rhythm, rocking, gently rocking, and the touching, here, there, everywhere, and the heat that grew and swelled between her legs, pushing in, growing, spreading upwards and outwards. One more feather touch: and she cried out and the explosion rocked her, she sobbed, she clasped, grasped, clung, throbbed with it. Above her and in her, the unknown creature to whom she arched her body groaned and came down; like a falling tower, covering her quite. Hair in her mouth and saliva pouring down her chin and her body convulsing still, she wept, at the pleasure, the generosity of it, the ease.

Between this point on the way south, this star exploding in darkness, and her destination, there was no further landmark, no station. Only the long rapid haul of the train on a straight track, only hours of dreamless sleep, uncharted. Anything could have happened, but did not.

In the morning, first thing, dawn breaking, there was the knock and the man coming in with a tray of tea and two digestive biscuits in a packet, and there, soon, would be London. She sat up, took the tray, pulling at her slipping nightdress. The door had been, she noticed, unlocked. The sheets were not unduly crumpled. She had slept well, even beautifully. The tea, though too strong, was wonderfully hot, the thick china cup good to the fingers. She unwrapped and ate the biscuits, because in the morning she did not usually eat biscuits, and began to pick up her scattered clothes, and to dress. She pulled up the blind, and the light outside was grey, the sky streaked behind gasometers and narrow streets of houses, the land flat beneath the sky as if a weight had pressed upon it from above.

Finn on his way home that night stopped his car for a moment in a side street and thought of Alice settling for her night in the train, and the train leaving, and Alice being carried swiftly south, and knew himself freed. They were always doing this to each other, it seemed: capturing each other, letting each other go. There was the intense closeness, the moment of almost uncomfortable intimacy, and then the urge to separateness, and the dread of separating, and then the departure (of one or the other) and the relief, the realisation of freedom. Sometimes he wondered why his life tired him so. Surely it would have been possible to have jogged along, to have settled down, to have known what was happening next? He had to be at work tomorrow, up at seven o'clock to get breakfast, see the children off to school, walk to his place of work; and here he was at eleven-thirty, eleven-forty, even, alone, in his car, in the dark, in a side street, not knowing why he had stopped, parked. The light of street lamps spilt upon cobbles; egg-yolk, he thought, searching for similies, as if Alice were here. An egg-stained, wet street. The moon up there like an egg.

The stones, the black stones of the city, crumbling like soot. No, it would not do. He could not find words for his sense of things crumbling, cracking, oozing. It was in him, not out there, not even in this stage-set street, its mediaeval narrowness. He opened the car door, to breathe in some fresh air. Stations always smelt, tinny like phone-booths. The smell of iron wheels and money. Or was that from when he had stood, a small boy labelled for a far destination, somewhere south, fingering the coins in his pocket, the heavy pennies, breathing in the coaldust and smoke? He got out, leaned against the car, looked up, up to the light chill sky, the moon sailing. Here, you did not look down a street, but up it; the eye always directed upward, as in fairy-tales, to see what might be reached. Which street was this? He remembered that he had once known somebody who lived here, in this street or the next, which ran parallel. A name in his address book avoided his memory. But a light shone high up, that was not the moon, that was shutters suddenly opened and a beam let out into the night. He remembered a door, a long list of names, bells, an answering wheeze of a voice; a heavy door opening inwards. Up there, now, high at the top of the building, somebody leaned, to look at the moon. His fingers felt at the names beside the door, felt for memory. The sky was full of pale clouds, drifting. Alice was set on her way south, rattled to sleep, to dream. He touched the top bell and after a moment's pause came a wheeze of assent and the door opened easily at his slight push, the magic word had been spoken, and he was inside. The hallway was curved at the far end, and just wide enough for him to pass the stacked bikes that were locked there and reach the bottom of the stairs. Stone stairs, their step slightly eroded, over centuries. His hand feeling for the rail, on one side. In castles, stairs went round a certain way, so that the defenders could rush down easily, sword in hand, and cut invaders down. But he was left-handed and that might have made a difference. In the darkness, his imaginary sword; against the rush from above, ambidextrous knight, counting on others' right-handed predictability. In bed, he liked to sleep on the left side, with Alice on his right (with whoever it was on his right) and women were surprised by it. Surprising the number of women, he thought, conditioned by right-handed husbands, to get into bed on the left. Was that it? Or was it a matter of bedside lights, and the elbow one leaned on to read, back turned to a snoring spouse, and a hand reached out at last to extinguish light? He went on up the stairs. Past doors, lit feebly; and in between, the darkness. Up and up, breathing faster, treading more slowly, where once he might have leapt to the very top. The door was open. He remembered it, painted that shade of yellow. Images tugged at his mind. A voice called out from inside – Come in. He went in, a man in a dream, somnambulant. Nobody sprang out to repel the invader. What if there were one there, though, flattened behind a hanging, sword in hand, moustache close over tightened lips, just waiting for the moment? When he, trousers dropped and pale flesh vulnerable, might be slit like a rabbit from throat to crotch? But he went in anyway, letting himself in for the next moment, and for all that might unfold from it.

She was standing in the middle of the room in a pair of trousers with purple legwarmers and nothing else, but with a shirt hanging from one hand. Had she pulled it off as he came up the stairs, before he rang, after he rang, as he came in through the door? Before looking at the moon or after? The shutters were closed again and the room was hot from the full glare of the gas fire. Her bed was in the corner, a different corner. She might simply have been going to bed. But in that case would surely have pulled something on before answering, before pressing the button that released the door? But there she was, casual, in the middle of the room, barefoot, in those legwarmers, as if she might have been doing exercises, limbering up. Her breasts seemed to stare at him. Perhaps it was ordinary, these days, perhaps it was usual, for women to walk about in their own rooms wearing only trousers, to welcome men in like that, without covering themselves. But he, rabbit in a sprung trap, erect as he would have been at twelve years old at the very word, the very thought, breasts, could not find it ordinary.

She said – Hello.

He could only think of covering with his cold hands those warm globes of flesh. She was faceless, nameless, an offering. He struggled to speak, heard his own voice a croak.

She said – This is a funny time for a visit. Have you got a cold?

She said – I was just going to bed.

He moved forward, unbuttoning his own coat, throwing it and his scarf aside, kicking shoes away, unzipping trousers; paused a moment in his undressing to find her, hold her, hold those breasts, cover her face with kisses, to follow the opening zip of her own trousers down, to support her as she stepped out of them; struggled with his own belt, hopped to remove socks (Alice had once said that anybody who made love in socks was ridiculous); naked as a peeled stick, he who had been so wrapped, so buttoned in clothes, led her from the little dropped piles of garments, towards the bed. And she, brown all over from a sunbed in the lunch hour, less poignantly naked than if she had been patched conventionally bikini-white at breasts and bottom, went with him as if she expected this, had been awaiting it. They rolled upon the covers until he twitched with one grand movement both bedspread and duvet aside; on chilled taut sheet they rolled upon each other, rubbed together, bare skin such a delight to him, a relief, after the daylong effort of clothes, talk, decisions. Hours ago, he had been in a flower-shop, pushing his face into the cold cluster of chrysan-themum's bloom, breathing in, nearly weeping from the chill, firm touch of the petals; now, he buried his face in her, warm bread flesh, astonishingly hot salt crevices, rock pools, her hair spread like weed; hunting for it, the exact taste, smell, sensation, chasing down the tunnels of the years, shedding age, losing experience, peeling from himself layer after layer as he had peeled clothes, leaving himself for a moment quite raw.

Alice set the thumbed sheets on the table before her, and the thin books, one upon the other, with places marked with paper strips, and moved the glass of water, that left a wet rim upon morocco leather, and stood up with the lamp behind her, on view. The room was full of people settling and scuffling, eyeing her. They awaited her, her signal; they expected her to wield power. The slight dampness at her arm-pits, beneath her silk shirt, let her know that she was nervous, more nervous than before a class, even than before a lecture audience. She thought, what they want is blood. Salt, sweat, essences. Myself, ground small, And I shall give them words irreducible as atoms, that will maybe baffle them, I shall go away intact. The time when poets had to give blood is surely over. Sylvia Plath put an end to it: shamed a whole public into consciousness at last, ended an era of Roman games. Now, we are allowed to defend ourselves. A world afraid to ask the final question, will no longer expect us to gas ourselves, to drink ourselves to death. But still, she sweated under her light shirt and in the palms of her hands, and somebody was introducing her, it was Giles, he was using words, personal, vivid, vision; woman, essence, truth. Feminist, he said, and the ranks of women sitting near the front sighed and settled, reassured. Classical, he said, and another section, the older, well-dressed men and women sitting in the comfortable chairs, revived. Love poems, he said, and a shudder seemed to go through the audience, a breath of shared desire. Love and poems. What we are all starved of. It was like offering them bread, wine; she saw their mouths, open to receive. And she, her life, her experience, her hours of work, was to feed them. Giles said something that brought a ripple of amusement, after that, orchestrating the overture, and sat down. He smiled at her. He was pleased with himself, with his wit, his sensitivity, his sense of occasion. Some of the women in the front row were glaring at him. What was a feminist poet doing, letting herself be introduced by a man? Had nothing changed? Was everything to be thus polluted, distorted, robbed of meaning? Alice thought, I should have thought, should have realised. And, love poems? Am I about to be fed to the lions after all?

The imagery of the unconscious, Giles had said, brought into the light of day. And she remembered the grey light over London, winter dawn, the coldness of air, the dampness as she had stepped from the train, carrying her overnight bag. A poet, stepping out with her bag full of images and her knickers unusually wet, surely, a wetness there that could not have come from dream, and the sight of a door easily opened, because not after all locked, as the notice had said, and a body still singing with caresses that could not, surely, have been imagined? Puzzled, she had glanced up and down the train. Looked for a man getting out on his own, from a compartment not far from hers. A man in an overcoat with the collar turned up perhaps, and no other sign but a certain gleaming eye? There was no one. Or rather, there was a woman with piles of luggage, and a couple travelling together, and a young woman being met by a young man who must be her fiancée; and then there was simply a crowd, dispersed, its separate elements lost because mingled together, and she was alone in it, moving towards the barrier, and now she would never know.

She cleared her throat. She would risk the newest ones, the ones still unpublished, that were like stepping stones through a torrent. They could knock her sideways, if they wanted, even drown her, but the stones themselves would remain, firm, showing the way to others if they dared. She began. There was the sound of her own voice trembling, balanced upon the silence. The words, spoken out loud for the first time in public, heard for the first time, that had been secrets, solutions, salves at a time when her flesh had seemed to burn needing them. Now they were clear, neutralised, now that the feeling had drained. She could watch with interest, to see what they became. She saw herself loose them, a flock of birds, to fly among the audience, white doves from the conjurer's hat. Her own voice settled, dropped in pitch; as she sent them forth. There was a breath from the audience, indrawn and then exhaled; she could hear them, like one entity, breathing. (And again, there, the flash of memory: of somebody who breathed above her, around her, invisible in darkness. Had it happened? Had it not?) In a moment, she would pause, sip water, pick up one of her published books and read a poem that would be familiar. One from the late sixties, when she had begun to pour out so much energy that it had seemed the poems would never stop, one to reassure them. Then, there had been the poetry of women in rooms, women who burned time away, waiting for their babies to grow up; drinking Nescafé, borrowing books, watching the time for *Play School*; and all the time, the great changes that they imagined ballooning between them, in the rooms, in the enclosed spaces, so that there was no gap left, no doubt; almost, no air to breathe, no time to sleep. Reading these poems again, she could almost taste it, touch it, that time; and see Laurie, smoking, in the corner by the gas fire, tense as a wire, and her little boy on the floor, and Emily, and Jeanne, her friends. She had seen, at that time, a production of Tchekhov's *Three Sisters* and had written this poem, 'Getting to Moscow'. It had won a prize. She had

92

had prize money, and spent it on boots. 'Boots!' had said Laurie, as if it should rather have been, bombs. Laced boots, to the knee, from Anello and Davide, in London. If she could not be free, she would at least have laced boots, and undo them in the evening, Finn watching. Even then.

A voice in the audience said clearly 'That's better' and there was a murmer of assent. Louise Burnett, sitting in the front row, her arms flung back across the backs of the chairs beside her, her chin lifted to listen, thought that the reading should have been for women only. It was from just behind Louise that the voice had come; a tall redheaded woman sat there, whom Alice perhaps knew. Sssh, sssh, came the voices from further back. Alice picked another safe one, read at so many meetings where poetry was exchanged. The murmurs were of assent, approval. This was the stuff of which her reviews had been made, this was what had established her. Women quoted from these poems, found in them words and phrases that made little ladders in their own lives, and climbed them. This, at least, she had done: made of the everyday, the ordinary, the boring, the oppressive, a poetry for herself, for others; saying, look, this is what we can do. Encouraged now at the smiles, at the upturned faces, she picked another type-written sheet from the small pile of her latest poems, and decided to risk it again.

– This has not been published. I wrote it last month.

And there were these dreams, these images, that had forced them-selves, it sometimes seemed, forced themselves upon her. After all these years, the images of a life that was neither waking nor sleeping, images culled from that narrow time between the two, things smoky, insubstantial, swift moving, filled with a power she did not under-stand. Reading, she wondered simultaneously if she should not rather have stayed silent. But, no; years ago, she had written:

> silence will no more still us
> our tongues will not be bound
> all sounds shall we speak
> and thus will you know us.

Never again, then, silence; the silence of fearing, of not-daring, of hoping for the best. Years, a whole decade, there had been now, of her speaking up, speaking out, writing down, publishing. And yet, this evening, her voice faltered, she heard it; there was a catch, a flaw, something that might fault her; and in the room, the discreet Georgian room, with its pillars, its fine carved fireplace, its wide doors, its plasterwork, it was heard and noted. Alice Linnell, one of the finest feminist poets of the time, was losing her grip.

A voice said loudly– 'Cop out.'

(Sssh. Sssh. The soothing, covering voices, the poetry establishment, the people who had hired this room, the ones in dinner clothes, who were going on somewhere else. Sssh. Sssh. We do not accept disturbance.)

Alice jerked her head up and stared into the audience. From where had the voice come? The redhaired woman stared back, equally surprised. Louise, in front of her, looked about, signalled to Alice to go on. Giles, on the other side of the desk, coughed, glanced at her too. His glance said – I'm sorry, how embarrassing, let us hope it doesn't happen again.

Stones. Objects. Round, hard, unbreakable, solid. One for you, and one for you, and one for you. What I have written, what I have known, become stones. Existing, indestructible. Gripping the paper, Alice went on, reading her newest long poem right through to the end.

– We're not interested in this stuff.

– Cop out. Cheat.

– This is terrible.

Were there now two voices? Her glance this time raked the audience, for enemies. For they all might become enemies, and she would go down among them, destroyed, invisible except for a storm of torn white paper, that would flutter and then blow away. Giles rose, beside her. The two women had been seen, identified. People, men, were gripping their arms, pushing them, trying to push them towards the door. Louise looked at Alice, and shrugged. One could not do everything. One had done so much already. One had survived said Louise's look, and one was not obliged to leap to one's feet all the time, not any more. Alice saw the two young women, one in a ragged fur coat, the other in a blue duffel jacket and red scarf, being pushed towards the door. Stop, she wanted to call out, stay here, talk to me, explain. But they did not see her; they were muttering to each other – Come on, we might as well go – and picking up bags and books, shuffling noisily out. They were too far away, they would not hear her. She had not arranged the reading, hired the room, paid for it, it was not her responsibility – And yet, here she was, moving out from behind the table, pushing her way forward, calling out to them after all; as if she had done too much, to remain silent, as if her body and its reflexes, at least, were programmed still to move always into the fray.

– What do you want to hear?

She saw a pale face, wiry dark hair, eyes glittering; and a wider, harder face, mouth pursed with scorn.

– Nothing. The response came back to her. Nothing. We've had a bellyful thanks, already. We don't want to hear any more arselicking fucking shit.

Giles said – Go on. Go on reading. Ignore them.

She picked up a magazine, in which a poem had been published that she had written about her children; wry, sad, funny, tender, it was. She would begin again, luring them back, the scattered audience, its attention divided, and tell them, poetry is stronger than division, words stronger than violence the image stronger than the flung missile which seeks to destroy it; singing her song, she would woo them back to her.

At Emily's, there was the familiar late-night disorder, wine bottles and plates of food half-emptied, but her guests had gone. Emily herself sat, her youngest child on her knee heavy with sleep, her late last baby, four or five years old now, his mouth still pursed and rosy as if he sucked still at the immense store of her maternal feeling. Martin was in the kitchen, washing up; just within earshot, as he called to them above the clatter of his sluicing and stacking.

– How'd it go? Still packing them in the aisles?

Alice was talking to Emily, low. She wanted to ask her – Emily, is it true? Did that really happen to me? And if so, what is its meaning?

She called back to Martin – It was okay except for some women treating me as a blackleg. Arselicking, they said I was. Otherwise, fine.

95

He came out of the kitchen, drying his hands on a tea-towel, sleeves rolled. He grinned at her in his malicious way. Thus would he taunt and tease Emily. He danced around them, gadfly, goading.

– Well, you are, aren't you? What could be more bourgeois-establishment than you? You're not only living with a man, you're actually married to him, you have pots of money, look at the coat you're wearing, you come down from Scotland on the night train, bet you had a first-class sleeper, you swan around showing these poor women how you've made out. What do you expect?

Emily said – Martin, that's not fair.

She would keep an eye on him, check him in his excesses; firm yet tolerant, she reined him in from her distance, from where she sat with her nearly sleeping son. Alice thought, she will not draw back, will always risk the confrontation, but so sure of herself, she is, that he will never be able to resist her, however he may dance and fret.

She said – Maybe it is. Everything he says is true.

– But you're earned all you have.

Martin said – On the backs of real feminist revolutionaries.

– That's rubbish, Martin. She hasn't exploited anybody. She's written fine poetry, and people have recognised it, that's all. And if you ask me, people who make a scene like that are simply jealous. They wish they could do the same, and they simply haven't the talent or the ability to work.

– You mean, they haven't got earning husbands and big houses and don't eat out of the hands of cynical publishers who jumped on the bandwagon of the women's movement.

– Martin, shut up. Alice, have a drink. Pour her some wine, Martin, for God's sake. Alice, you know him, he's just a nuisance.

Martin poured Beaujolais, handed her the stemmed glass. He smiled friendlily and raised his eyebrows.

Alice said – The problem is, having won the right to freedom of speech, does one have the right to say what one likes? That's what came up for me this evening.

Martin said – Nobody has freedom of speech. You may think you do, but you're being censored and manipulated all the time. You're a product of your age, no more, no less. You're a hybrid.

96

Emily said sharply – Well, at least she does something, at least she creates something, she doesn't sit around all day putting down other people.

– Aren't you going to put that child to bed? You know, Alice, if he was asleep, she'd wake him up so that she could sit and cuddle him all evening. She'll be going on pretending he's a baby till he's twenty-five, at this rate. She'd still be breast-feeding him if she'd half a chance.

–Well, if you'd had breasts, I wouldn't have stood a chance, would I? I wouldn't have been able to get near him.

Martin shaped his hands in the air before him – The best pair of tits in North London. What a pity they never grew. No, you're right. I'm only so nasty because I never got my stint at breast-feeding.

Then Alice remembered, that nothing was serious between these two, the bickering, the anger: all evaporated in a minute, puffed away quite lightly by an extraordinary breath of tenderness. She had nearly forgotten this. That just as friends, guests, onlookers were being drawn in, were about to bicker and shout and take sides, in their turn these two, Emily and Martin, would withdraw, and smile at each other, and then the cardboard edifices would topple the ranked opinions fall flat as stacked cards; it would be over.

Emily said – You take him to bed.

– All right. Come on, old son, old lump. Daddy'll take you up. That is, supposing I am your daddy. Anyway, I love you. There we go.

– Idiot. Emily watched them go, the child's head dark upon the man's slight shoulder, the arm coming up to clutch at the back of his neck. Ascending the stairs, out of the wide wrecked peace of the room in which they all lived, the man's back tense with carrying, the child all limp and loose, a pink foot dangling.

Alice saw Emily watch them go, her face narrowed with concern like that of a mother cat, attention all focussed, eyes wide.

– Em. How are you?

It was the time for more wine, and confidences. Martin came back, unbuttoning his shirt on a narrow, matted chest, said – I'm going to bed too, I'll leave you two to it. I've got to see a man in the morning.

The two women nodded to him, shuffled their chairs closer

97

immediately.

Emily said – He always says that, about seeing a man in the morning. And he does go, he does see them, God knows who they are, but they never seem to come up with anything. It gets him down, not being in work. He pretends. He won't talk about it. But it's why he's so prickly. He's got worse. I don't like him treating you badly, though. You know he loves you, don't you?

– If I hadn't known, I'd have guessed. Don't worry, you don't have to protect me from Martin, I know his bite of old. Or bark, do I mean.

Emily said – This wine. He bought it for Christmas. And it's still only November.

– I should have brought some. I meant to, and there wasn't time. Guzzling your Christmas wine like this.

– Alice, for God's sake. We only see you about once in two years, you're not going to be here at Christmas, you're my oldest friend, Martin loves you, however out of work he was he wouldn't be able to not buy the Beaujolais Nouveau when it comes in, and Christmas is months away, and I stockpile the family allowance. What contradictions our lives are made of, aren't they? Drink up, you must need it after this evening.

– What about you, are you working?

– Supply teaching. The woman's got cancer, so I'm all right for a bit. English and Social Studies, just down the road. I know, it's a horrible way to look at it, isn't it, but at least she's not going to leap up and demand her job back in a hurry.

Alice sat back. Whatever contradictions, whatever impossibilities there might be, there was Em. Sitting there opposite her still, after all these years, managing her life. Like a sailor in a storm, she thought, pulling in a sheet here, letting a sail billow there. Reckoning, eyeing the map, listening to forecasts, taking readings; calm, because it was all that she could be. Her blue, mariner's eyes fixed on horizons, on distances. She wanted, now, to tell Em. To unburden herself of what had weighed her down today, making her uncertain, tentative where once she would have been bold.

– Em.

– What?

(Late night bedroom talk, after parties, between men, over coffee, beside gas fires; how this brought it all back.)
– I had a weird experience last night.
– Good for you. Did you enjoy it?
– Well, yes. I did. But I can't tell whether it really happened or not.
– Some of the best ones don't.
– Yes, but this— Well, I'll tell you. It was on the train. I got the night train. I thought I'd locked the door on my compartment, only in the morning it didn't seem to be locked. And in the night, I thought that somebody came in, a man, and – well, fucked me.
– Alice, come on, you aren't telling me that you don't know whether a man fucked you or not.
– Well, yes. I mean, I was sure someone did. But it was impossible. And in the morning there was no one there. There was no one it could possibly have been. And it was like a dream.
– You probably dreamed it. The phantom lover. I mean, it's everybody's fantasy, isn't it, getting done on a train by a total stranger. Sealed compartments, and rattling through the night at a hundred miles an hour.
– A hundred and twenty-five, now.
– What? Oh, even better. The fastest phantom fuck. High speed. This is the age of the train.
– No, but Em, seriously, it matters to me, to know whether it was true or not. It's all right to have a fantasy like that, but to actually have it happen – so that there's a man somewhere who knows that's what he did in the night – that's different.
– Oh, I see. Like the Marquise von O. Well, she got pregnant, that was how she found out. I hope you're not. I've heard of phantom pregnancies, but it could turn out to be only too real. What happened to the Marquise von O in the end, I've forgotten?
Alice said – you think I'm joking, don't you? Or dreaming, or making it up. But, it felt real. It really did. In the morning, too.
– Did you come?
– Yes.
– That could have been in a dream.
– Yes, but the rest couldn't. I know there was somebody there. A

99

real person. A real man.

– Well, he must have been Houdini. Look, no hands.

– I'm not totally certain that I did lock the door. But, Em, I couldn't have, not really, I couldn't have just lain there and let a total stranger fuck me and then get up and go without a word. Could I?

–Ah, you mean it isn't quite in keeping with your persona as a well-known feminist poet?

– You sound like Martin.

– Well, it is rather rich, you must admit. Perhaps you have a secret power, to make all your fantasies materialise. That could be fun.

– You still don't believe me, do you?

– I don't know how to, really. Why worry, though? You had a good fuck on the night train from Scotland, got up in the morning, went about your business, it's all over now, it was fun – why worry?

– It's the passivity, I think.

– Okay in fantasies but not in fact?

– Something like that.

– Not very liberated.

– Not very, no.

Em drained her wine glass and set it down deliberately on the table, as if something had been settled.

– How about this, then. A different point of view. You conjured up this delightful man out of thin air, so that he arrived in your compartment, said not a word, gave you the time of your life, acted out your favourite fantasies, disappeared discreetly, left you free as air in the morning. Surely that's what men have always wanted from women? Or at least, lots of them have. I should count yourself lucky, if I were you, love. A sheer bonus, that's what it sounds like to me.

Alice looked across at her friend and saw that always, Emily would stretch out her hand to whatever was there in the way of experience and choose by which handle she grasped it. It was why she was there, herself, not compromised; yet not separated, either, not alcoholic, not bitter, not on tranquillisers, not raging against fate. She thought – Well, why not? A sheer bonus. Perhaps that was what it was, would turn out to be.

3

Finn let himself into his sleeping house that was warm still from his children's evening activity, strewn still with the wake of Alice's departure. The bottle, the glasses, the plates, the crusts, were still on the table, all at one end of the table, as if a snack had been quickly eaten, rather than a meal. He smelled still his daughter's shampoo, the toast he had made, the packet soup, burned milk from somebody's night drink, the slight singeing of clothes aired upon the boiler. The curtains had not been drawn. Strange how teenagers never drew curtains – as if they did not notice, or care, that the world stared in. He imagined them sitting on the floor, on squashed cushions, watching the television, biting mouthfuls without looking at what they ate, kicking each other occasionally. They had turned off fires, switched off the television at the wall, they were in their beds, breathing, heaped with covers. Only the cat got up, stretched, came towards him, its tail rigid. He would pick it up, put it out into the cold. The cat, whimpering as he touched it, knew this, pleaded, but gave in without struggle to the pleasure of his touch. He rubbed it behind the ears, stroked its belly, flattened its springy spine with the flat of his hand. Silence in the house, his house. Alice away. Himself truant, two in the morning, intruder, inspecting the place for clues. On the stairs, the smell of garlic; or was it from his own hands, on his breath? Alice went garlic-marked to London, ringed by his spell; would return, therefore recognisable, unchanged. The light flickered about him, fluorescent in the kitchen, bleaching surfaces. Objects were strange, left where they had dropped: a glove of Kate's, a book, paper from the overflowing basket. It seemed, that he was always going into rooms, these days, that people had just left; he sniffed, he guessed at their presences, yet did not meet them, not quite. They evaded him, his children; in an unobtrusive game of hide-and-seek they waited perhaps for him to give himself away.

Finn went into his own room, leaving the rest of the house in darkness. He had his own bed, his lair: so that when he slept with Alice, it was as a visitor – no toothbrush or pyjamas, no book he wanted to read – and when she came to sleep with him, she was mysterious, a woman on a one night stand, peeling off her clothes in alien surroundings, free to drop them in a silky heap on the floor. His room was colder than hers; so that she would come towards him shivering, goose-fleshed, hugging her breasts like hot-water-bottes, urgent for him to warm her through. In Alice's room, he went naked and missed his own things, was more like a man stranded somewhere for the night than a mysterious stranger; he thudded about on the soft carpet and wanted to borrow things, and jumped into bed after her, a homeless dog she teased him, missing its blanket and collar. And she would wait for him, watch him, a little irritated, the duvet up to her chin. It was not quite what she had planned, he thought; but then would go right down under the duvet and tickle her with his hair and growl, so that she would shriek and giggle as Kate had when little, and he would find her suddenly all moist, offered, close to him, like found treasure, and all would be well.

In his own room, it was tidy. If Alice loved profusion, confusion, he liked things ordered, stacked or in rows, and each thing in its place. He marvelled that they had lived together for all this time, when they first took their own rooms, so that the contrast was evident. Now, all the rooms in the house were like Alice's – scarfs curling from open drawers, knickers and socks in heaps, flowers brimming from bowls of stale water, books and records and pictures in a rich profusion which was, to Finn, chaos. But in here (and he closed the door, pulled off all his clothes once more, stood naked, shivering, folding them and placing them on the chair) was order. An island of order. And he, he was drained, sucked dry, fragile with spent emotion. He had bought flowers and seen Alice off and made love and driven home through the thick dark winter night, and he was now like a shell, light to float upon the shallows of sleep, for hours, for days, for ever. He pulled on a night shirt and tucked it between his thighs for warmth, and jumped into bed as he had every night of his life, whether the bed had creaked or sung or simply given gently with his weight, and whether a woman had sat there, or lain there, laughing at him, at the way he jumped. Burrowed, turned like a dog (Alice was right), wriggled and turned and butted at the pillow with his head, and finally tucked his hands between his legs, or somebody else's, and sighed, long and deep. In the darkness, now, visions flowered, exploded softly, dropped brilliant fragments to earth. He was quickly and easily asleep, shunted into the tunnel of the end of his long day at last.

Angela was awake. In her high-up flat, from which the light still beamed out like a lighthouse lamp, across gulfs, across precipices, she walked up and down. Now, she wore the shirt that she had been carrying when Finn had come in, and her legs and feet were bare. The heat from the puttering gas fire dried the air, slightly scorching her flesh. It was two in the morning, nearly, but she was wide awake, tidying up; folding clothes, stacking papers, putting shoes in tidy pairs. Making love made her energetic, alert; she felt like emptying out cupboards, washing kitchen shelves, singing, learning something new. But if she were to sing or bang, the neighbours downstairs would confront her angrily in the morning; so she hummed hymn tunes and folded up her clothes. She felt purged, yet whole; sleek, a fed cat licking its whiskers, settling to a long contented grooming routine, herself, then her house, her surroundings. Her light beamed out right across the city; and through her open shutters the full moon gazed equally in, so that they were twin beacons, twin signals. In between, the whole stacked dreaming city, spires and chimneys in the dark. A sleeping population, wrapped in its long northern winter night. No hint of morning, not for hours and hours, for it was dark still at seven these days, and streaked seaside sky only waking by eight, and darkness creeping back, an inward tide, by three in the afternoon. The dawn, like the sea, came in from the east. Sometimes she leaned on her high sill and watched it come, spilling red light upon the city. Sometimes she allowed herself to get quite cold, watching it, feeling the chill from the unshuttered glass, and then would bundle herself back into bed again, duvet to her chin, rolled and wrapped like a doll, and would watch her room fill with the uncertain light, the sky come pouring in. Up here, she lived like a bird, a rock-dweller. It was her perch, her ledge, and upon it she was safe. Sometimes it was visited, perched upon by others, and her door would fly open and there she would be, half-naked perhaps, doing Yoga or using her sunlamp, and the cold black visiting bird would be a man rushing in with his coat flapping open, ready to leap upon her and batter his wings and bear her to the ground. Finn Anderson. She only remembered his name because it was a curious one; more fish than bird, perhaps. His shoulder-blades, yes, with the sharpness of fins, and the bony coral reef of his spine. She knew his body with her hands better than she remembered any detail of his life. Once, she had given him her address. But how, then, had he come, so exact, homing, on this very night? How opened the door and flown in and covered her with his big cold hands and fed her so thoroughly, so well? A big fine bird stuffing fish into the gullet of another, she thought. Strange, how images prevail, how I see us, birds upon a clifftop, preening. Finn Anderson. His wife was famous, a poet. And he smelt of the cold, of late-night stations, of waiting traffic, of coins, of smoke. He rushed in (had he said something about a night train, a departure?) and walked straight up to her and covered her breasts with his hands. What did it mean, if anything? She thought, we could have talked, drunk, made coffee; instead, we touched each other's strung nerves to explosion point, and met in an ecstasy of relief, dumb as strangers, coming together and then flying instantly apart. He knew where to come. Could have phoned me, been tentative; as I could have said, well, perhaps, so? Some actions preclude words, predate arrangements. And what now, I wonder; if anything? Does such a moment pass like a dream into a realm of oblivion, is there a sequel, what might it be?

She laid her folded clothes into the top drawer and looked about her, to find something else to do. In the little kitchen adjoining her bedroom, she washed a few plates, rinsed them, placed them in the rack, then wiped the worktop clean with a wet cloth. Something in her longed to scrub, to scour, to do the kitchen floor perhaps, or pull everything out of the cupboards and gradually, neatly replace them. But she resisted. She sang, and rubbed her hands together, pink from the water, and washed her tights and knickers in the bathroom, and stared at her own face in the bathroom mirror, her mouth wide open to examine her fillings. Her body beneath the shirt smelled still to her of the warm pungency of sex, but the sperm was dried already and cracking on the insides of her legs. She thought, in a few minutes, this well-being will pass, and I will begin to want something else; it will no longer be enough to sing, and tidy the flat, and admire my teeth in the mirror. The old opening mouths of numberless needs, crying for attention. Before the spell wore off, she would cover herself, and sleep, though, holding her comfort tight against her belly, between her legs as when she was little she had held animals, worn, furred, angular, tight against her navel in the dark, their button eyes to her ribs, a leg between hers, teddies of a hundred uses, pandas, elephants, rabbits, lions. A whole circus parade; and new ones at Christmas to fill the gaps, to keep the cold out, to keep little Angela warm.

At work, in the daylight, in the morning, she would no more let the world know of the night visit of Finn Anderson than she would, twenty years ago, have made public the real uses of those Christmas animals. To nobody would she say – I stood there with the door open and no clothes on and a man I hardly know came in and made love to me. It was indeed easy, in the morning, to behave as if it had not happened. The women at work would not guess, would not know. For it was in her night world, the world of the high-up ledge perched high above the darkened, roaring sea, that Finn Anderson's visit belonged. In a world of isolation and bird-cries that floated and carried and were at last borne right away. When she came down her spiral stone stairway in the morning, booted, dressed, money for her bus ticket in her hand, she left that world behind, entered another. For her, the two could not meet, were incompatible. In the days and nights of her infancy had the two been split, parted; so that it would be danger, folly, carelessness, to bring them together. Angela, her mother and father had called her, Angela, their little bright blonde daughter: ignorant of the corner of darkness that she nurtured and hid, that would call a man, decades later, straight across a city to her, one night; ignorant of the lighthouse beam and the deeper darkness afterwards.

'Endings' noted the diligent pens of those who attended Alice's Creative Writing class that week: 'endings may be used as beginnings. Anything may be used as a beginning or an ending. Sometimes the end of all narrative may be condensed in the first sentence, the first page.'

A student interrupted, asked – But if you know what's happened, what it all leads up to already, then where's the suspense? Surely something has to be kept back, kept hidden till the end?

Angela on her morning bus had a similar thought, but did not voice it. Everything, she thought, has already happened between me and Finn Anderson. What should have been the climax is already over. What people lead up to and dream about and plan and hope for, has already happened. Nothing led up to it – or at least, only a chance encounter months ago, an address exchanged, some vague registering of attraction, nothing enough to merit such an event. I am still on my bus, going to work. There will be, can be, no development, surely? Whatever we have done, we have done back to front, according to the norms. Now, we will go backwards, perhaps. Eventually, perhaps, he will call on me, shy and hopeful, and bring me a bunch of flowers . . . .

And Finn himself, waking with a groan, remembered a hundred things before he remembered the night before: he thought of the time and the date (his mother's birthday) and the report that awaited him on his desk at work, and that Alice was not there, and that his blue socks had a hole in them and he must find others, and that Reagan was in Paris, and that the world might end, and that *The Elephant Man* was on at the theatre, and that he had cramp in his left foot, and that he had forgotten to buy loo paper yesterday and that it was colder than yesterday and that— But the dry patchiness on the insides of his thighs, a certain languor, reminded him. Angela – what was her other name? To whom he had gone, like, he thought, a homing pigeon. Suddenly finding himself in her part of town, her street, outside her house, ringing her doorbell. Minutes after seeing Alice off, strange. He who was no philanderer, after all. Alice, he thought, what would he say to Alice? Nothing. It was just one of those things. Delightful, but essentially meaningless. Meaningless because he would choose not to invest it with meaning, because he was in charge. Meaning could be doled out by him, then, and withheld? Yes, meaningless, because anything else was too complex, did not fit. Not a woman in this town, anyway, not in the same city as Alice. Elsewhere, perhaps, yes? Paris, or Madrid, or even London. Somewhere remote, where secrets might be hid: not here, where his life was, where he would risk his very self. He thought, yes, what I needed, a good fuck, a good screw. No preliminaries, and no necessary consequences, but a coupling in mid-air, as it were, in passage, in the narrow free time between one day and another, in darkness, in secrecy, outside of the structures of meaning. That was all right, then. How good it had been, how remarkable, how exactly right. How he had come in, and been greeted, received, accepted, and how easily let go. Perfect. He lay and wriggled his left foot to get it to return to life, and enjoyed his memories, now that they were cut loose of context and obligations. In a minute, he would get up, run a bath, call his children, make coffee. Life was a case of selecting pleasures, after all, creating them for oneself, knowing how to savour. He would make some good coffee, stronger than Alice liked it, and sit in front of the stove and sip it, reading an untouched newspaper that for once had been left for him alone, and enjoy his view of the universe. He would like to tell Alice – Guess what, while you were away . . . Could not tell how she would react, imagined her wise and congratulatory, glad that he had seized life, for once, seized and had. It was what one was supposed to do, in this day, in this age. Seize the moment, embrace and let go. The only thing one could be sure of, in a time like this: the exactness of naked bodies, the unambiguous messages of sex. He had become, overnight, a man of his time, of the era: selecting, consuming, and ignoring causality, cutting himself loose.

When he was young, it had been so different.

He and Alice, he and others before Alice, he fumbling towards women through some long dream of adolescence from which it was hard to awake, which pestered, which kept him enthralled. He, Finn, the long gangling one, the one with sticking-out ears and the too-short haircut his mother favoured, he of the shiny-kneed trousers and the pimple above the collar, he dreaming and lusting, always about to overflow, he in torment, embarrassment, anxiety, stress. There had been young women at parties, the parties of adolescence; pretty or plain (one knew immediately which was which), pretty giggling to plain, plain blushing, all of them ranged against a wall, shoulder to shoulder it seemed, impenetrable. Pink off-the-shoulder dresses and deep-hollowed collarbones and tight perms and lipstick. So that if you kissed it was to come away decorated. And if you went further, there were bones, straps, ribbons, elastic and finally astonishingly warm flesh. Girls were warmer than he, always; yet wore fewer clothes. Their blood temperature was higher, they ticked over like racehorses, their hearts beat fast as kittens'. And yet it was boys who had no control, and girls who were all control, all caution. They set the pace; measured, counted time, rang bells when it was time to go home or a hand had strayed an inch too far. They knew the rules, the limits; knew when to disqualify, knew what penalties to exact. Cased in whalebone, their silk purses dangling from their arms, they watched him come: disbelieving, it seemed, even mocking. He had to ask one of them to dance. And steer her like an L-driver through traffic jams, to impossible music, his immense black feet avoiding her satin toes. Close to his nose, her bare shoulder. Bare. They came half bare, and slipped stoles, shawls, wraps from their shoulders, and wriggled into their strapless moulds, settling their breasts like blancmanges into shape. If he had come half-undressed, strapless, shirtless, tieless even, they would have laughed him out of doors. His body had been all spots and eruptions, strange sproutings of hair, uncontrollable sweats and tremors. He believed thoroughly that he was repulsive; and yet knew that he could not retreat, become a monk, wrap himself in sackcloth, give up the game. It had to be played. In the backs of cars, in hallways, in cloakrooms, behind coats, out of doors in wind and rain, it had to be pursued. He had no sisters, nobody he could ask: what do girls want, and how do you do it? What is the secret, the password, the way through? Other boys, dinner-suited while he paraded in wretched flannels, glanced at him with mirror-eyes, showing him his own repulsiveness, giving no further clue. There were the jokes, the boasting; but since everybody lied, the truth slipped between them unmentioned and the lies were what counted after all. The stories, passed between them, had all a beginning, a middle and an end. The beginning – I could see she fancied me, she was the best looking one there, biggest tits you ever saw, blonde, you know – passed effortlessly into the middle – and then I said, and she said, and then I, and then she – and finally, the ending, teasing in its inexactness – well, of course I, you know, fantastic, it was, she was quite something, go all the way, of course we, what d'you take me for – The sagas proliferated; and wherever you heard them, had the baffling similarity of myths from many lands. There was a set progression; all you had to do was get in at the beginning, do the right thing from the start, and the rest would follow. There was a breathless narrative simplicity: so that if you overheard only a part of one of these stories, if only so much as a word was caught in passing, you knew exactly where you were, what stage the story had reached, what would happen next. Even from the tone of voice of the protagonist, the story-teller, all the rest could be known. And yet how, inarticulate as he was, could he manipulate all the grammar of it, however could he start, with that unerring confidence, as resonant as 'Once Upon a Time'?

At university, he discovered. The story progressed through the same stages, but the props were different, the scenes differently set, the signs other. There were pubs and halves of bitter and bicycles and the closing times of girls' colleges to be manipulated. There were sofas bonier than old clothes horses to be grappled with, and gas fires that singed one side of you, leaving the other freezing, and there was the breathless, give-away moment (pause before denouement, will he, won't he make it) at which one was supposed to undo a girl's bra with one hand, beneath at least two sweaters, while french kissing her and simultaneously unzipping one's trousers. The routines, the milestones were different; but the narrative clarity, the one-way system, was the same. Pass go and straight on till you reach the finishing post. Competitors who stop to philosophise, need to pee, fail to undo a brassiere, to be disqualified. The prize is at the end, and needs no describing: for the text book is in all hands already, the unexpurgated edition of *Lady Chatterly's Lover*, published in paperback the year he lost his virginity at last, two stumbling blocks removed in one swift movement, as censorship and his own inhibitions fell away. Lawrence told the same story, but filled in what women were supposed to feel too, which was a help. He learned that real women came with soft little cries, doing nothing to promote their own orgasm; that penises, and more particularly male buttocks (small ones) were irresistible, that flowers and rain and damp places in woods were encouraging, that some women had beaks between their legs and would do him harm. Reading and re-reading, his soft orange-and-white paperback copy often in his jacket pocket in case inspiration should fail, he sought out ruddy countrified-looking girls with upper-class accents and persuaded them to go for bicycle rides on damp days into nearby woods. Icy winds upon his own buttocks (small and white they were, but pimpled with gooseflesh) and the fear of discovery made him shrivel as Mellors never had; it was the wrong time of year; and the story was finally ended, concluded, with a triumphant cry upon a goatskin hearthrug (the smell was right, if not the atmosphere) in one of the women's colleges. The girl, Helena Thompson, a mathematician, had not given soft little cries as far as he remembered, but he himself had shouted out with the disbelieving excitement of the race-winner breasting the tape, all the remaining air shot out of him. Afterwards, they lay and looked lovingly at each other. For each, the story was completed, the 'happily ever after' within sight. This was what they had been created for, they said, to be at one with the universe; years of doubt and misery were over; the grail was theirs. They wandered about the university for some weeks with their arms around one another; in the mornings he looked at his long face in the mirror as he shaved, and marvelled at the fact that he was in love. It seemed that his spots were disappearing, that his face was maturing, that he grew more beautiful every day; and in her softness, her roundness, he saw beauty, for a well-fucked woman is beautiful, he said, and lovingly he silenced her when she moved away from him awkwardly into abstract thought. The evening that he came to knock at her door, bicycle-clipped and freezing, to take her in his arms again, and a preoccupied face looked out to say – Sorry, I've got too much work to do – he could hardly believe what he heard. She repeated it – I've got too much work to do. She did not even open the door to him, Helena Thompson, that night, but muttered round it and assumed he would go away; she shut herself away, her blue myopic eyes glazed with formulae, and left him to wander back down the corridors and free his locked bicycle and ride back alone in the

110

rain and dark. He did not know what to do. This was not supposed to happen. Suddenly, he had no freedom, no force, could not work himself, spent hours before mirrors squeezing spots, hung about for her on his bike in the road. Women were not supposed to put work before love before the grand dictates of sex; he still could not believe it – 'I've got too much work to do' – and fantasised endlessly her real words, her true, hidden self. Finn, at last. I've been waiting for you all evening. I can't bear the minutes spent without you. Oh, Finn—

But she passed him on her way to a lecture, she was in a little knot of girls and hardly looked his way, she carried books, mathematical books, she was not for him. He kicked his bicycle and hurled it in a rage against railings, and went in to hear his own lecture on the modern movement, shrunk to nothing it seemed within his trousers, and his hand too cold to hold the pen. He felt ill, cold, far from home. History seemed to him a record of absurd failures and petty treacheries. He heard that man was corrupt and perverse and needed control from above, and thought violently that woman was at the root of it. He needed – not her, perhaps, not Helena Thompson herself, but what she had seemed to offer, a safe way into the labyrinth of himself.

Now, he set himself to think of Alice, as if in conscious atonement for the night before. He had first met Alice not so long after the Helena Thompson episode. Looking at her across a room – had it been a bar, or a crowded room at a party? – he wondered if he was on the rebound. Fated perhaps to bound and rebound, from one woman to another, in a perpetual search for the reassurances of love. Alice talked a lot; that was what he first noticed. She was at the centre of a group, and she talked fast, wildly, in a high upper-class voice that made it hard to guess where she came from geographically; she wore black, as most people did in those days, black sweater (although perhaps not from Marks and Spencer's as most people's were), black corduroys. She smoked and talked and waved her hands about and looked foreign, inaccessible. At first, he was repelled by her. Upper-class bitch was the phrase that came most easily to mind. But there was also the swing of her fine dark hair and the tilt of her chin and some fire that flashed from her eyes, a glance that briefly included him. She cared – about something. That much he saw. All the rest was show, dazzle.

111

Self-protective. He moved closer to the group she was in, to share in it, but she as abruptly moved away, left the room, shrugged on a duffel-coat and was gone. Who was that, he easily asked. That? Alice Linnell, don't you know her? Had another party to go to. Another of these Roedean or Cheltenham birds. Professional virgins, most of them.

The man whose side she had left spoke brutally and nursed an empty glass. And, yes, even then, Finn thought, he had been repelled by it, the way they had evolved, between them, of describing the women who threatened to outdo them, or would not go to bed. Professional virgin, cock-tease, upper-class bitch. Even then, he had known. Yet could not protest, had nothing to put in the place of insult, not yet; could only stare after her in the darkness and feel suddenly bereft.

Later, he had let her know: that first time, I saw right through you, it was like seeing your skeleton, or your soul. You were talking, laughing, waving a glass about. You looked phoney and stuck-up. And then you looked in my direction just for a moment, and I saw you. And that was it. I had to get to know you. I had to find out.

And she, lying beside him by then and all her body's surfaces known to him, still looked up at him with a certain dark stare he could not fathom and said lightly – Well, I'm certainly glad you did.

All these years since, all this married time, and sometimes it seemed like a long, long way round to reach again that certainty, that flash of vision, of the time when he had first seen, first known her. Alice Linnell, don't you know her? As if everybody did, but he. Now, he knew her, inside and out, the warm inner and cool outer skin, the wit and the tears and the way her stomach rumbled after meals; and yet, the closer he got, the more mysterious was she. For instance, where was she now? What did she really think about? What lay between the words, between the lines, of those enigmatic statements for which she was known? Daily, they stepped over precipices, he thought; and the gaps, the leaps, were there in her poetry, and he feared them. Next, he would challenge her. Stop her on the threshold, homecoming. Say – what is this, what lurks, what lies in this blank, this unended line? Open all the cupboards of his fears.

112

He thought of Alice, and then with conscious luxury, allowed himself thoughts of Angela. What he had done with Angela fulfilled all his adolescent dreams. You dreamed, when you were young, spent nights wide awake and dry-eyed with lust, imagining. Then, when you were middle-aged, it all came to you, unasked and unplanned, and poured about you. Angela half-naked waiting for him in her tower, beaming out her lighthouse-beam across the city, Angela all breasts and eyes, and he with the password – open Sesame – and no questions asked. With Alice, for so long, it had seemed that there were complications. Words spun a web between them, a thicket, so that it seemed to him sometimes sad that the grand simplicity was lost. With Alice he had learned to say them, the print words, fuck and cunt and so on, not as swear words as he was used; but seriously now, for accuracy; and with her, perused the new illustrated sex books with their idealised drawings – no spots, or unwanted hair – for new ideas. With her, he learned of vaginal orgasms being replaced by clitoral, of the political implications, the right attitudes, of sex. With Alice, he discovered he could shit and hold a conversation at the same time, he naked on the lavatory, she chatty in the bath. He learned to contemplate bloodstained tampons and vaginal caps as ordinary parts of life, to walk naked around the rooms of a flat without drawing the curtains, to forget to care what people thought. Systematically, with her, he learned to trample on, obliterate, the silences, the pruderies, the taboos of his upbringing: and with them went the carefulness with money, the tidiness, the instantaneous sense of guilt at self-indulgence, the anxiety for what the future might bring. With Alice, it was as if he had been blown wide open, made vulnerable to the four winds, which might sweep everything he recognised away; and if there was at times a tinge of sadness, an echo of regret, he kept it from her, it was his.

When the children came in, he was sipping coffee, and the newspaper dangled from the table, open yet unread, and his eyes focussed upon them with difficulty. Kate banged the fridge door open and began rummaging inside for something to put in her sandwiches for school, swearing as she went. She was tall, and strode across the room, her

113

one plait bouncing. He heard her – oh, Christ, fucking hell, bloody fucking—

– What is it? What on earth's the matter?

– No bloody cheese, except this stinking thing, that smells like rotten fish, can't think why she keeps it – phew – nothing to eat here, why the hell neither of you does any shopping—

Reasonable, but the coffee speeding his heart, he said – Couldn't you pick up some from the corner shop? Some filled rolls, or something?

Alexander said – She's thrown away the Dolce Latte, Mum'll be furious.

Kate said – It stinks, it's been in there for months, I expect it's poisonous by now.

– That's how Mum likes it.

– Well, she isn't bloody here, is she, so why should we put up with it?

Finn said – Can we three have breakfast in peace?

The cat, a heavy marmalade tom, crouched on one corner of the table, licking the butter. Finn flapped the paper, but the cat resisted, daring him. Peace – or whatever it was you had when you were alone – began to crack. Finn felt his own fragility; he should not have to live with young barbarians. His daughter strode and banged and swore. There was good Italian cheese in the waste-paper basket. The door bell rang, on a long demanding note, Kate's friend come round to meet her, and Christ, said Kate, no bloody time now, or I'll miss the bus. They rushed past him and he sat here, a man laid open to the four winds. Soon he would close himself up carefully and go to work, and his riotous heart would beat on unnoticed, unsuspected. Angela, he thought. What was her other name? How some women seemed to offer peace. How the world was dark with chaos. How he longed— But Kate, in flying past him, coat unzipped and bag beneath her arm, bent and kissed him suddenly – See you, cocker – before she was gone, the sudden warm print of her lips upon his cheeks and Alexander, slower, methodical, placing crisps, egg, chocolate biscuit in his lunch bag said to him – Dad, I hope you have a really good, a *really* good day.

They went, his children, the young adults that had been his children, his sperm-and-egg nine-day wonders, his magical portion of the future, ambivalent delight: out in a minute and into the world, to catch buses and greet friends and sprint down pavements and sit in school with the dizzying facts of the universe spilling over their heads, all around them. Beached like a great whale on the shallows of the morning, he moved a little feebly to start with, and then struck out after them, into the world he had made.

4

It was cold and the light seemed barely filtered through grime as Alice came into King's Cross station, walking a little heavily so that her boots sounded with a military sharpness, for she carried two bags that weighed her down: there was a queue for the train, that stretched and wound around the station, there were placards everywhere, announcing time changes, but those were, she checked, for other trains: the 125, in its glossy yellow plastic newness, would run on time. It was nearly dark, anyway, late in the afternoon of a London day that had seemed dark from the outset, with only a little daylight breaking through at midday, pearling the river, lifting the heaviness of the sky. She had walked across Waterloo Bridge alone, coming back from the Hayward Gallery, and had looked down on the wideness of it, the flatness, the choppy grey river and its banks surprisingly far apart, the barges, the buildings themselves dwarfed and flattened by some trick of the light or of distance; even St Paul's, even Westminster, even the ugly new jutting buildings of the South Bank somehow insignificant beneath the weight and cloudiness of that just-lit sky, the scudding of that water. In the gallery, she had looked at drawings, mostly of the naked human, the naked female form. She had wanted something new – a new vision. Into her mind as she walked across the bridge came the phrase, unbidden, 'A new heaven and a new earth.' She savoured it, and strode, air beneath her and all around her, the stretch of the bridge surprisingly long, the distance a long way to walk. She had not eaten, at midday, not after the breakfast at Emily's, but

115

would eat now, as the train shot north through the increasing darkness, would find a table and eat slowly, going north. Yes, there had been the search, the seeking out: of one thing that would show, that might explain. What went on, what the logic was, in the deep places, the unknown places of the body; or was it perhaps in the heart? She wanted to know her own anatomy, how these things could be. But the drawings had been mostly drawn by artists who had contemplated the outside, the smooth or wrinkled, stretched or sagging, skin-deep, contoured, opaque, essentially irrelevant outer flesh. This told of what it was like to see, and to be seen. But to be plumbed, investigated, known, in total darkness? Not that.

She showed her ticket, heaved bags up again, walked alongside the length of the train, looking for the restaurant car. Here, she would sit, and watch the south of England darken and disappear, as she ordered food, let the events of last night's reading surface again in her mind. She wanted order, and the chance to be alone. It was hard to realise that any of it had happened, now that she was about to go home. The women's voices, as unlikely as the body of the man on the train: as if only half experienced, half understood. She swung herself up and into the train, which did not yet smell of trains and so had no resonance for her. A shell, only; a safe shell in which to travel, from one place to another, from here to there. She had not taken another night train, because she had wanted to be home tonight. There was a reason, had been. Home waited, a lit cave-mouth, a refuge. She would take off her clothes there, and sink into hot water, so that it closed over her head, and be reborn; and she would be greeted, welcomed, and it would not matter.

– Is this seat free?

– Oh, yes. Yes, I think so.

She did not want anyone opposite her. No, but the train was crowded, would be full. He threw up a mackintosh into the rack, stowed a small bag beneath the seats, glanced at her, settled down. Looked out of the window, away from her, so that she saw his reflection looking back. If she were to get out a book and read, now, he would not bother her, would not talk. Otherwise, there were all those hours; she could not bear the thought of it, hours of talk, desultory, trying hard, trying to

116

pass the time. But the only books she had were her own, copies of the two published books of poetry. She could have bought a newspaper, had not found the time. But on a long journey one must, must have something to read: to wear, to hide behind, to distract attention. She must have been mad, not to have even bought a paper. Would he have a paper? She should have said the seat was occupied, should have put a bag on it, then— He sat, and looked out.

She looked out too, into the growing darkness of the station, and saw his reflection looking back. It seemed to study hers with intentness; whereas in reality, he must be looking beyond, outside, to the people who moved out there, hurrying for the train. As the train began to move, so smoothly that only by looking out, seeing the station slide away, could one be sure of movement; he looked directly at her. The look that passed between them was opaque; either significant or not significant. She thought – a man sits down opposite me on a train, and it is the beginning of a story, either significant or not-significant. Is it inevitable, given the five hours of the journey, that we will talk, get to know each other? Is there anything I can do, to avoid this? On the way down, what seemed to have happened seemed to have been unavoidable. Now, she was not sure.

– Did you say something? Nervous, she thought that he had spoken perhaps, that she had not heard, not answered.

– No, I didn't say anything. I can't even ask if you mind if I close the window, or open it, since these trains are air-conditioned. I can't even ask you if you mind if I smoke.

– It's a non-smoker.

– I know. Would have been different in the nineteen-forties, wouldn't it?

– What would?

– Oh, the openings.

Again, unsure that she had heard aright, she said vaguely – Yes.

– I'm glad to have a chance to meet you.

– Oh. Why?

– I've been looking forward to it.

– What d'you mean? You don't know me.

– In a way, that's true.

117

He leaned back, looking pleased with himself. She thought, she had rarely seen someone look so pleased with himself, almost smug. She thought, if he were to vanish, that grin would remain, Cheshire-cat-like. One could get tired of it.

He said – You were on the night train coming down, the night before last.

– Yes. She said – I came down for a poetry reading. As if that made it any better.

– So did I.

– What, come down on the night train?

– Yes, for a poetry reading. But I never got to it. Other things happened instead. It didn't matter.

She considered in silence what he had said. A suspicion sprouted and bloomed in her mind and she held it there, warily, played with it, wondered what it might do.

She said – What time do we get in? And then wished she had not; assumed that he was going where she was.

– About ten-thirty. It takes less long in the daytime. At night, the trains must go all over the place. I can never think what they do, to pass the night. They must go all over the north of England, dropping mail bags here and there, passing the hours. Otherwise, how could it take so long?

The conversation seemed to be getting more normal. With relief, she uncrossed her legs. Then she realised that the relief was to do with the fact that he was going where she was going, would get in at the same time as she did, considered this normal. The discomfort began again. She thought – I could never ask, never be sure – But the suspicion bloomed and spread in her mind. It was possible, even likely. And if likely, then why not certain? She felt again the spreading warmth and wetness, the evidence, that had actually stained her clothes that morning so that how could her mind go untouched?

– What was the poetry reading?

She thought, asking the questions, I will take the initiative, I will take charge.

– What?

– You said you came down for a poetry reading.

118

– Oh, yes. There was a woman poet reading. A friend of mine wanted me to go. Only, as I said, other things happened. I never got to it, after all.

– Did your friend get to it?

– Yes, I believe so. I believe she did.

– I see.

– And what did your friend think?

– She didn't say. I did not see her, in the end.

– Doesn't it take a long time getting out of London? Even going this fast.

– It does. But you wait till we get to Darlington. Then, it really flies.

– Do you like poetry, then?

– I have a vested interest in it.

– Are you a publisher?

He looked at her quickly, a suspicion, a flash sideways, narrowed eyes. – No.

– I don't know what you mean, then.

– I simply mean, I have a vested interest in it existing.

Silence. She felt tired, suddenly. One could not ask questions all the way from London to Edinburgh, not even to keep somebody at bay. He sat back again and felt about in his pocket and pulled out a packet of chewing gum. He said, laughing – In the fifties, I could have offered you some of this.

She took a piece. Chewing was better than nothing, that was why it had been invented, chewing took up time.

She said, chewing, – Why did you say that about the fifties?

He said – There are no conventions any more. We have to use the old ones from time to time, don't you agree?

– And what if we don't?

As she spoke, she felt an abyss opening. She it was who chose dangerous ground. At the same time, the stirrings of it again, the discomfort, the desire, at the thought, at the memory, at the question in her mind.

He looked at her straightforwardly. – Then, we may flounder. Nothing wrong with floundering, except that it feels confusing, I suppose. Or perhaps we invent new ones, for later generations to reject.

— Do you always talk to people like this on trains?

— No. I don't always talk, and not to everybody. You have to be a bit selective, don't you?

— Why did you say that in a way you didn't know me?

— Because, in a way, I do.

— And what way is that?

— Well, you're reasonably well known, aren't you? I saw your photo in the paper once, I think.

— Oh, I see.

— What other way were you thinking of?

— No other way. I wondered what you meant, that was all.

— I know who you are, that's what I meant. But you don't know who I am, do you?

— No. Who are you then?

— Nobody that you would have heard of. My name's Liam Henderson, how d'you do?

— I didn't think you were a Scot.

— I'm well disguised, then. I pass, anywhere. Even in London, it seems.

— And you went all the way down to London, to hear a poetry reading that in the end you didn't go to?

— Among other things. I told you.

— What things, then?

— Ah, business. This and that.

— Things you have a vested interest in.

— That's right.

He stared back, the sharpness of his glance became cloudy, blue-green, meditative. He said — I'll tell you more when I know you better. Or differently, at least.

— Are you having dinner, sir?

Ah, yes, the white cloth spread suddenly between them, the waiter briskly there, pad in hand, the menu, the trappings.

He said — Now there's a convention we could use.

— Excuse me, sir?

— Yes, we're having dinner. Or at least, I am.

120

Alice said – I would like to order dinner, too. For it seemed all at once that the white cloth, the waiter, the menu appearing made them too neatly a couple, sitting face to face, dining, as if this was what went on.

– I think, if you sit here, you have to have dinner.

The waiter said -- Do you want to see the wine list?

And Alice thought – this is exactly as I imagined it, exactly. Without having realised, without having known.

Liam Henderson, the man opposite said – We might as well.

Dinner came in the right order: soup and then steak and vegetables, ice cream with chocolate sauce. Outside them, beyond the windows, the countryside grew quite dark, the land was flat fen, to be rushed through unseen. In between mouthfuls, in between sentences, whole tracts of land rushed past. They were sealed in, together, a table top between them, wine and water shivering in their glasses, forkfuls of food halfway to their mouths. It was easier to eat than to talk without eating, easier to swallow food than to feel one's mouth grow dry with effort. Opposite them, across the corridor, a family settled to eat: father, mother, aunt or friend, three daughters. The man handled all his females, playing with their laughter, their complaints. The mother unzipped her high-heeled boots and pulled them off and massaged her own feet, laughing. The youngest daughter grizzled and wanted to sleep. The aunt, or friend, looked alertly across at the man, her back very straight. They were from Yorkshire, all of them, might be getting out at York. Friendly, yet self-absorbed, each of them glanced from time to time across at them, the couple opposite, the tall woman with long dark hair, the equally tall, dark man. No, said the mother, you can't have soup *and* juice, it's one or the other, look, it says. The aunt, or friend, yawned and wanted a drink. A G-and-T wouldn't break the bank, would it? She would give her right arm for one. The man, all nervous energy, waved to the waiter, but the waiter had his own rhythm, his own progression, first one table, then the next. She would have to wait. They could go to the bar. though. The bar would be open. She and Carol could go to the bar. Carol said, I'll stay, you go, you and Roger. I'll stay with the girls. The girls pouted and woke up, about to be slighted. Roger said, I'll go. You sit here. The aunt, or friend, said, I'll go with you, Roger. The youngest girl moaned and said, I want a drink, I want a drink too. The mother said, look, the man's coming in a minute. Anyway, how the hell I'm ever going to get my boots on again. My feet are like pumpkins. Roger said, all right, all right, everybody happy? That's one G and T, and I'll have a pint, and Carol, what about you? Carol said, I don't know, maybe a gin and something, Jesus Christ London's exhausting, I don't know. The three little girls huddled up together, giggling, their blonde heads close and shoulders shaking. The train rushed on, northward, lit from within.

Alice said – Who are you, anyway?

– I told you. The great thing about trains is, you can meet anybody.

– So you can anyway, travelling; or even staying at home.

– Have you noticed, on planes and buses people don't talk? No, there's something special about trains. People expect something, on trains and on ships. There's an added romance. Perhaps it comes from the age of steam. Anyway, meeting on trains is special, don't you think?

Again, she wanted to ask him. Remembered the precise sensations of that other train journey; or were they already less precise because several times remembered, re-evoked; memories a little used, a little worn down, a little elaborated at the edges, a little untrue? She thought – now, I can never ask. It would be absurd. I have no reason for thinking that he was the one; only the flimsiest of reasons for thinking that there was anyone at all. Let it go, forget it. Let it drop away. But still, the rhythm of the train, quickening northward, would not let it go, would remind her. She chewed her steak over and over again and found it hard to swallow. The man opposite looked at her and said nothing, looked at her over his glass, but not as if he were thinking anything in particular; his gaze was vague, friendly, a little preoccupied.

Then he said – I rather like the idea of getting to know somebody backwards. In the reverse order to what is usually the case.

– What?

– Starting at what is usually the end.

– What do you mean?

– Well, here we are eating dinner together, travelling together, quite an intimate thing to be doing, wouldn't you say?

– But we only met by chance. We aren't travelling together, only going in the same direction.

– Is that so? All right, but here we are, anyway, eating dinner, if not together, at least at the same table, opposite each other, sharing, would you not agree to this much, at least some degree of the experience?

– Well, yes.

– And if we were to go backwards – in conventional terms, I mean – from here. This is not quite the end of the story, it's true, there are other degrees of intimacy, but usually, a man and a woman having dinner together might imply that those could exist already?

Alice began to blush, as she had not for years. She would not be able to ask, would never exactly know, but it would be suspected, it would be possible between them. She felt the quick heat in her cheeks and neck and covered them with the cool palms of her hands.

– What I would like, sometime, with somebody, is to go backwards from the convention, do it all the other way round. You see what I mean? It would be more interesting. All the things which usually bog people down would be over first. Sex, romance, meals in restaurants, assignations. The illusion of happily-ever-after wouldn't operate. The big O would no longer be a goal, but something that once happened and so could be taken for granted. Haven't you ever wanted to fall in love with somebody on a train? The trans-Siberian perhaps, or the one that goes across China, or the Blue Train, or even the Flying Scotsman. Doesn't your blood quicken as we rattle along, ticketyboom, tickety-boom, over the tracks?

– This one doesn't.

– No, this one doesn't, not exactly, this one is designed for the smooth sleeping of executives and businessmen, dreamlessly carried from Scotland to London and back, across territory in which nothing should have happened, past places which should not have had to exist. But its smoothness, you must admit, gives a tranquil sort of mood, rocks one with a kind of safety, carries one back to babyhood perhaps, lends the erotic, the infant's sense of ease?

123

She sat with her hands covering her cheeks still, most of the steak uneaten. She sipped water, with an invalidish care. Everything that he said was true, existed already in mind. She thought – I could have invented him. Even the way he talks has changed, as I thought it might.

She said – Surely you would only be going backwards through the rituals: not through the feelings. You wouldn't be really changing anything, because feelings progress, do not go backwards. You would have the outward forms, the expressions of them, but no real change inside.

– If you change the form, you change the content. You as a poet must see that.

Stubbornly, she said – It is the content that dictates the form. At the same time, she wondered whether she meant it. She thought – It is a game; each of us can make a statement and it does not matter whether or not it is true for us, so long as it takes the challenge a little further. We go on by these stepping stones; what they are made of is irrelevant, perhaps.

He said – What I mean is, that people's feelings are really trapped so often inside the forms, the rituals. What I was saying earlier, about convention. People felt certain things because they behaved in certain ways. The feelings were conventionalised. If you went backwards, say, through a courtship, an affair, you would have a chance to know what you were really feeling. Just as if we were to eat this meal backwards, or in the wrong order, ice cream then meat then vege-tables, then soup, we might have a chance to know whether we really liked ice cream, or carrots, or minestrone soup. The taste of the meat would not depend on having soup before it and a sweet after it. We might find we hated it, that we did not enjoy it at all, that it had been imposed on us, made palatable by the very order in which it appeared.

– So you want to start out by going to bed with somebody and end up with them becoming a stranger?

– In a way. If, by stranger, I can mean, somebody I see afresh, as if I had just met them, and that that is the way they would see me.

She allowed her plate to be taken away, leaning back a little as the waiter intervened between them. The sweet arrived, ice cream in a cold silver dish, cockily topped by a wafer; the same for each of them. It looked as if it would be too cold for her teeth, too sweet, and with an out-of-place flavour of summer; still, she would eat it because it was there.

– Coffee?

Again, the time might as well pass through coffee-drinking, stirring, passing sugar, adding milk.

– Yes, please.

Suddenly she imagined them both sitting naked in some bald parched place, eating raw meat, tearing at it with hands and teeth. There would be no feelings then, no order, only hunger and imperative need. Naked, he would be thin and hairy, as she was. They would be two of a kind, from the same litter, grown lean and alert through years of fending for themselves. The image came and went, and she smiled at it.

– What were you thinking?

She told him. It could do no harm. She said – It was your talking of meat, I suppose.

He smiled too, and said – You see us both as carnivores, then, as survivors.

–Perhaps, now, it will be the vegetarians who survive. I don't really like meat, actually. In the way that you said, I don't like it. It has to be decorated, flavoured, come after one thing and before another. That steak on its own would have been impossible. As it was, I had trouble chewing it. But then, I wonder how many things one actually does like on their own, just crudely themselves. Surely life is made up of contrasts and differences and nuances, and that's just as important? Sauces and things, to contribute different tastes, and lighting to change the look of a room, and clothes to express moods. Choices, not just a sort of crude necessity.

But still, she wanted to hold on to, to examine, that vision of the two of them, savages, in a place where no subtleties existed.

– Is that what you write about?

– Well, it comes into it. Women have been very involved in all those things.

125

– I was going to say, it sounds like a traditionally feminine universe. Making things look nice, taste palatable, fit in. The decorative arts and all that. I would have thought you would have been concerned with more essential things.

–That's just it, you have to go making things exclusive, making contradictions out of things which are not necessarily contradictory. Women have been involved in all those things, they've also been oppressed by them, it doesn't make them unimportant.

She spoke angrily, as if this should have been obvious. But thought, at the same time, that she was tired of this argument. Tired, as she had grown tired of cooking, of arranging, of orchestrating it all. Yes, it was important, yes, she wanted her universe to be harmonious, beautiful, in tune; but who was to do it, who make the monumental effort now? You lifted your hand from the task, and chaos began at once to creep in. She thought of the rooms, the houses of her friends, the do-it-yourself materials, women learning to patch, to mend, and that added to cooking, to folding clothes, to sending children out in the mornings properly dressed, to creating the right atmosphere for supper parties, to welcoming guests, feigning indifference to tiredness; finding the right food, the right object, the right word, the right look, the right response; thought of the whole immense effort required by bourgeois living, the exacting payment through flesh and blood and energy, the tax that women she knew had paid, over years, over decades. And there, now, were the same women, not doing it. Letting things fall apart, and fridges and cupboards go empty and children go ragged to school; going to prison for what they believed in, camping out in the cold and wet, instead. Saying other things. Worrying, even in prison, about the food in the cupboards. Carrying with them perhaps, even into captivity, the old injunctions about the way things ought to be.

– Yes, she said. I am. Concerned with more essential things. But at the same time, there are the pleasures of life. They cannot be discounted. You have to have both! We need both! You as well as me. Look at you sitting there, eating that meal, drinking that coffee. Somebody cooked that, produced it. You relied on them doing it, got on the train assuming that they would.

– I could have done without it.

– Really, she said. Really? Do you mean that? Could you do without being served, being serviced, being fed, being kept going? It's unusual, if so. Most people can't.

The train rushed into a long tunnel, and the lights blacked, then, so that for a long minute neither saw the other, there was only the sense of a hostile presence in darkness. After which, in a renewed flicker of artificial lighting that yellowed the immediate surrounding dark, they looked at each other a little blankly, as if each had forgotten what to say.

Alice looked at him, at the pale face and dark hair and rather heavy features in repose, at the gravity of his eyes at the moment, at the neck going down into the shirt collar, at the set of his head as it leaned back against the seat, and thought – I am going to have to make a decision, before I get off this train, about whether I am going to let this man into my life or not. Train journeys are trial runs, experiments. You can make things happen on them, and then go home, safe. Or you can get off at the end, and exchange addresses, telephone numbers, commitments. With your feet on firm ground, you can walk off with a stranger into another life.

But they were only halfway, they were only in York; and the family opposite were rummaging and collecting bags and thrusting stockinged feet into boots again and struggling, laughing, emerging from heaps of newspapers, magazines and coats as if they had slept the night there, made camp. The train began its long slowing glide into the station. There was still Newcastle, and the stations north. The carriage emptier, the night darker, the waiter less in attendance, the dinner cleared away, the seats around marked with the recent departures of others, crumpled papers, tissues, spilt coffee, a scarf left forgotten on a seat. Others retreated, and there was this deepening privacy. Alice thought – I do not know if I want it. Half of me would like to retreat too, now, and to go out anonymous into the night. Half of me is tired, wants no further commitments. The other half, alert, curious, eager for adventure, sits and waits and snuffs up the air like a wild animal, scenting danger, but every muscle in control.

127

Finn, at work, thought about telephoning Angela. The thought, which he had put out of his head three times during the morning, recurred during the afternoon; twice he stretched out a hand for the telephone, remembered he had decided that the night's occurrences should be left meaningless, without sequel, thought that Alice was on her way home even now, that his life with her would resume this evening, and did not even lift the receiver. But as the afternoon grew longer, as he stared out of his window across town towards the brief, shrinking gleam of light that lit the city in winter from the horizon (and as Alice stepped on to the train at King's Cross, carrying her bags) he thought: life is too short to let good things go. And dialled a number. The ringing sounded and sounded and no answer came. Then he remembered, of course, she goes out to work. Does something for the Social Work department, to do with fostering, or adoption. He put down the receiver, checked in his dream. Until now, had not seriously considered her working, her doing anything except await his call. Topless and barefoot, enclosed in her airless flat, exercising by the gas fire, remembering details of the night before, thinking of him; that was how he had thought of her. But she was a busy woman in her thirties, doing something useful, fully dressed and somewhere out there, in town. He thought – what would I have said? She would have answered, a little breathless, excited, and I would have allowed silences to develop, so that we could hear each other breathing; would have interrupted them only with endearments, so that I heard the ripple of them reach her at the other end; would have let her wait a while, then suggested meeting, heard her relieved acceptance of all I could spare her, of my time. But she was not there, was at work. (Helena Thompson, pale and ugly mathematician, for all her abundant breasts and smooth, eighteen-year-old flesh, had had too much work to do. Alice, shut in her room with her dusty typewriter looked out – what time is it, seven o'clock, goodness I'd no idea. I've had so much work to do—) Finn picked up the receiver, got the switchboard, asked for his own home number, called his daughter, Kate. Kate would be home from school by now, lolling in her room with a mug of tea and an enormous sandwich, biting the sandwich as she flicked through her homework books, and loud music

128

or chatter from the television filled the room. The television had been moved into Kate's room, where it stood on the floor with mugs of congealed tea standing on top of it. The record player, its lid open and records without covers all around it on another patch of floor, lived there too. Alex sat hunched in his room over his computer, the ZX he had bought him for his birthday, with yet another television set and a flickering pale grey screen. Alex would not hear the phone, being in another world, where space invaders pursued each other like asterisks across a cloudy field. Kate, screaming obscenities, would leg it to the telephone, longing for love and friendship, would call down it her nonchalant 'hello?', sigh deeply when she heard it was he, grumble as he asked her to do things for him. From behind her would come the beat or the wail of music, that trailed her like an aura. And the final slam of the receiver would tell him of a resentment he could never trace to source.

– Kate?

– Hello. Oh, it's you.

– Could you get something for supper, love?

– Couldn't you? I've got German *and* chemistry tonight.

– I may be late.

– Well, oh, shit, when's Mum coming home?

– Not till later. Not till about ten.

– Well, why can't you get it? I'm starving. There's nothing to eat in this bloody house, I told you this morning.

– Take some of the housekeeping money, and buy what you want. I don't mind what we have. Get what you like.

– If I really got what I wanted, it would be fish and chips, and just for me. Why don't you ask Alex? Why can't Alex go?

For a moment, he thought of the reasons. It would take ten minutes to explain to Alex what he was talking about. Alex did not know where anything was; money, shops, food, anything.

– Alex, said Kate, never does a bloody thing. I'll tell him to go.

– Look, love, it's just easier if you do. You're better at it. (As he spoke he knew the weakness of it.)

Kate, like Alice, poured easy scorn – That's bullshit. I'll tell him to go and get fish and chips. I've got too much homework to do. I'm not doing your bloody cooking. Okay, Dad, bye. 'Bye.

Slam. He imagined her, in stockinged feet, skidding back down the corridor, back to the warm and noisy confusion of her room. Marmalade on her fingers, and the books spread out to be marked with an easy, rapid pen, and the cat sitting purring by the gas fire, and heavy rock probably jarring the air. The door, like the telephone, slammed shut behind her. In her own world, shutting him out; again and again, as he had been shut out once, long ago, in another impenetrable time and irrecoverable place, shut in and left to wait intolerably until some door might open and time, moving on, include him in its flow.

He moved restlessly at his desk, doodling with a felt pen across the backs of envelopes. A client was due to telephone and would keep him perhaps till late, arguing about the details for a new conservatory, demanding all of his patience at this late hour when everything about him was running short, he felt, and when already, outside, there were the footsteps and cars starting of people going home from work. He sat up here in this attic, and doodled, and beneath his pen capitals appeared, rich with carved flowers and fruit, and pediments, bearing inscriptions, and broken columns, ending in human feet. As the telephone rang, he was turning one of the carved capitals into a hat, complete with hatpin; the voice came through to him, high-pitched and defensive, and his right hand drew on, fitting the hat to the voice, imagining the face in between. Somewhere, like an automatic answering machine, part of him received and noted down instructions; another, silenced, part, argued back in florid obscenities; his right hand held the phone, and his left hand manically drew, and in her room Angela closed shutters, lit lights, stretched out to do her yoga, turned her stereo up loud, and all the while Alice was coming back north, in the train that came nearer and nearer. Outside, a door slammed, a car accelerated. Yes, he said, and, no. Certainly. Of course, I'll see to it. Yes. I'll be in touch directly. Yes. Yes. Goodbye. Sometimes, saying goodbye, you could not silence the voices: they went on and on, through the evening and late into the night, complaining, demanding. Sometimes, they were there at two in the morning. Mr Anderson? A call for you. One moment. He slammed down the receiver. Was he no more, then, than the sum of all these pieces, a kaleidoscope, perpetually whirling, a man to be parcelled out according to others' needs? There was the pull too of the lit window, and the tug of the train coming north, and there was a certain hunger in him that made his stomach growl perpetually, also in complaint. Perhaps he would go straight home, eat with his children whatever revolting food they had bought for him, and await Alice. Perhaps he would not drive up into the old town, accelerate up narrow streets, watch for that high-up beacon light, and wait at Angela's door like a knight-errant, errant knight, heart beating mightily in his chest, stomach grumbling and breathing short? Perhaps, after all, he would take it home with him, his need, back to the domestic hearth where surely it belonged. There, like a good dog, it would lie down, hardly visible. There, it could be contained.

Kate said – Alex, you're to get the supper tonight. Dad said.
    – What? Shut up a minute, I can't concentrate.
    – You never bloody listen. You're useless. I said, you're to get the supper tonight. You can go out and get fish and chips, since you're so useless at anything else.
    – Hang on a minute, Kate. I've nearly got it, this programme.
    – Alex!
    – Okay, okay. Where's the money? Isn't he coming back? When's Mum coming back?
    – He's going to be late, he said, and Mum's coming later on the train. Go on, get moving, I'm starving.
    – You had bread and jam. You'll get fat.
    – No, I won't, and even if I do, who cares? Women can be fat just the same as anybody else.
    With his calm gravity, Alex said – I'd hate to be fat. And I'd hate to touch a fat woman. Rolls of flesh, just think. Like putty. Imagine, Kate, it could be you. Ugh. Yuck.
    – Alex, go and get the fish and chips.
    – I was reading a thing about diet. It said that heart disease starts in your teens, not when you're middle-aged. It said, fatty deposits start to build up around your heart and block your arteries. It can start when you're twelve. So it could have been happening to you for three years,

already. And to me for one. It could be too late. And we had spaghetti and sort of oily sauce last night, and fish and chips tonight, we have tons of junk food because they can't be bothered to cook for us, I should think we're building up fatty deposits all right.

– Look, just shut up and go and get something to eat, all right? I don't bloody care about fatty deposits. You're an awful hypochondriac. And turn off that bloody computer.

He turned a switch, and sighed, and the little darting figures died away. He said – I think they regret having children. Mum and Dad do.

– Oh, nonsense, they're just busy. Why don't you grow up.

– I don't think you can grow up, unless you have the proper sort of relationship with your parents when you're a child. It's like baby birds – they just fall out of the nest and die, if they're made to fly too soon. The parent birds have to look after them and feed them, and gradually show them how. Did you know, they predigest their food and then sort of sick it up and feed their babies with it? I saw this programme the other night.

Kate stamped with impatience, and her hair flew up and down. She pushed at him – at this small, immovable object, so slow, so deliberate, so infuriating, that was her brother. Ever since she could remember, she had been waiting for him to move. When he was a baby, inert and cooing in his pram, she had danced her impatience and wanted to shake him, to shout at him – grow up! Move, play with me, do something, grow up. And he had opened his eyes and smiled at her vacantly and somebody had said – Look at him, isn't he lovely, look at him smiling at you, Katie, look, he loves you, he knows who you are, his big sister, ah.

– Alex, go on, for God's sake. Just go. The money's in the kitchen. And come straight back, I'm starving.

– All right, all right, keep your hair on. I'm going. Only, it's true, what I said. They don't look after us properly. Lots of kids at school feel the same, you know. I wonder if it's to do with the economic state of the country and the fact that everything's going downhill?

She kept an eye on him until he had pulled on his trainers and khaki anorak, and pocketed the money, and gone.

As the King's Cross train pulled out of York, bound on its journey to the north, Finn started his car and turned it in the street, where the early dark was on him and the cobbles wet from the afternoon's brief rain. He could have gone out for a drink with Peter and Archie, sunk a couple of pints of Drybroughs as they had suggested, quenched that sense of aridity and fatigue he had felt when his client had hung up. Professional men, in bunches like grey birds, he thought, pacing close-shouldered in the rain towards their pub. No, not what he wanted. Not to hear the same jokes and the same after-hours stories and the same references to clients who should be nameless and institutions that went without saying. No. He turned the car, headed into the dense traffic on Princess Street, drove between ethereal Christmas decorations and the dazzle of shop windows, with the castle poised halfway up the sky on his right, giving himself the option to turn left and go home, or right and up into the old town. There were more left turns than right turns, that was as well. In a city where planning had regulated lives, in which men had tried through planning to eradicate the irrational, let chance, or town planning, dictate. He drove on, pressed on both sides by cars, buses, taxis. The lit monuments passed as in a dream, the castle and the Scott memorial; and there were the explosions of gold and silver, a Christmas tree like Danae's shower on the mound, paganism hardly disguised as Christianity, reindeer wild as jungle animals, rare as the unicorn, in effigy on all sides; the pagan feasts of this time of year disguised as Christmas, and he disguised as a rational man in a car, and a decision already taken masked as indecision, a destination already known hidden behind some trappings of old fears— He turned sharp right and drove up across the bridges, crossing the gulf between the new town and the old, leaving caution and restraint behind him, yet feeling the two parts of him, the divided inheritance he had, still sharply sounding each other out within him. In his native city, that evening, Finn felt all the protective disguises of the years drop away from him and remembered the old, buried fears that lay at the heart of them.

He leaned at Angela's door, his thumb upon the topmost bell, as he had imagined; but could not know if she would answer. She could be anywhere; anywhere in the whole city, anonymously going about her

133

life. She did not have to be here, for him. The bell could ring and go unanswered, and there be no muffled voice from far away 'Come in – push the door' and the door need not give, quite suddenly, to his touch. She had her own life. He tried, unsuccessfully, to remember it. If the voice did not sound, the door did not give, surely, he would die. He stood there, wracked with hope, that ate at his stomach and heart like indigestion.

– Who is it?

– It's me, Finn.

– Push the door, it's open. Come up.

From inside, from high up, the beckoning voice, as in a fairy tale. He had the password, could enter. He mounted the steep turning stairs as fast as he could, but feeling breathless. What could he say to her? Could there be endless wordless meetings like that of the night before; in which she would stand before him and he would leap upon her and they would both fall together through all the layers of words and looks and conversations that could have been, back into the wordless featherbed comfort of caresses? Or would he, now, have to begin to explain himself?

– I had to see you again.

– I've been thinking about you all day.

– I need you so much, I couldn't keep away.

All the things he could say were used, worn thin, ridiculous. He presented himself, excuseless, at her door. Perhaps she would just see, notice, understand, from his look, how he was; perhaps he could leave it all to her? He could have brought a bunch of flowers, a bottle, a book. Too late, he thought of it. The present, perhaps was himself. He would give himself at last, as he had never been able to, not with Alice, not with anybody. Lay himself open and be accepted, completely: of this he dreamed.

– Come in, she said. She was wearing her work clothes, he guessed; could not have long been in. She seemed less tanned, with lines about her eyes he had not noticed, and her hair drawn back, giving her a jawline, her blonde beauty a touch of hardness. She said – I've just made some tea. Or would you prefer a drink?

He wanted drink, the raw annihilating touch of alcohol, whisky if

134

she had it. She came back with it, like medicine in a glass, and her own mug of tea. He sipped whisky, felt it burning out anxiety, cauterising pain. She watched him; saw him, he felt, perhaps even judged.

She said – Tea would have been better for you. You look terrible.

– Tired, he mumbled, that's all; better now, nothing like a tot. How are you?

– I'm fine. But you know, it's not going to happen again.

– What isn't?

– Last night.

– You mean, you don't care anything for me, that was nothing, it's all over?

– No, I mean that it's not going to happen again. It's not part of my life. I don't want it. I don't want you, in that way. Once was fine, it was like a sort of weird dream, wasn't it, but we're not going on like that, that's all I wanted to say.

She sipped tea, warmed her hands, looked at him quite levelly. He wanted her crying, begging, out of control; lying beneath him, in total surrender. For the first time in his life, it occurred to him that he could, like any other man, rape. He faced her, shocked and bewildered.

– Why did you, then?

– Well, why did you? The same reason. Lust, like one beautiful blooming unique flower; dried to dust, by morning.

– I don't understand.

– Don't you, really? We both gave in to some irrational impulse, enjoyed it, probably would if we did it again; but it's not essentially anything to do with us, with our lives.

– Isn't it?

– You don't know me. I don't know you.

– Ah, yes, you do, I do—

– In the only way that matters? No, don't kid yourself, it isn't, you know. No, Finn Anderson, it's not there, not in the structures of our lives, that I do know.

– But, it could be! Why not? Why not? Why set your face against something in this deliberate way, why exclude possibilities, why not take a risk, dare something, follow a path even if you don't know

135

where it's going, why not take a chance?

She said – You drank that too quickly. Have some tea, now.

– No, I don't want any. He wanted to say – keep your bloody tea. Keep it, and your mealy mouthed puritanical claptrap, that denies me what I have always wanted, that always has, wherever I have run.

Angela said – People think they can have sex to escape from everything else; they think it's the one free act, with no consequences, that doesn't connect with anything else. Well, it isn't.

He cried – But, it wouldn't be like that, I'd care for you, I'd –

– Respect me?

– Yes of course, it wouldn't be all just making love, not all the time—

– You mean, we'd go to the cinema sometimes, and have clandestine little meals in restaurants?

– Stop making fun of me. You enjoyed it, anyway.

Now, he wished he had not come; not allowed himself to be a creature of impulse, driving up here so hastily, in the dark.

– Yes, I did. But it was as if you were anonymous, as if you were anybody. A faceless lover.

– Thanks very much.

– Oh, but you know very well what I mean. I was nobody, I was a body, to you. I was an image of what you wanted, that was all. Well, there's no sequence, to follow on from that, that's what I'm saying. I don't want to have an affair with you. I don't want one with anybody. Particularly not a married man with all the complications you have, I'd be all drawn into them in no time.

– But, you're—

– Free? Alone? Yes, and delighted to remain so.

– You keep interrupting everything I say. You don't give me a chance.

– To talk your way into my life? Yes, I know. I've already decided. Unilaterally.

– Relationships aren't unilateral. Ever.

– We don't have a relationship.

– Of course we do. You can't evade that, that *fact*, with all your dogmatic theories. We've done what we've done. Inevitably, we have

136

a relationship. What's to be done with it's open to question. But you can't deny it's there. You yourself said, it can't be an act with no consequences, unconnected with anything else. You're being illogical.

– Give me a minute, and I'll be being hysterical and emotional as well. We did it – had sex, made love, fucked, were intimate, whatever you want to call it, just once. There's no sequence, that's all.

–One swallow doesn't make a summer?

– If you like.

– But that one swallow's still a bird, with feathers and wings and a beak. It still exists, even if there aren't any more. You still have to be aware of it.

He thought – how absurd, to sit here arguing, when we could be delighting each other so. Anger rose in him, making him sarcastic, sharp. He wanted to taunt her, to draw blood. But at the same time longed for the old promise of tenderness, the mirage of eternal peace.

Determined, he said – I love you, I'm in love with you.

– Then do as I ask you. Drop it.

– Angela, it could be marvellous. Even more marvellous than last night. It was magical, last night, the way I came to you. There was something so extraordinary about it, it must have meant something. Things like that don't just happen for no reason.

She said – They happen because people stop thinking and go off into a sort of daze. You can't live in a daze. Believe me, I know. Yes, I know what you're going to say, about magic and trusting fate and letting yourself be open to things and letting go and trusting to whatever it is, some mystic thing, to hold us up, but I know it isn't like that. It means, to me, trusting myself, my life, the whole balance of it, to a man; saying, okay, come in and make a mess of everything I've made, stir it all up, I don't care, the world's well lost for love. And it isn't. You're not trustworthy. Your head is full of these romantic dreams and a bundle of unfulfilled needs that are nothing to do with me, and I don't want to be saddled with them. Everything you're saying simply makes me more convinced. Go and change, if you want to be friends with me, that's all I can say. I don't want a big love affair with all the soaring music over and the lights dimmed and that; I do

137

sometimes want friendship and I enjoy sex. But as soon as I saw you coming up those stairs this evening, I just knew it, here comes trouble. And I thought, no thanks.

– So you do feel something for me? You are scared of it. Otherwise you wouldn't be pushing me away so hard.

He spoke fast and nervously, excited by what she said, urging himself on to dare and risk it all; yet was like a man approaching the edge of a precipice, knowing the danger.

Angela said – Oh, God. How can I explain? The harder she says no, the more she means yes? Where've you been all these years? Hasn't that feminist wife of yours educated you one bit? No means no. N–O. Pure and simple. Nothing else. I'm not so much scared, as aware of trouble when I see it. I don't want my life made into a nasty mess, that's all. Look, you're quite a nice man, I liked making love with you, but you've got a long way to go. Right? Okay, well, then, goodbye.

– I shouldn't have come. I'm sorry.

– Look, pal, spare us the clichés, you sound like something out of a nineteen-forties film. Terribly stiff-upper-lip and hurt masculine pride. Go on, it's not that serious. I'll see you around, I expect. Cheer-oh, just now. Push the door right to at the bottom—

He went. Went and sat in the car with his hands on the steering wheel, the engine running, not going anywhere. The pain around his heart and stomach contracted, intensified; first he thought, I am going to have a heart attack, perhaps, then he knew, the pain was the wrench that produced tears, unfamiliar, rare, wet tears; it was like turning a rusty old tap that had been sealed, shut off for years, and at last coughs and chokes open, letting a brownish trickle of water flow. He leaned over the steering wheel and cried, feeling with astonishment the wetness on his cheeks, his own tears, real tears, the first of his adult life. He was amazed and impressed; as well as relieved, at the draining of pain, the easing of tension. There was even, as he let the rivers dry upon his cheeks, a sense of well-being. He glanced up at Angela's lit window, moved the gears, released the brake, and drove away back down the steep cobbled street again. He paused at the bottom of the street, blew his nose, laughed; and then accelerated away.

PART III

1

Halfway, halfway there. Half of the journey, as probably half of her life, before her, and half behind. She thought – I can decide now what happens, it is up to me. In spite of all appearances, the present moment, this time now, is mine. Half-wanting, half not-wanting: no, she thought, enough of this half and half, this in and out, this state. Briefly through her mind, like a whistle blowing and a flag waving and a hand slamming doors – we're off – came again the night-time memory, that would not fade.

She sat up, leaned forward, confronted him – Who are you? Tell me who you are really.

Spin around, spin again, Rumpelstiltskin is my name.

He said – You have known me for a long time, already. Had you forgotten? It's true, there was a long gap, where we did not see each other. What happened in between? I'd almost given up on you.

He looked tired, now; he looked the same age as she was, a middle-aged person after a busy day. He shifted in his seat, but did not take his gaze from her.

He said – Have you really forgotten my name?

She said – I never knew it. Really, I didn't. When did I last see you?

– Well. Let's see. I remember you sitting in a tree somewhere, biting your pencil. They were calling for you all over the garden. Quite rightly, you refused to get down. But that must have been long ago. Then, you were sent away somewhere, weren't you? I remember it being bloody hard to get through. I felt really out of touch, then.

– School, probably.

– Oh, was that it. Then, you were doing a lot of mad dashing about, looking for something, it seems. I couldn't catch up with you. Whenever I got to where you had been, you seemed to have gone on somewhere else. There was a long stream of parties. I used to get the addresses mixed up, and then when I got there, you had always just left, just gone somewhere; sometimes I saw you leaving with somebody, and the look of them made my heart sink. I think it was then that I really began to lose heart a bit. It was such hard work, trying to keep up with you. I didn't know what you wanted, any more, and I doubted sometimes whether you did. Every now and again I heard some rumour of you, some remark repeated by somebody else, that cheered me up, that sounded as if you were still going your own way; but those were difficult years. I have some vision of you sitting on a dark chair, somewhere, facing a wall. That was when I most nearly gave up. There seemed to be no room left for me at all. And then, quite suddenly – isn't this odd? – there you were, leaving that room, and coming in to another, that was full of wintry sunlight, and you were at a table, with sheets of paper all spread out in front of you; and I was so encouraged, just when I had nearly given up, that I came down your street and knocked on the door – do you remember? – and you looked up, just briefly, as I glanced in, and then I went on my way, reassured somewhat, even though you did have a long line of nappies in the back garden and rather a lot of shopping lists lying around, and I wasn't entirely happy about the way people dropped in for meals.

Alice said – Good God, you were right.

– So, I wondered if you would fill me in on the gaps. Why, each time I had most hopes of you, did you almost disappear? Why would you not talk to me? What was going on?

– I'll tell you. If we have the time.

– Time is relative. Train journeys are metaphorical. You can relax.

– But we are nearly in Newcastle, surely?

– Newcastle is movable, for the moment. Have we not fought you for centuries over the border? Why not let me organise the north of England for you just now.

– Okay. You want to hear it all?

– All as it presents itself to you. All as you see it at the moment. And, don't forget, I love you. Nothing can destroy that. I know, you did forget. But it doesn't matter, now.

There were a lot of us, then; I was one of many. I was Alice, but there were also Sue and Fenella and Christine and Jane. Aren't you interested in any of them? We're all there, together, on the college photograph of that year, sitting in rows. You must remember. We all still have the neat hair-do's with which we had come up, lots of hairpins, or perms, and we're smoothing down our pleated or straight skirts over our knees, hiding our breasts with folded arms, gazing defensively (it was early in the morning, to catch the sun) into the camera. You can see us there with all our hopes furled up inside us, invisible. I know mine were there. Early in our first term, that photograph was taken, and we were all like chrysalises, undeclared. The eccentrics, the wild beauties, the famous, the artists, the poets, all of us were hidden there beneath that freshman blandness, the wish to please. Here and there you might spot the odd stray wisp of hair, the pair of black stockings, the slightly longer, baggier sweater, the pale make-up, that might suggest a wish to deviate from the norm and be somebody else. But most of us, that third week of term, were still so impressed at being there, at being accepted, being grown up, being female, being academic, being away from home. We were half awake and fumbling still; finding our way down corridors, into lecture theatres, through library systems, into books. We'd unpacked our things and set them around our rooms, making fair copies of our rooms at home, our mothers' rooms, what we were used to. Only a few, a very few of us, had drink in our rooms, or cigarettes, or beds disguised as sofas or flowers given to us by men. We were good. We were timid. We were hopeful. We worked hard, we had to, had been told to, knew full well that this was the only way, as women, that we could be allowed into the world of men. Our work habits held over from school, where we'd been trained and groomed like race horses for the great exams, the Derbies and Grand Nationals of the system, taught to aim high and win, to settle for nothing less. We were proud of our brains and terrified of our bodies, on the whole, because they could let us down, weaken us, produce menstrual tension at the worst moment, give us headaches and backaches, periods and endless embarrassment of one sort or another. We all had, wouldn't you agree, in that photograph, the slightly strained expression of young

143

women from whom much has been expected. We had never allowed ourselves to relax.

So, there I am, wearing my good tweed suit, with my hair in a French roll with hairpins flying out at odd moments, arriving with my school trunk in yet another strange room, my room, the room which has been put aside for me alone. It was a good room, for people with scholarships and exhibitions were allowed two windows instead of one, and it was on the ground floor. In my entrance exam paper, I had written about William Yeats, about whom I dreamed: he was a tall old man with white hair and an Irish accent, who leaned elegantly against mantelpieces and read me his poetry aloud. In my interview, I had said that I was a writer, and chatted about the Brontes to my possible new tutor, who was also a poet in disguise. Just in time, we both remembered that we should be talking about other things; but I got my scholarship, and my room. I sat on the bed, that afternoon in early October, and wondered what would happen. I was alone. (You are right, I thought you had deserted me, years ago, upon some playing field, in the mud, beneath a windy sky.) Everything during the past few months, years even, had been geared towards getting here. Friends, family, holidays, all else had existed in the shadow of this, the great race. People had laid bets on me: a high flyer, they had said at my very first school, scholarship material, yes. Expert trainers had put me through my paces, wise buyers had put their money on me, I had scanned the right books, eliciting information, as steeple-chasers take hurdles in their stride. I had gobbled and digested ideas that made my brain race, I was stuffed with them, high on them, sure of myself, programmed to win. I had won. What now? I sat on the narrow sagging bed and looked through the window at autumn touching the gardens, the silver birches that sighed in the wind, and did not know what to do. I had arrived. And the room was stale with disuse, after summer. I opened windows with difficulty – they were barred (to keep me in, or others out?) and breathed the chill, fresh, October air. There were hours to go till supper. The corridors were full of unknown girls flapping black like young crows in their gowns, and of notices, telling me to go to unknown places. The corridors were a maze, leading somewhere: perhaps in the end, I think now, to some

144

great final library where all the secrets would be known. But I had not read Borges, then, or would have thought of him. Neither, believe it or not, had I heard of Freud, Virginia Woolf, my own fallopian tubes, the diaphragm, the revolution in Hungary, to mention a few. I knew all about the Treaty of Utrecht and Hume's political philosophy and the mediaeval Papacy. I had read Goethe, Racine, Bishop Berkely, John Locke, but not Lawrence, Joyce, Jung or Marie Stopes. As a racehorse, I had only taken the necessary hurdles, ignoring, not being shown, the forests or grassy plains I might have wandered on. I was nervous, keyed-up, fretted to be off – but where?

It took me twenty minutes, that evening, to find my way to hall, where supper was laid. A bell rang, and surely, following somebody, I would find my way? The corridors stretched ahead, there were corners, more corridors, and no signposts along the way. Eventually, a swing door and a smell of gravy showed me. The crows were massed here, perched in rows. I saw bright faces that did not know me, that turned quickly away, and black gowns that flapped. There was grace, and a scraping of chairs. The food passed was in mounds – mounds of potato, mounds of cabbage. Gravy swirled on plates, and people ate fast, talking all the time, leaning across each other and across the narrow tables. I was, for that first evening, alone. It was like school all over again: an exile. Depressed, scared, I trailed after all the others out of hall, the food lying like lead. I had my own room and my trunk of clothes and books, coffee pots and flower vases: but why? What should I do? What was the point of being here, after all? The great prize, dust and ashes in my hands. Girton. The name that had echoed through my childhood, through my life (my grandmother, who came down in nineteen – o – something, a raving beauty with a first and two blues, no less), tag now for something shrunken, accessible but meaningless, after all.

Suddenly, a voice hailed me, and I saw a girl coming quickly across the floor towards me whom I recognised. Smaller than me, blonde, with long hair coiled up neatly in a shining roll, she was Fenella; we had met at the interview; together, I remembered, we had been into the empty chapel one evening, to pray to get in. God, give me what I want. Side by side we had been, a little self-conscious, but determined

145

to do everything, everything, to make sure; hedging our bets, belt and braces, getting God in on the act, too. It had worked! We greeted each other. Our prayers had had this instant, evident effect; we had obviously done it right. Spun the wheel of fortune, read the signs and portents, propitiated the right powers. We were in, favoured, the elect.

– Hello!

She walked out beside me, and instantly I had a friend. You must, surely, remember Fenella? We had coffee, in her room – instant, too, out of mugs with flowers on them. I was in my friend's room, invited. We talked and talked, she questioning me, wanting to know everything. I was not used to anybody being this interested in my life, my family, everything that I had lived through up till now. She had a way of sitting, sideways up on the bed, cross legged, looking directly at me through narrowed lids; after about a fortnight of term, she let her hair down, abandoning the smooth pinned French roll, and her hair used to hang down on each side of her face, and sometimes in a curtain half across it, hiding her direct glance. She wore high roll-necked sweaters and smoked Embassy no. 6. Her eyes were greenish, her hair honey-coloured, her face round and innocent-looking. She had been in Paris. Her room was two corridors and a staircase away from mine, and we visited each other several times a day, adopting the slow-slouching gait of Girtonians, slip-slopping in backless mules down the shiny red pathways, keeping nun-like close to the wall. We came to recognise each other's step, each other's knock. We cut hall breakfast and breakfasted together, late, in our rooms, buying Swiss cereal, ground coffee, smoking cigarettes together in a haze of mid-morning satisfaction, missing lectures. We cycled down into town together, two abreast, our feet off the pedals and arms stiff to the handle bars, leaning back, streaming down the hill, laughing as the wind blew tears into our eyes, just making it through the changing lights, skidding then to a stop, one foot on the pavement, to shout a consultation to each other across the roar of traffic, to decide where to go next. The city was ours; the university was ours; suddenly, with Fenella there, I could stop wondering about what to do next, for the only time was the present, the moment our raison d'être, there was no point in doing

146

anything but what we were doing now. I was absorbed: in love with her, in a way, and so suddenly able to love myself. I shut my tweed suit up in a cupboard and spent my book allowance on scarlet drainpipe corduroy trousers and a black sweater that came nearly to my knees. It was 1960. The trappings of the fifties, of my teenage years, could be put away now: it was a new decade, I was launched, I was away. Everything that had been in my life till now paled before this moment, this time. The beauty of the city held me entranced, during those first autumn days. Suddenly, I could look out, see it, the outer world, and go out, be in it, revel in it, make it mine. We tore about on our bicycles, gesticulating among the traffic flow, going the wrong way up streets, helter-skeltering down the narrow passage-ways between the colleges. We stood on Clare bridge, one blue afternoon, our cycles in a heap together, and gazed down into the Cam. We made vows, plans, promises. We were in love – with a whole city, a whole decade, a whole new life. Everything was possible. All that mattered was to be in it, of it: to live!

Late at night, in her room or mine, we made instant coffee where other generations of undergraduates (my grandmother, in her shadowy other time, her long skirts, her purdah-like seclusion?) had drunk cocoa and smoked a last cigarette. We surveyed our day, exchanged anecdotes, told each other everything. Fenella told me of her months in Paris with her friend Elaine. Elaine was an art student; together they had escaped school and family, hitch-hiked, stayed on the top floors of cheap hotels, been to night clubs, picked up men, had philosophical discussions, learned to smoke and drink, adopted a whole new attitude to life. In Paris, there was Juliette Greco, there was Jean-Paul Sartre, there were Henry Miller's and Lawrence Durrell's forbidden books to be had upon the bookstalls, there was cheap wine, there was freedom. There was a boy called Jean-Claude. There were cellars, where people danced dumbly enfolded in each other in clouds of smoke. There was existentialism: at last, I thought, as she passed it on to me, haphazard, in snatches, in anecdotes, in passing, at last, the truth. It had no name, for me, this philosophy of life, but a hundred different faces; and these came to be the faces of my friends, of my present time, of my sudden adulthood, of my own life.

147

Of course.

Flap-flap. Flap-flap. I heard her in her slippers coming slowly down the corridor towards me, knew from her careful gait that she was carrying something, and my heart jumped up with anticipation, each time, to greet her and whatever new thing she would bring in with her.

– Guess what?

She came in, her hair streaming, in her blue jeans and big roll-neck sweater and fur slippers, carrying two mugs of coffee, a cigarette already between her lips and the smoke spiralling up before her face of concentration. She sat upon my bed, handed me a mug. I was so unused to it, to friendship, to sharing life in this way, that still in me there lurked the fear that it would end, that she would no longer want it, that it would all have been a mistake. (Now, two decades later, decades that have been filled with female friendship, I look back and realise that nothing in my life had told me that I could be close friends with a woman, that this was what it was like. Her liking for me stunned me. I could not believe that it was really me that she wanted. I was chosen, picked out by this extraordinary person, was loved for my own self, valued, thought brilliant and entertaining and fascinating in my own right, without effort; and it was not so much lack of self-confidence that made me so surprised but simply that, nothing had ever suggested to me that this was possible.)

– Guess what? said Fenella, coming in with the coffee, as she so often did. I was sprawled on my bed, in my uniform of corduroys and sweater, reading a book on modern architecture and listening to Bartok's Concerto for Strings and Orchestra on my crackly old record-player. The gas-fire had been on for hours, putter-putter in the corner, and the room was stuffy, curtains drawn to hide iron bars, the disorder I liked proliferating. I had a new style in 'working'; had abandoned sitting upright at a desk and taking notes in silence, as I had been taught at school, for lying down, smoking, reading a book and listening to music at the same time. I thought the Bartok sophisticated. Some of my other records – *Oklahoma*, *My Fair Lady*, *High Society*, I had already hidden. I was pleased with my 'ambience' as Fenella would put it. My book on Mies van der Rohe lay open, a postcard marking the page. I was reading architecture, for some strange reason of my father's, – you remember? – and she, Fenella, to my envy was reading English. Where she had poetry, I had these rigid shapes, these foreign, unwieldy ideas. But I did have these names to drop, these glossy books to read: that was something. I looked up from the paragraph I had been trying to assimilate for the third or fourth time.

– What?

– I'm in love!

– What! Are you? Who with? How?

The heaviness then of something sinking inside me: envy of her, jealousy that she should be lured elsewhere? Hard to know. I felt all at once excluded, threatened. It was, after all, a world of unsafety, of competition, of war.

– He's reading English. I met him after the Donne lecture.

We had arranged to meet, in town, and she had not come; I had waited for a while and then cycled up and down, lonely, freed, a little angry, but determined to pursue, like Camus' heroes, my lonely individual existence. So I had chained up my bicycle, walked by the river at King's, eyed black-sweatered young men, written a bleak poem in the sunlight. I had not had any lunch, out of some interest in self-deprivation, and had arrived back at college at four to devour half a cake that my mother had sent, drink four cups of coffee and smoke three cigarettes before falling asleep for half an hour out of confusion.

She sat on the end of my bed, her back very straight. Shook back her hair out of her eyes and blew Juliette Greco smoke trails. Suddenly, I was angry with her. In love! Posing like that, as if she were something special, when I knew, at least, that she was just an ordinary girl from Lancashire, less bright than I was, with a good line in Parisian-style patter and too much blonde hair.

– Well, then, who is it?

I was brusque, questioned her like a mother. She sighed, her gaze vague, remembering. She had a way of gazing into the middle distance with such a melting expression on her face that one could almost relive the experience with her.

– He's incredibly intelligent. And very thin. He looks like a sort of

149

starved baby. He talks all the time, very fast, says the most incredible things, I've never met such an intelligent person in my entire life.

I did not remind her that a week ago, she had said this about me. It seemed that my role now was to be eager and encouraging and see her off into the world of men. I felt all at once clumsy, schoolgirlish, left behind; my old self in her tweed skirt with her hair up came creeping back out of the cupboard – see, you never got rid of me, I've been here all the time. And there was Fenella with her dreamy look and her starved-baby young man, and another new world opening. The first of so many times: when she seemed to me to show me something new, something unimaginable, and then abandon me at its threshold. Suddenly, I was aware of her blonde beauty as a threat, I hated the way she looked. And hated myself, doing so.

– He's invited us to tea.

– Us?

– Well, of course. I told him all about you. He's dying to meet you. He's got a friend, who's in the school of architecture too, who's noticed you. He's heard about you from him. Oh, isn't life exciting?

It was her cry, of those days; mine too, in echo, claiming that right. Life was, because we made it so, because we drew it for each other in those colours, imagining it, allowing it, willing it to be so.

– When are we going? What's he called?

– Tomorrow. He's called Pete. He was at school in London, he's read absolutely everything, I've learned such a lot from him already. He's fabulous, really he is. You wait and see.

So, she trusted me, with Pete, with her life, with it all. I was included, invited too. We had been invited to tea in a man's college, with a man. (My grandmother, in her day, had been driven down into town in a closed carriage, taken to lectures, driven straight back: so that this could not happen. When she had invited her brother to tea, there was a chaperone there all the time. Things had been different, then.)

– Are you really in love?

– Yes! She was triumphant, certain, she had got there. Where we had dreamed of being, the end of all our hopes and aspirations, she had arrived, in one simple leap. She had met him after the lecture,

150

they had talked, she leaning on her bicycle, I could see her, her blonde head tilted, questioning, her eye upon him in such a way that no man could have looked away; there they had been, just for a few minutes, in Mill Lane, out in the light of day, and it had happened, just like that. They had walked together, she wheeling her bike, he carrying books. They had exchanged fascinating conversation all the way. He had said – Come to tea tomorrow. She had said – had she? – I have this fascinating friend, can she come too? They had parted, and it was done, a bond sealed, a future fashioned. I was impressed.

We stayed up later even than usual, that night, talking of men. Men, the real, the strange, the flesh-and-blood creatures that were everywhere here, at lectures, at the cinema, in the streets. There had been men in Paris, she let me know, and I felt left behind again. I had been at boarding school, locked in at night with three hundred girls to dream and plot and imagine our lives away. I had written to my cousin, showing off, 'frustrated as hell in this man-starved establishment'. I did not know what I meant, but knew that men were necessary, that one must have them. Now, here they were: inviting us to tea, and what else? I did not know what else; could not imagine the step from having tea with a fabulously intelligent young man to having my body (my body?) feverishly covered with burning caresses, as in my secret dreams. Suddenly, to have this happen was all that could matter. Sex, I knew it in a flash, would be the answer. The existentialist truth would lie there: everything stripped away, the meaning of life known. But, how to get there? I wanted to ask Fenella if she knew, but dared not. Perhaps she never dreamed of burning caresses, far less gave them to herself in anticipation ('his hot breath touched her naked flesh') every night before she fell asleep. I looked across at her, where she sat sipping her coffee, with her dreaming look. She was unknowable, suddenly removed. I did not know if she was female, or if I was, or what that meant, or if we did, apart from the surfaces, have anything in common. She looked back, coolly always, through her hair, through the smoke, across the distances between us.

– Well, she said, we'll see, won't we? Sleep well. *A demain.*

You see?

We cycled down, wearing our black sweaters and tight trousers, our hair loose in the wind. Fenella's flew out like a blonde wave behind her; mine blew into a black wild bush. As we dismounted and chained our bikes, our cheeks were flushed with wind. I felt exhilarated again, transformed: my new, delightful self, the old one locked away, forever. I was with her. We were adventuring. Life, and its possibilities, went on and on and on. I followed her, across cobbled courtyards. She had the room number on a piece of paper, looked at it as if she were reading a map. She marched straight ahead with determined steps and her hair thumping between her shoulder blades, and I guessed that she was nervous, only could not have known it. I understood now, that she had brought me because she was nervous; but was no longer insulted, only intrigued, only relieved, that I after all was the onlooker, the companion, rather than the star. She stopped, knocked. A door opened and music came out, a trickle of jazz, and a young man stuck his head round the door, which he clutched with a thin dirty hand with bitten fingernails. He had the round face of a cherub, curly hair, wide eyes, and an air of ill-health, for all the cheerfulness of his grin.

– Oh, it's you. Come in. Hi. Is this your friend? Hi. Fabulous. Come in. We're just having some Scotch. Or d'you want tea? You can have tea. This is Philippe. He's just going, aren't you, Philippe? Sorry, there isn't much space. Hang on, I'll move this stuff, then you can sit down. Sorry, it's a hell of a mess. I keep the curtains drawn because the light puts me off working. You can have them drawn back if you,want. Hang on, I've got some cups somewhere. Have some peanuts? Look, you can sit there, shove my stuff on the floor. Okay?

On the floor, in the half-light, sheaves of paper shifted and settled as he moved them for us to sit down. A huge man stood in the corner of the room, filling it; but sketched a farewell with one hand to Pete and went, eating peanuts from the palm of his hand, scattering some upon the floor. The afternoon sunlight made only a thin crack of brilliance between the drawn curtains. The gas fire was lit, and a whisky bottle, a tea pot and two mugs were set before it. In the room was a bed, a desk and a chair, and a sagging sofa, upon which we sat side by side, upright, our hands on our knees. Pete came and crouched close by Fenella and put an arm around her and kissed her on the lips. She

152

kissed him back, her hair falling around them both, and I sat, looking straight ahead, a strange feeling in the pit of my stomach, wishing I had not come. They kissed, for a long time, in silence. Then Pete straightened, pulled down his black sweater that hung about his narrow hips like a skirt, teetered a bit on his heels, looking down at us, and said

– Have some tea?

We drank tea, ate stale digestive biscuits and peanuts from the jar, and he poured us whisky in a toothmug, to share. I had never tasted whisky before and shivered and gagged as it went down. The half-empty Vat 69 bottle stood on the floor between us. The peanuts were stale and mousy tasting. Outside, the afternoon was hot still, an Indian summer. In here, it felt as if we were underground: I, and my friend, whom I would never understand, and the unknown young man who came and kissed her, quite as though she belonged to him.

He said – Would you like to hear *Aida?* And put on, with solemnity, record after record of the opera. We sat side by side on the sofa, Fenella and I, and he sprawled in an armchair opposite, his feet dangling over one end. When I got up after two records to look for the lavatory – ('the bog? oh, you'll have to go across the court, I think there's a woman's bog over there') he was on the sofa beside Fenella, and the chair was for me. I sat and did not watch them, and tried to listen to the music, tried to like it, and the whisky, and the darkness, and the smoke, and my best friend kissing a man. I thought – this is it, this is life, this is what it really is like; this is experience. It was one way of justifying everything, and it did me very well that year.

Back at college, after the long uphill bike ride in the cooling early evening, Fenella stretched and yawned in her room, smiling at me, enjoying herself. On her wall she had pinned a text which said: Here is a girl who has lived, loved, lost, and lived to love again.' I wanted to ask her if that was true. I wanted to know that it was lies, propaganda. But she looked so well-fed, so satisfied, throwing back her hair and stretching, that I had to believe it. I imagined her in Paris, with Jean-Claude. I glimpsed a life that was so unlike my own that it hurt; I ached with envy, from the outside. We went into hall together, slop-slop along the corridors, our gowns hanging off our shoulders

153

like dressing-gowns, our hair loose, and sat at a table far away from other people and kept an existential silence going between us until it became uncomfortable, and then she said – Well, what did you think?

I realised then that she did want my opinion: that for her it had been necessary that I was there, that it had not been Pete who had invited me.

– Pete?

– Yes.

– Well. Great. Really nice. Really intelligent.

– Did you really think so?

– Yes. Well, yes.

– He's not very beautiful is he? But I love his mind. That's what's so great; after all this time, all those years at school, to be in contact with men's minds. I think we have a lot to give each other. I've learned masses from him already. He knows all about Freud.

– Who?

– You know, Freud the Viennese psychoanalyst of course.

– Oh, yes.

– And he's read the whole of *Das Kapital*.

I wanted to ask – what was it like kissing him? Do you really like it? But instead, said – Gosh.

– In the original. In German.

– Really?

– He's lived in Germany. Studied, at Heidelberg. He knows masses of German poetry, Goethe, Heine, and all about the novella and masses about opera.

– He does know a lot.

– He's convinced that Lawrence is the greatest writer of the century. He's read all of him. Even *Lady Chatterly's Lover*, in the unexpurgated edition. He said that Lawrence had the key to our malaise, in his analysis of the relationships between men and women. I'm reading *Sons and Lovers* again. I realise I'd never really understood it before.

I did not ask her, when did he tell you all this? For, during the hours of that afternoon, all that Pete had said was – Great, and, Fabulous, and, Don't you love this bit? and, Listen to him here. He had kissed

154

Fenella frequently, with a strange, quick, nuzzling movement, more like a grown curly-headed young ram still suckling from its mother, with buttings and gruntings from time to time. She had responded quite silently, hidden by the curtain of her hair. *Aida* had shouted and cried above them, and I had heard the minutes tick past, and, finally, the hours.

– After lectures, we've talked, she said, although I had not questioned her. We just get through so much in a short time. Everything he says is sort of buzzing with ideas.

I was silent. My pudding, jam sponge with custard, sat in front of me, and I did not want it. I felt as if I had never had an idea in my life; and suddenly, urgently, wanted a young man for myself, who would buzz with ideas at me, fill me up with his books, quotations, music, whisky, kisses; so that I could tell Fenella, share it with her, be an equal. We drank coffee together that evening, long silences between sips, long pulls upon cigarettes, I creating long understanding gaps in which Fenella could talk about Pete. He was a genius. Wasn't it wonderful to live in a world surrounded by geniuses? Were they not desirable, necessary, compulsory, these beings with such brains and bodies, such flashing eyes, such curly hair? I decided, going to bed that night, alone with the puttering gas fire and my room full of smoke, that I would get one too.

I followed him into the bookshop, Bowes and Bowes on the corner of Trinity Street laying my bicycle down symbolically on top of his, where I had seen him prop it minutes before. I was pretty determined and systematic even then. He was tall and thin, black-bearded, wearing the compulsory black Marks and Spencer jumper, pale-faced, definitely an intellectual. He stood at the modern languages counter, leafing through a book; there was something in his stance that I immediately disliked, a certain weakness, but I decided to ignore it. He would do. I had seen him at the freshmen's fair, joining the Heretics, and at a party given by a poet: his credentials, so far, were fine. I stood a few yards away, also leafing through a book. It was a translation of Rilke's love poetry. I, too, was a poet, and adept at languages. I wore my red corduroys, my tight black roll-neck and a

155

pendant on a chain and flat black shoes for creeping up on people; my heart making a great commotion inside me, I said (casually) – Hello.

– Hello? He looked puzzled, but not unwelcoming.

– Haven't I seen you before somewhere?

He looked down at me – at least six foot tall, thin as a beanpole, with white hands coming out of his black sleeves. He said – I don't think so? There was that question at the end of everything he said, making it possible for me to pursue him.

– Yes, at that party, at Caroline Black's the other week.

There was nothing more to say. I turned, terrified, back to Rilke. Then, he understood.

– Are you reading languages? I haven't seen you at lectures.

– No, architecture, actually. But I love reading French and German, particularly poetry.

(Anything Pete can do, I can do. I searched in my mind for some fragments of Goethe, forced on me by a teacher at school. *Kennst du das Land?*)

– Architecture? There can't be many women doing that.

– There aren't. Only two, in the whole school. The others all failed their exams, apparently.

– Whew. You must be pretty bright, to get in to read architecture. (And read French and German, yes, and have a scholarship in history, and write poetry, and soon, thanks to Pete, quote Freud and Marx and Lawrence and talk about Wagner and existentialism and, thanks to Fenella, Paris, the left bank. Yes, I began to feel pleased with myself.)

Interested, he looked at me over his book. It was a copy of Kleist's Erzahlungen. Yes, I had heard of Kleist. Yes, I loved the German novella (thank you, Pete) and yes, I would love to go to a party tonight, only, I must check my diary, make sure I was free, there was so much on, wasn't there, one had to pick and choose.

– Fine, he said. Eight-thirty, I'll meet you at the main gate of Emma. We went out of the shop together, I buying the latest copy of Granta, he with a bundle of reading-list books under his arm. Waiting, while he paid for them, I began to feel proprietorial. I had done it; this one was mine. Fenella, I wanted to shout, look, I can do it too!

156

Friendly, linked by incipient coupledom, we left the shop together, to disentangle our bikes. My pedals were all caught up in his spokes, and his front wheel had come sideways to block mine. In the closeness of struggling with mudguards and chains, I caught a whiff of what he smelt like, and recoiled slightly; it was not unpleasant, not a body smell you could object to, just alien, not me, not recognisable in any way at all; not my father, brothers, relations, friends. A strange person. But, I had to go through with it, now, what I had begun.

The party, that night, was in his rooms, but he came out to meet me as he had promised, under the main gate at Emmanuel. I had tucked my bike away with twenty others, in a corner, and stood trying to flatten my hair and pull my wrinkling trousers down over my calves after the ride. I had decided, now, never to wear anything but these trousers, never to change into a skirt; it simplified life, but also allowed me a certain identity, a certain sureness of myself. My new self, so recently invented, discovered, wore red trousers and picked up men and name-dropped riotously, impressing everyone, and cycled at night with no lights on, and came back late to college to climb in. She was all that I had ever wanted to be: I was delighted with her. She drank and smoked and missed lectures and got up late in the morning and knew exactly what was wrong with the world. During all those years at boarding school, beneath the neat short hair and the uniform, she had been growing in me, growing, biding her time, pushing at the confines; and now, she was out. It was 1960, and this was Cambridge, and it was her life.

She – I – this person in red trousers – met her intended lover in the darkness between the lit spaces of rooms, walked close to him across courtyards, followed him up steps, entered the party. The room was full, of people, noise, smoke. Buddy Holly on the record player, hiccuping, dying. Wine filling cups and glasses, leaving a dark stain. Cigarettes lit quickly from the extinguishing butts of others, strangers' faces close in the flare of a match, sucking for nicotine, strangers holding each other close, swaying, breathing in each other's rank sweat smells, cheeks against the roughness of sweaters, beards in hair, eyes closed, feet shuffling, words muttered, songs crooned, all judgment set apart – I jumped in. It was what I wanted. It was the

157

anti-thesis of all my upbringing, it was exactly right. Larry (his name was Larry, as in Durrell, he told me) held me in his arms, in a loose, rather uncertain embrace. My face against his sweater found again the slightly warning smell I had caught across the entangled bikes, but my determined body ignored it. I danced with him, slow, hardly moving, the music thumping through us, in among the others, the faceless, nameless bodies, in among the sweat and smoke. I drank, to forget, to be unaware. He would kiss me, and I would swoon away, (being uncertain what might follow, anyway). The kiss would seal everything, solve everything; from it, we would emerge, a couple, no longer alone. I waited, embraced his bony chest, but nothing happened. He swayed, a little out of time with the music. I felt his glance go out across my head, focussing on something else. The tension in me slackened, the wine flowed, I did not care. Whatever he was looking at, whatever he was thinking, I had this prize, this man, and it was his party, and he was mine. We swayed on. My back began to ache, and somebody put on Chris Barber's 'Petite Fleur' and he began to sing the tune down my neck, a little as though he thought he ought to. Across the room, men were humming the tune into girls' ears, as they steered them to and fro, just moving, across the inches of carpeted floor. In bottles on the window sill and mantelpiece, candles dripped streams of hot wax down bottles, and the wine bottles that were not stuffed with candles dripped wine. It was hot, airless, and Larry's sweater scratched my cheek. But it was necessary, it was right. I waited, thinking that he might kiss me. All around, mouths were now glued to mouths, in a sucking, sighing, groaning continuum. Suddenly, he broke away – Would you like some cheese?

– Cheese?

– I bought some Brie, it's just exactly in the right condition, *coulant*, you know. I thought we might eat some before anybody else gets at it.

–Okay.

We ate the dripping Brie in our fingers and licked them afterwards, and drank tumblerfuls more of cheap red wine. Then we smoked Gauloises, his, from a blue packet in his trouser pocket, crumpled and sour, with the bits coming off on our tongues. I thought – after this, he will kiss me. I thought of the combined tastes of Brie and dark tobacco

158

and the strange smell of him, and rather dreaded it. But, instead, he wrapped the remains of the Brie up carefully and put it back in his cupboard. He said – Let's make some proper coffee. I can't stand drinking Nescaff all the time. It doesn't even deserve the name of coffee, in my opinion. The French would never call that, coffee. We are a nation of barbarians.

It was nearly eleven. Already, I would have to cycle back up the hill with no lights, risking police cars, and climb in to college through Evelyn Bond's window, risking night porters. I might as well stay. In the little kitchen I watched him grind, percolate, and pour coffee. The smell was good. There was still time, in which he might kiss me. I imagined him turning suddenly with a groan of desire and taking me in his arms.

He said – Sugar?

– No thanks. I must go soon. I'll have to climb in, anyway.

– Barbarous, these women's colleges. Mind you, they treat us all like children, with all these ridiculous rules. Of course, nobody on the continent would stand for it. Still, take your time over the coffee, it's an insult to good coffee to hurry it.

We sipped, and eyed each other.

I said – Do you like Lawrence?

– D.H. or T.E.?

– D.H., I meant.

– I find it all a bit torrid, actually. But then, I do think the novel's dying. It's all so old hat. I'm more interested in film. Film's the medium of the future. Are you interested in the cinema?

– I love going.

I thought of *War and Peace*, with Henry Fonda stumbling across battle fields, and my love affair with Yul Brynner of *The King and I*.

– I mean, do you like The Cinema? Have you seen the latest Bergman? What do you think of Antonioni? They're showing *L'Avventura* this week at the Arts.

I was silent, groping through ignorance. Wagner and Freud and Lawrence would not do, any more. There was a whole new language, a whole hidden culture yet more, endlessly more, to explore.

– I know, would you like to come, one evening? I'd like to see it

159

again. I saw it at the Everyman, of course, but I think one does need to see him at least twice, to get the symbolism. What do you think?

– Oh, yes. Yes, I'm sure you're right. I haven't seen many films. I've been at boarding school.

It was like saying, I've been in prison. I thought of the afternoon I had tried disguising my school uniform and going with my friend Rosie to *Look Back In Anger* and being caught by the school prefect at the door.

– But you're interested in the Nouvelle Vague, in the development in European cinema?

– Oh, yes, of course.

Not the sort of thing you should be concerning yourself with, had said the housemistress, punishing truants of seventeen.

– Would you like to come and see it, then?

– What?

– *L'Avventura*. The Antonioni.

– Oh. Oh, yes, love to.

He might have been talking about Italian food, for all I knew.

– See you at the Arts, then. Seven-thirty, Monday?

I cycled off through the dark near-emptiness of the provincial town at night, the moon lighting my way instead of the defunct front lamp. He had said goodbye with a wave of the hand, as if I were an acquaintance. I thought of Pete, kissing Fenella on the sofa, the long, secretive, greedy fastening of mouth on mouth. My thighs ached from pounding upright on the pedals; I panted upward, on up the long hill home. To Fenella, to my room, to my diary, to working it all out. The lights of cars swooping up behind, passing: either rapists or the police. I kept my eyes on the road. It was midnight, and the college was almost in darkness, just a light on here and there between the trees, otherwise, a black Gothic mass, captive maidens locked in for the night. I parked my bike in the shed and crept out across the moonlit grass, soaking my feet. Evelyn's window, third on the ground floor from the end of the wing where I lived behind my bars. Darkness: I imagined her asleep, waking at my tap, her white face and mouth in alarm, as she sat up, pushed the curtain aside, expected – what – a naked man in a mackintosh flashing his penis at her, a monster with his face pressed against the glass. A face distorted by a stocking mask:

the beast that walks the grounds at night anywhere where three hundred young women are locked in together for the night, the beast of our dreams.

– Evelyn! It's me. It's okay. Can you let me in?

– Who is it? God, you frightened me. I was asleep.

– Sorry, Eve. I was at a party. Sorry to wake you.

– It's okay.

She yawned, shifting back in the bed as I crawled through under the lifted sash and across her, my shoes wetting the eiderdown and leaving grass upon the sill, so that any detective would have known. I pulled the window down behind me, sat on the end of her bed. She switched the light on and blinked at me without her glasses, her face puffy with sleep and patched pink where it had rubbed against the pillow. She was like a baby, about to break into a roar of crying.

– Turn the light out. I'll go. Thanks for letting me in.

Hers was the only window on this wing without bars, and the price of her own freedom was to let whoever wanted come and go. A quiet girl, studying maths, she did not use the escape route herself, but waited with maternal patience while others tapped and entered and clambered across her at all hours of the night.

– Did you have a good party?

– Fabulous, thanks. Goodnight.

– Goodnight.

Fenella was awake, with her light on, reading George Herbert and smoking a cigarette, in her pink dressing gown with her hair loose on her shoulders and a brush trailing through it. The light was pink, too, from her coloured shade. Her room was half child's nursery, half night club; she herself, clean from a bath, the daughter her mother would have liked, apart from the Number 6.

– I thought you were never coming back. Did you have a marvellous time?

– Yes. Fantastic.

– Doesn't sound like it.

– Oh. Well, it was.

She said – Are you in love?

161

– No, I don't think so.

It was a confession of failure. Yet even I could not feel it, that night, the burning abstract passion just waiting to be unleashed. I thought of Larry's thin mouth set in his beard, and his thin white hands, and the way he had held me when we danced. My head ached with wine, and my legs from cycling; I was very tired.

–Oh, well, you probably will be. She was philosophical, looked at me kindly, from her vantage point.

– Did Pete come up?

– Yes. We had a wonderful evening. (Oh, yes, the pink lights, the romantic glow, the hair-brushing). He came on the bus. D'you know, he can't ride a bike? Isn't that odd? But we talked about – oh, everything. He is a genius. No doubt about it.

– I know, you said.

– D'you know, he said my room was full of phallic symbols? I'd never noticed before.

– What on earth d'you mean?

– The candles, that china thing I got in Paris, the pictures, look, the lamp, even my horse.

Her china horse reared on the mantelpiece, his nostrils flaring: but so had many china horses in girls' bedrooms at school.

– He said Freud would have been very interested.

– Oh. What's that supposed to mean, though?

– I don't know, a general sexual urge, I suppose. It was just interesting. An example of what one's unconscious tends to do.

– Well, in that case, anything could be a phallic symbol.

– Well, most things are. Apparently. Isn't it weird?

I said – I'm going to see the new Antonioni, on Monday.

– With Larry?

– Yes. He wants to see it for the second time, to be sure about the symbolism. I'm really looking forward to it. (Some time, somehow, I must find out what this meant, symbolism; but even with Fenella, it would be impossible to ask outright).

– D'you think you will fall in love with him?

– I don't know. I might. He's quite nice. We had lovely coffee.

Fenella said – It's wonderful, being in love. I've never felt so – well –

162

complete, in my life before.

I said – Goodnight.

She said, beaming at me, all love and pink light – *Bonsoir, chère amie. Dormez bien.*

We went to films, Larry and I, because films were his life, cinema his only passion; we sat in darkness, in silence, side by side, and were as one; we came out into twilight streets and lit cigarettes from the same flame and strode along in silence, because to talk too soon after a film was not done, and we gazed thoughtfully at each other in bars and over coffee, reliving in our minds the camera shots, the techniques (in his case) and the embraces, the naked grainy flesh on view (in mine). We saw films in the afternoon and came out to brew tea in his rooms (Earl Grey) and went back to see another film immediately, came out to eat spaghetti or drink sour glasses of wine and then in again, for the next showing. We saw Fellini, Antonioni, Bergman, Godard; French, German, Italian, Japanese reeled through our heads, we peered to read the odd white subtitles and guess at what was going on. There was the Russian Hamlet and the French Phaedra and there were the Westerns that were not westerns but really social comment, and there were the films that used footage of the concentration camps in Europe as if they were ordinary; there were films that made me sick, afraid, appalled, and that drew comments from him like: perceptive, insightful, daring. I had no time to work, and never went to the school of architecture except to stroll through in dark glasses showing him off as my new man. I hoped that somebody noticed. There was no time for meals, either, so we lived off Earl Grey tea, good South American coffee, stale bread and Brie and cheap red wine. Occasionally, we went out to eat spaghetti, the cheapest on the menu, and in between complicated sideways sucking bites, to discuss the film. It was all, all complicated. I laboured to wind the spaghetti neatly round my fork and prepared the appropriate comment in my mind. In fact, I had found the Antonioni film very boring, but blamed myself for that. Nothing happened. I could see nothing happening. People wandered about all over an island looking for each other, and that was that. All through the film, people got up and left the cinema, until it was nearly empty. Each time one left, banging the seat up, muttering, Larry called out clearly – Philistine! so I knew I could not say what I really thought.

– Such an accurate image of life, was what he said.

– Mmm, yes, wasn't it. I tangled the spaghetti round my fork, was about to bundle the whole lot into my mouth when it slipped and fell back on to my plate in a rush of wet tomato sauce. Larry lifted his in the air as if on a fork-lift truck, and tucked it in between his moustache and beard, leaving tomato stains on both. Watching, I experienced a sudden feeling of disgust. It was not what I wanted, no. And yet, each night, as I tore myself away from him, climbed on my bike, pushed and heaved and lumbered my way uphill, I thought of him embracing me, reaching out for me, in the cinema, in the street, as I straddled the bike seat and teetered, one foot on the pavement, to say goodnight. Over the last weeks we had sat together and watched countless couples, male and female, one of each, grappling naked with each other beneath sheets, kissing, sighing, groaning, and reaching for a cigarette afterwards. At last, I knew what to do: in the outward, social trappings of the event, if not in the event itself. It was all there, poised, ready in my mind, as countless film-makers had portrayed it and novelists suggested; but how, how on earth could it really be done?

And we went to parties, and copied the stances of the Antonioni, the Godard couples: expressing our alienation, the way we stood apart from each other, gazing with disgust at the throng, picking a little food, sipping a drink, eyeing the world over the rim of a glass. I began to wear a black dress that had belonged to my mother and pretend to be Monica Vitti, lowering my eyelids, sucking on my cigarette, undulating across the room while all the while my ennui burned in me; it was hard work, and sometimes I longed to flop down on the nearest bit of floor and simply chat. But Larry was upright, there, his pale eyelids fluttering above his grey eyes, his hands waving languidly in monosyllabic conversation. Yes, he was probably saying, but I do feel that the modern cinema has grasped the essential angst of our time. A girl was listening to him, in an attitude I recognised: head inclined forward and upward, hands clasped upon an empty glass, mouth a little open. I did not care. It was the fourth party that I had been to with him, and suddenly I saw Fenella across the room, suddenly I was myself again, freed for the moment, angry flesh and blood instead of celluloid, with all my unfashionable opinions still intact. Fenella, in black sweater and skintight black pants, her hair piled up on her head and dramatic black eye make-up. I looked for Pete, but saw behind her a tall thin young man whom I recognised as a school friend of his from another college. Fenella smiled, but carefully, as if not to disarrange her make-up, and he waved to me in a friendly, casual way, as if he had known me for years; I liked his wave with its jump of enthusiasm, like somebody greeting one at a railway station. I waved back, forgetting his name.

– Hello. Fenella was beside me, short in her flat ballet shoes, her shining coiled hair a masterpiece.

– Hello. I didn't know you were coming. Thank God you're here.

– Why? Aren't you enjoying yourself? Is that what's his name, Larry, over there?

I had not wanted her to meet him, for fear of her intense, scrutinising look.

– Hey, this is Jon, by the way, if you didn't know.

We shook hands. People rarely shook hands, I think. He seemed to bend over Fenella in a protective way, but then I noticed that this was probably only because the ceiling was low and he was so tall. He wore the uniform black Marks and Spencer sweater of that year, but a collar and tie as well, and his jeans looked as if they might have been ironed.

– I'd heard about you, he said. And didn't we meet at Pete's once? I hear you had to sit still all afternoon and listen to Aida.

Larry appeared at my right, carrying glasses, one for me; perhaps to establish our connection. I introduced Fenella and Jon. Jon listened intently to what people were saying, leaning forward a little, his eyes on the speaker, his lips compressed, as if it were an effort.

Larry said – Quite fun to *épater les bourgeois*, isn't it? Must just take someone a drink. Ciao.

We, the three of us, looked at each other. I thought I was blushing. Fenella looked protective in her turn, maternal; she smiled at me, as if saying, it's not your fault. Jon said – What a prick. Excuse me, I know he's your friend. Sorry, shouldn't have said that, it's my working class

165

origins showing again. But, strewth.

I looked at Larry's willowy departing back as he threaded his way through the crowd, and felt hot with anger. Then, there was Jon's look of concern, brown eyes signalling something – a regret, a promise of some sort; and there was Fenella, leading him away from me, as if that were enough. They began to dance, the two of them, shuffling together on the small space of floor between the table and the fireplace; she very upright, straining upward, her back like a ballet dancer's in its sprung tension, her blonde head shining against his chest, he leaning over, always leaning, as if to encircle her, as if to keep away all the rest. It was the first time I saw them together. He, with the humility, the attentiveness in his stance, she with something defiant, alert, determined. Her face turned against his chest and then tipped upward, right back so as to look up at him and say something, so that her heavy crown of hair weighed at the back of her neck and might fall down; but she laughed, with a deep chuckle at whatever it was he had said, and I turned away. I did not follow Larry, but went and sat at the kitchen table to talk to a young man from my year in the school of architecture, with whom I could be a work-mate, an equal. We tipped back wine and talked of lectures and crits and the latest design project, and each word was an effort for me, as if I were tugged back by whatever bound me to Jon and Fenella, as if the desire to sit there and watch them and be included was almost too strong. Later in the evening, I went back into the room, where they had been dancing. There was near-darkness, the few candles burning low and dripping wax, the flames blown about by the draught from the door. The music ran on, Chris Barber again, in a hard continuous blare. The two of them were there, on the bed against the wall that had been heaped with cushions, entwined together as if they were one person, kissing and kissing, their black clothes blending together, only Fenella's long loosened coil of hair to identify her, and the chuckle again, her robust and most self-satisfied laugh. Of course. As I stood for that minute and watched them, all capacity for surprise drained out of me. Anything could happen. In a minute, while one looked away, everything changed. Human relationships were quick and volatile and shifting as that: look, and then look away. The wheel turned, and the partners changed, and it did not matter, none of it mattered; and at the same time, it mattered more than anything ever had, and I was outside of it, still outside.

– Fenella.
– Hello. God, what time is it?
– Half eleven. I thought you might want some coffee.
She sat up in bed, wearing the sort of nightdress one might buy for a honeymoon, I thought, and stretched her arms, throwing back her tangled hair. The sun came through the blown curtain from her narrow window, lit her face, her arms, her hair, so that she was golden, grainy. I thought that she was entirely beautiful, I loved and despaired of her beauty. If anybody had told me that I was beautiful, then, I would not have believed them; beauty was blonde, was golden, was her, was Fenella. I sat down on top of her thrown-down under-clothes, on the only chair and held out the coffee, Nescafé made entirely with milk, the way she liked it. She sat up and warmed her hands on it, her hair tangling pale and dark gold all down her back, her sipping of it precise, and the steam rose around her. I wondered what it was like to be her; and, wondering, experienced myself again as somebody perpetually on the outside. I was the observer, brilliant perhaps, witty perhaps, a poet, an intellectual, a friend; but she, she was at the centre, essential, she was already where it all lived, beauty and love.
– Isn't life exciting?
I wanted, for her to tell me, for the explanation. Life is not like this, after all, it is like that. Love is this, not that. Love is not here, but there; the will o' the wisp, darting ahead, never to be grasped, the enigma never to be understood, hers however to hold in the cup of her hand, while I lumbered after her, with my butterfly nets, my ridicu-lous patience.
She sipped the coffee, and beamed at me, and was silent. I wanted to prompt her, for it to be over, so that we could get on with our lives.
– You and Jon?
– Isn't he fabulous? He reminds me of a changeling, of some fairy creature, an elf or something.

167

I thought of the last time: Pete as a starved baby.

– Yes, I see what you mean.

– Don't you think he's beautiful? A beautiful, beamish man.

– Yes, I do. Are you in love?

This time, I asked her the ritual question, began the liturgy.

– Oh, yes, of course.

As if there were no question.

– What about Pete?

I knew it was plodding, but I had to know.

–Oh, it wasn't the real thing. I didn't realise. He's very brilliant and everything, I think he possibly *is* a real genius, but I wasn't really in love with him. We gave each other a lot, I think. He and Jon are very great friends. They have a sort of secret society, with names for things, a sort of secret language. Jon thinks he's wonderful. Well, I do too. Only, this is quite different, with Jon. I feel sort of – transfigured – when I'm with him. As if we both exist in a kind of magic world, where nothing can go wrong. You know? I'm so happy.

– That's what it looked like, last night.

I felt that I had witnessed something holy, magical; the finding of the grail. Real love. It was what we had been reared on, this longing, this search: the gold at the end of the rainbow, the happy ever after, the kiss and the long awakening, it all. I was awed, impressed by her. Perhaps I did not need to find it myself, if I knew somebody who had. On the wall above her bed was still her text: Here is a girl who has lived, loved, lost and lived to love again. There she sat in her bed, warm and alive and drinking her milky coffee, making my world work for me, making it live. Lived, loved, lost and lived to love again. It was, it became, our credo. Live for the moment, take and enjoy passionately, follow your love wherever it may take you; the world is well lost for love, love justifies, sanctifies, allows, extends, protects. The magic circle, the hallowed dream: and our quest, our quest to the world's end. We gazed at each other triumphantly, delightedly. You too, her gaze promised me, will have it all. It is ours, the world and everything that is in it. Just you wait and see. The best men, the best love – we will gorge on it, stuff ourselves with it, you and I. Come too, her gaze said, and you will see. I would not be excluded: I would be with them, of them, a part of the magic circle, on the inside. All this would be mine too. Suddenly, she leapt out of bed, stripped off her nightdress, dropped it on the floor and stood there naked in the sunlight for a moment; then with a characteristic briskness began putting on her bra and pants. One movement, into the neat white bra cups, and fastening the elastic; one more, and pulling up the equally neat white knickers. She ran her fingers round inside the bra cups to be sure of comfort, patted her stomach, and stared at herself in the mirror, baring her teeth. Her hair fell about her like light. And I, as used by now to her nakedness as to my own, simply observed, simply awaited her. She pulled a sweater down over her head, and came out, blinking, as if born into the day.

– Run down and get us some ciggies, do, I'm dying for a smoke!

2

At the end of the summer term, at the end of our first year, I sat in a car with a young man beside me, and did not weep, but felt tears block my throat with incredible pain as I held them in. The Morris Minor was my mother's; I had borrowed it for May week, and in it, through the Cambridge countryside flowering wildly with cowparsley and elder, I had driven him around. I loved, I thought, every inch of him, from his red head six foot two off the ground to the soles of his worn-out sneakers. I loved his lean freckled body, lightly tanned between freckles, and the wild bush of his hair and his scowl. I loved his blue eyes slitted against the sun, or behind dark glasses. I loved the way he smelled, and snuffed it up at every opportunity as if he were something good to eat. When I had been with him, I did not want to wash, afterwards. I took his dirty shirts back to college with me, and buried my face in them before I plunged them into soapy water: he did not know what I was stealing, when I offered to do his washing. Oh, the secret pleasures of laundresses, the slavish joys. And when we spent long evenings together, 'working' as he put it, I would pretend to read my book, cramming for exams, and would eye him instead,

169

watching the movement of his hand in his hair as he read, waiting for him to look up. Then, he would look up, and catch my eye and be on me; together we would sprawl upon the sofa (a sagging sofa, spring-gutted in every college room) and kiss each other till we were sore and wet, and his hands would roam about over my breasts, outside my shirt, and I would feel his hardening lump there inside his trousers and do nothing about it, and we would kiss and kiss in an endless entangling of tongues, until the insides of each other's mouths were as well known to us as our own, until our lips were rubbed and slippery as rubber. Then, he would slide off with a sigh, and be unaccountably grumpy, and I would look at my watch and realise that I must rush to be back to college in time, and that would be that. I love you, we would tell each other, over and over again, in between moans, sighs, ecstasies. Was there any more? If so, how did one cross the great divide, and get to it? Neither of us knew. The shirts, sweaters, jeans, bras, pants all stayed in place. There was a pleasure in holding, kissing, rubbing, sighing, yes; but after a while a certain boredom, too, so that I was relieved when it was time to go. One more kiss, as I straddled my bicycle, my summer skirt hitched up high above my knees in the May night, and then I would watch him go, his white shirt ballooning out in the dusk above his narrow hips in the tight, faded jeans, and love the way he moved, almost as if I had created him.

— Oh, yes, I told Fenella fervently at last, with truth, oh, yes, I am in love.

He was beautiful, svelte, red, tawny animal, and he was mine. Or I had thought he was. Would we get married? There seemed to be only that one choice. Fenella and Jon talked about marriage, the safe house at the end of their road, the haven, the prize already theirs. I thought of marrying Andrew Reid, and it was like deciding to set up house with a beautiful sulky panther. If only I could tame him; but then, if he was nicer to me, more amenable, I would not love him so much. For what I loved, admired, was his cynicism, his ennui; it was the fashion, that year, and he was in the vanguard, from his cultivated slouch, in through doors with a hunch of the shoulders and hands jammed deep into jeans pockets, to the way he smoked cigarettes and

170

threw away the stubs. He was monosyllabic, terse to a degree. He nursed a secret pain that challenged me: for surely it was the challenge of all women to ease the pain of men, to understand.

I read Lawrence (for he too was reading English, and a Leavisite) and imagined and precisely located the sensations he described, the little flames, in the loins, in the womb, the flutterings, the earthquakes; but I did not know where my womb was, and the loins were hard to be sure of, and anyway when Andrew kissed me, everything happened quickly and urgently and on the surface, so that my sighs and moans of pleasure were simply copies of his. I was pleased because he was pleased; and I enjoyed the clean, wet, cool taste of the inside of his mouth, the smell of his skin, the softness of his wild hair. Most of all, I enjoyed parading him about: arms around each other, his at my shoulder, mine at his waist, we had strolled miles, showing each other off, proprietorial and proud.

Now, we sat in my mother's car, and he stared straight ahead (somewhere I had read about profiles on coins, and his was a fair imitation of some angry potentate). I tried to swallow tears as if they were a hard lump of matter that no human should ever have to ingest. He had said it. Everything was over between us. This was the end. I did not dare ask, why; or protest. Evidently, it had been some lack on my part.

He mumbled – It's just the way things are.

He had a phrase – that's the way the cookie crumbles; but did not use it then, at least. I did not ask why things were that way; but dumbly accepted. He made the rules; or rather, interpreted the feelings, and therefore led the way. Being a Leavisite, he had the last word on feelings. And if he felt no more love for me, then that was the way it was.

– About the ball.

We had – he had – tickets for the college May Ball; twelve pounds a go, and it was almost like getting married. I had bought a new dress, and had twirled in front of him, embarrassed only that his James Dean slouch looked odd suddenly in the shop full of taffeta and tulle. He was the reluctant bridegroom, I was bride. Then, I had known that all was not well; that the game we were playing was false. But I twirled desperate in my new dress with the huge skirt that would block doorways and the vast splodged roses of blue and green, I turned and flounced and dwarfed him, and he looked miserable and turned away when I paid the bill, and would not speak to me all the way back.

– We won't go, of course.

Of course. If you were suddenly not, after all, in love, then the ball was off too. Cinderella, I was back to hearthside and unwashed pots, my dream turned to rags.

– But, he said – Finn would like to take you. Finn Anderson.

– Would he?

It had all been discussed, then, between them; I had been passed on from one to the other, discreetly managed, handled. I thought in amazement of Finn, the young man who sat behind me in the school of architecture, the one with the blond crewcut and slit-eyed funny smile, who greeted me sometimes on my way in, the only one there who ever did. While close-knit groups of intense men in dark sweaters and big black glasses all huddled to examine drawings and tap their teeth with Rapidographs, so seriously; he would glance at me sometimes, and smile, it was true. It had been with Finn that I had sat at a kitchen table, months ago, at a party where I was with Larry, and joked and drank. He looked – unlike other people. A Scot, scandinavian, perhaps, a Viking anyway. His cheekbones from Eastern Europe, his eyes from the Steppes; the whole of him from some archaic sculpture somewhere, that I had not yet seen.

– Oh. You mean, he wants to take me to the May Ball?

– Yes. He asked me. He knew – well – that you and I were finishing. (How, when I did not myself?) He said, he would like to take you, very much. I was too surprised to be insulted: Cinderella reclaimed, recycled, allowed to prance and twirl after all.

– Well. Okay. Will you tell him? Or shall I?

– I will, if you like. I'll just give him the ticket. Good.

He was lighter, all at once: freed, about to spring away. Suddenly friendly, he bent and kissed me lightly on the lips. – Ciao. It's been good knowing you. I hope things go okay. That your parents aren't too much of a drag.

172

That morning, I had crowded with him and others outside the Senate House, to get a glimpse of the piece of paper that announced examination results. I had failed: the only one of my year, the only woman, the only failure. In my papers I had one, two, three per cent. My world, that day, lay cut about me in ruins, failure on both counts, the worlds of work and love both closed, and a bleak summer ahead. I settled determinedly into gloom that would take more than Finn Anderson and his ancient smile to move: just let him try.

The evening that I had met Andrew, Finn had been there. I was giving a party, with Fenella and Sandy, who lived on her corridor; I was cycling about town buying French cheese and bread and packets of cigarettes and black stockings to wear, and there they were, the two of them, lounging by the river bank, one red head and one blond, as if they had nothing to do. I was full of the generosity of party-giving, easy-going and inclusive, for once, without wondering what effect I might have. I skidded up behind them, scooting my bicycle so that I might not be said to be cycling where cycling was forbidden, and the wind blew the paper off the bread in my basket and tangled my hair as usual into a mop; in a hurry, and careless of my appearance, I greeted them – Hey, D'you want to come to a party?

They turned, faced me: one tall and freckled, with incredible hair and a pout, the other Nordic secretive, a mask of boyishness upon something else. I knew Finn, he sat behind me in the airless upper room of the School of Architecture and doodled black insects and men with squashed faces upon the margins of his paper; he wore home-made looking clothes and smiled often and sometimes looked exhausted. Andrew Reid I had seen, at English lectures. When the lectures at the school of architecture grew too frightening, when I began to know, once and for all, that I did not understand what was going on, I began to go to English faculty lectures, to sit in a row with Fenella and Pete and sometimes Jon, to be in a whole group of people who knew each other, who spoke the same language as I. When bending moments and the Bauhaus got too much for me, I defected. At lunchtimes, at the School of Architecture, groups of men and lecturers would go off together to select pubs, to talk about Corb and the Movement and draw boxes on the backs of envelopes, and drink pints of lager, and be men together. There was no place for me: sometimes they flirted, mostly they ignored me, and I dared ask for help with nothing, my Graphos pen, my measured drawing, my shadow projections, my hopeless female life. Sometimes I wondered why I had said I would be an architect, when I knew all along I was a poet; but like so many other things in my life, it seemed that it had to be so. You could not put 'poet' on a passport or an income tax form, or even say it out aloud at a party, not unless you were a man and queer and at King's and content to wear black shirts and white ties and be an outcast for the rest of your days. So, I went to hear Leavis, or rather to watch him pace and mutter, in among the groups of the elect, who were choosing the future of the culture; and shuffled in among hundreds to hear George Steiner, who really was audible, who spoke without a note for a solid hour about things I had never heard of before. I would stumble out among the others, elated with the glowing tumble of the words, not daring to ask who Lucasz was or if Freud and Marx were related to each other in some way. And, briefly, I had seen Andrew Reid, lounging, running his hands through his curly red hair, practising his style. I had registered him: accurately, so that confronted with the two of them, some inner mechanism said – that one. That one, with his affectations, his elegance, his inner misery, his long body, his style. They, both of them, perked up, were interested. A party? Where? When? Tonight? Should they bring a bottle? Yes, it was my party. Yes, I would do what I wanted, take charge, for once. I mounted, wobbled off with the bread overflowing, waved to them au revoir. They both watched me go: I had them, the evening ahead, my life, in the palm of my hand. As Fenella would have said – Isn't life exciting?

She was in her room, brushing her hair so that it all fell forward over her face making her for some minutes a frightening faceless zombie as she called to me come in, and I came. All in black, with gold ballet shoes, and no face. Our party was to be in a cellar, that we had hired: no ordinary undersized rooms, this time, no making do with the space between the door and the bed. We had asked everybody we knew. There would be candlelight, and red lamps, and masks upon the walls, and music both hot and cool, and cushions to fall back on and wine to flow black in the stained light and sweat to come running down the walls. We wanted it really decadent, really cool. And so Fenella had thrown aside the full crackling skirt she had been wearing recently as Jon's intended, and taken off the gold cross she had had for her confirmation, and was back in her black, her existentialist phase, brushing her hair out so that she could peer through it. Blonde in black, she had always a stunning two-edged effect, madonna in disguise, the round innocence of her face contradicted by the black strokes of make-up, the gymnastic litheness of her body, never languid, but something brisk about her softened, muted, in suspense.

I said – I've found two more men. I picked them up by the river, Andrew Reid and Finn Anderson. They're coming tonight.

– Good, good. The more the merrier. Which one have you got your eye on?

– Neither.

– You're not still hankering after Larry Whatsit? The limp one?

– Oh, no, of course not.

I had been warned off. Fenella had said to me one day that Pete had something very serious to tell me, and that I should go round to his room and hear it. I went, and Pete was sitting in his collapsed armchair as if to interview me. He had told me, very seriously, that he had only asked me to come for my own good. Nervous, intrigued, I had sat on the edge of the bed, waiting.

– That Larry you've been seeing. The one at the party the other night.

– What about him?

– I should warn you. He's no good. He's queer. It sticks out a mile he is.

– Queer?

I was shocked, so that my heart seemed to suffocate me. I wanted to deny it, but no, he's kissed me, he has, honestly, it's all all right, what a ghastly thing to say, no, no—

– Are you sure?

Pete was solemn, sad but wise. Yes, I'm sure. Maybe it takes another man to see it. But I had to tell you, for your own good.

175

– Oh, well. Well, thanks, Pete.

– You need a real man.

I agreed with him. For a moment I thought he was suggesting himself, but no, he was still in his role of mentor. He looked at me thoughtfully, his lips pursed. I remembered that he was a genius. He said – Have you thought of Nick?

– Nick Feinstein?

– He's crazy about you. He's a fabulous guy.

– Well, no, I hadn't, actually.

– Think about it. You want to give these public school guys a miss, you know. He wants to meet you very much, Nick does. I could fix it, if you like.

– No, no thanks, Pete.

Anger was slow in me, in those days; blocked off by so much surprise at what was happening that sometimes it took days to surface. But I was angry: at having been wrong about Larry, at looking a fool, at going round for months with somebody who was queer without having noticed, at Pete knowing better than I. I retreated, to work, to be with Fenella, in the spare moments when she was not with Jon, to retrench, to start again. A real man? There was only Jon, and he was occupied. I set myself to watch, to wait.

The party, my party: a thump of Elvis, somewhere deep in the gut. Heartbreak Hotel. We-e-ell, if my baby left me— The hesitation and then the drilling it home. Andrew Reid came slouching across towards me, almost straight away, as I had known he would, and the walls were damp, the candles sputtering, the couples already on cushions, the bread and cheese already being devoured off the red table cloth, the darkness already full and smoky with promise. We danced. We-ell don't you – step on ma blue suede shoes. With a lithe and limber showing off of bodies, of styles. He caught me, sent me spinning, twitched me back. His dancing was narcissistic, languid, a little off the beat, but his hands were strong, flicking me to and fro. The uneven stones of the cellar floor underfoot and I in my thin shoes spinning, stamping, go on, guess my name. The happy ending of all happy endings in sight: a close embrace of bodies, a seeking of lips, while the rough Spanish wine raged inside us and there were hours yet to go. One kiss, one long kiss, tongues and teeth and all, in those days, and you were coupled, for as long as it might take, until somebody said, Ciao, and sauntered off. I did not know any girls who did that, but maybe there were. Young men said it in practised offhandedness and took their priceless bodies elsewhere, vamping it. The dance was all come-and-get-me and then playing hard to get. We-ell there ain't no cure for this body of mine, but to have that girl that I love so fine – They, we, mouthed the words, skipped and pounded, at arm's length from each other, and between us there was the gulf, the void, the don't know of our inexperience. I wanted it over with, the gap filled: once and for all.

By ten o'clock, that night, we were up against a damp wall, Andrew Reid and I, and his hands were all over the top half of my body as if searching for something he might recognise, and my lips were glued to his in the wettest kiss of my life, saliva flowing, and my hands were on his back and in the hair at the nape of his neck, not daring to move further down, and we were caught, fixed like that, the kissing flowing on and on and on. The music changed: from Elvis through to Edith Piaf and on to Miles Davis – through all the sounds of our generation, seeking something. In my head went the thought, again and again – This is it. At last. I did not know him. It did not matter. I knew his red head and his wet lips and his pointed tongue and the smell of him through the sweat-soaked shirt, and that was all that mattered; we would get to know each other at leisure, anybody could talk, anybody could read books, drink coffee, swop life stories; this, according to our lights, was the real thing, the essence of it all.

I thought of Lady Chatterley and the delight she had in the gamekeeper's body, an admiration so keen for the beauty of his maleness that she tended to forget about herself. I thought of small white buttocks, loins, the heavy mystery of balls. The ruddy glow of maleness. Andrew was ruddy, ruddy as a fox, and burned like a long-distance runner in my arms. Embracing him was like being him, like feeling his feelings. Time enough, perhaps, for me to feel something later. But he, the male, the predator, set the pace. He was entirely beautiful; as Lawrence had said. I did my best to swoon at the beauty of him, to drop from my own consciousness, to be entirely with

177

him. But my legs and back began to ache, with stretching up to somebody so much taller than me, and I was relieved when he suggested we lay down on the cushions. Fenella and Sandy and I had laid the cushions there for that very purpose; or rather, I had, my body planning moves in advance. But now that I was there, I seemed to retreat, before his eagerness, and I was hardly there; existed only in lips and tongues, tasting, forever tasting, as if I licked an inexhaustible ice cream.

Later, in bed after the party, I lay in a sort of ecstasy, my head spinning from the wine, my whole weight sinking down again and again through the mattress, layers and layers and up again, and then down, down, further each time, into some abyss of softness. My mouth felt stretched to an abnormal size and my pants, without my having noticed it, were soaking wet. I was in bed in bra and knickers, for some reason, and had no memory of having arrived there. Fenella, perched on the end of my bed, advanced and receded, handing me a cup of coffee I could not reach. Was it night, or morning? A grey light came through the curtains. My body smelt strange; and then I remembered Andrew. Ah, yes, my life was transfigured, transformed. Andrew. The red hair of him, the length and strength of his back, his forearms, his thighs, the way he walked, his sulky hunch, his eyes, his lips, his tongue.

Fenella said – Are you all right?

I said something, but it came out strange.

– What? You sound very odd. Are you drunk?

– In love, I said, articulating it at last, and fell back asleep again.

So, all through the summer days, until that moment on the worn leather seats of my mother's car. Mornings, afternoons and evenings spent together, in the mute togetherness of being in love. Gazing at each other, kissing, walking entwined. When I was not with him, I looked for him, for that pigeon-toed long-legged lurch of his, for his head like a beacon in the streets. We were invited, together, to parties, teas, pubs. We were a couple. At last, I was no longer out there on my own, at sea, unanchored, in the vast spaces of adult life. I had Andrew. But I had him only in his immediate physical presence, and what went on, what he thought, what he felt, beneath that tawny skin, behind those screwed-up grey eyes, beneath the monosyllabic grunts of our discourse, I did not know. He said, that he was crazy about me. But never asked what I thought or felt, never initiated that. Fenella would sit for hours, cross-legged, smiling, quizzing me – yes, but what was it really like? What was it like growing up in a big family, what are your brothers like, have you any photos, oooh, do let's see, isn't your Mum beautiful, she looks like Ingrid Bergman, who's that? ah, there's you, you look different with your hair that short, did they make you cut it at school, who were your friends at school, did you have any, what did you talk about, you must have had *some*, go on, I can't imagine you without friends, goodness, I do envy you, coming from a big family, it must have been fabulous, tell me some more about it, tell me what you did when you were young, you and your brothers, go on, do. With Fenella I would talk and talk, and then suddenly stop, amazed that she should want to know, and glance at her entranced face, and be able to go on. She was really interested, in me, in my life, she really wanted to know. Was it possible? She really wanted to hear, about my brothers, my aunts and uncles, my grandmother, my dog, my room at home, my schooldays. With Jon waiting outside and the whole of Cambridge at her feet and the sun shining and only three years to spend here and a third of that gone already, still she wanted to know. For the first time, I had a life, an existence, that was not simply mine, in my own head; for Fenella teased it out of me, laughed, mocked, encouraged, asked, questioned, challenged. My life became hers, too. She knew my family tree as well as I did, remembered the names of all my cats, would quote back to me the stories I had told her. I could not believe it. Beneath her touch, in the light of her fascination with my life, all the details of it grew, burgeoned, flourished. My world was furnished, beautiful. I would never be alone in it again.

But with Andrew, it was as if we had neither past nor future, relations nor parents, childhood nor middle age. We were the golden present, fastened avidly upon itself. We were evanescent as the blossom that dropped from the trees; light and insubstantial as that, an accident in time and space, an event with no meaning but itself.

We were enclosed in the complete and unfurnished privacy of our own twinned existence. Nothing outside now existed. I knew he was the child of parents who lived permanently abroad, so that he grew up like an orphan, making out. I knew that he had cut himself badly with a scythe when young, blood flowing that accounted for the long scar on his body. I knew that he cared about certain books, certain poems. But that was all. He did not say, or ask. His life was sealed to me, put aside. And when I began to speak of my own, he looked bored, his pale lashes fluttering down over his eyes and veiling his look, protecting himself from the bourgeois clutter of it all. We lay in the long grass of that summer and basked in its sun, and the lust in us grew and abated, grew and abated, and we held each other close in an increasing desperation, and then it was over. He had given me a record for my birthday and once, a squashed rose, picked upon impulse and handed to me as if he would have liked, after all, to have given me more. I kept both, playing the record of the Modern Jazz Quartet over and over until it was stolen, fingering the browned and fated rose as I fingered the pain of my existence, until that too wore out. A petal remained, tucked into my diary, and a pencilled note he had once left me, and the laboriously written day-by-day account of the time we had spent together, and the knowledge that I had done it, lived, loved, lost, and would presumably live to love again.

With Finn, I acted the part that Andrew had bequeathed to me, adapting some of his mannerisms to my own use. I was bored, pained, desperate, the ennui of life eating at me, the existential moment my only salvation. He tried, to talk, to dance, to distract me. I wafted, an overgrown dying butterfly in my vast dress, and took up all the space going through doorways, and brushed all the wet grasses with my hem as I held him at arm's length and told him, monosyllabic and curt, of the disaster of my life.

He said – Well, if you never wanted to be an architect in the first place, now you're free, aren't you?

I had not thought of it like that; but had wallowed in my interesting failure, proof that I could do no right.

– What d'you really want?

– I don't know. Yes, I do. To be a writer. A poet. That's what I've

180

always wanted, ever since I can remember. But people always thought I'd grow out of it, I suppose.

– Hundreds of writers don't grow out of it. There are quite a few grown-up ones around.

– I'd given it up. I'd nearly given it up. I haven't written anything for months. I'd nearly forgotten. All that exam work, all that mechanics and stuff.

– Well, now you can, can't you?

– But I've failed! I've failed prelims! Everybody said, nobody ever fails prelims, and I did! D'you know what marks I got? They were rock-bottom. My parents are never going to forgive me. I've totally mucked it all up.

We were dancing, clumsily, treading on each other's toes. He said, reasonable – Well, does that matter, if you're going to be a writer? Surely you can just get on with it, now.

– And, breaking up with Andrew. I don't know, my life is just a mess. It's a write-off. After tonight, I think I might not even want to live.

We stopped dancing. I knew it, at once, the absurdity of what I said. He looked back, slit-eyed, inscrutable but friendly. He said – Shall we go and get some more champagne? We might as well enjoy ourselves, if this is your last night on earth.

– Okay.

It was good, after all, to be with a friend, who demanded nothing. I did not have to behave in any particular way, it seemed, but could be just as I was, moody, tired, easily distracted after all. The hours passed, from twilight through darkness and into dawn, and we talked. Dancing had been painful, a prolongued bumping and treading on toes, a disparity of aim between us that was embarrassing. We sat, and walked about, and looked at people in their charmed coupledom, and talked. I did not want to touch him, nor for him to come any nearer; and he kept his distance. I did not want him to fall in love with me. Because I did not want this, I could be myself, as I was that night: irritable, yet wanting to be amused. I flounced about in my overblown dress with my lacquered hair like a carapace upon my head, and smoked cigarettes from a long holder, and held him like a courtier at bay. But, we talked. And the masks, the carapaces, came down. He was, as Fenella was, a good listener, and perhaps for the same reason. It was the last night of our first year at Cambridge, last moment of the long-drawn, exhausting summer term, a last chance for confidences and reassurance, a last opportunity to share what we had, before going home to what was no longer home, before going out into the alien world. When dawn came up, showing the frowsty world of the evening in clear light, showing each trodden patch of grass, each cigarette butt, each trailing muddied hem, and on faces, each fuzz of stubble, each stain of make-up smeared: we were still the same people that we had been. We had not become, during the space of a few magical hours, a couple, as others were. All around us, the alchemical transformations, the pledges sealed, the twinnings, the couplings: absurd, illogical, but necessary, effects of a veritable Midsummer Night. Finn and I were still ourselves separate, conversational, wide awake but tired, the effects of drink and hours of talk marking us with temporary lines and shadows that would fade with a night's sleep. Nothing had changed. In the morning light, my dream world still lay in ruins about me. The year was still finished, and Andrew and I were still finished, and I had failed at architecture. The summer still lay ahead of me like a threat, before I could come back here again and take up my life. But at least I had told somebody, at least I had one more friend. I took his hand, at the end of the night, as the sun came back and warmed the streets again, and everything looked strange, sleepless, as if in a dream. It was a gesture of greeting, and farewell. I did not know if we would ever speak to each other like this again, or if I wanted it; I ran from it, that morning, as if it were dangerous. I wanted only to sleep now. To go home.

In the middle of the summer holidays, the vacation, the time that felt as empty to me as that word sounds, a letter came. It was stamped and postmarked from Greece, covered with the spiky black writing of the School of Architecture, that seemed to bend over in its urgency. I was lying as far from the house as I could get, at the bottom of the garden, half naked and reading Lawrence Durrell's Alexandrian Quartet. Above and around me raged the arguments, the disputes:

about my future. I should leave Cambridge and go to a sensible school of architecture at a local technical college, and start learning about bricks and mortar. I should get a job. I should go back to Girton for the long vac term and study hard to read history next year. I should take a look at myself. I should remember how lucky I was. I should stop smoking, and get my hair cut, and be some use around the house. I should get a nice boy friend, go to the tennis club. I should work harder, read fewer sexy books, go for more walks. I should spend less time on the telephone. I should go back to being what I had been, a nice girl, ambitious, hard-working, polite. Was this what Cambridge had brought me to? Two per cent in mechanics, and a set of nasty habits? My mother slaved in the kitchen, bottling fruit, and I scowled in as I passed the window. I did not want to bottle fruit. I did not want to be there. I telephoned Fenella, long distance, and we drawled to each other, exaggerating – My God, the boredom of it, how will we survive?

And Finn's letter came. It was six pages long, closely written in his manic black handwriting, with footnotes and PSs round the edge. He was in Greece. He was high, drunk, mindblown by the landscape, the Retsina, the heat. He was back in the cradle of it all, of the world; back where it all began. He loved me: Greece had made him realise it. He was crazy, hopeful, risking everything to tell me, without a cat in hell's chance but enjoying it anyway. He was in touch with the old gods, the original builders, the great architect, the oracle. He was strung out like a firework, he blazed, he was sure. He hoped I did not mind him saying all this – I could burn it if I liked. He was looking forward to seeing me next term. He was, Finn Anderson.

I bounded about the garden in bra and shorts, the letter in my hand already marked by my sweat as well as his. I was alarmed, flattered, delighted, appalled. He loved me. I could not get enough of it. Future, careers, studies, it could all go hang, as long as I was sufficiently loved. But, I did not want him, not to touch, not to have, not to gloat over. I did not want him in the way I had wanted Andrew. With Finn I wanted talk, meals, cigarettes, films and books, telephone calls, bottles of shared wine, perhaps, but nothing else. How could he do this to me? How could I so suddenly lose a friend and gain a whey-

183

faced lover? I read Durrell, down in the deep long tickly grass at the bottom of the garden, and closed my eyes from time to time against the red blurring sun, and got the letter out of my pocket to read again and again. He was eloquent, a poet. I liked his handwriting, its sprawl. I liked the way he told me everything he was doing and feeling, almost as a woman friend would have done. I liked his confidence, his new daring, the tang of his new self, sundrenched, pared down, Retsina soaked, that came to me through the wafery pages. But I did not, no, I did not love him.

My mother moved on from raspberries to red and black currants, and asked if I could spend a few hours picking, if I had so much free time. I sat beneath the net in the currant cage, stripped for action and maximum tan, my head full of Durrell's and Finn's phrases, interspersed; the eroticism of the encounters in the book I read, the inevitably prosaic nature of Finn's and my discourse. I thought of Andrew, down in the meadow grass on the banks of the Cam, his long hard body in its thin clothes pressed to mine. Why did nothing match, nothing fit? I pulled the blackcurrants from their skinny stalks in handfuls, staining my palms purple. The sun burned me across the shoulders. Why was I not in Alexandria, in Greece? The next week, I was to start a holiday job in an architect's office; a last effort to convert me, perhaps. I longed to tell Finn what I felt, how I hated what was happening to me. In my head, the phrases ran, the letters, the conversations. He would understand. Even in Greece, with purple seas and a sun overhead like a furnace and the taste of wine and olives in his mouth and architecture everywhere, he thought of me. I told him. I began, with the currant juice running down my arms, to talk to him. Late at night, I sat up writing him a letter. My life, laid out before him, plain. But no, it would not do; I could not love him, had to write him that hard truth, cause him that pain. We would be friends. I would always be his friend. I would always appreciate the evening we spent together, our unromantic first May Ball. But, as for all the rest, burning passion in the heat of day and in the eye of the sun, the love that burns and purges, makes drunk and clarifies, cauterises all the rest away: no.

In the architect's office I sat and boiled and wrote poetry under my drawing board, while pretending to make scale plans of lavatories. Outside the double-glazed windows, the sun turned in the sky, morning through to afternoon, and baked us all, and the hours dragged. I watched flies crawl up the pane and fall, crazed by the heat. In the evenings, I took a bus home and took off all my clothes and lay naked on the cool satin of my eiderdown and despaired. The poems I had written seemed, like the flies I had watched, to struggle and die. The plans I had drawn bored me utterly, so that I had done them as badly as ever. I did not want what was happening to me: longed for Cambridge, for friendship, love, real life. Day after day, the same. And I had posted my letter to Finn, so that there was no hope there; he would retreat now, wounded in his pride, and try his attentions elsewhere. He was not the love of my life, but he was somebody. I telephoned Fenella, and she was out. Her mother sounded surprised, critical. Are you calling all the way from Surrey? She was out with Roger, her first boyfriend. Roger! I was appalled. How could she, out of sheer boredom, go from Jon to Roger why was she not in, and languishing, and therefore available to talk to me? Fenella, I appealed to her, Fenella, what is happening to us, where is our wonderful life, our golden youth, where the moment of perfection, where the dream? But she was out, and did not answer. I was alone again, in exile, imprisoned, and who would rescue me now?

    – Is Jon coming up this evening?
    – I don't know.
Fenella lay on the bed, painting her nails with varnish, very concentrated. We were back, back after the vacation, back where we could start it all again, living, living this intensely, living as we wanted to live. There was something about her voice, though, its casualness.
    – I s'pose he may drop in.
They had become a cult, an institution. Everybody knew them, everybody saw them: the couple who had made it, the perfect pair. Everywhere they went, he with his arm about her shoulders, she so much smaller with her arms around his waist, both of them stepping in time, his stride shortened to match hers, they had the smiles, the

envy, the adulation of us all. Jon and Fenella. Their names, linked, upon party invitations, upon lists, in the minds of all who knew them. You could see them coming, down streets, across college courts, from far off: he with his long-legged skip in ironed blue jeans, topping her by feet, she with her blonde floating hair at his waist-height, close to his side. And I, I was with them, of them, and yet not, I was their friend and confidante, I loved them both, listened to them both, was rarely made to feel left on the outside. I was their go-between. When Fenella was out and Jon called, he would have coffee with me, and talk about Fenella. When she came in, late at night, from her evenings curled with him in front of his gas fire in Trinity Great Court, she would sit on the end of my bed and tell me, so that I would be included. And they were the proof to me, to all the rest of us, that it could be done, the circle be squared, the other half found, human loneliness be annihilated in the closeness of another of the opposite sex.

– Didn't he say?

I realised, then, how much I wanted to see him, to talk, to catch up.

– I haven't seen him.

– Fenella! Why?

– Oh, because, because. For God's sake don't you cross-question me. It was only the first evening of term; but it was a time at which we would have got together, the three of us, hugged each other, exclaimed with delight, before I left them alone. During our second year, we had settled down to an almost domestic existence, in its regularity. I was reading history, saved from the school of architecture at Kingston Tech and from weeks spent in architects' offices by my director of studies, who was a poet. I was still a poet in hiding, not allowed to read English, not to join that elite; but at least, in history, one could use words. So I went to lectures with Jon and his friends, and we talked of the American revolution and de Toqueville and John Locke and the Civil War, leaning upon bridges, upon bicycles, upon table tops, stirring coffee, sipping pints. I no longer had to sit in among the rows of keen young men in the school of architecture and try to make museums out of squash courts and design housing for barren stretches of the East Anglian coast. History was easy. History

186

did not have to be planned, invented, only discovered, remembered. History was what had made us, not what we had to make. And at least half the students of history and some of the teachers, were women. History included us, to some extent; whereas architecture, as far as I could see, did not. I no longer saw Finn so often, for he sat behind somebody else now, some other man; I, the last of an endangered species, had flown. I had, now, work, friends, a safe place to be, with Fenella and Jon; I did not need anything else. Love, passion, the obsessions of last year (in which the *Lady Chatterley's Lover* trial had dragged on in London, deciding what we could read, how we could think, how we could behave) had waned. Sexual involvement was perhaps not, after all, the one dire necessity of life. I kept men at arm's length, returned like a good child to Jon and Fenella, resisted their attempts from time to time to pair me off. Nobody was worthy of me, but them. I was their mascot, watchdog, ally. And with them, I need never be alone.

– Look, Fenella said – I want you to tell him.

It was after Christmas, and we came back to our cold college, wrapped in sweaters, scarves, thick stockings, to crouch around our gas fires and warm our hands at mugs of coffee several times a day.

– If he comes, I'm out.

– But why?

– Because, I'm going out with Pat.

– Pat Fanshaw? You aren't.

– Yes, I am. He's asked me to a party. I want you to tell Jon.

– But, Fenella, you can't!

– Why not? I'm not married to him.

But, you were going to be, but, you said you would, but, it was true love, but, how can I believe in it if you don't, but, what will he say, feel, do?

– Go on, Alice, you tell him.

– What, that you're going out with Pat Fanshaw?

– Well, not necessarily going out with, but I've gone out with. He's coming for me in a few minutes. He's got a car.

So, she would not even have to go out on a bicycle like the rest of us, wrapped and muffled and waterproofed, eyes and nose running,

187

hands blue and hair tangled; but would step safe, dry, warm, thinly shod, into a car. I was shocked. That was why she was painting her nails, then. That was why she wore a skirt, and nylons, and shoes. It was a betrayal of me, as well as of Jon. I was left trousered, thick-socked, unmade-up, a scruffy beatnik left over from another era. She was going out with Pat Fanshaw, in a car.

– It's an MG. A red one. He has it for the Sailing Club.

– Fenella, why should I tell Jon?

– Because he'll take it better, coming from you. Anyway, he doesn't own me. He'll have to realise.

He doesn't own me. Neither did I own her. We could be left, both of us emptyhanded, while she went off in a red MG, wearing nylons. I felt furiously angry with her, and also, mysteriously afraid. But, with an easy wave, she went. Ciao for now. *Au revoir, chère amie.* See you when I get in, if you're still awake.

I sat for a while in her room, that was suddenly emptied of her. There were the clothes she had taken off, left lying on the chair, the corduroys and thick sweater she had abandoned. There were all her things, still half unpacked. She had not been able to wait five minutes before running off with Pat Fanshaw; had thrown everything down, changed, done her nails, greeted me casually, and gone. And there was the little photograph of Jon, still at her bedside, there was the china horse he had given her, to match the phallic symbol one, there the flowers he had sent to greet her on arrival. There was her room, her pink, childish, messy, intimate, familiar room, that smelled of her perfume – Miss Dior, lavish for tonight – and of burned milk from hasty coffee-making, and of cigarette smoke. I no longer wanted to be in it; would not wait for Jon there, but walked out, slamming the door. My own room was bleak, beside hers, with nothing unpacked and no fire on, as I had gone in straight away to join her, where she was. I took out some books and ornaments and put them around, and lit the fire, and sat close beside it on my dirty off-white sheepskin rug that reminded me of Andrew, and stared at the uneven flickering columns of yellow and red and pale blue, the false flames. My fire made a wheezing sound, and then a series of little explosions, over and over again, as if it were talking to me. I liked it, in the silence. I did not want to hear Jon's feet coming down the corridor, though, so I put on a record of Art Blakey and the Jazz Messengers, drew the curtains, and sat down, safely covered by the noise, to smoke. Suddenly, I noticed, on my little table behind the door, one white carnation, its stem stuck into a milk bottle and a piece of paper tucked underneath it. A carnation, in winter? Its whiteness cold, crisp, its stem blue-green, its solitary perfection a little austere. I had worn one at the May Ball in the summer, and crushed its scent out of it dancing with Finn, pressing up against his chest, it had flowered and died between us, drooped in the morning. I knew, at once, that it was from him. Welcome back, said the note. His handwriting big and spiked, announcing him. That was all. He must have cycled up here, in the biting cold of the afternoon before I arrived, found a milk bottle, left it for me here like one solitary footprint in snow, reminder of his existence. Surprised, touched, I smelled it, its hothouse whiteness just flecked with red, so out of place in my cold room, and thought of what it must have been like buying it, deciding, coming up here, taking that step.

When Jon came, I was lying on the floor in front of my fire, reading, my carnation in front of me like a still life. If Fenella had red MGs, then at least I had white carnations. The absurd competition still flared between us, scoring points, so that sometimes, it was hard to decipher what was real. Jon's footsteps were real, coming down the corridor, turning the corner, rapid, sure of himself, sure of a welcome, sure of Fenella here waiting for him, sure of his future. I knew them, now, as well as I knew hers. Knock-knock; he hardly paused before coming in, and then was in, towering over me. Greeting; surprise; disappointment; all that, in the space of a few seconds. Where is she, then? His face asked me, even as he welcomed me a little cere-moniously, cutting his brief hug even shorter than usual, looking around.

– Hey, Jon, it's good to see you. How's things?

– Good to see you, too. Where's Fenella? I thought she'd be here.

– Did you? Isn't she in her room?

– I've been to her room. All her things were there, thrown about rather, as if she'd come in in a hurry, and then gone somewhere. The light was on. I thought she might be back in a minute, might have gone to the gyp room or the bog or something, but she never came. Have you any idea where she might be?

– No, no idea. I expect she'll be back. Perhaps she went along to the library.

– Her coat was there, the thick one, you know, with the hood, so she must be in, somewhere.

– Yes, I guess so.

– Come on, Alice, you must know where she is, you must have seen her, surely, since she arrived.

– Yes, I saw her. We had coffee together, after hall. Then I came along here, to unpack. Then I got stuck in to reading. Have you seen this, it's the new *Granta*, there's some good poetry?

– Look, screw poetry, you're not telling me. Where is she?

I was sitting up on the hearth rug now, threatened by his tallness, his distress; and he squatted down, at my level, looking at me. I could no longer do it, lie to him, protect him, put it off, pretend.

– She's gone out.

– Where?

– I don't know. She went out, after hall.

– But she's left all her outdoor things behind!

– She went out in a car. To a party. With Pat Fanshaw. He came to pick her up. She did ask me to tell you, actually.

He was white-faced, taller than ever, still breathing out the cold, he was up, he was off after her, I had never seen anyone look so desperate, suddenly, so ill. He was still wearing his scarf and gloves and bicycle clips, he was pinch-faced, on her trail, he was straining narrow and fierce as a hunting dog, to be off.

– Where's this party? When did she go? Who's this Fanshaw berk? Why didn't you tell me straight away?

– I honestly don't know where the party is, she didn't tell me. Wait, Jon, have some coffee, do.

– I don't want any coffee. I'm going to find her. Even if I have to cycle all over Cambridge to do so. Fanshaw, Christ, what a name. And he's got a car, has he, he's one of those castrated upper-class idiots from the Sailing Club, I suppose, what the hell's she doing with him? I'm sorry, I can't stay, I can't talk to you, I've got to find her. Christ, I haven't even seen her since I came up. It's only the first bloody night of term, and I haven't seen her for four weeks. Look, I'll see you tomorrow. I'm sorry. I have to go.

And he was gone, banging the door behind him as I had banged Fenella's, and that was the first of the nights on which he came looking for her and she was not there, and I heard him, watched him suffering, and could do nothing. Sometimes, he waited in her room, and left her angry messages, scrawled on her essay paper, his writing swarming all over with his dismay; sometimes he came down to me, and sat groaning, accusing himself, unable to find a reason for it that was not his own fault, convinced that he had driven her away. Sometimes he telephoned, to see if she was there, to check up on her; sometimes he cycled round the college and did not come in, for fear of what he might find, but would leave messages in her pigeon hole, accusations, pleas. And she was out. Dancing, driving, dining in restaurants, drinking coffee with clean-cut young men in yellow sweaters, going to sherry parties, with her hair up, wearing her new clothes. I did not recognise her; it was like seeing her in disguise. Patiently, painfully, I waited for her to return, her old self, my devil-may-care recklessly cycling friend. But she made hair appointments, went punctually to lectures, stepped sedately into parked and waiting cars. And Jon and I, left alone with each other, could only glare at each other, furious in our disappointment, alone in a world that no longer contained her, that was no longer enough.

Then, I did not see him for a while. It was a relief; not to be responsible for what was happening, not to have to console him, not to lie, to cover her, not to be involved. It was cold, snowing, and I stayed in, and invited other women to tea and coffee, and wore my slippers all day and read in the college library, and went to hall to eat. I worked; I immersed myself in history, catching up on a whole missed year. It was easy, after all. Being at college, you only had to stay in, and work, and watch the snowflakes fall outside the window, and you were safe. It was Pete, who came to find me, after several weeks, to tell me what was going on. He had no real overcoat, only a kind of mackintosh that came below his knees and might have belonged to a

191

tramp, and he looked strangely pathetic, defenceless, in the cold. His ungloved hands were blueish and frail. His face, paler than ever, with the nicotine stains showing clearer on his lip, like pee stains in snow.

He said – Coffee, great, I've run out, God, I was dying for some. It's about Jon. I'm afraid he's going to do himself in. Can't you talk to her?

– Fenella?

I was rigid all at once, listening. No. People did not do that, not really, not people I knew. Not Jon. Not possibly. But yes, students did gas themselves, it had happened only last term, to a man we both knew. But, not really. Not friends, not people who were loved, real people, solid flesh and blood.

I said – I can't make her change her mind. But, where is he?

– Rushing about all over the place like a maniac, looking for her, always trying to track her down. Doesn't she realise how much he needs her?

– I think she's had enough.

Of being paired, twinned, married? Of assumptions, plans? Of being half of a whole and never entirely alone, entirely free? I did not know; she had not told me. I had only seen her from afar, launched on her dizzy new course, going from one young man to another and in and out of cars, dates, cinemas, parties, coming in only to change her clothes. I did not understand, myself: how one could give up real love so lightly.

– But she's going around with these idiots, I've heard. He's worth ten of them, those berks in sports cars.

– I know. But it's her business. It's up to her.

– It's not, not if he's this depressed, not if he's talking about killing himself. Christ, he's my best friend, you don't think I'm going to sit around and watch that silly little bitch drive him crazy?

Pete, the genius: expert on Shakespeare and Milton, who had read all of Goethe in the original, who knew about Marxist criticism and the nouveau roman and Kant. I watched him wave his hands about, gesticulating in the huge mackintosh, like a puppet. I knew, he was right. Lawrence had said it, that the deep bond between man and woman was the central spring of all life, the sexual connection the one thing sacred. I knew that Pete was, as I was, deeply shocked. Our principles, our morality, did not allow for this. Yet, I hated the way he spoke about Fenella, and would defend her right to go out in sports cars if she chose.

– Will you talk to him?

He was enjoying the drama of this, too; as he had enjoyed telling me that Larry was 'queer'. He liked to be there, at the hub of our lives, controlling things. The critic, securely based in the new criticism; the arbiter of life.

– To Jon? Well, of course, if he wants to talk to me. I thought he'd been avoiding me, lately. I didn't know he was that low.

– Well, of course he is. It was the love of his life, she'd changed his whole existence. Honestly, Alice, he's such a fabulous guy.

He was telling me, then, how much he loved him. Suddenly I felt a strong respect for him, that he should come all this way on the bus, in the cold, at night, in his thin coat and cotton jeans, to save his friend, to tell me – I love him, too.

– Well, I'll go and see him tomorrow.

I did not know what I would say. I saw Fenella in my mind, quick as a flash, in and out, her wave to me, her grin of delight, as she left that morning for a day out in the country with one of her Sailing Club men, all navy-blue and neat, with her hair up and make-up, lipstick, somehow emphasising the carefree face she wore. Perhaps the carefree look was a studied one: a face drawn hastily upon her real face, to impress me and others. I thought so, now. And she was out of my reach, away from me. My friend, at the end of a long college corridor, passing me with somebody else. It was as if the pang of our rejection went right through me and Pete as well as Jon, as we moped behind her, unable to understand.

– Surely she has a right, though, to go out with whoever she likes? I asked myself this, as much as him. I did not know.

– But, she's being unfaithful to Jon.

Unfaithful. Yes, and to me, to our way of life. But, what did it mean? It was as if the standards of the playground – I'm your friend, no you're not, she is, I hate you – had been elevated to the status of a general morality. I thought – are we kids, then, or grownups? Pete's furrowed frown as he lit another cigarette and stood there gloomy as a policeman in his borrowed mac, told me that we were grownups, that it was for real. He was telling me, this is the most serious thing in life. Unfaithful. His whole existence. Suicide attempt. Love of his life. And I was impressed. I thought – then, this is it. This is serious. I must tell her, must let her know. Unfaithful, one could be, perhaps, out of passion, out of uncontrollable longings. But, surely, not for fun?

Fenella threw off her jacket and skirt and stood in her new petticoat, her stockings and high-heeled shoes. She still wore her confirmation gold cross around her neck and her hair was up in a high bun, coming down in long wisps. She dabbed a powder puff under her armpits and laughed at me through the cloud.

– Are you going out again?

– Yes, Jasper's taking me out to dinner. We're going to Trumpington. There's a drinks party first, in Christopher's rooms. Oh, Alice, isn't life wonderful!

Her old cry, her enthusiasm for it, all of it, whatever it was, undimmed.

– What about Jon? I heard he's very depressed. He's out looking for you nearly every night.

– Well, I can't help that. I did tell him. I wrote to him. Look, I can't spend all my time at Cambridge behaving as if I'm married! You must see. I just want to enjoy myself. It's so nice, going out to reasonable places, eating good food, not having to bike everywhere, not having to take care of somebody, not having to watch out for every damn word I say, you can't imagine. I'm sick of sitting around living off cigarettes and instant coffee and taking life seriously all the time. Oh, I don't mean you. But, it's a different world, it's so much more fun. Oh, God, I'm going to be late. Still, I suppose he'll wait for me.

– Aren't you going to marry Jon?

Stuck still in the world she described, of instant coffee and serious talk, I resented, deeply, her ability to have fun. She looked at her delicate little gold wrist watch and began quickly to scoop up the straying strands of hair. I was more than ever irritated by her beauty, and the quick way she moved, and how her clothes fitted, how she was.

— Oh, I don't know. Don't ask me. I haven't a clue.

She pulled a green sheath dress on, that I had not seen before, and stood before me asking me to zip her in.

— Is this new? I haven't seen it?

— Joshua Taylor's. My father sent me a cheque. He's delighted I'm getting out of blue jeans for once.

— It's nice.

I hated it, what it did to me, the sense of inferiority it reached. I zipped her, noticing that she had lost weight. She hopped about in her heels, collecting things. The evening before me, without her, became hollow.

— What're you going to do? She asked me, guessing.

— Pete asked me to go and talk to Jon.

— Well, give him my regards. No, my love. Tell him, if you can, not to be such a lunatic.

— You did love him, didn't you?

— Oh, I don't know. Yes. Probably. But I can't do it, I can't be what he wants, it's just no good my trying. I think it's probably impossible, anyway. I *can't*, don't try and make me!

And she was gone, with a clicketing small stride, her coat over her arm, her handbag clutched, her hair high and regal, her small stature showing her even more determined: propped, armoured, prepared, going out to get what she wanted, whatever anybody thought. I was left, again, in her room, with the light on, curtains still undrawn, and the text still there upon the wall: here is a girl who has lived, loved—

I wanted to take it down and tear it into small pieces and scatter it all around me, and then run.

All that cold spring, out of the depths of winter and into the longer days, the shorter nights, there was Jon and his pain. On sharp evenings, I cycled down streets, along towpaths, looking for him. I sat up late with him, over cooling mugs of coffee, and heard him talk with Pete, with others, I discussed: the problem. And the river was always there, the thick deep dark current of it, under the bridges, between the innocent green banks, all the way down beneath overhanging trees and through thick weed, to Grantchester and the meadows: the river, in which a body could drown and float quite gently away from us, leaving nothing.

He talked about it, often. Well, there's nothing left for me now but the river.

I would come out of a cinema or theatre late, and be met by Pete: he's talking about the river again; and we would go out scouring the town for him, looking for signs, tracking down his desperation. Two by two, like detectives, over the bridges, down the narrow alleyways, along the banks, where nobody was. There, look, that must be him. No, it's too short. It's just somebody going home. No, he's not here. Should we go up to Freeman's Common? There's be nobody to see him, up there. No, look, let's pack it in for tonight, he might just have gone back to his rooms.

Jon, and the river. Jon, and Fenella, and the course of true love. The grail: found, held, then discarded. It was as if we passionately wanted the story to end happily, the fairytale ending to hold, love, true love to be vindicated, the princess to end up in the prince's arms. We needed it, as disciples need proof of the god's divinity: we could not bear the feet of clay. Everything, that we read, heard, saw, told us, this is the way it should be; and Jon and Fenella were there to prove it.

Run, Fenella, run for it. Totter in high heels if you must, paint your face for disguise and pick up your possessions and run: run from the impossible dream! Looking back, I cannot help but cheer her on.

3

That year, with Fenella gone from me into her new world of rich young men, sailing and right-wing Union politics, I was adrift again and toying with occupations: writing for *Varsity*, hanging about the edge of dramatic societies, talking to new people after hall, going to parties out of curiosity: taking with me everywhere, and with an increasing sense of discomfort, my virginity. It was no longer a question of finding some passionate Lawrentian perfection in the summer grass: it was a cold year, and summer grey and rainy after the long-drawn winter, and I no longer, I thought, believed in Love. Sex existed still, an unknown. It was an intellectual necessity; something to know about, at least. Back in our early days, we had debated, Fenella and I (out on the grass of the Girton lawn, between the magnolia and the lilac, an innocent early summer day). I had asked her – Which do you think is more important, sex or friendship?

She said – Friendship.

I said – I should think, sex.

I suspected, envious, that she knew more about it than I did.

I said – I should think, sex is the ultimate. The only way one really ever knows.

– Knows what?

– Well, oneself, and the other person.

I remember her grey eyes, grey-green, level, her gaze, her straight eyebrows; in those days she had the habit of pondering everything long and seriously before answering, so that everybody turned and listened when she at last spoke.

She said – I think, friendship would last, where sex doesn't.

It was impatient – But, lasting isn't everything! Isn't it the moment that matters?

The moment. How we glorified it; how we loved, or I loved, evanescence, transience, those beautiful words. How I wanted, from life: the Moment. Stuff of poetry, of dream, of ecstasy, suffering, and loss. If you had your Moment, then nothing else mattered. But Fenella was talking about duration. And so sure of her was I at that time, that I did not care, how time slipped past, how we moved on from that place to another, how we disagreed. The moment, of the photograph, the poem, the shared memory, one of a thousand others that have slipped away; and the continuum, unnoticed to me then, the day-to-day.

When I took up with Nick Ripley, it was despite so much of what I had told Fenella I thought, that I was almost glad she was so seldom there to tell, now. It was at a party in London that we met, not in Cambridge, it was on the top floor of a tall house in Fulham, and the floor shook beneath the booted stamping feet, so that bottles were shaken over and wine dripped upon an uncertain kitchen floor, and the record player jumped its needle in a groove every now and again. Love, love me do – o. – I love you – ou. We sang along, under our breath, ignoring the gaps. There were Londoners there, in among the people from Cambridge; it was our last year as undergraduates and this, the real world, London, awaited us. Parties here were more drunken, noisier, went on longer, there was an increased sense of excitement, of the open-endedness of it all. You could go on till dawn, and then roar off on a motorbike to London airport or Brighton for breakfast. Harold Wilson made a speech about 'white-hot technology'. We were in it, of it, at home in our era, living it up, alive. London awaited us, with its promise of jobs, money, freedom. We would work with the BBC – they wanted thousands of people to work for BBC2 – or join publishing firms, or go into professional journalism. Some of us would dare further afield, head for the States and never come back without a Masters and a new accent and a roll of greenbacked notes. At the moment, we played with it all, with the ease of children out of the kindergarten playing at real school knowing that the uniforms, curriculum and status will one day be for them.

He leaned against a rickety table at my side, Nick Ripley did and pushed a glass of purplish wine at me, Moroccan red – Have some of this stuff?

– Thanks.

– Might as well. It's pretty poisonous, but it does the trick. Know anybody here?

– Jenny, and Sue. They invited me. Oh, and quite a few other people, faces I know. Cambridge people. Do you?

– Jenny's a vague relation of mine. Pretty weird set-up here. I s'pose we might as well dance?

We did; my face against another rough sweater smelling of smoke. He did not want to jive or do the twist, preferring an antique rocking from side to side, foot to foot, so that I could feel the tension of his body from head to knee. He told me, between records, that he was a medical student, from Caius. We sat in a corner, smoking cigarettes, our knees crooked up, touching each other. It was somehow like being too weary, too bored of the whole routine, to take the long route,

198

getting to know each other. We were here, so we might as well. I nuzzled up to him as if he were long-awaited, long-deserved. It was easy, speechless, pleasant, drunken, nobody's business but ours. As the party stretched around us, through the night, we lay on the floor on bumpy cushions, talked, kissed, slept, while people walked over us, loudly exclaiming to each other – Have you seen so-and-so? Christ, isn't there any more wine? Or, the bastard promised to wait for me. Or they rushed over us, to go to the bathroom and be sick. There were sounds of laughing, rowing, retching, and the regular pulling of the lavatory chain, all night. The floor smelt of stale ash and cat's piss. Nick's sweater smelt of himself and me. His cheek was smooth against mine, as if he never needed to shave, and his long cool fingers stroked me a little absent-mindedly, and as the grey London dawn came up outside the dirty windows, we were asleep, together in a cramped cat-nap, to awake into a new day.

Spending the night with somebody even fully dressed on a dirty floor in a room that stinks by morning, creates intimacy. When we awoke, it was to wonder what to do next together. It was to assume that in Cambridge, we would see each other, would continue. I flattened my hair and tied it beneath a white silk scarf, borrowed black leather boots from my hostess, added dark glasses to my already pale face, and set out with him into London. The night had transformed the day. I did not ask, now, whether I loved him, but considered him an inevitability; he was what happened next. We sat on benches and strolled by the Serpentine, and talked. He was a nihilist. He had read not only Marx and Kant, bu Heidegger, Sartre, Kierkegaard, Martin Buber. Did I like Mahler? Did I appreciate Bruckner? They were the only composers worth listening to. Modern jazz was all right, but had become essentially a bourgeois panacea, white men taking over black men's music, using it to blur the edges of despair. As the Beat generation, Ginsberg, Corso, had taken genuine existentialist despair and made it fashionable. Poetry was only worth anything if it expressed the essence of the void. Had I read *Being and Nothingness*? No? I could not mean it, that I liked Dylan Thomas. He would lend me a useful book, called *Black Ship to Hell*. All the while, we talked, and walked in the chill spring sunshine, and the trees, grass, ducks, other people of that day passed by unnoticed, like a film as a back drop to real life. Real life was our talk, ourselves. I sensed, as he talked, that he would somehow transform my life; and I needed it transformed, or needed a new reading list, a new set of attitudes, a new belief. For if Fenella had disappeared, if true love no longer existed, if poetry was useless unless it expressed the void, then it was clear, which way I must go. There was also the matter of still being a virgin; I had to do something about that, as I had to get through finals, in order to emerge into the real world.

We kissed, his cold tongue like peppermint in my mouth, the freshness of him always apparent, and his cheeks with a bloom like a young boy's, even after a night of so little sleep. His eye was brown and bright, his laugh merry, even when his words were at their most desperate. We took the train, together, to Cambridge, and sat reading opposite each other, having bought ourselves suitably nihilistic books. Bishops Stortford, Audley End, and into the flattening fen countryside, to begin again, one more time, one more term: my excitement was high, I greeted each landmark, was nearly sick with the pleasure of it as we caught the bus up from the station, through town, look, there's this, there's that, there's so-and-so; but hid it from him as I would hide all pleasure, all dismay. We sat on the swaying top of the bus, still reading, and my stomach rumbled as we had not eaten all day, Nick not considering it necessary, and I thought of rushing down to Fenella's room again, and telling her, I thought of my own room, and the fruit cake my mother had put in my luggage, and how I would make coffee and share it out and dig myself in, home again, home, after the exile. But Nick only looked up from his book as we came into the centre of town, hooked his bag up under one arm, briefly touched my cheek – See you – and got off the bus outside his college. Of course, we would meet again. His casualness was a way of saying, that is assumed. See you. From the bus stop, he waved up to me, as my bus began again on its trundling way uphill. I felt a physical pang, at parting from him. Perhaps I loved him. I wanted, anyway, his presence at my side, that day, as it had been there through the night as we had lain together like exhausted animals upon the hearth, our dreams perhaps meeting, entwining, as our bodies twitched and slept.

In his room, there was always darkness, and very loud music, either Mahler's Fifth Symphony or Bruckner's First. There was a skull on the table, that he used as an ashtray. There were rows of medical books from libraries, stolen over the last three years, and rows also of dog-eared paperbacks on philosophy. He had a neat small bed, sheets tucked in as if in a dormitory, and striped pyjamas under the pillow, and a Bible. He said that he kept it there, in case. His desk was neat, with stacked clean paper. There was no sign of food or drink. Upon the washstand, he had a new toothbrush, its bristles not flattened like mine, and smokers' toothpaste, and dental floss. I noticed it all as I took a drink of water, and checked myself in the mirror. We sat, side by side, and the Mahler poured its desperation over us, and far down, behind the curtained windows, there was the normal sound of traffic in the market place, and the shouts of vendors, and buses braking and starting up again. Far down. It was like being in a tower, high up above the world. He rarely went out, but lay full-length on the bed, blowing smoke rings up towards the ceiling, and read me bits out of the books he was reading. Then, he would turn towards me with deliberation, and kiss me with his cool clean mouth, and touch me with the accuracy of a medical student, trying me out. One evening, he said, as we lay together on the narrow shelf, poised above the drop to the floor – If you come back tomorrow night, I'll make love to you properly.

It was a promise. Or, a threat. I cycled back to college, that night, once more elated, and my lips sore in the wind from kissing, knowing that I was at the point of no return. At last. All I had to do, was be there. All other decisions, manipulations, ploys, conditions, had been removed. By tomorrow, I would know. I did not tell Fenella, but went straight to my room to get a good night's sleep after reading a chapter of Heidegger. The darkness, once my light was out, sang with shapes and sounds, was full of rustles and creaks and red dancing patterns before my eyes, and phrases, promises – if you come back tomorrow night, I'll make love to you properly. Again, and again, and again, before I slept.

We got down to it straight away, having locked the door. Then, he had to unlock the door to pad in shirt-tails down the corridor to the lavatory, and I sat shivering on the bed, on the rough outer blanket, my knees to my chin. He came back, wearing his shirt and a condom, covering himself with his hands. We lay together on the outside of the bed, where last night the erotic words had been whispered, and struggled. I tried to relax into his toothpaste kisses, to feel the cool regularity of his breath in my mouth as his lips covered mine, and conjured phrases from Lawrence to my mind, forsaking Heidegger at this moment, forgetting Sartre. He was butting and poking at me with a painful, quick motion, and I did not know what to do.

– What's the matter?
– I've never done this before.
– Neither have I.
– I thought you had.
– I thought *you* had.
– Oh, God. Look, I'm sorry. Did that hurt?
– Go on, go ahead, it's okay.

The sudden tearing pain of it was enormous. I lay biting my lips, bound to silence, because if a porter should discover us the penalty was instant expulsion from the University, from life. He was suddenly limp, warm, inert. Liquid trickled between us, glueing us, warm and comfortable after the dry rip of that pain.

– Thanks. That was great.
– Thank *you*.

Did I love him? I lay, considering it, his weight covering me, his bony hips clashing with mine, the tension in him all gone, just for that time. Perhaps, probably, one could not help loving someone who so suddenly surrendered himself like this, who simply lay there, gasping with relief. I put my arms round him and wondered, how long we would lie there, and what would happen next. Eventually, he sat up, put on the light, sat on the edge of the bed, elbows on knees and the shrivelled rubber on his penis dangling. He took it off and threw it in the bin. I lay there, trying to remember – I have become a woman. We were both of us streaked and striped with blood, as if after a battle, and the sheets were marked, and I was surprised we had not made indelible bloodstains upon the floor, like the ones at Holyrood House, marking a historic event.

I said – Should we get cleaned up?

– I'll have to do something about those sheets. We can't let the bedder see them.

– I could wash them, if you like.

– Okay. Look, you use the basin first, if you like.

He began picking up our discarded clothes from the floor and sorting them into neat piles, his and hers. Oddly, I felt quite at ease with him, naked, even as I bent over the basin, breasts dangling, and tried to wash my soreness away. He washed briskly, in his turn, and zipped himself into his trousers as if after a pee, and slicked down his hair in the mirror. We dressed in silence, then he put on the Mahler.

I said – I'm terribly hungry.

So he bought me a curry; we went to the Taj Mahal, I walking gingerly, unused to my new discomfort, and felt blood leaking down my leg, and worried about it showing through my trousers, and sat edgily upon the velvet Indian chair, anxious about what might show there when I stood up. Nick ordered Chicken Vindalloo, that night. I had no idea what the various names meant, and so listened to his advice, chose what he chose, and sat sweating, my mouth burning and throat on fire, sipping as much water as I could get, while my cunt twitched with pain at every slight movement and the blood oozed out upon the velvet chair. But Nick smiled at me, with his beautiful white teeth, and I smiled back, grim with pride. That night, I cycled back to college poised above the bicycle seat, avoiding all contact, and wedged into my basket, trophy and prize, carried the bloody sheets, so that all traces might be washed away, in one of the anonymous college washing machines, some moment when nobody was around.

– I've done it, I've slept with Nick Ripley.

– Oh, Alice, you haven't.

Slept, I thought, was hardly a fit description for that short and violent action, after which we had got up so speedily. And Fenella was suddenly solicitous, even disapproving. I noticed, we no longer asked each other – are you in love? I was telling her – I am an adult, equal with you. She looked at me, at once loving and contrite, across a room in which books and clothing lay about, which I had had no time to put away. I had been proud of myself, and suddenly, now, I was sad.

– Oh, Al. What's happening to us?

It was she who said it, voicing my question of past weeks and months. What was happening to us? We were growing older, were about to graduate; were women, perhaps, not girls; we no longer leapt dizzily to greet each other down corridors, loving every minute; something had claimed us, slowed us, divided us from each other.

– I don't know. Are you happy?

– I don't know. Are you?

Once, it had gone without saying. She began picking up and folding my clothes, as if they were her own. I saw the chaos of my room, hardly inhabited since I had started spending my afternoons and evenings at Nick's, lying on my back listening to Mahler and him reading aloud.

– Next year. After a silence, she spoke decisively. Next, year, let's get a flat. Let's live in London, and share a flat. Shall we?

It was, that moment, as if everything had suddenly opened and flowered around me: my future. Layer upon layer, level upon level, each one becoming reality, and all flowering out from that centre, which was us, now. I could think of nothing better.

– Oh, yes! Let's! We can get jobs and we can be free! Oh, Fenella, what a fantastic idea!

We would have a salon. The literati and cognoscenti, as she put it, of London, would flock to our door. I would write, and she would get a brilliant job in publishing. We would have candlelit tables and bowls of flowers and wine. We would have lovers, friends, everything. We would have our degrees, our adulthood, our beauty, our fame: for what could fail, if we had each other? The morning was transformed, as mornings had been once, when we first met, when we first showed each other, what life could be like. Isn't life exciting? It was. I believed it, believed her; but cycled down to find my nihilist lover, all the same.

– Of course, death really is the only rational solution.

He lay full length, smoking a pipe, a new development which seemed

204

to lend weight to what he said. Thought – puff – word – puff – thought – puff puff, was how it went. I loved the smell of his pipe tobacco, but it could not be shared the way cigarettes could, was not lit by that desperate common sucking at a single match. I sat in the chair. The curtains were drawn, but summer evening and the slight wind pulled at them, so that flashes of light kept on assailing the room, in spite of him. The skull on the table watched us, and the air was full of particles of lit dust, dancing.

I said – I suppose so, yes.

– Listen to this. This man says—

But I, I was tired of the arguments in favour of death. I did not want to see him, flesh and bones and fresh pink lips and glinting brown eyes, dead; I wanted warmth, contact, pain if necessary, but life.

He read me another chunk, proving that life was absurd, arbitrary, that we were accidents, that the only free action was to choose death.

I said – I really should be doing some work, you know.

I could not, after all, write my mediaeval history paper on the death wish; nor quote Heidegger instead of Elizabeth on her parliaments.

– All right, go if you want.

– What about you?

– I'll be up all night for my anatomy paper. You could stay and test me if you like.

I could, as I had done before, sit there trying to keep my eyes open, questioning him, the heavy medical textbooks in front of me, hearing him list each bone in my body, each muscle, each nerve. I could, worse, hear him on pathology, until every twinge in me signalled disease and death. He would sit, on such occasions, staring at the blowing curtains, his eyes fixed and lips moving rapidly, the Latin words flowing out of him, as with my finger (with all its numbered bones and nerves) kept pace along the page. He had, it seemed, lost interest in my anatomy. I wondered, if that brief spasm of his inside my body, the muscular contraction people called the act of love, would recur; he showed no signs of wanting it, and I sat tensed, doubting my own ability. He had delivered me of my virginity, and I had freed him of his. Perhaps he had wanted to know, as a doctor, whether it all worked as the books said. But yet there remained with

me the memory of him all spread out over me and in me, all unconscious, with a smile of relaxation upon his lips and his fear, for the
moment, gone; there remained the echo of that thought, that perhaps,
then, I loved him; so perfectly, at that one moment, had he been
himself. We had been there together, in that pain and confusion, he
butting, pushing, I resisting, we had both been scared, lost for a
moment, and then united in some common relief. There was that.

– I think I'd better go. It's only three weeks to Finals, after all. If I
go now, I'll be back in time for Hall, and there'll be time to work
afterwards.

He said – I work better with you here, I think.

I looked at him. With him there, I did nothing. I had six history
papers to write, in three weeks time; my head was a jumble of dates,
edicts, scraps of mediaeval latin. I was afraid, of failing again, of being
cast out, of not reaching the haven of my 'salon' with Fenella; all of
this.

– I really think I'd better go.

– I want to make love to you. Passionately.

There was no resisting that: mediaeval history, dinner in hall, had no
chance. I let him draw me to him, felt his lips, his hands, the
insistence, suddenly of his body. He held me, very hard, as if to
demonstrate how necessary this was; his thin, long-fingered hands
upon my shoulders and at my waist. Something began in me, a slight,
slight flicker of desire. It was good to be wanted this much. His teeth
bared against mine, his tongue like a lizard's, in and out, and the
hard, pressing bulge of his penis. Down on the hard bed, quick in the
space between a passerby's footsteps and the rap on the door of a
porter, roughly in and out, in and out, till my new soreness raged
again, and his fingers hard and clinical, feeling, pressing, made me
want to close my whole self against him and wriggle away; in between
pathology and anatomy, in between Charles V and the Papacy, in the
narrow narrow space, in the channel that was left to us, the insistence
of it: come! I retreated, into some far corner of myself, blaming myself,
close to tears.

– What's the matter? You didn't enjoy it.

– I don't know.

206

I did know, but it was, then, unsayable. There were no words, no explanations. Feelings, the blind, dumb protest of the body, did not count. My mind was full of the accusations – 'frigid' 'professional virgin' 'cock-tease'; the words I heard all about me, used against women like me. Account for yourself. Explain it. Above all, enjoy it. Come!

– Well, I'll get on with revising, then. See you.

– See you.

I went. Down the stairs and along the corridor and out, into the evening sunlight, the outer world; across the courtyards of his college, passing men with gowns trailing from their shoulders, who eyed me curiously and did not speak; past the gates, past the guardians, past the watch towers, out into the street.

– Hello.

It was some minutes before I realised that the pad of footsteps just behind me meant that someone was trying to catch me up. I was pacing along quite blindly, my head down, forgetting my bicycle that was locked to the railings, not thinking where I was going; I was going somewhere, away, out, beyond, but did not know where, or why; it hardly mattered.

– Hello!

– Oh, hello.

– I haven't seen you for ages.

It was Finn, Finn Anderson. Standing there blushing (or hot) in the sunshine, staring at me, friendly, wondering what to say.

– No. No. I haven't been around much. I mean, I'm not in the school of architecture any more.

– You haven't been, for two years. It's different. It was nice, when you were there. Nice having women there, I mean, it seemed more normal.

– Oh. Yes.

– How are you?

I looked at him, and longed to run away. His squint into the sunshine meant perhaps that he would not be able to see me. And I did have my dark glasses.

– Not too bad.

– Finals coming up.

– Yes. I've masses of work still to do.

– So've I.

– But you go on for five years, don't you?

– Seven, altogether. A marathon. This is only stage one.

– Gosh. Like medics.

But unlike medics, in that he could stand in the street in the sunlight and talk like a human being.

He said – I wouldn't fancy being a medic. All those dead bodies to cut up.

– Yes! Although, they don't look so bad, soaked in formaldehyde, I've seen them.

I did not, though, want to talk about bodies, dead or alive.

– Hey.

– What?

– You wouldn't like to have a drink, would you? Have you got time?

– Well, I was on my way back to hall.

– Well, in that case, perhaps another—

– No, actually, I'd like to.

We walked along together, and turned into Rose Crescent, as if by common consent, leaving the close roar of traffic in the narrow street behind. A smell of meat and garlic came to us instantly; we both stopped, sniffed, looked at each other; I had not eaten all day, since breakfast with Fenella, and my stomach seemed to turn to water.

– Shall we have some?

– Spaghetti? Yes!

And all at once, I was with him, we were a couple, a man and a woman, entering a restaurant, being shown a table, sitting down one on each side of a white tablecloth, with knives and forks and glasses and a waiter for our order, and all the trappings, all the effects. I did not want this. I picked up the menu and stared at it.

I said – I'm going out with somebody, he's a medic, he's revising for his anatomy exam at the moment, I was just on my way back to college.

He said – Oh. I knew you were going out with someone, Andrew told me, he'd seen you around.

– Andrew Reid?

– Yes. He said he didn't much like the look of the person you were with.

– Oh. Well, I'm in love with him. I think I'll have spaghetti bolognese, and I'm paying for myself.

– Okay. Well, I'll have the same. Actually, I'm in love with somebody too. She's at the Tech.

– Oh.

We assessed each other, across the table. Both in love, therefore equal, therefore safe. I was at once relieved and disappointed; it might have been good to have been courted tonight and to have refused.

– She's an art student. But, tonight she's gone out with somebody else.

– Oh.

– So, there's no reason, is there, why we shouldn't have supper together? Seeing that we were both so hungry? I think I'd missed hall by now, anyway. I expect you would have, by the time you got back, waiting for the bus and everything.

– I had my – oh, my bike.

Chained to the railings at Caius, as I was not. The waiter poured wine into tumblers, and we drank. It seemed to rush through me to my empty stomach, and touch my sore, numbed genitals to life. I crossed my legs under the table and looked at Finn, and suddenly wanted to cry, looking at him as he sat there rolling his spaghetti ineffectually around his fork, dropping it all again, smiling at me, eyebrows raised in dismay at how difficult it was to eat.

– Look, try rolling it up against a spoon, it's much easier.

– Ah, okay. So it is.

Pleased with ourselves, we stuffed our mouths with spaghetti, and did not bother to speak to each other for some time. The tears which had pricked at my eyes rolled down in to my napkin and I wiped them away, and I did not know whether or not he had noticed, not for years.

So, we began to see each other, to eat meals, to go to films, to have coffee at odd moments when we met in the street. In between, as we reminded ourselves and each other, our love affairs, our real lives: in between my hours spent with Nick, still, in between the peaks of his love affair with the blonde art student at the Tech. It was a relaxation, always, to be with him. It did not matter, it seemed, what I said, what I wore, what I wanted to do; it was fine by him. In his acceptance of all that I said or did, I saw his admiration for what I was: so that it was like meeting Fenella all over again, like being welcomed. He wanted, as Fenella had, to hear all about me. He wanted to tell me all about himself, more than Fenella did. So, we talked. We talked hard, and listened, and spun stories between us, the stories of our lives; also of our parents, brothers, aunts, uncles, grandparents, pets, schools, friends. Unlike Fenella, who had envied my big family and begged me for more stories of it, he had a big family of his own, with as many stories. Sometimes, the stories could keep us going for hours, into the night, so that time passed in a flash, and suddenly it was ten-thirty and time for him to go. I sat in my chair and watched him put on his bicycle clips and heard him apologise about leaving me the coffee mugs to wash, and he was my brother, my friend. It was safe. I could keep him at arm's length, there, across the room, we could sit in chairs, opposite each other, and talk, and be equals. At ten-thirty I saw him off, to tramp with the other marching men out down the corridors of Girton, past the porter and into the night, to pick bicycles from the heaps of them thrown down, or to catch the bus. Only lovers stayed in after ten-thirty and were seen out, under cover of darkness, from downstairs windows, smuggled with kisses and choked laughter out of the way. He was not a lover: or I could not have talked to him, could not have been myself with him, in this way. There was, as I told Fenella, an essential difference, a line which could never be crossed.

– How are things going with Nick?

– Oh, fine. What about you and Deirdre?

– Fine, fine. I'm going out with her tomorrow. We're going to the jazz club do, in King Street. Should be good.

– Oh. Should be good. Well, hope you have a nice time.

– Thanks. I hope you and Nick have a nice time, too.

And so it went, all through our last term, right up until the end.

He saw us off to Paris, Fenella and me; stood at Victoria in the early

morning, waving, as we took our last trip together, from Cambridge
out into the world. We both had our hair up in beehives, lacquered
stiff from the party the night before, and we wore dark glasses and
carried slight bags of luggage, so as not to look like tourists; and Finn
was pale from sleeplessness and carried a rolled up copy of the
Guardian, to read when we had gone. We were all three full of coffee
and our heads heavy with the alcohol of the night before, our tongues
furred with the smoke.

Fenella said – Paris. By tonight, we shall be in Paris.

She leaned right back against the seat, and stuck her legs out in front
of her. She was on to the next stage, entirely there already; I envied
her her easy ability to leave. Jon had left for the States, a week ago; we
had said goodbye almost formally, at a party. The gravity of it:
farewell. And Fenella, reaching up just once to kiss him goodbye and
going off at once to dance with somebody else, taking once again her
small, resolute steps into the future.

Paris. I knew what it meant to her. To me, it was all new: the
delight was, that I was travelling with her, that we had our plan of a
shared flat to come back to, that the year was ours. We had our
degrees, and had arranged to do a postgraduate teaching diploma
(me) and a secretarial course (her), as being a poet and a publisher
seemed respectively hard to attain, just like that. Our parents had
insisted, on further qualifications. Finn had marched me round
London, only days before, to push me into one of the London University colleges. Evidently, arts degrees from Cambridge did not
instantly open the doors we had imagined; still, doors there were,
entrances all, and we would use them, typing, teaching, if need be, but
keeping our further plans alive.

Paris. And she in her turn marched me to the tall thin hotel in
which she had stayed with Elaine those years before, in which you
could still stay for ten francs, sharing a sagging bed, going down two
flights to the bog on the stairs where water rushed all night and the
floor was strewn with used paper and shit, and somebody coughed in
the small hours on the other side of a thin wall. We walked about
Paris, eating as little as possible, so that some days I felt my legs
would not carry me and each food shop made me salivate, and we

looked at it. Sacré Coeur and Montmartre, the Marais, Vert Galant were her places of pilgrimage. The left bank kept us busy for hours, days, as we looked at books along the Seine, searching for the forbidden ones, Pierre Louys or Genet, Henry Miller, de Sade. We sat in Notre Dame and prayed, that life might go on. We lit candles, overcome all at once with piety or the urge to propitiate. We sat on benches and on warmed stones beside the Seine, reading our erotica, glaring through dark glasses at any man that approached, we made sandwiches last all day, we counted out francs each morning like misers and wrote down what we had spent. Each night, we went to a restaurant in a dark little street near the Place Saint-Michel, and ate a bowl of spaghetti or a bowl of soup. At night, we sat up late, one on each side of the humpy bed, each clinging to the edge of the mattress for equilibrium, and wrote our diaries, smoking Gauloises, our hair coming down, neither telling the other what we wrote. On the other side of the thin partition, there was an old man coughing or brushing his teeth, or a couple making love. We noted everything, for the future. Each sound, each smell: the people we saw in cafés, that we encountered on the stairs, the men who followed us in the street, and everything we ate. Late, with diaries written and the light out and the racket from the street reaching us with the heat through half-open shutters, we lay each on the side of the bed, trying not to roll down into the middle, and slept. I woke to her hair spread out on the shared bolster pillow, its colour and texture so unlike my own that I studied it as something separate, something unknown. She would lie, spread out, spilling into my half of the bed, sleeping like a child. And I would get up, leaving her there, and go out into the early morning, dodge between the cars and mopeds, cross the street and go to a café and buy myself a large café-crème, and a croissant. It was the one thing I did alone, that I hid from her. When I got back, each morning, she was just waking, at nine or ten o'clock, and I would come in, full of my illicit breakfast, and we would start our day. Fed, full of warm coffee, with the crumbs of the croissant still there to be teased out from between my teeth, I could contemplate the long day of walking, looking, at buildings, pictures, people, cafés, shops, the day that would stretch on hungry until evening, when we allowed ourselves our frugal meal. For she was fully tuned to asceticism, it seemed, where I was weak; I watched her lose weight, her summer dresses grow looser on her, her cheeks pulled in beneath the cheekbones, as her hair grew blonder than ever in the summer sun, and never dared to tell her of my breakfasts, that kept me going, that secretly used my store of francs.

We were both of us staring into a cake-shop window, when we met Pierre. Gradually, patisseries had taken over from fine art. We had examined the paintings at the Jeu de Paume, the sculpture in the Louvre, and now, increasingly, we turned our attention to food. In the cooked food shops, artichoke hearts in aspic, chicken salad, whole chickens on spits, stuffed tomatoes, ratatouille; in the windows of restaurants, the menus, with the words – *Plat de Jour*, *potage bonne femme*, *roti de porc*, a whole pornography of taste; but above all, the patisseries. *Tarte aux pommes*, *chaussons de pommes*, *pain au chocolat*, *pain au raisin*, *coeurs d'Alsace*, *tarte aux mirabelles*, *tarte aux fraises*: the list, the variation, was endless. In the mornings, we watched the crisp stacked loaves being carried out, and stood to breathe in the hot smell of them that filled the street; at lunch time, there was the smell of the restaurants, garlic and juices of meat, wine poured sizzling over joints, the pink tender insides of the huge sides of beef; but in the afternoons, in the early evenings, it was the patisseries that drew us. The feeling of *crème patissière* between one's teeth, against one's palate; the bitter dark centre of *pain au chocolat* suddenly found; the pastry, that crumbled against one's lips, that was buttery, short, as English pastry never was, that made us want to taste it, again and again. Sometimes, we fled from the shops: sat by the Seine, smelling the river smells, facing away from the city, watching the barges, lighting another bitter cheap cigarette to keep away the thoughts of food, reading the salty passages of our books. Gradually, it seemed to me that Henry Miller was writing of food, not sex: of dark roasted meat, of wine sauces, of charcoal grilled steaks, raw at the centre, of a hunger more basic. We both read *Tropic of Cancer* and tried hard to thrill to it; but it seemed remote, curious, the stuff of an alien obsession, either because we were too hungry for basic fare or because we were female, I was never quite sure. And, Pierre Louys, whose *fin de siècle* titillations I enjoyed, was

213

surely writing about patisserie, not flesh.

Anyway, Pierre came up behind us both, as we gazed in at a particularly good patisserie one day in Montparnasse, one we often looked at because new stores of delicacies were always arriving in the window, to be laid out there fresh and tempting, even late in the day.

Fenella was saying – If you could choose anything – anything – what would you have?

– I don't know, I think the *tarte aux mireilles*, today, look, that one up there without a single slice taken out of it. I could eat the whole thing, actually, what about you?

– Look, she's just brought some more *chaussons de pommes*. They must have just been made, this afternoon.

– Oh, come on, surely we could just once—

– No. I've only got fifty francs left. And we want to stay here, don't we, we don't want to go home!

– Okay, yes, you're right.

I wondered when, if ever, I could confess to her that each morning, in secret, with increasing pleasure, I sat in a café with a steaming cup before me and actually bit into the horn of a fresh *croissant au beurre*? As the days went past and our supply of money shrank, it seemed more of a treachery.

– Can I offer you something?

He was just behind us; how long had he been there, listening to what we said? It seemed useless to deny our greed.

– Wouldn't you like a cake each?

It was as if he spoke to two little girls out of kindergarten. And he was, must be, at least forty. Why not?

We looked at each other; chances like this did not come every day.

Fenella said – I'll have a *chausson de pommes*, please.

I said – I think, a slice of the *tarte aux mireilles*.

Both of us knew, at that point, that we gave up *pain au chocolat, gateau au marrons, baba au rhum*. But the choice was made. He went in, followed by the two of us, paid, and carried out the slices, on thin paper, with great care.

He watched us eat: in the street, licking up each crumb, pursuing each grain from cheeks and chin, devouring rather than savouring, not speaking, each of us deep in our complicity of silence.

He said – I see you appreciate French food.

– Oh, yes.

– Are you on holiday here? Are you students? Are you sisters? Where are you staying?

They were questions that we had parried, refused, so many times, turning our backs on the importunate stares of men. But, eating his cakes, it seemed churlish not to reply.

– We're trying to stay in Paris as long as possible. We're students. We're at the Hotel du Cheval Blanc, Rue de la Huchette.

– Only we won't be able to stay there much longer, because we're running out of money.

– I don't suppose you – either of you – would be interested, would you, in the job of cook? Seeing as you enjoy food so much? I am looking for somebody to cook for me, you see. I had not thought of taking an English cook, there might be some risk involved, I thought, in that I might have to eat green jelly everyday, or, what is it called now, Spotted Dick. But seeing that you might need somewhere to live, and that you like food, I wondered—

Fenella and I looked at each other with our quick, calculating, shall we – shan't we glance. It summed up, arranged so many things. Yes or no? What do you think? Shall we risk it? Might as well. Without a word, before strangers, thus we asked each other and agreed upon plans of action; she with her head cocked a little on one side, I with a narrowing of the eyes or a quick nod, then she with a smile. Or, the other way round. In front of the man, now, we performed this rapid pantomime, and came to our conclusion.

– Okay, where do you live? You'll have to have both of us. We'll go and get our stuff from our hotel, shall we? Perhaps you could give us a hand.

He was a painter, he said, and the woman he had lived with for years had just moved out, leaving him with a broken heart and no food. He loved to eat, but had not the temperament for cooking. Cooking, he believed, required a certain temperament. He would explain later, what that meant. Meanwhile, we could have a bed each in his salon, and he would give each morning the money to do the

215

'courses' and we would cook for him and we would all eat together each evening, so that he would be free to spend the day in his studio. The rest of the time, we could do as we liked. There were only two things he could not stand: undercooked eggs, and tripes. Apart from, he was sure, many unmentionable *specialités anglaises*, which we would do well not to inflict on him.

We agreed.

– Food, Fenella. Just think breakfast, lunch, tea, supper. Food shopping every morning, buying just what we like! Isn't it wonderful!

– But, can you actually cook? I can only do eggs really, scrambled, boiled, poached, fried. And he doesn't like eggs all that much.

– I'm sure we could knock up something. I've seen my mother do omelettes. And roast meat's easy, all you do is put it in the oven. Anyway, if we get stuck, there are all those shops that sell ready-cooked things, we could get stuff there.

– He'd know. He'd know we hadn't made it.

– Does it matter? He gives us the money, we produce something to eat. That's all he wants, isn't it?

– French cooking's hells complicated. I wouldn't know how to begin.

– Maybe he's got some recipe books. We could have a go. If he's out in his studio all day, he won't know if we have to throw stuff away. Just as long as there's something on the table when he gets in.

We moved in. He, Pierre, slept on a shelf suspended above his salon, reached by a ladder, and we had sofas covered with cushions, down below. Beneath his bed, there was a small wash place, and next to it, the kitchen; so that everything effectively happened in one room: Fenella and I, wriggling into our clothes under cover of our nighties, as he made coffee, zipping himself into his trousers, scratching himself with one hand. Coffee was the one thing he must do himself, because we would ruin it; and when he had brought it carefully to place on a rickety table before us, the three of us would sit, half-dressed, our eyes full of sleep, and sip up the syrupy black brew he had made. His eyes upon us; but there were two of us, and besides, he was a painter, so perhaps he had an objective interest in looking at young women. He leaned over Fenella, reaching an ashtray. And she, with her blonde hair upon her shoulders, sat barefoot in a thin shift dress, warm with sleep. I thought – he will fall in love with Fenella. Of course. But he only yawned, having settled himself with cigarettes and ash-tray, and opened his copy of yesterday's *Le Monde*, excluding us as if we were children. No, he was too old to fall in love with Fenella. We could relax, perhaps; perhaps here, we were not only fed, but safe.

Our meals consisted of very many tomato salads and pieces of grilled steak, and finished with patisserie. Pierre picked and chewed and read *Le Monde* and occasionally got up to fetch the olive-oil bottle, and glanced at us, drank wine, said little. Fenella and I ate, as quickly as possible, as much as possible, glancing across at each other in amazement and congratulation; we were like stray cats, indoors after the days of hunger, daring to believe that it might last. Pierre picked his teeth and smoked, and we sat, elbows on the table, talking English to each other in subdued voices, and then got up together to remove the plates and wash up. Then Pierre would return to his studio for the afternoon, and we would loll behind closed shutters, play Brassens records, plan the next meal. It was a little like waiting for something to happen; the holidays went on, Paris was out there, outside the window and across the little courtyard downstairs, only now we hardly bothered to go out, now, like slave girls, we lay about and grew fat. Each morning, Pierre gave us money, and we went out briskly to buy: to queue at the butcher's and listen to women arguing, to wait at the boulangerie while the great new split loaves were carried out from the ovens at the back in the baker's arms, and to pick over lettuces, tomatoes, artichokes, apples, pears, at the fruit shop, crossing the road before we had to pass the Boucherie Chevaline with its horse's head over the door like a death mask and its slabs of dark red meat. We spent a long time choosing our cakes, but without the obsessive attention to detail of our hungry days; now, if a croissant or a tart were not perfect, there would always be another one tomorrow, another shop to try.

– You two are costing me a fortune. He grumbled at me, one evening, while Fenella was in the bath, which was shared with the White Russian woman across the landing. When we took baths, it was a long performance: you went in, introduced yourself each time to the

217

White Russian, who was eighty, listened to a lecture on Russian history as it had occurred to her family, ate a sweet from a jar on the ornate sideboard among the photographs, showed eventually by waving towels and soap that you wanted a bath, and were shown into the tiny bathroom, like a cupboard, where you sat in deep hot water with your feet propped up the wall to get your shoulders under water and heard the White Russian singing in her kitchen in a deep voice, through the wall. Fenella had gone off to do this, with her shampoo and a book and her knickers to wash, so I was alone with Pierre for a while.

    – You said you wanted us to cook for you.

    – Yes, but the best steak every day? I'm not a rich man.

I said – We could try something else, I suppose.

What could one eat? I thought of my mother, thinking up each day something different for us all to eat, every day for years and years and years.

    – We could do spaghetti.

    – All right, tomorrow do spaghetti. Only remember, pasta must be as the Italians say, *al dente*, or it is fit only to be thrown away.

    I hoped he had not noticed the signs of rich cream sauces that had curdled, gone into lumps, and been scraped away down the drain, the heavy grey pastry that we had buried at the bottom of the garbage bin, the carrots we had forgotten and burned, so that they had stuck to the pan.

He said – Fenella told me that you are a writer.

    – Oh. Yes.

    – What do you write?

    – Poems, mostly.

    – I would like to read your poems. But, would I understand them, in English? Also, what could they be, the poems of a young woman, a young English woman, I wonder? A young woman with no experience. You have many disadvantages.

I said – I know.

It was like an apology, and he took it as such.

    – So, we are both artists. I wonder, would you be interested to see my paintings?

218

– Oh, yes, I'd love to.

In fact, I was scared to, because of what I might see, because of what I might not understand. Modern art was terrifying, because one should understand, and comments had to be made. He looked at me sharply, hearing my insincerity perhaps.

– Do not be alarmed, it will not bite you.

Together we went down, across the narrow cobbled yard in the darkness, and up the ladder, one behind the other and my skirt blowing up, into the attic space above a garage that was his studio. He straightened, switched on lights. We were in a brilliant, white square of light that intensified the outer darkness. In the fierce light, he pulled paintings out from a stack against the wall and thrust them, one after the other, in front of me. I saw, splashes of paint, thrown upon the canvas: a random violence. The biggest painting, on the far wall, was a firework display of colour and energy, full of wild movements of the brush. In most of the others, there was a single long brush stroke, in space, in emptiness. It was as if a bird had dashed itself against glass, again and again. It was like a bloodstain, recurring. It was as if he came up here, day after day, and threw himself into some paroxysm, leaving over and again, this mark. I did not know what to say. I stood, and looked, respectful and silent as someone in a church who feels the atmosphere and does not know the responses. And he moved the paintings around with rough movements, suddenly turning one face to the wall, suddenly pulling out another, confronting me with it again.

There was nothing to say. I tried, and discarded, phrases in my mind, sentences constructed in polite French, questions, intelligent remarks. But he did not ask, did not even glance at me for a response. He rummaged through his paintings, sometimes muttering to himself so that I could not hear. At last, he presented me with a pure long stain, blood upon white, and I recoiled from it, so that he noticed. He came and stood beside me, his hand upon my shoulder holding me in place. His physical presence surprised and held me still. We both stared at the painting, and I felt his fingers tighten, close to the nape of my neck. I could not move, nor go, until I had said something.

– *C'est bien intéressant.*

219

He let go. He stacked all the paintings again, face to the wall, and the space between us existed once again, was possible. I turned to go, to descend the ladder and go back to normality and Fenella, clean from her bath.

– Attends. It's not for nothing I show you my paintings. This is myself, my life. I bring you here to show you, to ask you. You are an artist. Your friend, Fenella, she is ordinary, an ordinary girl. You are a poet. If you stay with me, you will be a great writer, you will see. Let her go home and you stay, stay with me in Paris, and together we will work, and you will be great, a great writer. That I promise.

He was close again, but no longer threatening; I looked back at him in amazement, that he should know so little about me and should yet offer me, quite suddenly, this new view of my life. It was absurd; it stirred and flattered me, but was yet absurd, unreal. He did not know of my life, my shared flat with Fenella, my friends, England, London, the realities that bounded me already.

– You are young. You have all your life, now. You can choose. To go back to England and be ordinary, too, to live a nice ordinary life, marry, have children, whatever you will, or to stay here with me and write. That is the choice, I see it clearly. You will not turn it down, you will not be stupid. That much I see of you. Now. You tell me tomorrow, please.

He held me hard against him in the courtyard, against the doorway, far down in the yellow light that fell from the White Russian's window, beneath the tall black buildings, the patch of sky. He was taller than me and very strong, and yet his kiss had none of the clutching urgency with which he had gripped me in front of his painting. Once he had me there, he relaxed, sure of himself. It was the first kiss I had had from a man, not a boy: I thought this, while he probed and tasted and withdrew, in his own time, leaving me with this sense, that there was a difference, complete and qualitative. He let go, and I looked at his long dark face in the yellow light, and saw that he was thoughtful, meditative now, as if he really was thinking about me.

– Tomorrow, we will go to the Louvre. I will show you, what is worth looking at. You will tell me that you will stay?

It was a question, now.

– I don't know. How can I? Anyway, you're old, you're forty, at least, aren't you, how can I possibly?

– Forty is not so old. As you will one day discover. And remember this: you will not get this chance often in life. Very quickly, for a woman, there comes the only choice, to be mediocre, a mediocrity, nothing. I have seen this happen. And what can you do in England? What care for art is there in England? Whereas here, in Paris, you will be at the centre, the centre of the world.

I said, in French – But my language, I write in English.

– Ah, that does not matter. It is not the language we use that matters. We can be bourgeois idiots in any language. No, if you stay here, it will be your soul that speaks, and your body, not your mind. You will find your true language, the language of you as a poet, that I promise you. If you return to England, never. Never.

I did not tell Fenella, that night, of the choice that had been put to me; she slept, across the room, her washed hair spun upon the pillow like that of a girl in a fairy tale, and she somehow unreachable, untouched, as I would never be. I could not understand why Pierre had not asked her to stay, not offered her, instead of me, the elixir: life and fame. Perhaps, because she was so far from being ordinary that he saw no danger for her there. Yet – your friend, Fenella, an ordinary girl, ordinary. I could not understand it, not of Fenella, not of my extraordinary, beautiful friend. Was it that I was a writer, was that it? I stood before the tiny mirror in the washing space, early in the morning, cleaned my teeth and looked at my face. It could be trans-figured, here, by love, sex, work, fame, all I ever wanted. Yet, I could no more stay here and live with Pierre, Fenella gone, than I could change my birth date, my ancestors, my whole inheritance of looks and abilities. He was wrong, had to be: it was not in me. Mediocre, a mediocrity, nothing. I have seen it happen. Very quickly, for a woman. His words, and the fear that came with hearing them, that it might be true, and the dream, then, the dream that I had had since I was six years old, be shown to be a lie.

We breakfasted off our sour black coffee and rolls, Pierre watching me. It was a hot, hot day. And this morning, we were to go, all three of

221

us, to the Louvre, to look at what was worth looking at; and today, I was to decide upon the pattern of the rest of my life.

Choose, said the magician: this way or that; love, poetry and exile or safety, friendship, home. Choose, because you are at the turning point; choose today, because tomorrow will be already the future. Choose, before the flower fades, before the fruit falls, before another minute passes; choose while the spell holds you. Or know that it is forever too late.

You see? You see how it goes?

Fenella said to me, at the end of the morning – I can't stand being shown round museums. Can you? Wasn't it ghastly? I thought we were never going to get away from him. God, what a morning. Look at this, not that, that is essential, this is great art, that is nothing, *cela ne vaut pas la peine*. Christ! Who does he think he is? I'm exhausted. Come on, let's run, before he comes back, and get ourselves some lunch.

We had trotted through the vast halls of the Louvre, to get away from Pierre, in the end. It had all been like eating too much cake: we were force-fed, suffering from indigestion. For we had a particular way of going round galleries and museums, Fenella and I did: it was, to leave each other at the entrance, arrange to meet in an hour or two at the exit, and in between, if we should meet at a particular painting or object, to behave as if we did not know each other, and pass on. Neither of us would have dreamed of commenting, let alone arguing about anything. But Pierre took each of us by the elbow and steered us towards his favourites, preventing us from pausing or even glancing in any other direction.

– Europe before the Renaissance was barbaric. It is not worth looking at anything earlier than the fifteenth century. In the Renaissance, the spirit of man freed itself from its chains. Chains of superstition and mediaeval bigotry. Mediaeval art was enslaved to superstition, you can see it.

And so, we marched past Giotto to get to Michelangelo, ignored the beautiful painted icons, the sorrowful Christs of the thirteenth, the robust sculpture of the twelfth century, the Madonnas with small adult Christs upright upon their knees, the pietas, the deaths of saints.

222

Fenella sulked, trailed behind, casting glances at what was forbidden, because barbaric. I strode beside Pierre, looking where I was told to look, trying hard.

I said at one point – What about Notre Dame?

–Notre Dame is a sacred cow. It is for the tourists. You can go, you can go and sigh in the holy darkness, soak in the atmosphere, all right, if you like. But do not expect me to go with you.

– But why, Pierre, why does it have to be either – or? Why can't you like both, the mediaeval and the Renaissance?

He glanced down at me: down, because he was taller, and because I was there to be instructed.

He said – Why? Why can the irrational and the rational not be reconciled? Why cannot barbarism and civilisation go hand in hand? Why not agree with both superstition and logic, chains and freedom, bigotry and intelligence, blind faith and rational discourse? Why? You ask me? Why cannot I like it all? Because, my dear, you have to choose. It is, as you put it, either, or. If you choose this – your lifeless religion, your sighing for nostalgia in Notre Dame – you choose everything that has enslaved man for centuries. The blind faith in something external, that must be propitiated, that has a supernatural power over his fate. No, if there is God, it is in here – here – inside. In the flesh, in the mind, in the stone, in the paint. That is why I bring you here, I show you, that you may understand.

– I see. Well, yes, if you put it like that, I suppose you are right.

– Of course. I have had time to think about these things. You, you are young, a young woman, you have nothing, nothing yet. But you will have, in time.

I walked along beside him and tried, that morning, to strip my mind of everything but the Renaissance: to glorify if I could the struggling form of rational man as Pierre described him, pushing his way out of the stone.

It was hard work; my legs ached and my neck stiffened with looking in the right direction, and I wanted to sit down, talk about something else, have a pee. And at last, I glimpsed Fenella beckoning me from another room – come quick, he's not looking – and I escaped.

She said to me, as we came out into the sunshine – Thank God for that.

I said – He'll be terribly hurt.

– So what, serve him right. Pompous idiot.

Then, I told her what Pierre had suggested. He says, you see, that if I stayed with him I'd become a great writer. That in England, I wouldn't have a hope.

– Al, you can't mean it! You can't have taken him seriously! Anyway, he's ancient, isn't he, he's quite repulsive, and you'd spend your entire time being dragged round museums being told what to look at. And, what to say, what to think, what to write, what to read.

– He's not as repulsive as all that. And, forty isn't old.

– But, his teeth, haven't you seen them? How can you?

I never told her, of kissing Pierre in the courtyard, of the curiously relaxing sense that he knew what he was doing, even if I did not.

– He could be right, though, about living in Paris. Look at Henry Miller and Durrell and all of them.

Fenella said – But London, Al, think of London. We're going to live there, and be free. We're going to have our salon, aren't we, and have all London at our feet?

– The literati and cognoscenti.

– Yes! And no-one's going to tell you which pictures to like and how to cook the dinner. A leetle bit too much salt, I think, Fé – né – lah, and, you English, you have but one use for the olive oil, and that, to oil your arse.

She imitated Pierre, and it was then that I understood how threatened she felt, by any thought of my departure from our plan. It was the first time I had seen that perhaps she needed me as I did her. And she mocked, scolded, ridiculed, pleaded, in order to get me back to her.

It was a relief. We swung along in step, laughing in the sunshine, laughing at Pierre and the Louvre and Art and men and the Renaissance and the French and olive oil in the food; suddenly freed into a light-hearted complicity with her, I felt I had only just escaped: young, free, female, English, philistine if need be, we marched along the right bank, up the Quai du Louvre, to find ourselves a café, shops, fun: whatever might be the antidote to gloomy palaces. We bought earrings and postcards, ice cream and coffee, we sat and roared with laughter at each other in the sun. Just up the street, there was the shop that sold rabbits and cockerels, canaries and white mice and geese in cages, so that our shouts of laughter were echoed by crows and clucks; everything that day seemed ridiculous, hilarious: exactly right. We walked on the hot cobbles, down by the thick green Seine, and watched men fishing and sleeping in the sun, and lovers gobbling each other up, and dogs stopping to piss only yards away from them, and past it all, past us and them, the slow coal-carrying barges going downstream. Behind us, above us, the traffic streams, the palaces; and we turned our backs, we threw sticks and pebbles into the river, and sat with our legs dangling, burning on the stone, and knew ourselves freed, free.

Fenella said – Well, where shall we go next?

– What d'you mean? We can't just not go back to Pierre's, can we? He must be wondering where we are. Anyway, all our stuff's there. And, what about money?

– Stop fussing! You sound just like my mother. Did you remember to say thankyou? We'll go back and get our stuff and say goodbye, and then we'll – oh, we could hire a car, go south, go anywhere. Anywhere. What do you think?

I thought of Pierre, and his sudden lapse last night into physical need, and the way that had made him human, and the choice he had shown me – this way, or that, with me or against me, bond or free. I thought of the slightly sickening feeling of him kissing me, as if I might gag or choke with it; and the longing I had had to relax into it, just for a minute, just for a while, just while nobody was looking and I was not to be held responsible: to let go.

– Alice!

– Yes, okay.

It was decided, already. Perhaps, even in the Louvre, or at breakfast (no, you cannot drink coffee with milk, that is for babies) or, even, last night (it will be your soul that speaks, your body, not your mind) it had been decided. Once and forever? For the time being, at least.

Fenella said – I've got the money he gave me for shopping today.

– We can't just—

225

– Can't we? Don't you think he owes it to us, for all those hours we've sat around with out mouths open listening to him laying down the law?

I did not, but dared not contradict her. We bought ice creams tall and bright as knickerbocker glories, in the next café, and planned our lives.

4

Smoke curled up every morning from the power station across the river, and the skies were grey, pink, blue, streaked with aeroplane trails, with smoke clouds, marked with sunsets like bonfires, black and pierced with stars. I leaned from our kitchen window often and looked out over the wet slate roofs, and fell in love with London. Everything – cats, pigeons, the washing drooping down there in the little squashed gardens – was there for us. It was all part of this decor: our freedom and squalor, our world.

– Another day. I leaned, looked, delighted in it, and Fenella, in her thick dressing gown against the cold, poured boiling milk on to coffee, pushed the mugs about on the table, stretched and yawned.

– Shut the window, Al! It's cold.

Yet nothing she said to me ever had the force of a complaint. We had never said it, but it was as if, once and for all, we had decided to accept each other, just as we were. I lived, with her, in a world in which everything I did was justified; and, as she accepted me, so I accepted her, her sudden disappearances and reappearances, evenings spent out with young men who simply collected her in their cars and drove away, rendezvous with people I had never heard of. We did not question each other: and the invisible lines, of privacy, of our own lives, held. We were, the two of us, accomplices in a larger plan than anything we had yet talked of; it had no name, then, no boundaries, no conditions, and yet, the rules were implicit. If I had had sisters, or if she had, perhaps we would have recognised it more readily, perhaps it would have seemed less remarkable. As it was, we lived then in a state of enchantment, in which, being together, we were able to be both strong and free: facing outwards into the world, full of enthusiasm to greet and conquer it, ready to take risks, with the safety behind us of each other, our shared two rooms, our front door, home. Yet, from our time in Paris, I knew there were limits, that I was to play at encounters yet not commit myself seriously elsewhere. There were rules, for I had nearly infringed them, I had nearly given in.

But then, one morning, it was Finn Anderson who sat at our breakfast table, drinking the coffee I had made, one weekend when Fenella was away; Finn who had come down from Scotland to sleep the night with me in the big bed in the next room, who had stood to wash at the sink while I boiled the kettle, who stood behind me in the little kitchen, doing up his shirt, while I leaned from the window, looking out on to my power station, my roofs. It was as sudden as that; and he sat there glinting in the sun like a cat that has been let in, and I made breakfast, and it was all normal, usual, as if expected, it was what had happened next. Only he and I, we had not kept one to each side of the invisible fine line down the middle of the bed that had separated me and Fenella, but had rolled together, doing what men and women had to do, at some point, if the story were to go on at all. We had walked, all evening and into the night, down the King's Road and along to the edge of the river, up over Putney Bridge, along the banks, and had talked, and talked, until finally it was dawn, and we were tired, and the locked door on the empty street was there to be unlocked, and the stairs to be climbed, and the bed to be rolled upon, and love to be made, before rest, before sleep. That was how it had been. And now, there I was, in this new landscape with my old friend, moved on into something entirely new on account of what had not, surely, been a decision, the night before. We were shy with each other, uncertain, loving, relieved, appalled. It had been, rather than pleasure or pain, like a sigh of relief. We had talked and walked to our standstill, to our falling down together, and he had come into me with a groan, and we had both fallen asleep, I some time after him, and the strange unfamiliar weight of him was there in the morning, and, waking, I missed Fenella; and from then on, it seemed, everything was changed.

I told her, when she returned. She had been for a weekend's sailing with a young man of Catholic upbringing who would neck passionately with her until eleven at night and then go to his bed. Her glance, upon the doorstep, told me that all her efforts had done nothing to change this situation, that he was still impossibly pure. And I told her, that I had slept with Finn, in her bed; almost, I did not say it, by mistake.

– Oh, Al.

Again, her tone of condolence: of my mistakes? I could not tell. Something saddened in her, when I did not live up to her expectations. Her hopes of me dropped again. Sleeping with Finn Anderson was not, evidently, what she had had in mind for me.

– Are you in love?

– I don't know.

For he, he was in love with me. I saw it, and it terrified and flattered me, it was what I had waited for and what I did not want. I saw it in his glance and felt it in the way he touched me: and I had wanted him at arm's length from me, across a room, talking, joking, being there, but not this close, not warm and wet up against me, no. But we walked, in the day time, with our arms around each other now. We sat in pubs and gazed at each other, when once we would have teased, told stories, read books. Yet, it was a relief: as if at last a question had been answered, something restless settled, an anxiety calmed. He was my friend. I was safe with him. He loved me. So, everything, against all expectations, would be all right.

Fenella said it – I know, you're bound to get married, now.

– Married? Oh, I don't suppose so.

But the word, the image, lingered. Married and therefore safe, married and therefore not alone, not lost, not wondering, not making things up from day to day; married and so predictable, married and so real. Married, paired, twinned: the great gulfs bridged, the uncertainties silenced. Yes, I thought, perhaps we will get married. Not yet, but one day. One day, later in another life.

It surprised me, how once one had said that it would happen, it happened, after that. The simple fact of attachment, of friendship, of

228

this light, slight fleshly bond, taken up, emphasised, talked about, planned, made public. Soon, before we had got used to the idea, there was the announcement in the newspaper, and there were my parents talking to his parents, there were long-distance telephone calls, lists, plans, preparations: a ring, a date, a service, all of it, quite suddenly applied to us. It seemed remarkably easy, to get married. All you had to do was mention it, and everybody else did the rest. Suddenly, all was changed. My shared flat with Fenella, our life in London, was to come this abruptly to an end; my job, to which I was entitled after a year of teacher training, would be given to somebody else. I would move back to Cambridge, to be with Finn as he did his final years at the school of architecture. I would be Mrs. I would be a wife. I might even have children. Everything, everything would be changed.

Before our wedding, I had a recurrent dream. I was approaching a church, in the dream, and I was moving as if by clockwork: I was to go into the church and be married to somebody, a stranger. I could not ask, or guess, who the stranger was. I came up the aisle, approaching the unknown man, my bridegroom. Suddenly, in the congregation, I saw Finn; his blond head, his smile, yet his glance towards me inscrutable. Finn! I called out to him, my friend and colleague, to help me, to save me from this inevitability. But he sat there, smiled at me but did not move. I had to go on, on with it: but awoke. And each time, dreaming this, there was the terror, of my own powerlessness: there was no turning back.

And there is none: not unless a stranger comes in and calls out from the back of the church, as in Jane Eyre – stop! Thereby reversing the processes, turning back the story, saying, this will not go on. Stop! But nobody told us to stop. The questions were answered, promises given, vows made, rings exchanged: and we looked at each other, and meant it, and if there had been any margin of doubt in me, there was no more, for I blocked it out, that day. If there had been a small voice whispering of other things, I no longer heard it. I looked at Finn and no longer wondered what inner voices he heard, because all was overt now, all was planned, deliberate, made public, there was no more room for doubt. It was like launching out to sea with someone, and a crowd upon the shore, waving, cheering, certain that you must go; it is

229

no time, then to wonder if your companion can sail, or swim. I see us, launched, and the multitudes (my relations, his, our friends from Cambridge, Fenella in gold silk my bridesmaid, swigging champagne) seeing us off, growing smaller and smaller on a distant shore, until the shore becomes so remote that we turn our faces in the direction we are going, which is quite unknown, and face, deliberate, daring, into the wind. The feet of water between the shore and the small boat becomes yards, the depths become immeasurable. It is too late to look back, even. I feel relieved that it is he, my friend, who is there, and not the stranger of my fears and dreams, not the 'husband' against whose word there would be no redress. He is another human being, recognisable: pale-faced, today, perhaps daunted, as I am, perhaps scared. We are in it together. For ever? I do not know what that means.

He asked me to marry him, yes, it was that way round, in a pub, as I remember it; I tipped my chair and moved my half of bitter around in a pool of wet upon the table, and from the odd sensation that his question gave me, concluded that I would say, yes. Yes, I will have another half of bitter, go to the pictures with you, go to bed with you, marry you. It was easy to say. Yes made things move on, gave life a glow of colour, made people's eyes blaze as they looked at you; yes was what came naturally, what moved with the flow. Yes, I said, frequently (like Molly Bloom, and sanctioned by her) yes, I will, yes. It was simple. He asked me – would you like to marry me? And I said – yes. We ordered another pint each, and decided to buy a stripped pine table we had seen outside a junk shop that morning. We paid cash, and carried the table along with us for a while, down the pavement, and then realised that we would have to find somewhere to put it, somewhere to live. I would have liked to have sat down with him then and there and begun living: one on each side of a table, out on the pavement, there on the street. But the table led to telling people, to announcements, to plans. You cannot sit there in the street outside a junk shop and begin to share your life. You cannot even be married sitting in a pub, in between the halves of bitter. We did not know what we had started: but other people did.

– Getting married? When, where, and, let's see the ring. Where will you live, eat, sleep, work; what will you live off, how will you manage, what will you do? All the questions that nobody bothers to ask you, otherwise. You have gone public; you are public knowledge, shameless as if you walked skin-naked, labelled and shockingly visible as Adam and Eve. I had to become a wife, and he, my husband, hus-band, strange word, he my white-skinned fragile youthful friend with spots still and a frequent hangover and a dreaming, somnambulant air: labelled now, with obligations and a role to play. Husband, provider, father even. I thought, even then, he did not look ready. I wanted, to spare him, to let him off. But I, I would dissemble and strain to be a wife, a wife for life, a woman, whatever that was, one half of a couple, the couple that was man and wife, legal, inevitable, indissoluble, all that.

We had been married about a month, when I sat in the bath in our small upper-floor flat, and wept. We had had our honeymoon, and a bottle of champagne flat for breakfast, and a lot of rather sore fucking, because we thought that was what we had to do, and we had talked, at last, over bottles of Guinness, over sandwiches, on long cold walks along beaches, and crouched close to the fire at night. We were children, going through initiations: cast out, with suddenly nobody there to tell us what to do. And like children, we huddled close, telling each other stories. In the loneliness, against the outer darkness, we held each other close; and in the holding, reached out for our unknown selves, striving to discover what we were. The blood and the pain of rituals: he cutting himself shaving, cursing in front of the bathroom mirror, coming out dotted with cotton wool, I bleeding in the bed, bleeding from a period, seeing his alarm, stuffing myself with tampons in the bathroom, out of sight. What we did not know about each other: stains upon sheets, marks upon cotton, white surfaces dotted and flecked and hastily hidden, hastily stuffed away: what men did not know about women, boys about girls, all this, to be found out and suffered and somehow come to grips with: cystitis, the pain of peeing, the shame of sex not being pleasure, all we had been told coming up sharp and ugly against all that we really were, and the shame of confessing it, the words that did not exist yet and the words that would not do.

231

I sat in the bath, in our new flat, our first home, and poured water in up to my chin where I sat with my knees up in front of me, self-protective, and cried. I did not know, could not say, why. Finn came in; after knocking. He sat on the edge of the bath, his face all worried young exhausted concern. What is the matter with you? Why are you not well? Why is it my fault? What on earth should I do? And I could not tell him, but cried, adding to the bathwater, enjoying at least my luxury of tears.

– I'll make you a cup of tea. And, would you like a boiled egg?

He went, to the kitchen, to be busy. I would come out, fragile as a new wife, and sip tea, and tap open my egg with a small spoon, and be cossetted. I would enter a universe delicate with shifting meanings, with shed and unshed tears, with apologies, endearments; I would be wrapped, cherished. But meanwhile, hunched in the bath, I cried to myself as I heard him moving in the kitchen – oh, I don't want to be married, I don't want to be married at all. He could not hear, so it was all right; but I heard, I knew, I had said it. I was pregnant already, married, totally changed, and there was no going back: yet somewhere inside me still there was my old self, the one I recognised, before this crying, depending, tea-sipping, egg-tapping began. I did not know what to do with her: she seemed less easy to relegate than the tweed-clad hardworking schoolgirl I had shut away in my cupboard at Girton, she was noisier, older, less willing to fit in. But, if I ignored her, perhaps she would go away?

If you go back to England, you will never be a writer, never. You will become mediocre. It was like a curse that he had put on me, that night in the white lit studio in Paris: a malediction. Not that I thought about it. For, being married, one had to put away childish things: dreams, hopes, plans for future careers as one put away old diaries, old friends. Suddenly everybody we knew was in couples, inviting each other to dinner. I was back in Cambridge, but a different city this time, one made up of couples and dinners, babies, men at work. Poetry was not part of this day-to-day, would perhaps never be again. It was, as Pierre had said, a case of either–or. You had to choose, and I had chosen; though there was the strong sense of something having chosen

me.
- Finn. Are you awake?
- I wasn't. But I am now.
- I can't sleep.
- Well, do you have to wake me up to tell me that?
- I feel lonely.
- Well, I'm here.

His arms went around me, he held me hard and went down again into the depths of sleep like somebody drowning, pulling me with him. But still I lay awake. Night after night, and staring up at the ceiling, while he lay so heavily asleep beside me and sighed and snored sometimes, and turned roughly, pulling the bedclothes off. I was not used yet to sleeping with somebody else in this way: with no boundaries, no demarcations. The bed was shared, the room was shared, the flat was shared, everything belonged to both of us, there was no separateness any more. I had my own clothes and my typewriter and my washing things, but everything else, plates, cups, sheets, books, letters, friends, past, present, we seemed to share. There was no corner, no margin: no gap, allowed.

- Finn!
- Oh, look, for God's sake, can we try to get some sleep?

So it went, for years. I waking, he sleeping; I talking, he protesting; I kicking free, he with his arm around me holding me down.

There is also another picture. In which, young and resilient and good friends after all, we laugh with each other and sit at tables eating meals and smiling at each other and talking, always talking. There are the moments of sheer surprise in such pleasure, as we learn the ways of each other's bodies, release them into delight.

- It's good, isn't it?
- Amazing.

All this. And, gradually, the space that was there, once, which had not been filled, not as I took my marriage vows (only unto thee, forsaking all other, so long as we both shall live) not as we set off on our honeymoon, not when I learned of my pregnancy, not even when we pleased each other most, was not evident any more, had perhaps never existed. We were a couple. Our house was open, as you said, our

233

friends came in couples, I cooked huge meals, great bubbling pots of stew, pies, home-made bread, and the opened bottles, and wine flowed, and with it, hospitality, ease, the outward sign of the abundance we had, with each other, together, after all. We had done it. Got married, stayed married, become what we were supposed to be. We lived in this house of fertility, of richness. And if there was one small locked door in that house, cobwebs hiding it now, and the key lost somewhere, forgotten; nobody need know. We could forget it, even though we passed it sometimes, and a glance between us told us that it was there. The attic room. The door behind which something is locked away, something is hidden; the room to which, in the fairy story, the girl goes to prick her finger and discover chaos. Sensibly, perhaps, I did not go near it, for a long time. We are told, we are forewarned, of the dangers that turning a forbidden key may bring. All the stories are at our disposal, after all.

Fenella was one of our first and most frequent visitors, and examined me when she came with a loving, exacting stare. What had become of me? What was marriage? How did it work? She sat at our table and drank our coffee out of our mugs, and looked around her at our flat, our life; and she smiled at me very maternally, and unpacked the expensive, delicious things from London she had brought – wine, avocados, Oxford marmalade, a new book – and settled in with a deep sigh of satisfaction to spend her weekend with us. We were at once her old friends and a marriage on show. We toasted her in her own wine, and talked. We said, we. We do, we think, we did this last week. Fenella said, I. But was wistful, perhaps, and envious. When Finn was out of the room, she turned her head just a fraction, to glance at me, rapid, enquiring – and you, Al, what about you? But there was no language for this, any more, for my saying, I, I feel, I think, I know. I, would have been treachery. To we, to what we had made, with difficulty sometimes and sometimes with ease and delight. I became, to her, a married woman. She wrote her letters to me – Mrs Finn Anderson. And in our house, she was circumspect, a visitor; sitting there with her legs crossed, a little as if she were interviewing us, and smiling, her head on one side, her shining bun of hair pinned high. She was nyloned, lipsticked, elegant, straight from a London publishing house where she now rang up authors to invite them to dinner. Some weekends, she drove up to Scotland with young men in fast cars; others, it was the Isle of Wight and Cowes. She smoked still, holding her cigarette a little away from her as if she disliked it, and then taking one more long sensuous puff. She was slimmer, older, smarter, she was successful, in the terms she had chosen for herself, she was my friend, and I ached at the distance between us; but there it was, I was married, she was not, it was how life was.

Her curious glance said – Are you in love? But she no longer spoke it. We were grown-up now, playing our roles, absorbed in them, making them real.

– Fenella, we'd like you to be the first person to know. Wouldn't we, love? We're having a baby.

– Oh, Al, oh, Finn, how wonderful, what marvellous news. When? She did not say: already? Or: what can have possessed you? No more did anybody else. Having babies was the next step on from being married, it was what everybody was doing, it needed no justification. I rushed about with her, buying maternity dresses, choosing colours, longing to buy things for the baby too. Finn sat at home at his drawing board, smoking, preparing for his exams; there was nothing for fathers to rush out and buy, there was nothing he could do. Inside me, his child grew and grew, quite arbitrarily, a seed becoming a person, and moved, kicked, pushed at the walls of flesh, felt something give way, perhaps, that should not have, and fell, fell away, fell out, fell dying into the harsh world. Blood stained our carpet, our floor, where I had paced, howling. Fenella was gone, back into her London world, where things were under control. And he was there, he was the person in charge, the one who waited however outside the doors of the hospital to hear what, who had to scrub up the blood.

Afterwards, there was a white silence, an emptiness between us. I lay in a room and looked out on apple trees, and felt summer rush past me, leaving me behind. Nothing was as it seemed, nothing. But the hand stretched out to me, the hand I held till my own knuckles were taut, the hand that did not withdraw, was his. I could hardly see his face, for faces had become blurs, voices indistinguishable. I did not know if I were ill, or perhaps dying, or perhaps saved: anything was possible. I was on an island, and there was Finn with me, marooned, and the white glassy sea stretched forever right up to the horizon where it met the sky, with no line, no division, none at all.

Babies, afterwards, were everywhere, in prams, outside shops, inside shops, on buses, babies smiling, babies crying, the soft hands the faces of babies, babies under the summer sun. I walked among them carefully, picking my way, being nice to them, the babies of my friends, trying not to scare them with my snarl of the walking wounded. Babies, result of sexual intercourse, between man and woman, the outward and visible signs of love. Babies with the right numbers of arms and legs, babies that worked. No sign anywhere that any of them had come slithering out filthy on a tide of blood. No, the world was full of nice, clean, tidy, washed, plump babies. Sometimes, I had to leave the room: or the shop, bus, train, park, and hide from them. They came to dinner, and were left in our empty bedroom, packed up tight in their carry cots among the coats. They were in pubs, at parties; yelling sometimes, their fists waving in among the people making love, drinking, having rows. They bobbed up, smiling, chuckling, wailing, wherever I was, so that that year the population was doubling, tripling, it was a bumper year, a surprise crop, a bonanza, babies galore and still coming, look, out of these fat women, these bellies, these fertile splitting cunts, still more.

But Finn and I, we did not have a baby. We had a gap, a hole, a blank. We had something unmentionable. People coughed and looked away and apologised when our blank appeared. What a lovely   .
Aren't you lucky, clever, proud, to have such a   . Who's a lovely   then? My belly had swelled and somebody had kicked about inside it, enjoying him or herself, and then something had happened; stop, somebody had cried, you cannot go on; and there it did stop. So there was no cause for congratulation, or commiseration, there was nothing you could even mention (such a shame about poor blank) nothing you could call by name, and so rescue, bury, mourn, have.

A woman I knew a little came down the street towards me one day as I wheeled my blank before me, and greeted me with her jolly smile and wave, and said outright – How bloody about your miscarriage, I heard you'd had one, what rotten luck.

She passed on, to her shopping, but I stopped in the street and cried. She had said it, she had named it, she had spoken out loud and in broad daylight the words that described what had happened to Finn and me, and our blank was defined, called something, was rotten luck. I went on, from that moment, my tears drying quickly in the summer wind, and the space that had swelled in front of me, invisibly getting in my way, began to shrink and diminish, until I was almost a normal size again.

Finn said – What would you like to do? Shall we try and have another one?

I did not know. How could one try, for what happened naturally to everybody without the slightest effort? How, make an effort, for what was at one moment air, inconsequential, and the next moment, growing flesh? I saw us trying hard, grinding our bodies together with the application of workmen, making babies. Was what we had between us too slight, too frail; would the fragility of our bridge not stand the weight? There was him, now, separate, a separate person, and there was me. Our separate, different bodies, with their different histories, temperaments, tastes; all that we had inherited, to make us different, so that how could we be merged and let this alchemy, this deep magic, take place? I did not know, how babies were made; and neither, I thought, did he. And yet there they were, all around us, more of them each minute, so that the whole world, surely, was made of nappies and bottles and bibs and cots and pins; the impedimenta of babies, filling all available space. Babies grasping, yelling, demanding, growing, pushing the rest of us out. Babies sucking, shitting, peeing. Babies' hands curled against mothers' breasts. The skin, the hair, the touch, the smell, of babies. There was no getting away from it, that even if you could not, you had to pretend you could.

I said to him – I think we'll have to, don't you?

When our daughter was born, there was, as you know, a revolution going on far away and getting nearer, there was the sound of it that reached me dimly in the hospital: where I lay and felt the child slip

237

from me like a fish, so easily, where I waited to see what happened next. The sunlight was brilliant outside, an early summer, green May on the banks of the Cam, and in here, in the narrow ward, I awoke to a new day: that of my child's existence in the world. Finn came in and said, there is a revolution in France: and there was our daughter, alive after all, whole, unscathed, leader of revolutions, newest person in the world. He had been asleep, Finn had; sleeping through the birth, after nights of exhaustion; unconscious as the thousands took to the streets. We were locked in, together, with this new fact, of our child: behind blinds, through curtains, we peered out into the street. What was going on there, out in the streets, who was marching past, who of our generation was in it, of it; stones in hand, arms flung up to protect faces? Who went to prison, who made speeches and talked of a new era, who was hurt, who got away free? We lifted the blind and glanced out through the narrow slot; from in here where everything was white, clean, scrubbed, disinfected, quiet, suitable for babies. We passed the tiny child one to the other, in awe, having first washed our hands. She looked at us solemnly with narrow violet eyes. It was like living with a very old woman, who knows but is not saying. And we waited, for her descent into real babyhood, fatness, noise, normality. Her hands were the delicate waving antennae of the frailest of the human race; her glance was old. She was an old bush woman in the desert, telling stories in the secret silence of her own mind; she was a space traveller, who sees and measures but cannot explain. We lived with her as if in a temple, waiting on her. And close to us, the radios blared, newspapers piled up, television news showed us people running, talking, falling flat. Something was changing forever, but outside, still far away. We waited for it, too, to see if it would reach us, the wave coming right up the beach; but it turned, retreated, and we were not swept away.

We had done it, we had become parents; and the world had changed in the night. Now, we woke often, went to see if she was breathing, began glancing at each other with anxiety, pride and care; checked temperatures, warmed bottles, propped ourselves awake for night-time feeds. We did not go out. Life, new life, this fragile, vulnerable thing, kept us watching and waking. It was like having a flame to keep alight; and passing it to and fro, wearied as runners long-distance carrying fire through darkness. And, asking myself, why then did we both believe that life was this tentative, this frail: I come back to all that had made us, back in the days when the bombs fell and our parents snatched us up, tense with their own anxiety so that we knew at once that nothing was easy, nothing turned out right. I do not know. It is one strand, perhaps of many. Life, ours, hers, that passionate, precious thing, that flame, that one right to be fought for, that absolute priority, the one command: live!

– She's lovely. But isn't she thin? Aren't you scared, of looking after something so small?

As a child, I had looked after tadpoles, newts, baby frogs, birds found with broken wings in the undergrowth, stray kittens, all with varying success; but nobody had ever told me this often how difficult it was.

– She was premature. She's putting on weight.

True, her skeletal frame was filling gradually, so that before my eyes I watched a human being made, a bone sculpture covered a little each day with living clay. Her hands became less transparent, her eyes less huge in her face, her ribs invisible, her other-world stare less strange. But she was not the chubby baby the world expected, that was out there in its millions, in prams, replete and fat. She was from some other place, of starvation, of need. She was yellow but turning pink, ancient but becoming young, dying but coming to life, emaciated but fattening, solidifying; this I saw, Finn saw, happening each day; but still people leaned, looked, exclaimed with horror, pitied us, admired us, could not stand it, not the unadorned human form.

I took her to the doctor, months after the point of anxiety had passed, and the clinics had despatched us into normal life. I had this small female creature to look after, and something was wrong, and I wanted to know what it was. The doctor, a young man with a long list of university patients, students with problems, graduate wives, took time, was patient; I, as patient, impatiently wanted to know.

He said – What's the trouble?

– I don't know. Could you examine her, please?

– All right. But, is anything particular the matter? She seems to be putting on weight fine, growing all right, she looks well?

He undressed her, gently feeling her all over. She was pink, by now, really quite human, quite believable. She gurgled at him and did not mind being touched all over, and I stood and watched in my impatience, my hands tense.

– She seems fine. What are you worried about?

– Well, I don't know, perhaps it's me. Could you just give me a check-up, too? I wanted all at once to lie there, and be probed, examined, said to be fine.

– If you like. Are you not feeling well?

– It's not exactly that. I just have a sense that something's wrong. I don't know, I might have something. If it's not her—

I was glad that it was not her, not my pink real growing baby; relieved that it must be me. Cancer, probably. I lay back, awaiting verdicts. It was good to lie there, and be seen, and know that in a minute I would know.

– You're fine, too. Perhaps a little anaemic. I'll give you some pills for that. But, in general, you feel you could do with a little help, eh?

– Yes. Help, yes, I think so.

A mother, to hold me in her arms, to soothe me to sleep. I wanted to be a baby. I wanted to start again. Something like that.

He gave me an address, and made notes himself, and a phone call. At that time, people were going in droves to analysts, psychotherapists; it was a moment for digging up the past and breaking it open and for going over relics with fine brushes, delicate tools, handling them with care. Several of our friends were beginning to talk about 'my shrink'. My shrink says, my shrink thinks, sorry, I have to blow, I'm seeing my shrink this afternoon. Suddenly, we met each other in a glare of sibling rivalry, competing. Neuroses like hothouse blooms, and we carried them proudly about with us all day. But this is to look from the outside; inside, the pain, the need, the sense of insufficiency; so that we shared, also, a vulnerability. Life was not all right. Life was not as it had appeared, it was not enough to fling oneself into it and swim with the tide, forgetting what had gone before. It was a matter of remembering, unearthing, painfully coming to the light of day. We were adult; we were parents; in order to do it at all, we had to know. To be reborn ourselves, so that we could bring up our children; not to be born this time in the middle of a war with parents who might be killed any minute, and the times against us, but to emerge into safety, a world of ease.

I sat in a black leather chair, facing the wall, early in the morning, late in that year, my throat full of a lump of terror, and did not know where to begin. This part you know. She sat behind me, my new mother, so that I could not look at her. She had a soothing voice that lulled me, but what she said was incomprehensible. I wanted her to hold me to her bosom, and simply sing. But she spoke, and asked me, and I began to speak, until everything that I said seemed to have equal weight and equal meaning. I presented it all to her, my life, a helping a day, and she examined it, analysed it, handed it back to me. I brought her my dreams as a good dog retrieves what's thrown for it; and she filleted them for me neat as a kipper, and I had them back. And we were not alone. Behind us, somewhere in the room, floating between the bookshelves, breathing in the airless spaces and looking over our shoulders, was Freud. Freud says, Freud would say, Freud thinks, according to Freud. (Just wait till your father gets home, then you'll get what for.) I wanted to summon him out: come on, I know you're in there! Like God the father, skulking among the columns. But he only whispered in his hoarse German and nudged her, and had his eyes on me, and would not let me go.

She said – Freud would say, you are trying to be the man and the woman, both at once. It is a matter for you of becoming the real woman. This may take some time.

I believed her. I heaved my bicycle against her fence each day, and rang her bell and went up her stairs with my heart heavy as doom, to sit for another hour in the black chair and confront this fact. It might take me forever, to become a woman. It might be impossible. There was the whole of my past, all my childhood, all my relationships and every dream I had ever had, to go through first. I cycled through the snow, home again in the mean hours before breakfast, to feed my child and drink coffee with my husband and talk to my friends and do the mounds of washing and washing up that awaited me and cook food and invite couples and finally go to bed; all the time knowing that in spite of appearances, I was evidently not really a woman. Was it

241

worth it? Was the whole assault course worth while? She assured me that it was. Being a woman was not self-evident; like having babies, so that I wondered how on earth others managed it, and had time to do other things as well. It was like reading an Elizabeth David recipe in *French Country Cooking* (which I did) and dashing around town hunting for all the ingredients (fresh black pepper, freshly ground, always, and fresh basil always, and ask your butcher to cut the meat this way) and spending the whole day cooking, and then finding that the whole dish tasted like English stew anyway, and you had fooled nobody. I came in exhausted, and unloaded the ingredients on to the kitchen table, and read my recipe book, sitting on a high stool in my long skirt, with the flies buzzing or the snow falling, according to the season, and poured in red wine to make a marinade, added all the right herbs, tasted, stirred, simmered, scalded, to get it right. And my bread rose, higher each time, the dough more elastic, the feel of it so right to the hand as I kneaded, the smell of it baking filling my kitchen, so that friends poured in, doesn't it smell wonderful in here, your house always smells so good; and my child began to look like everyone else's, my marriage better than everyone else's, so that surely, surely, I was nearly there? But Freud lurked in the corners, muttering. I did not tell Finn, for she had told me that I would undo the good of my therapy, if I talked to anyone else about it. I kept the secret, like masturbation, like poetry, like magic. I came in to breakfast and looked across at Finn in increasing despair; he poured me coffee, and sighed more often, and said that, really, he had to be off to work. And, if it was not doing me any good—

I said, only – She says, it gets worse before it gets better. You have to go down into the neurosis.

I saw myself, naked and clutching a small towel, lowering myself like an inititate into a black and stinking bath of some sort, in order to come out purged. Finn looked gloomy. It was five pounds an hour, and he breakfasted alone each day, and saw me come in, cold from cycling, chilled from what I now knew.

He said – Are you sure you do?

– Well, Freud says, apparently— But he was gone.

My dreams, crowning the effort I made, flourished and multiplied, so that I could carry a fresh crop of them to her each morning, proud of myself and of the insights they brought. Increasingly, I dreamed of trains, horses, towers, volcanoes, houses, aeroplanes launching. I was proud of the accuracy of my symbolism; learning a new language in my sleep. Trains rushed into tunnels with increasing regularity, as if a fascist had taken over British Rail, and I was on them, on my way. But, she was cautious.

– Good, good. That is a very interesting dream. But we cannot rush things. This may, you understand, take some time. The unconscious is a delicate thing, it cannot be rushed. Yes, this may be a long process. I think it would be a good thing if you were to write them, write them down. Take some time each morning. Never mind that there are things waiting to be done. You are a writer, you say. Well, write. Write your thoughts, your dreams. Two hours each morning, will you do this?

I rushed home. So, Freud would allow me to be a writer! I pushed all the dirty dishes to one end of the table, cleared myself this space, this square of table, and began. My child slept: out there in her pram in the frosty morning, her cheeks turning red as plums, beneath the rigid washing on the line. A space, a silence: the first for years. And I had not only a mother, now, but a teacher, to whom I would bring my written work. Two hours a day, while the world slept and turned and anything could happen; but I was absorbed. I cycled back – and the mornings grew lighter, spring on its way, the grey streets pearly, a stillness I now loved – and brought her my sheets, my sheaves, and she read them, and said nothing. One day, I wrote to Freud, care of her. I was full, now, of rebellious thought: a sullen daughter, not caring to do what she was told. I said: I don't think you are right about women, Sir, I think there are some things you ought to know. How would you like to have things made so difficult for you? Perhaps you have not noticed, that historically and for centuries, we have been supposed to do hundreds of things we do not like? Doing these things, like a servant, is nothing to do with being a woman. It's really quite easy. All this about penis envy, for example. We didn't want your wretched little penises, only the power and respect that went with them. Didn't you know?

243

Freud never answered, and neither did she: except to say – what you have written is very interesting. Very interesting indeed. It shows the next stage of the neurosis, you see, that is when we rebel, when we object, when we challenge the very basis of the system. We are becoming adolescent, we challenge the authority of the parent. Freud, of course, foresaw all this.

Of course. But I felt cheated, wanted my letter back, so that I could improve my argument and answer back.

– This is another aspect. As children we try to be everything, to be omnipotent. We want to be both male and female. We want the love of our mother. We want the penis so that we can make love to our mother. We hate the father who has the penis. But we must become the object of the father's desire. How can we do this? We start to challenge the father. Next, we must humble ourselves, to the authority of the penis, of the father.

I thought, blast the penis. I had lost the first round, given up my letter, my thoughts, seen, as she put it, my shit, that was so precious to me, flushed down the lavatory as waste. There seemed to be no way out. In my dreams, I was in tunnels now with trains rushing towards me, I was a white-faced heroine tied down upon the track and it all coming at me, out of the past, out of the future; my life a Clapham Junction of railway tracks upon which some absurd Western played again and again. From this position, spreadeagled there upon the sleepers, I began to write, what I wanted to write, what forced its way out of me, what would not be gainsaid: not for her, not for Freud, but for me, for my survival, after all.

ENDINGS

1

– Thankyou for telling me. I recognised some of the landmarks, but there was a lot I didn't know.

– How could you have? You're not a woman, after all.

– Not at the moment. But I might have been, once, might be again, for all I know, so it's good to have the information. You've certainly been into it all thoroughly. I'm sorry it took you so long, and that there were so many difficulties on the way. We are trying to iron out the major problems at the moment, make it all a bit more possible. But it's hard to do that, unless you're on the inside. If you hadn't shut me out for so long, I could have been more use.

– But I couldn't help it, you must see that. I did the best I could. I did keep on trying. I kept in touch to the best of my ability. It was just, for a lot of the time, like swimming against a strong current, that was all.

– Well, I congratulate you. And, by the way, that little storm in London, that business, well, I heard about it on my way, the objections raised. I think that is only temporary. People are bound to get upset at times.

– If we have the right to speak, if we are free to speak, do we have the right to say anything?

He laughed. – After all you've told me, you still don't think you know?

– Perhaps, I do.

– I should think so. By the way, did you notice, we crossed the Border while you were telling me your story. We're in my country now.

– So we are. And you still haven't told me your name.

– Yes, I did. It's Liam. For the time being, at least.

– But, didn't you have others? Weren't you – she searched –

247

Michael, Michael Foley?

– I was.

– And others? Have you been others, at other times? Were you Ned, and—

– I might have been. But, whoever I've been, I've always been your friend.

– I begin to see that. Will we meet again, like this?

– Somehow I rather doubt it. Of course, I'll be around. But somehow, I don't foresee the need. I'll say goodbye in a minute. Will you give my regards to Finn Anderson, when you see him, when you get home?

– Well, yes, but wait, aren't you going to Edinburgh? Surely the train doesn't stop again on the way?

– I'm not going all the way to Edinburgh tonight, no. It's been good to spend the time with you. I'll be in touch, even if you don't see me quite this way, again.

– Wait, I must know, it's important, was it you, I mean did you, the other night, was it—?

But there was no reply. He rose from his seat and quite suddenly opened the carriage door upon the darkness rocketing past outside, and as the air rushed in, stepped out. The door banged shut, and it was no longer the smooth door of a modern train, as she saw it, but an old-fashioned carriage door, heavy upon its hinges, that swung open above the track. The smell of the air was of cold and iron and steam. She fell back upon the seat, astounded. There was no doubt about it, he had stood up, and let himself out where there was no door, and gone; without a sound, without a thud upon the track, without a cry. She asked the ticket collector, who went through the empty carriages, taking the last tickets, before they arrived.

– Excuse me, but the man who was sitting here?

– Yes?

– Where was he supposed to get out?

The man peered at the little ticket above the seat, that said 'King's Cross – Edinburgh'.

– I didn't see any man sitting here. The seat seems to be booked.

– Well, it's the seat I booked. He was sitting in my seat.

– Well, he wasn't sitting here, then, was he?

– But, until a minute ago, he was.

– But you said that was your seat.

– No, it was only the one I was supposed to be in. We swopped over, without realising.

– Sorry, but what exactly do you want to know?

– Whether he was supposed to be going to Edinburgh. He just got off.

– Got off? He can't have. There's been no stop since Newcastle, not on this train.

– Are you sure?

– Course I'm sure. Sometimes, they stop in Berwick, and Dunbar, but not this one. We'll be in Edinburgh in a few minutes, excuse me, won't you, I have to go right up the train. I expect you'll find your gentleman's in the lavatory, if you want him. Goodbye just now.

– Goodbye. Thanks.

There was no pursuing him, not now. She settled back in her seat, closing her eyes, waiting to arrive. There was a curious sense of peace now, as if all things might be resolved.

2

The place that they were in was, as she had foreseen, hard and cold, and she had crouched there, in the same position, for so long that her thighs ached and her feet were like stones, as if she were rooted there, in her place. She was small, and compact, her body folded over upon itself, calves against thighs, elbows close to knees, arms wrapped around, hand joining wrist, head tucked down upon arms, only her eyes moving. Her eyes moved because they had to, because they watched the fire. It was only feet away, and it lived and flowered because she watched it, had her eye on it, because she was there. It was why she did not move. It was why she was at once alert and relaxed, squatting there, her bare feet upon bare ground, her own firm base. She watched the fire; was with it, in it, without getting any warmer, as if to warm herself were not the point. The point was to keep her eyes upon it: through them to give it herself, what was inside her. It was beautiful, in its red-yellow-blue complexity, in its dying and rising and its feeding of itself off new sticks, its sudden flaring tall, its crackling and spitting of damp twigs. It was like a beast, tethered, that she watched over. There was nothing else. All else was stone, earth, and sullen sky. Tall trees made a circle around her, around the fire. Stones, also in a circle, held the fire in. A bird flew out of the trees screaming, and the night fell. Stars began to wink chilly from afar. She sat, and sat, and felt the iron compactness of her body in its guardian pose. Soon, she must fetch more wood, or the fire would die down. Soon, she must move, use her legs to carry her, use her arms to take the bundles of wood, feed the fire with it, branch by branch, tease it till it flared high again and its light was pitted hard against the encroaching shadow from the trees. Her own shadow would fly up tall against the stones, she would be tall as the trees, and vulnerable. She did not want to uncurl, to move. Her head down upon her knees was safe, was curled, ducked, protected. But the fire would die. Already, the black sticks dropped, toppled. The blue flame at the centre spurted and then shrank into a quiet muttering, a fizz of near-extinction. There was the fire, at the centre, and the stones, which held it, and there were the trees, which held the space, in which it all and she was, compact. She knew that there was somebody else, but not here. Somebody expected, known, but absent. That person would not come until the fire was stoked. Brave, suddenly freed, from immobility, she stood, waved a stick held high against the encroaching darkness, was herself a beacon full of glittering light and movement waved against the night. She shouted in her throat to make the glitter stronger and the movement more sure, and stamped to fill her arms with the fuel that would feed the fire. Her arms were made of bark, like the thick sticks she held, so that it was hard to know what scratched and what bled and where, if anywhere was the softness. She stood erect and cast the wood, piece by piece, into the heart of the fire.

The pieces thudded and crashed and the fire fell open to receive them, and the flames ran greedily along the edges, eating what they could find. She stood close, her body afire now, hot and red with the molten heat, singed in its extremities, and felt the sparks fly up among the stars. She heard movement, then, behind her, steps that thudded upon the earth. The other, who was not-her, expected, came. At the same time, it was she who came, out of the far darkness, burdened and breathing heavily, entering the circle of trees and the burning air of the fire, coming close. There was a coming together out of darkness that was hard to distinguish, who came, who met. It was so habitual, so usual, that she could not tell. The third thing, that was heavy and bleeding, fell between them, open on the ground. It had been carried so that she felt its heaviness, its downward-dragging weight, just as she had felt her own flesh with her arms of bark; and when it was flung down upon the ground, she felt the relief of no longer bearing its weight. Then it seemed that water was coming into her mouth and pouring out, she was inhabited by a flood of something, that opened her lips and wet her all over, at the same time as a sensation gripped her stomach as if to turn it inside out. The stomach part pulled up towards the wet outer lip part in great heaves, as if both would join together and then in turn join with the thing that lay there on the ground before the fire, that the fire was beginning to singe and heat; and then, as if that whole would join, in turn, with something else, bigger, other, different, so that out of all the pieces something more powerful would be made. Her hands were gripping now the wet hot edges of the thing upon the ground, and the boiling up hot insides of it spoke to her own insides, promising them, and the spray flew from her lips as she worked, tugging and cutting and tearing it apart, so that now what she felt was hard and hairy, now it was liquid hot as the liquid inside herself. The other, who was not herself, plunged both hands in too and was cutting, tearing, so that the movement of them both became the same, so that once again it was hard to know whose, for they were like one, only with four hands and feet and two mouths that worked as the hands worked and the feet worked, each part doing what it did. Then, the smells began, as the flames ate the wood and turned to eat what was next, and what was next sprang to new life, a life of writhing spitting movement, blackening from red there among the flames, and the sensations poured down her nostrils and into her mouth, their mouth, and through every orifice, smells, tastes, the

251

richness of it, the spirit of what was dead and came now alive again in the fire. There was the running of juices everywhere and the promise of it, there were the aching cavities to be filled; and then, and then, there was the promise kept, the contact of flesh to flesh, the warm charred dead running flesh from the fire embracing the live hungry eating flesh, meat to meat, tongue and lips and teeth and throat and stomach, embracing, becoming one. She ate and ate in a trance of pleasure, stuffing the hot meat into her mouth through the avid opening of lips and teeth, the blood and juices running down her chin, her throat, splashing on to her breasts, trickling down her stomach; and the other, opposite, was doing the same so that she ate also what he ate and knew the pleasure he knew as meat went in through snapping white teeth in the darkness of his beard, and the wetness flowed down the hair of his face and body so that the hairiness of him and the feel of it was hers as her own smoothness was, and they were as one. Now, the tall trees receded and the night was appeased. Now, the fire died down because it had fed and had fed them. Now, the circle of stones could hold embers, ashes, the quieter smouldering remnants of the fire, now that the heat was inside them, was them, now that it flamed and flickered in their bellies, now that they had it there. The sky grew paler, as if the stars met and joined up, making white pathways, dusty patterns of light. The crack of the sticks as the fire fell apart, hardly disturbed the silence. One long branch flowered still with flame, to keep the noises and the feelings from the trees at bay. One of them would wave it, if need be, and make a giant figure suddenly of them both, shadows coupling to threaten what might come. They were powerful, now. She was in it, of it, the power. Now, she no longer crouched wary, folded upon herself, watching, like a part of the earth that had stuck in a crusted lump. Now, like the fire which was in her, she lay back and was hot inside and out with the power of the fire and the speed of the animal she had eaten, and the power of the fire and the speed of the animal was what joined the two of them already, herself and the other, so that although they did not touch yet they were in it, of it, it was what made them. She flowered in all her extremities as the fire had done when all the brands were struck alight, and she was full and hot at the centre with the flesh of the beast.

Outside her, there was the cold greyness of night, but it could not chill her now. And he was the same, so that there was now no not-her, no other; the only place that had not been filled now was filled, the only cavity filled, flesh to flesh, easily, just as the whole world fitted, sky to earth, with no gap anywhere. The fire that had just played with her and then fed her, leapt suddenly right inside her as the sparks had flown up into the sky, and then fell away; she slept with him at last in the warm embers, as the flickers and last flares of it died away.

Soon, in the morning, there was a world lit first in a cold grey light, that grew warmer and then was slightly coloured and then brilliant so that each separate thing was hard and clear in the light. The fire smoked still, and steam rose from the grass and the air was chalky blue. Birds sang in the trees. She had not known for certain that the sun would rise again, but there it was, warming her, warming the earth now: another day.

The child in the tree, who had waited so long to see this, smiled out right across the world.

And Finn opened the door.

– How was it? How was your journey?

– Fine. I'm late, aren't I? The train was held up, after we crossed the border.

She came in, unbuttoning her coat. The iron touch of the winter night; and then the door opening, the warmth of this interior. The clock ticked in the hall; he must have wound it up.

– How are you? How was the reading?

– Oh – strange. Peculiar. I'll tell you. Are the children home?

– In bed. Sudden enthusiasm for an early night. They've been hairwashing and so forth, I think we've entered a new era. Maximum dirt seems to be over.

Alice hung up her coat and ran her fingers through her hair and came up close to him to look up into his face and was checked there, suddenly, by what she saw.

– Did something happen while I was away?

– Well, things don't stand still, you know, just because you aren't there. Yes, – something did.

253

They looked at each other: a little wary, wondering what to ask. Finn kissed her quickly on the lips, perhaps to avoid her stare.

She said – You seem a little distracted.

The house, around them, seemed very large and quiet, with recesses neither had had the energy to explore. She wanted to go round it turning lights on, burning electricity, inhabiting it all.

Finn said – I'm glad you're back.

– I'm glad to be back.

They hugged, then, as if to discover by the close contact what words would not yet frame. This time, it was she who smelt of the cold and foreign outside to Finn; he snuffed up the metallic smoky smell of trains from her hair, felt her cold face with his, clasped her through her thick clothes with his hands in the middle of her back. He felt her spine, and the tense uprightness of her as she stood there. His own need seemed to have vanished: he was a man opening a door to let a stranger in; felt what was open in him swing gently to and fro, admitting what came. He thought, as he held Alice, of the beacon light of Angela's room across the city; he knew that he would go back, and be different, and that all would be well, that he was capable of infinite change, infinite adaptability; in the morning he would ring, and tell her, and all would be well, for she would laugh and say, you did make a balls-up of that, love, didn't you; and he was young again, for nothing was irreparable, nothing lost. In Alice's embrace, he was sure of this: feeling himself a man in transition, halfway; losing a tail perhaps and growing legs, he thought, and laughed to himself, tadpole becoming Frog Prince overnight, whom a simple embrace would make human.

Alice said – I met somebody on the train.

– Did you?

– Told him the story of my life. Or part of it.

– Was I in it?

– Yes. Yes, you were.

– Who else was?

– Oh, lots of people. All the people I've ever known.

– Sounds a good story. Am I still in it?

– Aren't you? I think you are.

254

– I do, too.

Balance, then: between the story of their lives, and other stories, branching, flowering, stories of themselves with others, of others with yet others, of the whole teeming peopled world. Balance, tonight in the darkened kitchen, where late at night they watched each other, a little wary still, and there at the centre, blooming mysterious as an untended fire, were the flame-coloured chrysanthemums he had brought her.

– I brought you some flowers, he said. Don't you remember?

By the same Author